Unlikely Killer

Ricki Thomas

A Wild Wolf Publication

Published by Wild Wolf Publishing in 2010

ISBN: 978-1-907954-01-6

www.wildwolfpublishing.com

As always, to my children, Ems, Alz, Joe, and Tom, for being there, putting up with me, and continuously blessing me with their wonderful presence. My Mum also, for being my rock. And to all the readers in Winterton who refused to give the first edit back ... because they wanted to pass it on to their friends ... that was special!

I would also like to thank two members of Humberside Police: DSI Ray Higgins, who let me have an interesting and informative couple of hours 'interviewing' him regarding forensics and points of query I had relating to the story. He and his colleague, Christine Kelk, were then generous enough to read the entire manuscript, with Christine updating me most days with constructive points to assist me on the final re-write. To both, I am truly grateful, for their time, their expertise, and their kindness.

More titles from Wild Wolf Publishing

Hunters & Hearts by James & John Iverson - *Based upon the extraordinary true story of Emil Iverson, explorer, athlete and head coach of the Chicago Blackhawks*

11:59 by David Williams - *A late night radio talk show host is drawn into a dark and seedy underworld*

Sinistrari by Giles Richard Ekins - *A tale of Victorian horror and murder featuring the infamous Jack the Ripper*

Rhone by John A Karr - *Gods and mortals clash on Mars*

Taralisu by Ryan Tullis - *A passionate and heartbreaking tale of a serial killer*

Emerald by M L Hamilton - *Epic fantasy of gut-wrenching sacrifice*

The Killing Moon by Rod Glenn & Jamie Mitchell - *The Road meets Mad Max ... Beyond Northern England*

Full of Sin by Karl Kadaszffy - *Some monsters aren't born - they're made*

The Venturi Effect by Andrew Linzee Gordon - *After you die it takes seven years for you to go to Heaven*

A Sick Work of Art by Claire Lewis - *When does art become a crime? How far is too far?*

Suicide City by Jake Pattison - *A darkly humorous tale of mass suicide in Gateshead*

Otherwise Kill Me by John F McDonald - *A bloody and surreal story of a schizophrenic doorman*

Bully by A J Kirby - *A supernatural tale of revenge from beyond the grave*

The Stately Pantheon by Kirsty Neary - *A dark tale of sex, addiction and power*

Turn of the Sentry by A M Boyle - *An edgy urban fantasy that will challenge the way you see the world*

The Tyranny of the Blood by Jo Reed - *A dark fantasy dealing with time travel, hereditary madness and eugenics*

The King of America: Epic Edition by Rod Glenn - *A futuristic thriller of betrayal and redemption amidst an America gripped by revolution*

Monday 12th May

An intense stab of pain shot through her abdomen, followed by a warm, sticky sensation seeping urgently over her skin. She instinctively looked up, darting, confused, noting the bearded man standing before her, his incredulous stare fixed on her body. Annabel followed his gaze, horrified to see the pastel blues of her clothing colouring a deep, glistening scarlet, the rich redness of her blood.

Swaying lightly with stunned faintness, Annabel's body buckled against the open car door, she collapsed painfully into the driver's seat. She wanted to scream, the reality of the situation horrifying her, but her breath was choked, and no sound emerged from her paling lips.

Greg Keeley was becoming increasingly agitated, he found himself unable to stand still, pacing the room mindlessly. Where was she? And where were the children? He had returned from work an hour before to an empty house. No dinner had been prepared, the beds were unmade, the dog was whimpering for food. Very unlike Annabel.

The telephone shrilled in the hall and Greg raced through to answer, hoping that it would be his wife with an explanation. But it wasn't, it was his mother-in-law. "Oh, Gail, sorry, I thought it might be Annabel."

"Is she not there? I've been waiting for her to pick the kids up, she was supposed to be back hours ago." Gail's voice was irritated, contrasting with Greg's worried overtones.

He scratched his head through his thick, fair hair, his fingers wandering nonchalantly through to the ends to meet his full beard. "Hours ago? Where did she go?"

"She dropped the kids off at eleven, stopped for a quick cup of tea, then she went into Oxford to do some shopping. Said she'd only be a couple of hours. I wouldn't normally mind, but I have to go to my yoga class soon and …"

"Eleven this morning? She should have been back way before now."

"Greg, are you okay?" Gail Rackham's timid voice faltered slightly, it hadn't occurred to her before that something may have happened to Annabel, she'd been too busy running after the children. The uncomfortable silence was palpable for a few beats too long.

Greg hated to worry Gail, she had never coped with problems too well, her undulating depression assuring she was well medicated at all times, but he couldn't hide the concern in his voice. "Gail, this isn't like Annabel, she tells me everything, she's never unreliable. Look, hang the phone up, I'm going to ring around some friends, see if anyone knows where she is."

"Greg, she's probably just lost track of time, pregnant women can be a bit vague sometimes." She chuckled insincerely as the words tumbled out, aware that her loving daughter would never be away from her children too long without a good explanation. "Okay, Greg, I'm going to hang up. Let me know what happens, won't you?"

Greg replaced the receiver and unconsciously reached again to stroke at his beard, deep in thought. His left hand flicked through the address book, locating his wife's best friend, Trudy's details, and he lifted the receiver to dial her. He found his fingers dialling nine, nine, nine instead.

The voice crackled on the other end of the line. "Emergency. What service do you require?"

"Police. Please hurry."

"What is your name, caller?"

"Gregor Keeley. Phone number eight five two, four, four, one. Caisten. Can we get on with this?"

"Just putting you through, Sir."

A short pause was followed by another woman's voice, still crackly, but clearer. "Hello, Police department, can I …"

"Please. My wife has gone missing, I'm really worried, I …"

"You'd like to report a missing person?"

The car was racing along the A354, much too fast for the pounding downpour that rattled against the bonnet and roof of the muddied Ford Escort. Occasionally Annabel slowed to a more sensible pace, yet the intimidating voice growled at her, demanding she speed up, faster, faster. She was frantic. Her warm blood still seeped over her skin, through her clothing, meeting the spent pool that soaked the drivers seat, but the gushing had stopped, her body already repairing the damage. She felt frail, but the bursts of adrenaline caused by fear kept her heartbeat quickened, although the blood loss had subsided.

A traffic police car, concealed in a lay-by, came into view as the car swung around a bend, and Annabel automatically lifted her foot from the accelerator. "Turn off here, just before Milborne St Andrew. Left." The urgency in the voice startled her, her foot slammed onto the brake pedal as she steered strongly into the corner. Overshooting marginally, Annabel steered into the skid, fighting to regain control of the car, and soon she was accelerating again, hurtling along the wizened country lane. A flash of blue in the mirror brought the police car to Annabel's attention, and she relaxed slightly, maybe if they stopped her she could escape this hellish nightmare. She relaxed from the accelerator once more.

Panic filled screaming. "Don't slow down. No Police. Get away. Fast." She knew she had no choice but to comply, her foot thrust forward, the trees raced by. "No Police. You've got to get away."

"I thought I'd bring the kids back, then I can go straight to yoga class." Gail Rackham herded the three tired children through the dimly lit doorway, she stepped past her son-in-law into the comfortably decorated hall. Greg's face was contorted with worry, his mind abandoned as he closed the door. "Greg, I was just dropping the kids off, I'm not stopping." Gail pawed at the latch, reopening the door. She trotted along the path towards her car.

"I called the police." Greg called out, he couldn't bear to be alone with this anxiety any longer.

Gail stopped abruptly. "The police! About Annabel? Isn't it a bit soon?"

Greg let out a long, burdensome sigh, his shoulders sagging hopelessly. "That's what they said, but I begged them to do something straight away. This isn't like Annabel, you know that, and I'm worried sick."

Grasping that her yoga class was going to have to wait a week, Gail reluctantly retraced her steps and entered the house. She patted Greg's arm in a shallow gesture of camaraderie.

The Escort ploughed along the narrow lane, which ran through the Dorset village of Briantspuddle. Normally Annabel's adoration of England's beauty would have spurred her to park the car and take a stroll around, she would have loved the ambience of the quaint, flower-adorned cottages. But the menacing voice in her ears shouted at her to speed up every time she relaxed. The car thundered across the crossroads, jolting the shock absorbers to scream an angry objection. A T-junction sprang from nowhere, Annabel instinctively slammed the brakes on, but it was too late to stop, the car skidded across the road as Annabel hauled the steering wheel to the right. Relieved to have regained control, the intermittent flashing lights in the mirror indicated the police car was still on her tail. "No Police. Faster."

A brown sign loomed to the left signalling a local tourist attraction. 'Clouds Hill' the bold white lettering stated, and Annabel felt a vague recognition of the name. Maybe she'd seen it in the brochures they'd collected for their annual holiday, after all, Dorset had been a potential destination. "Faster. Faster. No Police."

Annabel checked the mirror, the police car was gaining on them. She pressed her foot harder, the aging engine objecting as the car hurtled along the straight, delicately undulating road. "Faster. Make this car fly."

Beads of sweat glistened on her forehead as they, travelling at ninety, shot into the thirty mile per hour zone. As Bovington Tank Museum raced towards them on the left, an ancient Rover nosed out from a side road, the equally ancient driver not noticing the Escort. Swerving to the right desperately, Annabel overtook and continued along the road, away from Bovington.

"There's another junction." Annabel's voice was breathless, a mixture of fear and unexpected excitement.

"Right. Go right." Annabel obeyed without hesitation, and they immediately met another junction. "Go right again. Find somewhere to hide, get the pigs off our trail."

Annabel glanced in the mirror, the lights still flashed intermittently, but the police car was trapped behind an articulated lorry. She slowed to a stop, the traffic at the junction was heavy, an endless stream of vehicles in both directions, but an angry scream unnerved her. "Don't stop the car."

Recklessly, Annabel swung the Escort into the flow, squeezing her eyes shut in abandoned hope. Angry horns objected disdainfully, but a new, enthusiastic tone in her instructor's voice dispelled them. "Quick, there's a lay-by, left, in there, get in there."

Swinging the car into the tight pathway, Annabel manoeuvred down the steep track, towards a mildewed and craggy wooden fence, bordering an expanse of farmland. Slowing to a crawl, she bumped the car over the rugged soil, and stopped, discreetly hidden under the sweeping branches of a mature oak tree. Annabel breathed a sigh of exhausted relief, but balked when she heard the wailing police car speed into the distance behind her. They could have saved her from this hell. Now she was alone, who was going to help her now? "Get some sleep. You've lost a lot of blood." Annabel nodded her head lamely, her eyes drooping, she had no difficulty complying with the latest order, the blood loss had drained her.

Morrell Close in Caisten, Oxfordshire, was a desirable area, yet also a nosy one. Curtains jerked back and doors opened a shade as the police car slowed to a stop beside number thirty-nine. It was just past ten in the evening when the two constables knocked on the front door. Greg, tired from nervously pacing the lounge carpet for the past few hours, hurriedly opened the door, lightly guiding his eager mother-in-law aside.

"Mr Keeley?"

"Yes, yes, come in. Where have you been? We've been waiting ages." Greg impatiently stepped back for the constables to pass into the dim hallway. Glancing up, PC Jane Allan noticed two young children sitting in the darkness at the top of the staircase, chins on hands, tearful confusion glistening in their huge dark eyes. She smiled reassuringly, they reminded her of her own two boys, and she couldn't imagine the bewilderment they must be feeling.

Once in the brightness of the homely, practical lounge, Gail took the lead and gestured to the settee. The constables sat attentively, although Greg remained standing, unable to keep himself from fidgeting. He flitted mindlessly from one place to the next, touching photo frames, moving ornaments, his desperation palpable. "It's not like her, you know." He spoke to himself.

Uncomfortable with the edgy atmosphere, PC Jerome Taylor stood again. "Mr Keeley. I am PC Taylor, this is PC Allan. I understand your wife hasn't returned home from a shopping trip, and the circumstances are highly unusual for her. Have you rung round her friends?"

Greg shot a look at Taylor. "You don't know Annabel." He was snapping, he was an impatient man, especially under duress. "Something is wrong. I know it is. I believe she's in danger." He was aware that he was the centre of attention, an air of surprise filled the room.

Allan and Taylor exchanged a glance before Taylor continued. "Okay, Sir, okay. Have you any idea where Annabel could be?"

Greg eyed the man before him with disdain. "If I had any idea, don't you think I would have tried that already?"

Allan raised herself from the sofa in her colleague's defence. "Mr Keeley, I can understand your concern. Please calm down so we can assess the situation fully. Please, will you take a seat?"

"I'm sorry, it's just not like her. She's been gone for over eleven hours now, Annabel would never be away that long without letting anyone know where she was."

Allan sat, her legs complaining from the long shift. "Does she have a mobile phone?"

Greg looked at his feet and sighed, forlorn. "It's on her dressing table, upstairs, she's always forgetting to take it out."

Taylor produced his notepad from the breast pocket of his tunic. "Mr Keeley, could I take your full name please?"

"For God's sake, it's Annabel we need to find, not my life history."

Gail reached out and tugged on Greg's rolled shirt sleeve. "Greg, stop it. These questions need to be asked, the man is only doing his job. Just answer as best you can and then they can start looking for her."

Greg tugged his arm away, he sagged heavily into the free armchair. "Gregor Hilton Keeley."

PC Taylor, seating himself once more, smiled at Gail. "And you are?"

"Gail Rackham, Gail Annabel Rackham, I'm Annabel's mother."

"Thank you. What is Annabel's full name?"

"Annabel Elizabeth Keeley."

"How old is she?"

"Thirty three, just gone last week. She's pregnant, you know. Did he tell you that?" A fleeting martyr's smile passed Gail's reddened lips.

"How far gone, how pregnant?" Taylor was scribbling briskly in his notebook.

"Four months, it's due in October."

"Right. What is the registration number of her car she was driving?"

Gail glanced at Greg, he answered readily. "It's a Ford Escort one point four L, black, number T two four seven S K D."

Allan rose and moved to the doorway, she leant through and radioed the details to the control room, additionally requesting a check on recent incidents involving vehicles.

Annabel hugged her knees in the driver's seat of her car, her bare legs were cold now that the chill of the late spring night had fallen with the dark sky. The glistening scarlet on her clothing, although drying, was tacky, and some of the gore had drenched her powder blue cardigan, cooling her to a shiver. The seat was sodden from hours of spillage, Annabel felt uncomfortable, restless, scared, but any motion towards the welcomingly dry passenger seat had been met with the controlling voice of her unseen master demanding her stillness. Once she had tried to

11

look behind her, but the shattering voice screamed terrifyingly in her ears, leaving her head ringing, chastised. A tear trickled silently down her pallid cheek, and dripped from her chin to mingle with the spent crimson on her skirt.

The car was resourcefully concealed amongst the drooping branches of the oak tree, and the blackness of its paintwork blended into the fading twilight. The only sounds were the scuttling animals, the swooping birds, out in the silky darkness to hunt their prey.

"Mrs Rackham, as far as you know, you were the last person to see Mrs Keeley."

Gail swallowed hard, this sounded far too much like a murder investigation for her nerves to cope with. She wanted a drink to calm her, but knew Greg would object. Her voice cracked as she spoke, timid and retiring. "Yes. She arrived at my house at about eleven this morning. I'd just made a pot of tea, so she had a quick cup with me, then said she'd better rush off. She was going into Oxford to do some shopping."

Taylor scribbled the words in his own version of shorthand. "What sort of shopping, do you know?"

"She had to go and get a present from Argos for Katie, it's her birthday on Sunday and Annabel's arranging a party for her."

"Katie is your daughter?" This was directed at Greg, but it was Gail who answered.

"Yes, she'll be eight. She had to get things to put in the party bags, you know, and some party food. She was going to have a look at some maternity departments too, her clothes are getting too tight, what with the baby."

"What sort of mood was she in when she left?" PC Taylor glanced at Greg, he'd opened the curtains slightly and was staring into the darkness.

Gail considered for a moment, her forehead creased with recollection. "She was fine, quite excited, really. Her kids are her life, you know, and she loved things like parties for them."

Greg swung round, his face fierce. "For God's sake, don't talk about her in the past tense, she's not gone, you know." Gail could feel his eyes boring into her, his nostrils flaring with each breath. Silently, he let his anger subside through his fists, he traipsed to his armchair, and slumped, the fight over.

"I'm sorry, it was just a turn of words. Constable, Annabel adores those children. She said if she was late could I pick Katie and Samson up from school. Of course I agreed, but I asked her not to be too late, I'm meant to be at yoga tonight, well, I was supposed to be." Gail snatched a peek at Greg, but he was now concentrating on the streamlined fireplace, seeing nothing. "She said she'd be as quick as possible. Well, it got to three and she still wasn't back, so I put Petra in the buggy and took her to the school, got the kids. Eventually I had to feed them, give them dinner, because I still hadn't heard from her. Well, at seven I phoned Greg, see if she'd got home."

"Thank you, Mrs Rackham. Mr Keeley, do you have a recent photo of Annabel?"

Mindless, Greg leaned towards the fireplace he was still studying sightlessly, and removed a framed picture from the mantel. He handed it to Taylor. The frame showed a pretty blonde woman with smiling hazel eyes. Her bone structure was heavy, yet appealing, and she was laughing to the camera. Her shoulder length locks intermingled with Greg's darker blonde hair, his wide beard caressing her tanned skin. The Greg in the picture was a cheerful man, a man in love. The Greg who studied the fireplace whilst rubbing his hands together nervously was distraught.

Gail, eager to contend for the limelight, forced a lonesome tear from her eye, and daubed it away expressively as she gestured to the photo. "It was our present to them, my husband and I arranged it to celebrate their tenth wedding anniversary this year."

"When was it taken?"

"Three weeks ago. Their anniversary was on the twentieth of April. Ten years." Her voice subsided as she urged another drop from her eye.

Tuesday 13th May

Annabel heard the rustling noise outside the car, her eyes opened, squinting against the brightness, as the deep, fitful slumber she had slipped into the night before drifted away. She searched through the windscreen in the direction of the sound. Sinking into the still sodden seat a little to avoid being noticed, she observed a grey lady with her bounding dog through the branches of the trees that shrouded the car. Needlessly holding her breath until the stranger was out of sight, she pushed herself up, stretching away the sleepiness. Her abdomen was pulsing with intense pain, her expression reflected the discomfort, and it reminded her that, although she was no longer asleep, the nightmare continued.

Annabel steeled herself to consider the bloodbath on her clothing. The bleeding seemed to have stemmed, there was no fresh redness to note, but still the exhaustion ebbed through her.

The voice wasn't as urgent, it had a kinder tone this morning, gentle, even loosely compassionate. "Got to keep your head low. You must wait until mid morning to move on. Go back to sleep. Try and sleep."

Annabel was now accustomed to the demands of the unseen tormentor in her ears, she dared not object, she was terrified of the outcome, but her bladder was bursting. Too frightened to move, she slackened her pelvic floor and felt the hot liquid mingle with the dried blood on her skirt and seat. Relieved, she closed her eyes against the morning brightness, breathing deeply, desperate to encourage the sleepiness to return.

"Kidlington Police Station, can I help you?"

"I, um, I hope so." The woman's voice was timid, apologetic. "I wasn't sure if I should say anything or not, my husband said not to get involved, but I couldn't sleep last night for worrying."

"Yes madam." Paula Curtis sighed inwardly, here we go, another late night party.

"It's just, it's just I was shopping yesterday, I'd been shopping, then I saw a woman covered in blood, real scared, she was. There was a man with her, right close he was."

The civilian employed by the police straightened her back and edged towards the control panel. She waved her hand at her supervisor to attract some attention to the importance of the call she was taking. "Madam," Paula glanced at the note in front of her, noting the name the emergency room operator had given her, "Mrs Murray, where was this?"

"Westgate Car Park. Top floor, right at the top."

"You say the woman seemed distressed?"

"Real scared, blood all over her, all over her clothes. Loads of it, there was"

"Right. You say there was a man, what was he doing?" Paula beckoned the desk sergeant who was striding towards her.

"I couldn't see really, he was right in front of her, he just seemed to be looking at her, I think. Oh, I don't know, really."

"Can you remember what they looked like?"

"I think she was blonde, yes, I think so, but I was more looking at the blood than her face, think she was quite tall, though, seemed tall."

"Can you remember him?"

"Him, yes, he turned towards me briefly. He had a big beard, a really big beard, a light brown, big beard." She spoke in earnest, delighted that her story was of interest to the police.

Having managed to drift back to sleep for a couple more hours, Annabel was still awash with tiredness. The crimson spillage had been vast, and this, alongside hunger and thirst, was taking a toll on her body. But any hopes of sleeping some more were dashed. "You must start the car, now, you've got to go, now."

Sighing silently as she straightened herself, she turned the key obediently in the ignition, and on the second turn the cold engine chugged into life. She reversed the car from its hiding place amongst the branches, and backed out of the narrow pathway, righting the car on the verge of the empty road.

"What way should I go?" Her voice was shallow, resigned.

A brief hesitation, then. "Go back the way you came yesterday. Got to go back that way, that's the best thing."

A couple of vans passed, and Annabel pulled across to the right, then immediately a left, retracing her steps towards Bovington.

Within a minute the car had reached the Tank Museum, this time on the right, and now the sense of urgency had gone, they were travelling slowly enough for Annabel to glance at the imposing metal creatures on display at the entrance. She felt unusually calm, until she noticed the policeman patrolling the roadside. The panic in the voice returned. "He was talking into his radio. That policeman. He's seen you. They're gonna chase you again. Get out of here, you've got to get out. They mustn't catch you. Speed up. Listen to me, move."

Annabel pushed fiercely on the accelerator, the car racing, speeding, as they sailed along the undulating road towards Clouds Hill. She automatically relaxed her foot when the speedometer reached sixty miles an hour, but the hysteria held out. "Faster, go faster. They can't catch you, they mustn't. Listen to me."

Once more the car increased its speed, hurrying, flying, it hurtled to the base of a shallow dip in the road, and climbed rapidly to the next gentle crest. Suddenly a motorbike and two bicycles came into view, Annabel tried to avoid them but the road wasn't wide enough, she hit something, the sound of crunching metal rang through the air as she fought the steering wheel to maintain control of the car. Her foot pumped the brake as her widened eyes watched the skidding motorbike in the rear view mirror. Her struggling tamed the car, but it was over for the biker, he'd ploughed along the road, his leathers shredding against the gravel, until the crest of the newest rise shielded her view of the accident.

Her heart already palpitating wildly, the voice only managed to terrify her more. Screaming. "Get out of here, drive fast, speed up. Listen to me. You've got to get out of here." The Escort thundered into the distance, and Annabel was devastated. She'd never broken the law, it wasn't in her. What had she become?

Detective Inspector Krein was routinely ploughing through his post when the desk sergeant rang through from the control desk to inform him of Mrs Murray's call. He listened to the details, intrigued. He could hear his colleague of three years, Detective Sergeant Raynor, chatting outside the office, and he shouted for him through the door.

"Boss?" Raynor leant through, his handsome face questioning.

"Raynor. We've just had a call in from a, er, Mrs Murray, said she saw a woman covered in blood in the Westgate car park yesterday. There was a bearded man with the woman. I'm sure I overheard somewhere that some guy reported his wife missing yesterday, made quite a fuss about it. Can you get me some more details on the missing wife?"

"Sure, Boss. Have you got the full details of the last phone call?"

Krein showed Raynor his scribbled notes, the young man nodded and left the office. Krein rose from his untidy desk and traipsed along the corridor towards the drinks machine, deep in thought. From all indications so far, it seemed he may finally have an attempted homicide to investigate, and he was unsure if he was excited or terrified. Maybe a bit of both. He drew a strong black coffee from the gurgling machine, and returned to his office. Unaware of how long the simple task had taken, he was surprised to find promotion hungry Raynor waiting beside his desk.

"Raynor! Back already?" Krein sank into his chair and leant towards his colleague.

"Boss. I've got the statements from the husband and mother of the missing woman, Annabel Keeley. Here's a photo, she's blonde, and the notes say she's tall like the woman Mrs Murray noticed. Said she was going shopping in Oxford, mother said that when they shop in Oxford they usually park at the Westgate."

Krein took the statements, his mind skimming quickly, yet thoroughly, through the words, and cocked his head. "Nothing solid to go on, but quite a coincidence. Let's go and see this Murray woman. Try her with Annabel's photo." He pulled his jacket from the back of the chair and shrugged it over his toned arms, grabbed his car keys, and they headed for the car park.

The crest of the hill on the road between Clouds Hill and Bovington Camp was cordoned off, and a diversion in place. Two ambulances and a police car were waiting by the crumpled motorbike. The two boys who had been cycling towards the tank museum were wrapped in blankets at the side of the road, waiting for their parents to arrive in a second police car to accompany them to the local hospital. Neither was physically injured, but both were suffering from shock at the horrific scene they had witnessed.

Two paramedics were working methodically on the young man who had been knocked from his recently purchased Harley Davidson Sportster, his pride and joy. They already suspected his injuries would prove fatal, his internal bleeding was severe, but their duty was to do their utmost to preserve life at the scene of the accident. When his spine, neck and head were fully supported, they carefully slid him onto the waiting stretcher and wheeled him to the ambulance. He had a saline drip fed into the back of his hand to keep him hydrated, and one of the paramedics continued to artificially respire him.

A police constable was appraising the wreckage of the Sportster, the front had been smashed by the impact with the mysterious car, and there was intensive damage to the right hand side of the motorbike from skidding along the road for nearly twenty meters before hitting the verge. The constable had already radioed for assistance, this was a clear case of hit and run, but by the condition of the motorcyclist the charge may be death by dangerous driving. The designated Scene of Crime Officer was on his way.

Annabel, following haphazard directions from the nervous, yet intimidating voice, had raced through the back lanes and managed to stumble across the A352 again. Passing the dirt track the car had sheltered in the previous night, she drove through the small town of Wool. Reaching a roundabout, she turned left into a narrow, countryside lane and the voice issued a new demand.

She needed to find somewhere to hide the car. Almost too tired to care any more, Annabel found a break in the hedging and had drove through, across the bumpy, sprouting field, to a copse of trees at the far end. She concealed the car from the road in the sheltering lower branches.

Realising she had once more shunned help, Annabel felt more alone than ever. She had left the scene of a road accident, that was illegal, she'd never broken the law in her life, but she'd had no choice. The voice terrified her, she didn't dare disobey. "Well done. This is a good place to hide, they won't look here."

Annabel was pleased, her aggressor was so angry all the time, this calm and complimentary voice refreshing. But her security was false, the taunting anger had returned. Sneering, grating. "Now I want you to try to get away from here, I might go with you, I might not. They'll be after you even more now. They'll know the car. They'll know you just killed a man, you naughty girl." The deep voice was jeering as she trembled. "They'll put you away for the rest of your life, and you don't want that, do you? Oh, and you need different clothes, you can't walk round in those, nobody must notice you."

"I do want to get these clothes off." Her voice was quiet, speaking more to herself than anyone else. The dried blood was uncomfortable to sit on, and the wet patches chilled her legs.

"You're not listening to me." The voice boomed, and then repeated slowly, menacingly. "You - need - different - clothes."

Annabel slammed her fists against the steering wheel. "I heard you, I'm just thinking." Surprised her outburst hadn't brought punishment, Annabel thought for a few seconds, then with relief she remembered the holdall her husband kept in the boot of the car. He had a spare outfit for his frequent fishing trips, in case he got caught in a downpour and needed a clean set of clothes. She mentioned them quietly.

"Good, yes. That's lucky. No, not luck. All things happen for a reason, this was all meant to be like this. This is fate. Listen to me. It's fate. That man back there was meant to die. You were born to kill him." A light laugh. "I am born to murder." Raucous laughter.

Unable to handle the sinister racket in her ears, Annabel tightly clasped her hands to her head until the curdling hysterics abated. "I'm going to get changed now." She spoke timidly, desperate not to encourage any more demonic laughter. Annabel tentatively opened the car door open and stepped thankfully into the warm, scented air, avoiding the low branches surrounding the car, as she stepped cautiously towards the back. Her legs were stiff, her skin crackly with dried blood, her abdomen ached and grumbled. Supporting herself by leaning against the car, she staggered to the boot, and opened it wide. Greg's dark green holdall was bulging at the seams, and she unzipped it, pulling out a tatty pair of jeans, the ancient Levi's that he'd once charmed her in, an oversized T-shirt, and a hefty Arran sweater. At the bottom of the bag lay a pair of woollen socks, and some well-worn trainers.

With relief, Annabel slipped her blood-encrusted skirt down her long, athletic legs, scraping the excess gore and excrement with it, then let her cardigan fall to the ground. She dragged the T-shirt over her fitted vest top, and shrugged into the warming sweater. The clean, homely smelling warmth enveloped her immediately, and she thought of her children, of the baby inside her bloodstained belly.

A sudden wash of exhaustion flooded through Annabel's weak body. Her feet staggered on the soft undergrowth, she leant heavily on the car to support herself. Then she felt the piercing pain. No warning. The sharp, stabbing in her belly, the harsh, ripping sensation. Her hands clasped at her abdomen, trying to drag the pain away, and she sank to her knees. Watching the copious, thick blood ooze from her body, her eyes were wide, horrified as her insides fell out, churning, spilling out onto the damp undergrowth. Annabel screamed in desperation, the effort using the last of her energy, but no one could help her, she was alone, this was it, this was the end. She stumbled down against the expelled contents of her body, her frightened eyes wide, but now unseeing. The blackness enveloped her, the birds ceased to chatter, and then she felt nothing.

Christine Murray was a timid woman. Her home was a small, two-bedroom housing association terrace, which she shared reluctantly with her husband of thirty years. He was a heavy drinker, spending any spare money in the local, as well as money they couldn't spare. She managed to cope somehow, taking in work at home whenever she could find some, but she'd become downtrodden over the years, accepting unenthusiastically that was the way her life was meant to be. Detective Inspector Krein waved his identity badge at her, and she stepped aside to let him, followed by Raynor, through the unclean doorway. She proudly glanced at the neighbour's houses to see who was watching, before quietly closing the door.

They exchanged pleasantries while Mrs Murray prepared a large pot of tea, and, sitting in the cluttered lounge, Krein got to the part he'd been waiting for. "So, Mrs Murray, what time did you see this woman at the Westgate car park?"

She fidgeted constantly, her fingers feeling her arms, her blouse, her fingers, her nails. "Well, it was probably about eleven thirty, eleven forty five, maybe. I'd just been into town, you know, Sainsburys, and I was going back to my car." Her words tumbled out easily, she was proud to be helping.

DS Raynor scribbled the details on his notebook. Krein continued. "What floor were you parked on?" He already knew, but he needed her to relax.

"Top floor, I always park there because it's easier to get parked, I'm not very good at parking. Bill, um, my husband, says I need a wide berth." Her smile was wide, but the nervousness was overwhelming.

"Where were you when you saw the woman?"

"I'd just come through the door at the top of the stairs, I had to use the stairs because the blasted lift is broken again. Anyway I saw her straight away, she looked quite shocked actually, and there was a lot of blood. You know, I couldn't take my eyes away."

"You saw a man with her, I believe?" Slowly, don't get her excited.

"Yes, yes, there he was, right next to her, he sort of had his hands out, on her I think. I don't know."

"What did you do when you saw her?" Krein knew the answer would be nothing, the public had become scared and selfish during his time on the force.

As expected a flash of guilt registered on Mrs Murray's face. "Well, I didn't know what to do, did I? The woman saw me, I saw her looking, she was scared, real scared, but so was I, so I turned and ran, down the stairs, back into the shopping centre. In fact I dropped my bag on the way."

"Your bag?"

"My bag of shopping. Bill had a right go when I got home, I had to do him an omelette because we had no meat, someone nicked the bag, you see, I went back for it. My Bill likes his meat in the evening, he accused me of trying to feed him rabbit food."

"So you didn't go to help the woman?" He once would have been incredulous, but after years of experience he was used to the apathy, and his tone was flat.

"I know I should have, but I was scared. Thought the bloke would get me too, so I just ran away." Mrs Murray was bringing tendrils of hair across her mouth and sucking on them childishly.

Krein uncrossed his legs, he leant his elbows on his knees and considered Mrs Murray's life-burned face. "Why did you not notify the police at that point?" It wasn't an accusation, and she visibly relaxed.

"I thought no-one would believe me, in fact I wasn't sure I hadn't been dreaming, lord knows, everyone tells me off for living in a dream world, and Bill said it was probably just my imagination. And he said if it wasn't then I was to keep out of it. But when I couldn't sleep last night, I knew I had to do something, well, I wouldn't have been able to live with myself, that poor girl. I called you first thing, as soon as Bill had gone to work."

Krein knew he'd extracted as much information as he was going to get. "Okay. Can you remember what the woman looked like? You said you saw her looking at you."

"I didn't get that good a look, the weather was real murky, you know, rainy. She was blonde, her hair was sort of longish, well, shoulder length. Her eyes were bright, really wide open, because she was scared I suppose."

"Can you remember what she was wearing?"

"Couldn't tell you, well, definitely a skirt, but it was red from blood."

"How do you know she wasn't just wearing a red skirt?"

Mrs Murray fidgeted with her fingers again, anxious. "I could tell. I just could, it was a big patch of red, it wasn't all red. Blue. Her cardigan was pale blue. That's right, the skirt was too. Pale blue. I remember now. But there was so much blood."

"Thank you Mrs Murray, I know this is hard." He needed her to relax again. "Now, the man, what can you remember about him?"

"His beard, he had a big beard, wild, it was, light brown, dark blond, whatever. His hair was longer, quite shaggy. He wasn't bad looking, I suppose, I only got a brief look. He wasn't huge, not six foot, but not much less. His eyes were wild too, he had glasses on, but you could still see his eyes from the side."

"Can you remember what he was wearing, or if he was carrying anything?"

"Yes, I can. He had a smart suit on, real posh. It was pale grey. I didn't see anything in his hands. Oh yes, there was, there was something glistening,"

"Any idea what it was?" Krein wondered how much of what she was saying was true, and how much fabrication to make herself more important.

"Don't know, maybe keys, could have been a knife, I suppose, really, I'm not sure."

"Mrs Murray, if you were to see this man again, would you recognise him?"

"Definitely, I'll remember his face forever, I think."

Krein knew it wouldn't be ethical to show Mrs Murray the photograph of Gregor and Annabel, it would be seen as influencing a witness. He carefully brought the framed photo from his bag and concealed Gregor's face with a scrap of paper. "Would you be prepared to come to an identity parade, we have a suspect who fits your description of the man."

Raynor looked at his boss in confusion, they had no suspect at all! But he checked himself, Krein's mind always worked faster, and more logically than everybody else's.

23

"Mrs Murray," Krein displayed the un-obscured half of the photo, "could you tell me, is this the woman you saw yesterday?"

Christine Murray gasped, she held her hand to her mouth. "Oh isn't she pretty when she smiles! Yes, I would swear that's the same woman." Krein was so tempted to uncover Greg's photo, the deep blonde beard was such a giveaway. But he replaced the photo in his bag and thanked Mrs Murray for her time.

Krein rapped on the heavy, oak door of thirty-nine Morrell Close, Caisten, the door swung wide immediately. Gail moved aside as soon as she'd seen the identity badge Krein waved at her.

"Good afternoon, Madam, I'm Detective Inspector Krein, this is Detective Sergeant Raynor. We are here about Annabel Keeley."

"Oh, hello, I'm Annabel's mother, Gail Rackham, please come in." Krein hoped the shock had not registered on his face, he was usually a master of keeping his expressions blank, but this lady looked no-where near the mid-fifties that she must be.

Krein and Raynor followed the tall, elegant, yet demure woman through the white stained Georgian door to the lounge, they nodded their regards to the unkempt man curled in an armchair, his eyes bland, his demeanour broken.

"Greg, they're here about Annabel." Gail motioned to the settee for Krein and Raynor to sit, and sat herself in the spare armchair. Soon a little girl made her way onto, what Krein supposed, was her grandmother's lap.

"Are you Mr Gregor Keeley?"

"Yes, sir, and you are?" Greg seemed disinterested which bristled Krein.

"Detective Inspector Krein, Detective Sergeant Raynor." Krein noticed Keeley's wild beard with interest, it was far scruffier than it was in the photograph of him with the missing woman he had in his briefcase. He thought back to his conversation earlier with Mrs Murray, her description of the man who was with the lady she'd seen. Wild, light brown or dark blond beard, longer shaggy hair, not six foot but not far off. Was

Gregor Keeley attractive? Maybe, not his idea of handsome, but he supposed a middle-aged woman may find him so.

"Have you any news of Annabel, have you found her?" A flicker of hope registered in his voice.

"No sir, but we do have a possible sighting, at the Westgate car park yesterday. We're looking into it."

Gail's eyes lit up. "Really, was she okay?"

"It's too early to tell, Mrs Rackham. Mr Keeley, could you tell me where you were yesterday please?"

Greg looked shocked at the question. "Me? I was at work, of course."

"Where do you work? And what do you do there?"

"I'm an accountant, I work in Witney at Gordon and MacIntyre Chartered Accountants. I was working on one of our major client's accounts yesterday, assisting with notes for their audit."

Krein was suspicious, this didn't feel right. This Keeley guy had just offered a hell of a lot of unprompted information. He glanced at DS Raynor, noticing by the look on his face that Raynor was thinking the same thing.

"Were you at the Witney offices between eleven and twelve in the morning yesterday?"

"Yes, well no, I wasn't, actually, not the main offices, I took the accounts to a nearby office the company owns so that I could work with no distraction, the office above Timberlakes Jewellers. But I was in Witney."

"Were you with anybody?"

"This is ridiculous, you're treating me as if I'm under suspicion. Gail, take Petra away, please. I don't want her hearing this." Gail lifted the little girl from her lap and led the confused child from the room: their footsteps sounded lightly on the stairs.

"Mr Keeley, I can understand your concern, but these are routine questions that we have to ask to get a better idea of what happened yesterday. We need the complete picture. Were you alone?"

"Yes, okay, I was on my own. My telephone in the office rings all day, my secretary is hopeless at keeping calls back. These accounts are intricate, I needed solitude to be able to concentrate, okay, nothing wrong with that."

"Do you have anybody who could verify your whereabouts between eleven and twelve yesterday?"

Greg sighed, his head settled in his hands, before moving them down to stroke at his beard, smoothing it into shape roughly. "No. My secretary knew where I was, though. She could have contacted me at any time."

"Mr Keeley, do you need to wear glasses at any time?"

"You what? What the hell are you getting at now?"

"Please answer the question."

"Yes, not that I can see the point of asking that. I am slightly short sighted. I wear contact lenses, usually at weekends, and glasses at work."

"What were you wearing yesterday?"

Greg shifted uncomfortably on the seat, his hands were now smoothing his unbrushed hair. "Jesus, this is ridiculous. I was wearing my bloody grey work suit, I have three suits. Yesterday I wore the grey one."

"Could you show it to me please?"

Greg stormed out of the room and thundered up the stairs, muttering under his breath. Presently he arrived back holding a pale grey suit, which still hung neatly from a coat hanger. Krein lifted the legs closer, three tiny brownish red spots dotted the left trouser leg, mid thigh height. He held the material up to show Raynor and Greg. "Do you know what these marks are on your trousers?"

Greg's face paled visibly, his eyes flickered between the two policemen. His voice was strained, delayed. "No, I've no idea."

"Miss Packard, my name is Detective Inspector Krein, this is Detective Sergeant Raynor. We are investigating a missing person, and we have reason to believe you may be able to help us with our enquiries."

Bella Packard was quite beautiful, her long dark hair was rich and full, her figure was slim yet curvy in all the right places, her clothing immaculate. She had chocolate brown eyes that looked demure between her thick lashes. She took a moment or two to register what the policeman had said, then moved aside to let the men through.

Once settled on the sofa in the small, tidy lounge of Bella's modern flat, Krein explained the reason for his visit. Her boss's wife was missing, he needed to know if she could verify his whereabouts between eleven and twelve the previous day.

"Mr Keeley worked in the other office yesterday, he often goes there when he needs quiet, says it gives him time to think without distraction."

"Where is this other office?"

"Above Timberlakes Jewellers in the High Street."

"That's not far from Gordon and MacIntyre is it?"

"No, it's four buildings along, towards the town centre."

"Do you have a car park at your offices?" This was the type of interview Krein liked: short and to the point.

"Yes, round the back."

"Was Mr Keeley's car in the car park between eleven and twelve yesterday morning?"

Bella thought for a moment, and slowly shook her head. "No, he didn't have his car yesterday, his wife sometimes needs it, so he leaves it at home and comes in by train."

DS Raynor was looking at the photographs displayed in frames on the wall, they were of Bella Packard, but far more blatant than he would expect from the wholesome woman in front of him, she obviously did light glamour modelling as a sideline. Following Raynor's interest, Krein wondered if Keeley knew what his secretary got up to afters hours. Was there anything between Keeley and his pretty assistant? She was such a beauty, she must turn heads wherever she goes.

"Is there anybody you can think of who could verify that Mr Keeley was at the Timberlake office?"

Bella thought deeply again before speaking. "I'm sorry, but I can't think of anyone. Mr Keeley likes to be alone. Sometimes he doesn't even take calls when he works there."

"Doesn't take calls?"

"Well, when he's there I often phone through with questions, or people he may like to speak to, but yesterday the phone was just ringing. He often ignores the phone, hates being disturbed, which makes my job harder. In fact, to be honest I think he unplugs it, otherwise I'm sure the ringing would annoy him."

"He doesn't have a mobile?"

She pondered for a moment. "Not that I know of, I've not seen him with one."

"Did you see Mr Keeley at all yesterday?"

"Yes. He came in about half nine, like he always does, he collected some papers, then left for the other office."

"Can you remember what he was wearing?"

Again, she thought, her eyes narrowed as she mentally pictured Greg the day before. "Yes, he had his pale grey suit on yesterday. He wears it a lot, I think it's his favourite."

"Did you notice any stains on the left trouser leg of the suit?"

Bella flushed, her eyes flittered down as she avoided Krein's interrogating stare. "I'm sorry, Mr Krein, but I don't usually look at Mr Keeley's trousers. I'm good at my job, and he respects me for that."

Krein stepped back in surprise, he strongly suspected that Greg had something going with his assistant. Was this relevant? Maybe he wanted his wife out of the way? "I'm sorry, I didn't mean to offend you, I think you misheard the question. Just one more, and we'll be on our way. Could you tell me if Mr Keeley was wearing glasses yesterday."

"Yes, he always does. Now, if you'd please excuse me, I have to be back at work in a few minutes."

The Scene of Crime Officer had arrived at the site of the motorbike accident. He had been called in to try and assess what had happened an hour earlier, at twenty past eleven in the morning. He had briefly surveyed the wreckage of the Sportster, now he was waiting for a forensics team to come and take samples of the black paint that was scratched into the mudguard and handlebars of the chrome bike: these were probably from the car that caused the tragedy.

The first constable to attend the scene had managed to get a rough idea from the two young boys about what had taken place. They'd stated that a black car had come speeding over the crest of the hill in the opposite direction, towards Clouds hill, just as the motorcycle was overtaking the boys, who'd been riding side by side. The bike had collided with the front right hand side of the car, had flipped onto it's side and skidded along the road, throwing the rider into the verge. Neither of them had managed to remember the registration number of the car.

He had already heard that the motorcyclist had been pronounced dead on arrival at the hospital. The police had been notified to locate the mysterious vehicle.

Krein and Raynor hadn't needed to arrest Greg Keeley. When they asked if he would mind answering some questions at the police station, he bowed his head, resigned, and agreed to go without argument. Krein had been taken aback, he'd expected an outburst after the fuss Greg had kicked up earlier.

The three men were sitting in a grubby interview room, Krein and Raynor on one side of the graffiti covered wooden table, Greg on the other. Greg sat with his legs wide, one elbow on each knee, resting his head in his hands.

"Mr Keeley, could you please tell me if you took any telephone calls in the Timberlake office yesterday, or if you made any outgoing calls?"

"I pulled the connection out at the socket, like I usually do when I work there. Otherwise there would be no point me going there."

"How did you get to work yesterday?"

"I took the train, there's a direct line between Caisten and Witney. I use it quite often when Annabel needs the car."

"Did you leave the office at any time yesterday?"

"No. I collected the accounts at about nine thirty from the main offices, then walked directly to Timberlakes."

"Do you recall seeing anybody on your way there?"

"No, no-one." Greg knew this sounded bad, he wrenched his fingers nervously through his beard.

"Even at Timberlakes? Someone who could verify you were there."

Greg was resigned. "It's a separate side entrance, they don't know when the offices are occupied and when they're not."

"What time did you leave the office?"

"About five, I think. I took the accounts back to the main office, then caught the five twenty train back to Caisten. I was home about six, that's when I realised something was wrong."

"Did you go to Oxford at all yesterday?"

"I already told you, I was in the office all day, and I didn't have the car anyway."

"There is a train link from Witney to Oxford, Mr Keeley."

"No, I didn't leave the office. Look, if I wanted to kill my wife I wouldn't have done it in Oxford, would I!" Greg was increasingly frustrated at the time they were wasting on him.

"Interesting, Mr Keeley! Nobody's suggested that Annabel is dead. Do you know how those three stains got on your suit trousers."

Greg rolled his eyes, ashamed of his blunder. "Maybe it's red ink from my pen, when I reconcile accounts I always use a red pen, and I was using one yesterday."

"Okay, well we've sent them for analysis, should know the results soon. Mr Keeley, are you and Miss Bella Packard intimately involved with each other at all, having relations of sorts?"

Greg sprang up from his seat, anger flashing through his eyes. Krein noted how wild they were when he was angered. "That is none of your bloody business. Now either you bloody arrest me, or you bloody well let me go, because I've had enough of this crap."

"If that's how you feel, Mr Keeley, we will have no choice but to arrest you, but I'm sure you don't want that, do you?" Krein's gut feeling was that Greg was innocent, but he needed to rule him out first.

PC Flynn had the tedious task of trying to locate the curious car that had caused the accident near Clouds Hill. He was a passenger in the squad car that his colleague PC Collins was driving. His heart skipped when he noticed an unusual break in the low hedge on the left of the small country lane, not far from Wool. The muddied grass showed light tyre tracks on the verge leading to the gap.

"Whoa, Jack, there's something just up there."

Jack Collins slowed the Astra and pulled up beside the hole in the boundary, the tyre tracks continued through the shooting crops across the field, leading to a copse a couple of hundred meters away.

Jack reversed the car back slightly and manoeuvred through the hedge to follow the tracks, his heart racing with anticipation. He remained in first gear as the car bounced slowly over the uneven ground. As they neared the copse, the back end of a vehicle came into view, hidden underneath the drooping boughs of a willow tree. Sam Flynn radioed the find back to headquarters, requesting back up. They parked behind the car, and Sam moved the branches aside to get a clear reading of the registration plate. T two four seven S K D. Sam radioed it through, and within seconds excitement broke out at the police station. This was the car registered to a Mr Gregor Keeley, husband of a missing woman from Oxford. Annabel Keeley.

Detective Inspector Louis Reed had slipped on the regulation paper suit to collect the scattered clothes inside the cordoned crime scene for forensic testing. He was used to the odd brawl, stabbing, he'd even once had a case of poisoning, but the carnage around him was revolting. The driver's door of the black escort was wide open, the seat was drenched with rich, red blood, now drying black at the edges.

Beside the car lay a pale blue floral skirt, heavily soaked with blood, but also with excrement, and a pale blue cardigan, still blood stained, but not as copiously. A pair of women's shoes, low heel, navy, slightly tapered toe, both containing traces of blood, lay haphazardly by the trunk of the willow tree shadowing the car. A small Swiss army knife was found, sharp jagged blade extended, covered in blood. An empty clutch bag lay open beside the car, it's navy darkened with patches of blood.

The area had been cordoned off as soon as assistance had arrived, and a specialist search team were on their hands and knees, combing the area with their fingertips, searching for vital clues. So far there was no body. Where was this poor woman?

A police photographer had taken numerous pictures of the scene, from every conceivable angle, so Reed, gloved, placed the

31

articles carefully in paper bags for investigation. A curdled, sickened growl emerged from a colleague, and Reed guessed he'd found some evidence.

He hastened through the tangled undergrowth, recoiling as his eyes met the bloodied lump of flesh in the parted leaves of the bush. It was a fully formed foetus, still attached to the undersized placenta by a pale blue cord. The body was limp and lifeless. A tiny, perfect human foetus. The constable released the branches and turned aside, retching. The photographer approached with his camera.

Greg was tired, so tired. He couldn't believe what was happening to him. He loved Annabel with all his heart, he'd never do anything to hurt her, but in the space of a day, not only had she gone missing, but he was suspected of doing something awful to her. So far Krein had admitted that a witness had seen Annabel covered in blood, and a man who strongly resembled Greg had been next to her. Why, oh why, hadn't he worked in the main office yesterday. He sat in the stark room, his head leaning heavily, propped on his forearms, on the filthy wooden table, alone. Krein had been called out of the room a short while ago.

The door opened, Krein entered, closely followed by Raynor, who was carrying a tray laden with three mugs of strong coffee. "Keeley, we've received some news." Krein passed a mug to Greg. "You might need this. Your car has been found. It's in a copse between Dorchester and Bournemouth, near a place called Wool."

Greg rose from the hard chair with a gasp. "And Annabel. What about Annabel?"

"There is no sign of her, but I'm very sorry to say it doesn't look good." Krein glanced at his notes. "A pale blue skirt and cardigan were left beside the car, along with some low heeled navy court shoes, size eight, and, well, that's all the news I have right now." Krein couldn't bring himself to tell Keeley about the foetus and the knife.

Greg sat heavily, hearing the words and attempting to find some hope in them. "Annie's favourite skirt is pale blue, she wears it all the time because it's comfortable around her bump, you know, the baby."

Krein shuddered at the mention of the child, he sidetracked a little, guilty. "We have a special search team there at the moment looking for clues, or anything they can send for forensic testing, but I have to tell you, Mr Keeley, the clothes were bloodied: we now believe that Annabel may be injured somewhere."

"Blood. Annie. No. Not my Annie. You must be wrong, it must be the wrong car, just a coincidence, this sort of thing doesn't happen in real life, Annie's probably at home waiting for me, I …"

"Mr Keeley, we're doing all we can, but we need to act quickly. Do you know of anybody who resembles yourself who Annabel is in contact with?"

"Resembles me? Do you mean …?" Greg looked up, his eyes tired and worn.

The guilt was clear in Krein's voice. "Yes. You can't possibly have been in Dorset this morning, so obviously we apologise for the inconvenience you've had today. So, do you know of a man resembling yourself?"

"No, I'm sorry, I don't." Greg began to cry, deep and sorrowful, like a forlorn child. Anguish for his wife, relief for himself.

Wednesday 14th May

On Krein's request, Greg had supplied details of Annabel's credit card and company, the fraud department had been contacted, and asked to call Krein if the card was used at all. However, Krein was still surprised at the phone call he had just taken from the MBNA.

Annabel Keeley's credit card had been used in Wareham Railway Station to purchase a ticket to Havant the night before, then in the early morning it had been used again in Havant to buy a ticket to London. According to the constable sent to inspect the transaction slip, the signature was a good copy, if not a little shaky, but could well have been forged. An expert would need to compare the handwriting with Annabel's signature. The constable had interviewed the ticket officer at Wareham Station, but he couldn't remember anything untoward. Mrs Keeley's credit card simply said A. Keeley on it, with no reference to gender, so a male or female could have used it. Keeley was a dead woman, Krein was sure, and her killer was making his or her way to London. He'd no idea where in the city the killer may be heading to, he needed a witness somewhere, a sighting. Would this have to go public?

Katie Joyce had just nipped across the street to her nearest newsagent in her home suburb of Clapham, to get a daily paper. It was still chilly in the morning at this time of year, but that didn't deter her from lazily shrugging an overcoat over her pyjamas and slipping on her trainers, instead of dressing properly. She hadn't even brushed her hair, but very soon she was regretting that. The man who was beside the shop window was gorgeous.

Katie eyed him flirtatiously, and pushed past to enter the newsagents, but he didn't seem to notice her. Damn, she thought, why hadn't she made herself up before leaving. Irritated at her lack of foresight she grabbed a paper, and headed for the back of the long queue, waiting her turn, whilst admiring him through the glass. He was about six foot, no, a bit less, she estimated. His hair, covered by a beanie hat, was blond, in quite a shaggy style, just as she liked. He wore a baggy jumper, jeans, and his face was lovely, he looked so sensitive. Her heart leaped as he momentarily glanced through the window at her: Katie felt her cheeks burning, yet still she couldn't take her eyes off him.

However, Katie had no idea what was going through the man's mind. He was tired, very tired, he'd had a long journey, slow, tedious and uncomfortable. The train service had been poor, the usual delays, and he'd only managed to snatch a couple of hours sleep overnight.

As Katie surveyed him, engrossed in the headlines on the billboard outside the shop, she had no inkling that his head was being plagued by nagging voices, and he didn't like it: he was trying desperately to keep in control. His face was strained, confused, he was full of angst.

Katie could see he was troubled, she glanced at her own newspaper to see what headlines could be so important to him. "Lawrence of Arabia Style Death 73 Years On." What did that mean? And why did it bother the handsome man so much?

He fished in his pocket, pulling out some change, and entered the shop. Rudely, he pushed through the crowd and took a tabloid from the display. He checked the price and threw a few coins on the counter in front of the dumbfounded queue, and left.

Katie despondently watched him as he headed along the road, hoping that he lived nearby so they may cross paths again. She checked her watch, she'd make sure she arrived at the newsagent the same time tomorrow, maybe she would try and make conversation. He was far too stunning to give up easily.

He reached a bench near the train station and sat, studying the front-page article intently. Seventy-three years ago yesterday, exactly, at eleven twenty two in the morning of the thirteenth of May, Thomas Lawrence had been in an accident, falling from his Brough motorcycle. This happened near his home on the road between Clouds Hill and Bovington. He had died six days later of his injuries. At eleven twenty yesterday the thirteenth of May, in exactly the same place, Alan Benton, a baker from Bovington, had been knocked from his Harley Davidson Sportster 1000cc by a black car. He died from his injuries. Opening the paper to page three, he read the full story. There had been speculation at the time that T E Lawrence had been murdered, a rumoured phantom black car had been at the scene of his accident. This was never proven, but it was such a coincidence that another motorcyclist had been involved in an accident with a black car at the same time seventy-three years on.

He folded the paper and laid it on the bench beside him. The booming voice was back in his head, loud, overbearing, but somehow friendly. 'Now do you realise that this is your future, this is your destiny.' His mind tentatively asked; who was this person speaking to him so clearly? 'I'm God, of course!' The voice almost bemused, as if he should never have had to ask the question.

Then the feeble voice that kept trying to come through in his head was back, irritating and timid, but he ignored it, it was irrelevant now God himself was telling him what he had to do. His new duty was to re-create killings. They must be the same time, the same place, and the same method. He must find a library and be directed by the books, and by God himself, because he needed to select the next person to die in a destiny killing carefully. This was what he was born for.

Katie Joyce could not believe her luck. She hadn't seen him come in, but there he was, at the table, quietly reading through a stack of books. She nudged her colleague, who was busily sorting through the returned books, ready to replace them on the shelves. Caroline, lost in a dream world, jumped at the interruption.

Katie nodded towards the man. " Hey Caz, check him out. Is that sex on legs or what?"

Caroline sniggered and rolled her eyes. Katie was always falling in love with some new handsome guy. "Oh give it a rest, Katie, you're bloody sex mad, you are."

"I saw him in the paper shop this morning, I thought I'd missed my chance, but here he is. You never know, maybe he saw me this morning and followed me here, maybe he fancies me."

"Don't be so silly, and anyway, if he did follow you, don't you think that's a bit weird?" Caroline took another look at the man. He didn't seem weird, appearing quite pleasant really, but you had to be so careful nowadays.

"No, it would be romantic. Now how can I get his attention, show I'm interested?" She pondered to herself, her mind whirring.

Greg Keeley lay in his bed, it was ten thirty and Gail had already breakfasted the children, taken the older two to school, and three year old Petra to the playgroup. The house was empty, and the bed felt more so without Annabel's firm, athletic body next to his. Greg saw no reason to get up. Work didn't matter now: how could it? Without Annabel by his side, life couldn't mean anything. The phone trilled beside the bed, Greg stared at it, unsure, until it had rung five times, then he leant across and picked up the receiver.

"Hello."

"Is that Mr Gregor Keeley?"

Greg wriggled himself up until he was sitting, energised and hopeful on hearing Krein's voice.

"We have heard from Annabel's credit card company, the MBNA. The card has been used twice since the car was found, once last night, and the second time this morning."

"Really? So Annie's okay?" Greg sat up straight, a light smile underneath his moustache.

"We really can't tell at this stage, although we've sent the signature for analysis. I need to check with you that it's alright to not cancel the card. If we don't, we can keep track of where it's used."

"Of course, of course, whatever it takes. Where was it used?"

Krein referred to his scribbled notes. "Er, once in Wareham, then in Havant for a train ticket to London."

Greg pulled his feet from under the heavy covers and swung them off the bed. "London - she must be making her way home, she'll probably be making her way to Paddington to come home."

Krein sighed inwardly. There was no hope of that. Annabel would never come home, but he felt it unfair to dash Mr Keeley's hopes with what must be the bare truth. Keeley would come to realise as time went on, and sooner or later they would have the body to confirm his theory. "I will keep you informed. Mr Keeley."

Greg replaced the receiver, his smile wide, he had no idea about the severity of the bloodbath that was found in and beside his car, he had no knowledge that the police had recovered a foetus. His child. All he could believe was that his wonderful Annie would be home soon. Should he go and wait for her at Caisten Station?

He slammed the book shut in disgust, and several people turned to stare as he growled. "That's just not good enough!"

Caroline caught Katie's eye and mouthed. 'Stressy!' But Katie mouthed back. 'No! This is my chance'. She came out from behind the checking desk, and sauntered to where the man sat, now engrossed in a different book.

"Hello, sir." She breezed confidently, although she was anything but. He glared at her, surprised, eyeing her quizzically, and his gaze moved towards the door, becoming vacant once more.

"Sir?" Katie leant closer, levelling her neat cleavage with his eyes.

He returned his gaze towards her and looked, she felt, into her soul. "You called me sir." His voice was gentle, kind.

Katie giggled. "That's because I don't know your name! Look, I work here, and you looked like you were having difficulty a minute ago. Is there anything I can do to help?" She wanted to offer him more than help.

A slow smile spread across his face. The nagging little voice in his head tried to get through, but he ignored it, and pulled one of the books forward. "You know, you might be able to help me, I hope so." Katie was enjoying the delicate, fragile tone in his voice. "The only one I can find doesn't happen until the twenty seventh of May, but I need one earlier than that."

"I'm sorry, sir, I'm not quite with you." Katie glanced down at the book and noticed the title was 'Unsolved Cases'. She wasn't familiar with it.

A stronger voice came into his head, loud and clear, this one he didn't want to avoid, because this was God. It was God, and God was telling him that he must act normally. The girl started to speak, so he held his hands up against his ears, he wanted to hear God, not her. The message was clear, he had to make friends with her. Fate had made her talk to him, maybe she was to be his next victim. The voice drained away and he realised that the girl's hand was on his shoulder.

"Are you okay?" Katie was concerned about his anxious eyes: he looked haunted.

But suddenly he was back with her, the faraway look dissipated. "Oh, I'm so sorry, I must be confusing you." He examined her face, smiling. "I just get these huge headaches sometimes, you know, when I concentrate really hard. I'm so sorry if I alarmed you, but it's okay now."

Katie grinned and pulled out a seat next to him, shrugging into it neatly. "So, what can I help you with? And my name's Katie, by the way."

"Hi Katie, I'm," he blinked away from her, and turned back, "Paul. I'm conducting a research into the dates that crimes are committed on, and, er days. I want to see if there's any correlation." Katie wasn't really hearing his words, she was too busy looking into his pale, enigmatic eyes. "I need to find a murder between the fourteenth of May and the twenty seventh of May, and I can't."

Katie regarded him blankly.

"No," his smile subsided, "of course you can't help, silly me. Is it okay if I stay here and keep looking?"

Katie grinned again. "Of course, Paul. I'll tell you what, I'll go and look for some more crime books, maybe there'll be something else in another one."

Katie had collected as many crime and murder books as she could find, and throughout the morning had assisted Paul in any way he had wanted, although crimes and killings didn't interest her in the slightest. Being in close proximity to Paul made the work worthwhile. He didn't say much, a few grunts of thanks, but he was engrossed in his studies, scribbling notes here and there, collating details, names, dates.

Lunchtime neared, and Katie had braved asking Paul if he would like to join her on her break. He hesitated, and stared at the pile of books before him. She chuckled seductively. "Don't worry about them. I'll clear it with Caroline that you can leave them there for an hour or so."

He remained anxious, his eyes flitting over the titles, and finally grabbed his notes and threw them on the table in frustration. "This is too disorganised, I need a better way of keeping notes. This won't do."

Katie laughed again, this was one very intense young man. "Have you got some money? You can pick up one of those electronic personal organisers really cheap nowadays." His questioning eyes surveyed her face. "They're like little computers, you just type what you want on them and save it. Easy."

Paul retook the notes from the table, folding them in half. "Excellent idea, I'll use a credit card, then it doesn't matter what it costs."

So after clearing the arrangements with Caroline, Katie and Paul left, braving the downpour to head straight for the nearest electrical store. Katie helped him to select a suitable model, he paid and they made their way to a nearby cafe for a bite to eat.

Krein was contacted immediately by the MBNA. Annabel's credit card had been used again, this time in a CMC Electrical Store in Clapham. On contacting the shop by telephone, they confirmed that a hand held electronic organiser had been purchased, at the cost of one hundred and twenty-four pounds, ninety-nine pence. Nonchalantly, Krein scratched his head as he digested the brief description of the man and woman who had purchased the item.

Raynor entered the room and threw a pre-packed sandwich at Krein, who brushed it aside as he updated Raynor on the latest news. Raynor listened with interest. "So, it was a bloke and a woman. What did the woman look like? Could it be Annabel?"

Krein glanced at the notes again to remind himself of the description. "Small, petite, dark haired, no way is that Annabel."

Realisation crept across Raynor's face, he paled visibly, partly with horror, but also a touch of excitement. "But she might be the man's next victim." His sentence petered out, and Krein made no acknowledgement.

Krein had instructed Raynor to contact the nearest police station to the CMC Electrical Store in Clapham, ask if they could get a formal statement on the description of the couple who had used Annabel's card. The shop had had already given a brief summary to the MBNA, but Krein needed other details, like who had used the card, did she see which way they headed when they left the shop, that sort of thing. PC Bates was the man sent to do the task.

He sat in a small room at the back of the shop, with Felicity Barnum, the young girl who had served the couple, and drilled her memory to get as much detail as he could. She thought, although wasn't sure, that the couple may have turned right when they left the shop, she commented that the man was very handsome, so she had watched him admiringly. And it was definitely the man who had signed the slip.

"Signed?"

"Oh, chip and pin's broken down at the moment."

"Right. When he signed the transaction slip, did he do it with ease." Bates followed the list of questions he had been supplied with.

Felicity pondered for a moment. "He was a little shaky, I suppose, but I checked the signature against the card and it was similar.

Leaving the shop, PC Bates turned right, he glanced around, trying to guess where the couple may have gone to after buying a personal organiser. He entered a couple of cafes, but it was fruitless. Nobody of the description of either the man, nor the woman, had been noticed by anyone. Bates returned to his station, and soon Krein received a copy of the statement by email. He perused the document, realising it wasn't much help, and filed it in the growing case folder.

41

Katie felt like a complete fool, how could someone as streetwise as her have been duped like this? She was twenty two, well aware of the dangers of meeting strange people, especially in London, yet here she was, trussed up like a turkey in her own flat, and all because she hadn't heeded the warning signals that, in retrospect, were quite obvious.

She was on her own now: he had left the flat taking her keys and the money from her handbag with him, promising to be back soon, assuring her not to worry.

"Don't worry! Bollocks!" She spat to herself. How could she not worry when she was a pawn in some madman's game?

Paul, if that was his real name, his hesitation from before very realistic now, had made her telephone the library and tell them she had twisted her ankle, so wouldn't be in for a couple of days. Caroline had laughed, not detecting the tremor in Katie's voice, and suggested that Katie have 'fun' that evening. She plainly thought she was skiving.

Why, oh why, hadn't she just paid for lunch at Coopers when he mentioned, embarrassed, that he had left his money at the bed and breakfast he was staying in. Why had she been stupid enough to invite him for a sandwich at her flat. The door slamming launched her back to the present, and moments later Paul shuffled into the bedroom. He sank heavily to the bed, dropping a carrier bag onto the duvet.

Studying her in earnest, he groped in the carrier for the new organiser. He clicked a couple of buttons, stared at the screen for a moment, and returned his gaze to his prisoner. "You're safe." Katie's brow furrowed, not grasping his meaning. "I couldn't find any more murders, and you're too young for the next one. I did find one for today, but it was John Wayne Gacy, and he only killed boys, and that was in America anyway. So you're safe."

Relief shone from Katie's eyes. He didn't intend to kill her. But then reality hit again, she was still his hostage, she was still in potential danger. "Can you untie me then?" Her voice was hopefully cheerful, the fear she felt hidden from her jailor.

Paul heard the voice coming through, not the weak voice he always suppressed, but the stronger one, God's voice. 'Don't untie her. You have to shut her up, she'll tell the police, you don't want that.'

"How do I shut her up?" He shouted. Katie's face darkened, horror rising from the pit of her stomach. "I can't kill her, it's not the right date. I can't do it, don't make me."

Struggling, Katie's mind whirred: she had to do something to stop him, he was obviously troubled. Her memory darted to a book she'd skimmed through recently, it was about mental illness, and it had never occurred to her that it would be necessary to dip into the knowledge it had furnished her with. Maybe she could talk some sense into him. "Paul, nobody is making you do anything."

Paul glared at her, a glint in his eye silenced her. "Shut up." He drawled slowly, and returned his concentration to the organiser. It now held the information he had gleaned at the library, neatly documented in a hastily prepared spreadsheet.

Krein was frustrated, this case was so unusual. In his twenty-eight years on the force, he'd never been involved with a situation like this. A couple of domestics that fatally got out of hand, a couple of bodies in the Thames, but not a potential serial killer. This guy was different: there was a chilling air to the notes Krein read, and re-read, in the case folder. What did they have to go on? A rough description of a couple who used the victim's card in an electrical store. Did they need to discover Annabel's body, or was she still alive somewhere? How could he know? He strutted impatiently across his office, his hand clutching his forehead, deep in thought. "Goddamn this!"

Raynor sighed heavily, words evading him. Krein always took things to heart, he hated being unable solve a case: it really goaded him. Raynor was careful not to get personally involved with his work: he adored the job, it was a challenge, but he never took worries home to his wife.

"The thing that worries me the most," Krein glanced at Raynor with tired eyes, "is that we don't know if the dark-haired girl is an accomplice or a potential victim. We just have to wait here, hoping her body isn't our next grisly find."

Paul looked up sharply. "How old are you?"

"Twenty two." Katie's voice was subdued.

"Bingo! You're not pregnant, but you'll do. You've got until the thirty-first of May."

Tuesday 20th May

Greg was a broken man. Six days before he had been certain Annie was making her way home, he had patrolled Caisten train station for several hours, it gradually dawning on him that the wait was pointless. Detective Inspector Krein hadn't told him much, but it seemed from what he didn't say that they were tracking the credit card transactions to find a killer, not Annie. Was Annie's body lying out there somewhere, alone, cold, waiting to be discovered? Greg shook the thought from his head.

Gail had temporarily moved in with him. Her husband had tried to discourage her, but Gail knew Greg wouldn't be able to cope with children alone at this difficult time. It was eight days since they had last seen Annabel, and the local newspapers had ceased printing articles about her: late trains and vandalised parks seeming more important.

Strangely, Greg had come to respect Krein over the past week. At first he'd labelled him an insensitive bully, but Krein had proven himself to be attentive, making constant visits to Greg to update him on the investigation. Greg appreciated that these visits were more than duty bound: Krein was simply ensuring that he was coping.

In contrast, Krein was acutely embarrassed he'd initially suspected Greg, He knew that Greg was within his rights to complain, so he was being especially respectful to him to protect his own credibility.

The case would remain open until the man, or couple, were arrested, but the credit card hadn't been used again, and they had little else to go on. The Dorset Police Authority had tirelessly searched the fields near Wool, but no further evidence had turned up. A tabloid had suggested Annabel's body may have been dumped in the nearby English Channel, but there were no plans for a search yet.

Some forensic test results had been received back. Greg's Escort had been found to contain numerous hairs, both animal and human, but even after eliminating the Keeley family's hairs, they were too abundant for a speedy analysis. Annabel had been overly generous in offering lifts to friends and family. The details of the DNA found on the root of each strand was recorded, but so far none had matched any that of any known criminal.

A handwriting analyst had compared the signature at Annabel's bank to the transaction slip retrieved from the electrical store. He admitted they were similar, but very shaky, almost contrived. The document had been taken for further forensic testing, and using a solution of the chemical triketohydrindene hydrate they had managed to develop half a thumbprint, but it wasn't a clear specimen, which didn't surprise Krein: paper surfaces are renowned for being difficult to extract prints from.

Katie was uncomfortable and tired, she watched as Paul, carrying the small, black holdall she used for her trips to the gym, entered her bedroom. He sat on the edge of the bed, as he always did, and opened his electronic organiser. The room was silent, bar the whirring of the machine. Katie shifted her position, her legs were numbed, and she pushed her dry tongue into the gag that was in place for the majority of the day. He only removed it to feed her. She supposed, having counted the nights since her confinement, that this was day six of her imprisonment. She had long since ceased screaming, she had stopped hoping for escape. Paul scared her. His demeanour was kind, considerate, but the way he talked to himself was eerie, and his dark eyes were hard and unfeeling, maybe even dangerous.

Paul chuckled lightly, he pressed a button and lay the organiser on the bed. "All plans made, Rose, I'm all ready to go." Katie, unable to speak through the gag, stared at him, her drawn face emotionless. He unzipped the holdall and pulled out a couple of small boxes, which he threw on the bed, followed by four syringes. Katie winced, a bead of sweat prickled her brow as her body involuntarily shuddered.

PC Smith was fed up. Why did he always get the boring jobs to do? He finished filling in the police report and threw it in the filing tray. Sergeant Cross strolled towards him and Smith mustered a begrudging smile.

"Was that the report for the break-in at that chemist shop?" Cross glanced at the document in the tray.

"Yep."

"Anything nicked?" Cross was squinting, he'd left his glasses on his desk.

Smith retrieved the report and scanned through the paragraphs. He laughed, "I had to write them in capital letters or you wouldn't be able to understand them! There were two vials of methadone hydrochloride, and two vials of amitriptyline hydrochloride. Oh, and she said she thought there were less syringes than she remembered."

Cross took the document and looked over it, the blurring words dancing before him. "Isn't methadone what recovering drug abusers use?"

"Apparently, yes, it's a narcotic replacement. Mrs Rashime, the pharmacist, said it was on the Controlled Drugs List."

"What's the other one, that ami-whatever hydro stuff?"

"Er, she said that one was an antidepressant, or something like that."

Cross laughed as he threw the report back in the tray. "So we're looking for a depressed ex-junkie! We'll have hundreds of suspects round here then!"

Katie watched, resigned, as Paul half filled the syringe from one of the vials. He topped it up with the fluid from another vial. She had no idea what the drugs about to be administered to her, she supposed, were. Paul stood, tapping the vial to raise the air bubble, and glowered at her. "You're coming with me." Katie stared as he bent down, removing the gag from her mouth. She licked her dry, cracked lips with her parched tongue, then nodded towards a glass of water that lay by her feet. Paul held it to her chin and she drank, hungrily, the cold hitting her stomach painfully.

He continued. "We're going on a train, but we're going to have to use your credit card. I don't want any messing, so," Paul held the syringe in beside her face, "we are going to pretend to be in love, I will keep my arm around you at all times, and my hand, complete with this syringe, will be in your coat pocket. If you make one slight move that makes me suspicious, I will inject it into your leg. It will kill you within minutes."

Katie's eyes dropped to the floor, she wanted to cry, but a numbing veil hung over her. "Where are we going?" Her words were quiet, the question irrelevant.

"You have to go back to your cottage, Rose. Behave yourself, and you'll be back home in no time."

Caroline Merris sorted through the returned books mindlessly, and her thoughts wandered to her colleague, Katie. She hadn't come to work for nearly a week now, and no further telephone calls had explained her absence. Caroline had tried calling her numerous times, on both her landline and mobile, and she had even been to her flat, but she'd met no response.

Caroline automatically stamped the open book in front of her, smiling at the customer, and returned to the sorting. What line did she take now? Did she send a formal warning to Katie to force a reply? No, that was too harsh. She could ask human resources if they had any contact details for her relatives, maybe they would know what was going on. Caroline considered this carefully, she was concerned about getting her colleague into trouble. Katie may be a bit flippant, but she was a fast worker, and, Caroline reflected, a good friend. Decided, Caroline found the number for the human resources department of Lambeth Council, picked up the phone, and briefly explained the circumstances, casting Katie Joyce in a competent light.

Grimacing at her business partner across the beauty salon they co-owned, Joanna Joyce laid the receiver down. "Bloody daughter of mine's gone AWOL again. That was the Council, they say she ain't been in for nearly a week. I tell you, Maur, I always thought it'd get easier once they'd left home, but it bloody doesn't."

"You gotta go out then, love?" Maureen continued to manicure her client's long nails.

"Nah, I'll wait until me lunch-break, she's probably just holed up with some new fella, or something like that."

Katie shrugged on the olive trench coat that Paul held open for her. She had bought it several years before, but hadn't worn it for almost as long. She'd disliked it, but today it felt comforting and homely. Paul had skilfully pulled her filthy hair into a neat ponytail before, and had also daubed some make-up on her face with an accomplished hand to cover the dark circles under her eyes and the gauntness of her cheeks.

He pulled the door to her cosy flat open, slipped his arm around her waist, and tucked his hand, clasping the syringe, into her pocket. Her body shuddered with repulsion as she felt his touch. Paul grabbed the gorged holdall from the floor, and swung it over his shoulder. As they stepped into the communal corridor, Katie glanced at the clock on the wall, the time was ten forty five, and from the abundant birdsong, she supposed it was morning.

Joanna Joyce gratefully finished her morning shift at the salon at twelve noon, and resentfully walked towards her daughter's rented flat. She rang the doorbell, but the familiar chime didn't ring out. Suspecting the batteries to be old, she rapped on the door. There was no answer, and no sign of life from the rooms inside. Joanna sighed deeply and rooted in her handbag for her set of spare keys. Opening the door, she spotted some batteries lying beside doorbell chime box. She was immediately suspicious, although she had no idea what of.

Tentatively, Joanna edged into the kitchen and through to the lounge. This worried her more, the flat was scrubbed and cleaned beautifully, it was impeccably neat. Her Katie was not a tidy person by nature, and a more comforting sight would have been scattered clothes and food-encrusted dishes. Joanna called out Katie's name softly, her harsh accent cutting the silence.

Entering the only bedroom, she could see that the bed, although nicely made, had a few ruffles in the covers, as if somebody had been sitting on it. Passing the uncluttered dressing table opposite the bed, Joanna felt uncomfortable with its waxen shine. Something was going on, but what? What was her bloody daughter up to?

Fed up and wishing she had just been able to put her feet up over a mug of tea, Joanna realised she would have to return after work and scour the flat in more detail, see if any holiday brochures or likewise would explain Katie's absence.

"Bloody kids!" She exclaimed under her breath as she snatched the keys and her bag, and slammed the front door behind her, hastening back to the salon.

Paul guided Katie to the ticket office at Liverpool Street Station. He pulled her credit card from the back pocket of his jeans and threw it on the counter. "One single, one return to Saxmundham please."

The man remained silent as he typed on the till, three tickets spilled out, and he took the credit card from the counter. He fed it through the till, and placed the receipt on the counter with a pen. Katie nervously glanced at Paul, and leant over the receipt, shielding it from his view. Instead of signing her name, she wrote 'PLEASE HELP ME' boldly. Without even comparing the slip to the credit card, the man slipped it into the till and chucked the tickets across the counter. Tears prickled at Katie's eyes: she was more terrified than ever.

Paul and Katie stepped off the bus, amazingly he had managed to keep his arm wrapped around her waist for the entire journey. Katie was tired and hungry, but the fear had subsided to complacency. Having tried for help and been ignored, there wasn't much more she could do. Paul glanced around the small village of Peasenhall. It was pleasantly quaint. The main central road, which they stood beside, was flagged by old, character filled cottages, and a small stream trickled alongside.

Gripping Katie firmly, Paul steered her back along the road in the direction they had come from. An elderly man nodded hello with a smile as he walked by, but Paul ignored him, his face stern. They crossed the stream on a rickety footbridge, and waded through the long, scratchy grass, towards a large barn-like structure. Dirty and black, it was in bad disrepair. Paul's eyes scanned the area for onlookers, and, comfortable they hadn't been watched, dragged Katie up to the building, through the burgeoning weeds.

As they turned the peeling corner of the building, Paul spied a rotting board that clumsily covered an entrance. He tugged at the weakened wood, it breaking off in his fingers, creating a gap large enough for them to squeeze through.

The smell was stale, dank, and the coolness hit them with a shiver. Their eyes adjusting slowly, the only light in the building came from their bodged entry hole, bundles of hay became apparent in the darkness. For the first time in many hours Paul released Katie from his grip. "Sit." He demanded, and she sank into a prickly bale wearily.

Paul crouched down and opened the hold-all, he pulled out the rope that had bound Katie for the previous six days, and tied it firmly, attaching the knot to a metal ring he found jutting from the side of the barn. He brought the soggy gag from the bag and placed it over her mouth, pinching her hair as he fixed it solidly. Katie didn't resist at all, and she uttered no noise.

His prisoner securely tethered, Paul stood, hands on hips, and surveyed her, the smile on his lips not reaching his eyes. "Welcome home, Rose, you're back where you belong. You needn't worry about anything, because I'll take care of you."

Katie glared at Paul, the darkness protecting him from seeing the hate in her eyes: she detested him calling her Rose. "This is where you'll stay for the next eleven days, then you are going to have an exciting trip. You're going to your destiny, as I fulfil mine."

Eleven days? Katie's thoughts whirled, what could that mean? What was happening in eleven days? What date was it? If she could determine his plan, she may be able to outwit him. Katie strained to work out what the date must be, and, although not sure, she estimated it was the twentieth of May. Eleven days ahead would be the thirty first of May. What significance was that?

"I'm going to bring food soon, I want you to eat as much as you can, because in a couple of days I have to go away for a while. I don't want to come back here and find you starved to death. You mustn't die, do you hear me?"

51

Katie wearily nodded, he didn't make sense. Thirty first of May. Hold on, he'd said that date before, he'd said it at her flat. If only she could get her hands on his organiser, he did a lot of work on that, she was sure the significance of the date could be found on there.

Friday 23rd May

Paul confused Katie. She knew he was ill, after all, regular people didn't go around tying up librarians, or rabbit on about important dates and destiny: but he was so kind. Not once did he swear at her, he ensured she ate, and ate well, and he was always considerate enough to make sure she had a drink nearby. He wasn't interested in talking, but his presence was strangely unthreatening. Only his unusual outbursts, and not knowing what they meant, worried her.

She assumed she'd been there a few days, the light and dark was fairly interchangeable in this new prison, so she had lost a definite track of time, Paul had been busy making an odd structure from the hay bales in the centre of the barn. She couldn't work out what it was meant to be, but he had promised she would find out. Today she did.

Paul untied the ropes bounding her sore wrists to the metal bar, and carefully led her towards the newly built structure. She could feel the hay prickling her skin as Paul pushed her inside his formation.

"Sit." Katie followed the instruction and sat tentatively. She heard the sound of metal against metal, then the cold feeling of chains against her skin. She realised with calm submission that she was again being bound, this time with metal shackles as well as rope.

"My next duty is in four days. I don't want to leave you alone, but I still have to find the woman, and make her my friend. I estimate that will take up to four days to do. I'm sorry, but please don't be too lonely. Just try and sleep, it'll pass in no time."

Katie made no response. Paul walked away, but soon she felt his warmth beside her once more: he placed a cold object by her leg. "Here's a bucket of water, if you get thirsty, lean your head in, you will be able to sip through the gag. I can't leave any food, because if I take your gag off, you might scream. I can't risk getting caught. I will feed you well when I get back, a good meal, lots of lovely things to make up for leaving you."

Paul moved away. In the slim stream of light through the broken barrier of the makeshift entrance, Katie could see Paul lift a large object, then place it in front of her. Another was placed on top, and soon all beads of light had been blocked off. Terrified, Katie realised that Paul had built a cocoon for her to stay in, and a claustrophobic shudder ran through her body. Even if she was able to lose the gag and scream, it was unlikely anybody would hear her. She moved her hands a little, a metallic sound grated at her ears, and she groped about, feeling a metal hoop that was set in the ground. Her hands were chained to it. Katie had to give credit to Paul, he was thorough.

Caroline Merris strode through the doors of the small salon and hesitated by the dated reception desk. Maureen caught her eye.

"Yes love, can I help ya?" Maureen was excited, most of the salon's clients were aged, and only wanting perms or colouring for their greying hair. What a contrast, this young girl had a lovely head of luscious locks.

"I'm looking for Katie Joyce's mother, I think she works here."

Maureen's face fell. "Yes, love, I'll just get her."

Joanna had already heard and was sauntering towards them. She nodded at Caroline. "I'm Joanna Joyce. What do you want?"

Caroline glanced at Maureen, soon realising she had no intention of giving them any privacy. She focused on Joanna. "My name is Caroline Merris, I work with Katie."

"Oh God! What's the bleeding girl done this time?"

Caroline balked, she was expecting a little more consideration for her friend. "I, um, just wondered if you've seen her recently, it's just she hasn't been to work for nine days now, and I haven't been ..."

"No, not seen her at all. Some woman from the council rung the other day so I went to Katie's flat, but she weren't there. I meant to go back in the evening, but, tell the truth, I forgot all about it, what with all my shopping and whatnot."

And suddenly Caroline realised how lucky she was to have her own, caring mother. She grasped to re-compose herself. "I think we should contact the police, see if anything has happened, report her as missing ..."

"Missing! That bloody daughter of mine is always bleeding missing! Used to bloody slide down electric cables out of her bedroom window at night to go out and meet the boys."

Caroline shook her head slowly. "Well, I think I shall go to the police station anyway." She turned to leave.

Maureen nudged Joanna. "Oy, you wally. You should go with her - think of all those hunky men in uniform. I can hold fort here."

Joanna laughed. "Hey Karen, or whatever your name is, hold up. I'll come with you, might bag myself a fella." Caroline stopped walking, but didn't look back: she was disgusted. No wonder Katie hadn't mentioned her mother. She waited for Joanna to put her coat on.

PC Smith groaned as the two women left the station. "Jesus H Christ, that was painful!"

Sergeant Cross continued writing on a pad, his concentration intact. "What's that then?"

"Oh, some girl's gone missing. Her colleague is worried, but her mum says she's always going off with some man or other." Smith had failed to take the conversation seriously.

"Nothing I should know about then?" Cross signed his letter and folded it in three.

Smith dropped the statements on Cross's desk without conviction. "May as well a glance through, but, well, in your own time, know what I mean." He laughed and headed for the door. "Coffee?"

Paul had used the last of Katie's cash to purchase a bus ticket to Saxmundham. Fortunately he had the return ticket to Liverpool Street, so he'd reached London before he needed any more money. He took Katie's credit card from the side pocket of his holdall, a note of the pin number folded loosely around it. Feeding the card into the machine, he typed in the code, withdrawing two hundred pounds.

Paul ambled to a nearby newsagent, picked up a copy of The Mail, and paid. The change paid for a Zone C ticket, he stepped onto the escalator running down towards the platforms.

Sergeant Cross lived up to his name: he was furious. That imbecile Smith had to be the biggest idiot of the century. Cross slammed the statements onto his desk and marched through to the control room.

"Sue, radio Smith. I want him back here, pronto."

Cross returned to his desk, and glanced at the statements again. Joanna Joyce's was piffle, but Caroline Merris's was more sinister. The description of the man that Caroline had last seen Katie with was haunting, and that bloody ignoramus, Smith, should have noticed the similarities. Cross rooted through the filing cabinet and pulled out the statement Smith had taken from the girl at the CMC Electrical. Carefully, he read and re-read the details of the couple using Annabel Keeley's credit card.

The man: five-foot ten-ish, blond, shoulder length, unkempt hair. Good looking. Jeans, jumper, trainers. Could be anyone. Except it matched the description of the man Katie Joyce had last been seen with on the day she went missing.

The woman: five-foot two-ish, long, dark hair, brown eyes, pretty. Black trouser suit. Could be anyone. Except it matched the description of Katie Joyce, and she had been wearing a black trouser suit on the day she went missing.

Krein had taken the call with interest, it was about time there was some movement in the Annabel Keeley case. A Sergeant Cross from Clapham South police station was concerned because a young girl, Katie Joyce, had been reported missing by her mother and a work colleague. Katie's mother had shown the police around her daughter's flat on Lillieshall Road, she was concerned that it was unusually tidy.

Rooting through Katie's paperwork, constables located the name of her bank, and on investigation her credit card was found to have been used today, in London, to obtain two hundred pounds. Oddly, it had also been used in Liverpool Street station in London, to purchase train tickets to a place named Saxmundham, in Suffolk, three days before.

Krein's phone trilled, he leant over and snatched the receiver, deep in thought. "Krein."

"DI Krein, sir, it's Sergeant Cross at Clapham South again. I have some more information I thought you should know."

Krein waited, fixated, his pen hovering over a memo pad. "Go on."

"Barclaycard have received the receipt for the transaction on the twentieth of May, the one buying train tickets to Saxmundham. Get this, sir. Instead of a signature, 'please help me' is written in capital letters."

Krein stood up, adrenaline flowing through his veins as the atmosphere chilled eerily. "Sergeant Cross, thank you. Can you call Barclaycard and get them to report any further usage of the card to my number? Oh, and I also want the full details of where the card was used to obtain the cash today."

Cross agreed, his irritation that a detective inspector he didn't even know was bossing him around was undetectable. He surmised Krein's investigation was important, so he wasn't about to be precious just yet.

Paul had already phoned Eastbourne Council to ask them to recommend a nursing home suitable for his grandmother, who was suffering from Alzheimers. He'd told them money wasn't a problem. They'd suggested three: Bayside House, Summers Grange, and The Risings Nursing Home, all in Eastbourne itself. That was a good start, but he needed the names of the residents, because it was his duty to find an eighty five year old lady. The only way to do this, he guessed, would be to gain access to the homes, one by one, until he found the right lady to help him on his path to destiny.

Paul picked his bag up and left the phone booth: he headed away from Eastbourne Railway Station, on the lookout for a shop that sold torches. He would also need gloves.

Darkness had fallen and Paul remained crouched under the dangling branches of a willow tree in the gardens of The Risings

Nursing Home. A light was on in the entrance hall, and another in a room towards the back. A few of the upstairs rooms had light shining through the curtains, and Paul assumed that these were the bedrooms of the elderly residents. The door of the downstairs back room opened, Paul silently observed a middle aged lady bring a black rubbish bag out and place it in the bin. She returned to the house.

Knowing he now had a chance of entering un-noticed, Paul crept closer to the door and carefully, quietly, tried the handle. A lock on the inside of the door held it shut. Paul was prepared to wait, he had time. The sky was clear and black, the night cold, and a gentle breeze lapped around Paul's body. He had long since ceased feeling any discomfort, the important thing was finding the information needed for his next job.

It took an hour, or so, but his patience was worthwhile, because the door opened again: the same lady came out and traipsed across the garden to the small car park. Paul saw the opportunity and slipped through the doorway, into an unattractive, yet functional kitchen. Hearing the woman's footsteps returning, Paul opened a narrow door, and dived into a spacious, musty smelling larder. He pulled the door to as the footsteps plodded into the kitchen, silencing his nervous breath as the back door slammed shut, the bolt scraping back across.

Paul could hear the woman pottering about for a short while, pans clattering as they were put away, and taps running as she cleaned. With effort, Paul remained noiseless, although his legs were cramped and uncomfortable, and he breathed out heavily, relieved, when the light of the kitchen snapped off, veiling the larder in a deep blackness. Paul waited a few seconds more, he opened the cupboard and stepped into the darkened room.

Stealthily, he stepped into the main body of the Victorian house: he needed to find the reception desk, or an office, wherever the personal details of the residents were kept. He reached an expansive hallway, it's polished wooden floorboards hindering his attempts at silence. Trying various doors, the third opened to a room containing two cumbersome filing cabinets. Deftly, he sifted through a rack of files, eventually pulling out a well-worn book.

Scanning the pages, relief flooded him as he found the lady he was looking for: 'Room 12: BLESSING, Maud Ethel. Reg. 14/7/07. DOB 10/1/1923. NoK ANTON, Julia (daughter)'

Paul soaked Maud Blessing's details into his memory, remembering them with clarity. She was eighty-five. This nursing home specialised in Alzheimers care. Perfect. And by coincidence her daughter was named Julia. No, not coincidence, it was fate. Maud Blessing had lived her entire life for the moment he was arranging: she was destined to be Paul and God's next duty.

Saturday 24th May

Elaine Baylis could not help but be attracted to the handsome man who stood before her. But then again, she had a job to do, and letting Maud Blessing's long lost great-grandson visit without checking with Mrs Anton, well, that was strictly against the rules.

Paul grinned at Elaine amicably. "Come on, Maud would be thrilled to see me, you know she would. It would do her the world of good."

Elaine glanced at the visitor's book, tempted to break the rules just this once, after all, he was gorgeous, and it would mean she could get to know him better. "I don't know," she hesitated, "I'll be in such trouble. Why can't I just phone her daughter and check it's okay?"

Paul's smile diminished, his brow knitted sorrowfully as he leant towards Elaine, his voice lowering to a whisper. "I didn't want to say anything, after all, it's embarrassing for me, and embarrassing for my mother. I should imagine Mrs Anton would be ashamed too, if she were to hear of this." Elaine's eyes scanned his, intrigued. "You see, my mother is Julia Anton's illegitimate daughter. Julia fell pregnant while she was at boarding school, which was a disgrace in those days. She was sent away to have the baby, my mother, and the baby was adopted. After my mother had given birth to me, she tried to trace her birth family."

Elaine placed her hand gently over Paul's, he continued to speak, his expression fraught. "Well, she found Maud, my great granny, first, and Maud took to us both, I was still a baby, straight away, but when Mum was introduced to Julia, well, Julia wanted nothing to do with her." Elaine's face softened as she clutched his hand sympathetically. "When Maud was put into this home, I remember the date well, the fourteenth of July two thousand and seven, well, Mum and I had no idea where she had gone. For all we knew, she could be dead. But now, I am so pleased, because after such a long search, I have finally found her again." His voice cracked with emotion, a rogue tear wandering down his cheek was hastily wiped away.

Elaine felt torn, she felt desperately sorry for this gentle man, he seemed genuine, but she needed to find a way of verifying his story. Maud's illness was so advanced she couldn't tell day from night, she wouldn't be able to help. Paul interrupted her dilemma. "Look, all you have to do is check the date she was admitted, that will prove I am who I say I am, won't it? Well, as good as, anyway."

Her snap decision made, Elaine relented: she felt she had no right to keep the two people apart. "Hold on then, if the date's right, then I'll let you visit her, but keep a low profile because I'll be in big trouble if this gets out. Fourteenth of July last year, you say?"

Paul rushed into the stiflingly warm room, held his arms out wide, and ran towards Maud. "Oh, Granny, my dear Granny, I have missed you so much. It's Paul, Granny, it's me, I've missed you so." Paul hugged the old lady, who sat awkwardly in her bedside chair, gently. Elaine was certain she saw the twitches of a smile on Maud's lips, so she relaxed her guard, closing the door quietly behind her. That was her good deed done for the day.

Katie leant over the bucket in the blackness of her prison, she carefully lowered her face to the water, sucking on the saturated gag until her thirst was quenched. She had no idea how long it had been since Paul left, realistically it may only have been five minutes, but it seemed a lot longer than that. Gauging a sense of time with most of her senses dulled was impossible.

Katie wondered if anybody back home had noticed her missing yet. Before they'd taken the train journey, she knew Paul had imprisoned her for over a week, but now she had completely lost track of time. All she knew for certain now was that Paul had told her he would come back, and that he planned something with her on the thirty first of May, something to do with a duty. Even though Paul was her captor, Katie found it difficult to hate the good-looking man: perhaps she even felt wretched for him that he had this mental disorder, whatever it was. Maybe when he had finished with her, maybe he would let her help him, get him fixed or something.

Her stomach growled and the pain shifted through her abdomen. She was starving, and the water didn't satisfy her hunger at all. Katie felt lonely and cold, and, unaware that her own mind was lapping towards Stockholm Syndrome, she wanted Paul to return soon. He may not talk much, but at least he was company, and no one had ever shown such care towards her before.

Whenever he heard footsteps in the corridor outside Maud's room, he would talk cheerily, as if he were updating her on his latest accomplishments, but as soon as the steps dissipated, his stories halted. The innocent, yet vacant and gnarled woman sat, oblivious to his hateful stare. Her bony fingers were clenched unknowingly into fists, her head lopped to one side, her eyes were unseeing. Maud's legs, propped on a low footstool, were unmoving, but her mouth churned periodically, a dribble of saliva seeping over her chin. Footsteps echoed on the stairs, methodically clipping towards the room, Paul launched into an animated story again.

"You just wouldn't believe it, Granny, I was so pleased when …" The footsteps stopped and the door handle creaked. "Oh Granny, you've done it again."

Elaine entered, her heart leapt at the sight of the lovely young man wiping Maud's mouth with a tissue. He adores her, she thought to herself. "Mr, er …"

Paul flinched convincingly. "Joyce. Paul Joyce."

"I'm sorry, Mr Joyce, but it's really time you went, now. Mrs Anton will be here soon, she comes every Saturday."

Sighing, Paul rose, he stooped towards Maud, his lips brushing her cheek lightly, and stepped towards the door. He forced a tear to his eye, which Elaine noticed as planned. "I have to thank you, so, so much. Will you let me come back and visit my dear Granny again?" He was laying this on too thickly, but Elaine fell for his lies with ease.

She smiled widely and chuckled. "I think that would make Maud's day. Not until Monday, though, I'm off tomorrow."

"Are you working Tuesday?" Elaine nodded in reply. "Then let me come Tuesday, I have an engagement Monday, so if I come Tuesday, I can spend more time with her." Her agreeable smile signed Maud Blessing's death warrant.

Tuesday 27th May

She felt so, so weary, not through lack of sleep, but starvation. Her body had ceased to crave food, the gnawing pains long gone with acceptance of her fate. Her listlessness smothered her, her mind no longer caring if she live or die. Katie wished Paul would come back, she needed him: his presence would stop this numbness.

Lethargically, Katie dipped her head into the bucket. There was scarcely any water left, and her lips pushed forward, probing for the liquid in the darkness through the damp gag. Finally the material saturated, and her tongue lapped gently at the stale water. She swallowed painfully. Barely satiated, Katie's final surge of strength abated, she felt herself falling once more into a deep slumber. Her tense face relaxed as her body succumbed to the ebbing sleepiness, cooling as her nose settled into the water. She choked lightly, her throat gurgling soundlessly, and the blackness around her darkened. A feeble spasm rippled through her body. Katie drew her final watery breath, and the loneliness was gone.

Elaine had been surprised at how excited she was when she had arrived for her shift that morning. Mr Joyce, or should she be familiar and call him Paul, well, he was coming to see Maud again. They hadn't arranged a time, so Elaine busied herself with mundane chores, unsuccessfully trying not to think about his kind face, his slim, dare she say it, sexy body.

A man in his mid eighties, one of the newer residents, wandered into the hallway, his gentle face vague as he roamed aimlessly. Observing his frail body, it was difficult for Elaine to believe that Albert Cheeseman had been a Sergeant Major in World War II, he was now in the middling stages of Alzheimers. Elaine enjoyed that sweet stage, with most of the residents, anyway. Some were confused and had a tendency to violence when frustrated, but most, like Mr Cheeseman, were like children, in awe of their surroundings, pleasant, and wondrous.

Elaine stepped out from behind the reception desk and hurried towards Mr Cheeseman. "Albert, dear, where do you think you're going?" She laid her arm loosely on his shoulders and took his hand, tenderly guiding him towards the day room. "Come on, dear, you mustn't be wondering around on your own, must you? Let's sit you back down." Albert smiled appreciatively, and made no objection to being steered back in the direction he had come from. The main door squeaked open, Elaine glanced over her shoulder, and her heart flipped when she spotted Paul. He smiled, sending a deep fluttering through her stomach.

"Be with you in a minute, Mr Joyce," she grinned, her heart now racing, "I'll just settle Mr Cheeseman in the day room."

Paul put his holdall on the floor and mindlessly perused the notice board until Elaine returned. They exchanged a few pleasantries, and she led him through the maze of corridors, and up the stairs, finally reaching Maud's room. Opening the door, she stood aside to let him in.

"How long can I stay?" Paul's cold eyes were settled on the old lady, Elaine failing to notice the unusual sense of urgency in his voice.

She glanced needlessly at her watch. "I'm here until six this evening, after the dinner shift. As long as you're gone before, I don't know, five forty-five when Sarah gets in to take over, well, you can stay until then."

"Perfect. That's plenty of time." The coldness abated as his face crinkled into a smile.

Desperate to continue the conversation, but with no more words to say, Elaine turned to leave. Suddenly she stopped, an excuse found. "Oh, she has lunch at twelve, and dinner at four thirty. Would you like me to sit with you?" Hopeful.

Paul patted the holdall. "Oh, she won't need meals today, I've brought some treats for her, we'll have our meals alone, if that's okay?"

This wasn't going to plan. Elaine struggled for another reason to spend time with him. "Um, I should warn you, Mr Joyce, but it's quite difficult with Maud now, she finds swallowing difficult, it's a bit like feeding a baby, I guess." Being childless, it was a true supposition, but a correct one all the same.

Paul was starting to feel agitated, his manner became abrupt. "It's okay, I spoke to Mum, she's a nurse, she advised me what food to bring. We'll be fine." He glanced over his shoulder at Maud. "Won't we, Granny."

Resigned in defeat, Elaine stepped out and closed the door behind her. "Damn!"

Paul wasted no time. He waited until Elaine's footsteps dissipated, and strolled across the small room towards the frail lady, who sat, as she had three days previously, in her bedside chair. He placed Katie Joyce's sports bag on the bed, unzipped it, and lifted out a couple of cans of diet cola, some fruit, some crisps, and a bar of milk chocolate, placing them on the bedside table, followed by a small length of rope. Next, he pulled out a carrier bag, unfolded it, and retrieved two small vials of liquid, and two syringes from inside.

Just as he had done for Katie before their journey to Peasenhall, he filled one of the syringes with a mixture from the vials, and, once it was full, did the same with the second syringe. Paul opened the drawer of the bedside cabinet, slipping both syringes inside, and re-wrapped the vials, returning them to the holdall. He took the bag from the bed, and dropped it onto the floor.

Paul smiled, he paused for a moment to listen for any disturbances, but the silence eased him, and he continued with his plans. Leaning across the bed, he lifted the blanket, pulling it towards the end of the bed, exposing the fresh cotton sheets. Placing his hands underneath Maud's arms, he dragged her awkwardly onto the bed, straining to lift her gnarled body. He laid her gently against the headboard, the pillows sinking lightly with the weight of her head as it lopped to one side. A dribble of spittle ran down her chin. He didn't wipe it away, he didn't have an audience this time.

As quietly as possible, Paul dragged the still warm chair towards the door, he hooked the back under the handle, and tried the door. It wouldn't budge: he rubbed his hands together, relieved to be able to stop worrying about interruptions.

Settling himself softly on the side of the bed, Paul rolled the sleeve of Maud's flannelette nightdress as high as it would go, he opened the bedside drawer and removed one of the syringes.

Having once been a blood donor, Paul knew roughly how to locate a vein on the inside of the elbow, and he tied a tourniquet at the top of her arm with the rope. He squeezed Maud's hand into a fist repeatedly until her veins bulged expectantly, finally inserting the needle through her papery skin. The syringe empty, he took the second one and dispensed it into her blood stream.

Paul pressed lightly on the tiny puncture mark until it stopped bleeding, and wiped the area with a tissue, rolling the nightdress sleeve back into place. During the entire operation, Maud had made no sound, and no physical objection. She just stared, her unseeing eyes wide open, unable to defend herself even if she'd realised she was being murdered.

Paul took the spent syringes and replaced them in the carrier bag, along with the vials. He stuffed the bag back into the holdall, took the food from the bedside table and placed it on top, arranging it neatly to conceal the carrier bag. In hindsight, he retrieved a can of cola, cracking it open and taking a large gulp to quench his thirst.

"From now on I will call you Julia. You will die today, of poisoning, just as Julia Bradnum did exactly fifty-six years ago. She didn't have Alzheimers but, like her, you are eighty-five. You were placed on this earth, dear Julia, for me to fulfil my duties to God, and now it is just a matter of time until I have finished with you. And as with the original Julia, your passing will be seen as a sad, but timely death. John Bodkin Adams was never tried for Julia's death, and nor shall I be for yours. You will die peacefully, I've made sure of that, I did my research. Just relax, don't be scared."

Paul strode to the door and removed the chair, quietly dragging it back beside the bed. He slumped into it, satisfied, and took another long swig of the cola, glancing at Maud once his thirst was quenched. Her breathing was shallow, slightly quickened, and Paul smiled at her tenderly. She was dying, and he knew that God would be pleased with him.

Felicity Barnham, who had served the hunted man and Katie Joyce at CMC Electrical Stores just under two weeks before, had been interviewed again, and on the strength of her very basic description, and Caroline Merris's more detailed account, a photofit had been prepared of the man. During the past couple of days constables had spent hours talking to, and showing, the likeness, along with a recent photo of Katie, to staff at Liverpool Street station.

Suffolk Constabulary had also taken copies of the two pictures to Saxmundham train station, but nobody could clearly remember having seen either the man, or Katie. A few witnesses vaguely recollected that they *may* have seen them, but no specific, definite sightings.

Krein was at a loss. Although his line manager, Detective Chief Inspector MacReavie, was now officially in charge of Annabel's case, Krein was still doing most of the legwork, not that there was much to do at the moment. After all, without a precise witness account, without either credit card being used, and without Annabel or Katie's bodies being found, the only option he had was to wait, and hope for a lucky break soon.

The forensic examinations of Gregor Keeley's Escort were now finished, and the results had given them no clear leads. It had been verified from medical records that the blood in the car was from Annabel, and the foetus had been proven to be hers and Greg's. Only Annabel's blood had been found in and around the car, and although the details of all the other DNA found had been fed into the National DNA Database, the daily matches had so far brought no results.

It was a possibility to eliminate many of the hairs found in the car by taking the DNA of all Annabel's known friends and acquaintances, but this would be a costly exercise, one that the Thames Valley Police Force could well do without if they could possibly avoid it. There were no untoward fingerprints, nothing at all that could help them any further, found in Katie Joyce's unusually immaculate flat, and even if they had a hundred fingerprints and a hundred DNA samples, without a suspect to compare them with, they were of no use.

Krein had still not admitted to Gregor Keeley that the foetus had been found near the Escort. He reasoned uncomfortably that it must be obvious to Greg, now, that his wife would not be found alive, and subsequently he would also have to come to terms with the fact that his fourth child would never be born. But to tell a man that his child had been ripped from the womb so sickeningly, how could Krein tell him that? It would come out one day, but Gregor Keeley wasn't coping well at the moment: he couldn't make it worse for him.

Paul was quietly reading a book to Maud, he had found it in her bedside cabinet. He wanted her to feel comforted in her last hours, he wished her to die happy. She wasn't conscious anymore, her blank eyes had closed a short while before, her breathing slight, and, on feeling her wrist, Paul had noted that her heartbeat was slow, occasionally irregular. She had suffered a mild seizure, but that had passed in moments. A sharp knocking on the door jolted Paul, he felt a bead of sweat spring to his brow. "Come in." He hadn't noticed any footsteps approaching, he'd have to be more careful.

Elaine popped her head around the door, she frowned. "Why is Maud in bed?"

Paul raised his finger to his lips to quieten Elaine, and whispered, "We had a light lunch, then her eyes started to droop. I lifted her into the bed for a nap. I thought a quick snooze wouldn't hurt her."

Elaine opened the door fully, stepping closer, relaxed, and smiled, charmed by his gentle caring. "Okay, that's no problem. Has she been good? Did she eat without too much difficulty?"

Paul bristled, wishing the girl would just leave them alone. He tried consciously not to rouse suspicion by speaking abruptly. "She's been fine, she had some banana, a small piece of chocolate, and half a yoghurt. She seemed to enjoy them all." He held up the book for Elaine to see. "I was just reading this novel to her, she always liked to be read to, especially once her eyes began to fail. I know she's asleep, but I thought she would appreciate it anyway."

Mildly myopic, Elaine squinted towards the book. "Emma by Jane Austen, oh, that's a lovely story. She is lucky to have you, you know."

Paul stared at her, his irritation plain. "I know. So can you let us carry on."

The smile left her lips, the glare made her uncomfortable. She mumbled as she backed through the door. "I'll leave you to it."

Once the door was closed, Paul laid the book on the bed, bent down, and opened a side pocket on the holdall from which he pulled out a pair of scissors and another carrier bag. He took them across the room to the mirror that sat on a wooden chest of drawers, grasped a bunch of his mussy blond hair, and chopped at it roughly, close to the darker roots. He placed the shorn locks inside the carrier bag, and took another clump of hair.

With Mr Cheeseman on one arm, and Mr Aldredge on the other, Elaine led the two childlike men from the dining room to the day room and helped them into their seats. She had just finished supervising dinner time for the residents who could still leave their rooms easily, and, glancing at her watch, she noticed it was half past five, nearly home time.

Walking towards the reception desk, she decided to give Mr Joyce another ten minutes with Maud until she reminded him to leave, but was surprised to see an envelope addressed to her on the desk. Picking it up, she tore it open and scanned the hurried letter within:

'Dear Elaine. Thank you for today, it has been wonderful, and most satisfactory, we had a lovely time. ~~Juli~~ Maud was great company, but I must admit that I seem to have worn her out, she has fallen asleep again after her dinner. I have laid her down and left her to it. Unable to find you, I have left this note, and hopefully I will see you again soon, next Tuesday if that's okay. Best regards, Paul Joyce.'

Elaine chuckled to herself, enamoured with the pleasant letter, although the writing was quite scruffy, almost illegible. How was she going to wait a whole week before seeing that lovely man again?

Wednesday 28th May

It had been a long night for Sarah Johnston in The Ridings Nursing Home. There had been several disturbances amongst the residents, one man had tried to escape, a lady had had a fall in her bedroom, breaking her hip in the process, so had been admitted to hospital. The unusual events had kept many of the residents awake, and Sarah had not been able to do her normal nightly rounds because of the extra work. Finding the lifeless Maud Blessing in her bed this morning was the last straw: Sarah hated this job sometimes.

By the time Elaine's shift began, Doctor Waring had officially pronounced that Maud Blessing was dead, he was sure that she had suffered a heart attack. She'd done well to reach the age of eighty-five, especially with her Alzheimers being so advanced. Elaine was mildly surprised at the diagnosis, usually pneumonia caused the early death of people afflicted with the vicious disease, but, as Sarah mused, Maud was very elderly, she was bound to go soon.

Elaine pulled the tattered note from her handbag, as she had done countless times since the previous day, and unfolded it privately. Would Julia Anton inform Paul Joyce of his great grandmother's death? She doubted it. How could she contact him to let him know? Poor Paul. Poor Maud. At least they got to spend her last day together.

It was mid afternoon by the time Paul finally arrived back in Peasenhall, the journey had been tiresome, and the uncommonly hot weather had increased his discomfort. Gratefully, he stepped off the bus, stretched his legs, and crossed the road, heading for the village shop. Rose, or was it Katie, would be ravenous by now, having not eaten for, what, four, or was it five, days. He dropped the shopping into a bag, and sauntered back to the derelict barn, eager to see his precious prisoner.

Moving the rotten wood aside, he clambered through the makeshift doorway, and was hit by a foul odour. He dropped the shopping, and scrabbled towards the hay and rubble structure which housed Katie. Throwing the bales aside, he ripped his torch from his pocket urgently, sensing a problem. His fears were confirmed.

"No! Rose, no!" Paul grabbed Katie's shoulders and wrenched her head from the bucket, shoving her on the bales with disgust. Her body was rigid, but moveable, and her head slumped awkwardly to one side as she fell. Tentatively, his heart racing with shock, Paul leant over and tore the gag from her dripping face, throwing the sodden rag aside. Vainly, he hoped her chest would rise with life, but the morbid blue tinge of her waterlogged, swollen cheeks told him his hopes were futile. Katie had drowned in the water he'd left to keep her alive.

Paul stood up, he angrily kicked the bucket aside, the murderous water splashing over the dry, musky hay. Tearing at his hair, his voice was shaky, the quavering pitiful. "What do I do now, tell me God, help me here. What the hell do I do now?"

A rogue tear rolled down his cheek, and Paul slumped heavily beside Katie's still body. He shined the light over her once more, observing that she was as pretty in death as she had been in life. The torch fell from his hands, he wiped the tear away roughly, before holding his head tightly and rocking back and forth. He needed to hear God more than ever now, he was clueless of what to do next. He needed instructions.

Soon God's voice exploded confidently, and relief flooded over Paul. It didn't make a difference that Katie was already dead, he could still complete his task. In three days time it would be the thirty first of May, the day he was due to recreate Rose Harsent's death. Paul was to use his imagination and behave as if Katie was still alive on the sacred day. He was to take Katie's body to Providence house and mutilate it, just as Rose Harsent's had been one hundred and six years before. In fact, her early death was a good thing, at least she wouldn't struggle, and there wouldn't be too much blood.

Saturday 31st May

Maud Blessing's demise had passed without comment. Because there were no suspicions over her death, no autopsy was required. The medical certificate signed by Doctor Waring stated she had died from myocardial infarction, a heart attack, probably caused by the arrhythmia that she had suffered from for the past two years.

Julia Anton wasn't particularly upset to lose her mother. She had loved her dearly, but realistically Maud had died years before when the vice like Alzheimers had seized her. The lady Julia had visited every Saturday for the past ten months was simply an empty shell. Methodically, Julia registered the death the next day, placed a small obituary in the local paper, and busied herself with the funeral arrangements. Maud's house had been sold a year before to pay for the costly nursing home fees, and Julia was the only child, so the will would be straightforward. If anything, the only emotion Julia allowed herself to feel was relief that her mother wasn't suffering, trapped in a foetal body, any longer.

Paul scanned the details of his duties for that evening on his organiser, and clicked it off. It was an unnecessary act, every element was already embedded in his memory, but the day was going slowly and he was eager for the evening to come.

The previous day he had ventured to the nearby Halesworth, and had been ecstatic to find a delicate, floor skimming, black dress in an antique shop. Rose Harsent had been a maid at Providence House, so finding the ideal garment was surely fate.

Carefully, he had removed Katie's soiled trouser suit, and dragged the gown over her floppy limbs, lifting her slightly to tug it down to her feet. The weather had been uncommonly warm, and her smell had become offensive, but his feelings for her had only increased, this was going to be the most perfectly recreated duty yet.

Once dressed, Paul propped Katie's body against a bale of hay, and scraped her matted, greasy waves into a neat chignon. It was difficult, with every tug her body flopped to the side, but the

73

result was splendid. He evened the bluish tinge of her skin with foundation purchased in Halesworth, and blackened her eyes dramatically with several layers of mascara. Paul stood back, taking in her new, peaceful beauty, admiring his handiwork.

The Katie he had chosen had been a stunning woman, her bone structure was proud, and her melting eyes soulful, but the replacement Rose he had created from her body was even more captivating. There was an air of sophistication about her, but it was touched with vulnerability. Katie now had a compelling tranquillity that only death could provide her. Paul realised he loved her. Very much.

"Mister Krein …"

"Detective Inspector!" His temper was short with frustration.

"Sorry, this is Karen Parsons from the MBNA bank, I'm calling regarding a credit card registered under the name of A Keeley."

Krein sat up straight, was this the call he had been waiting for? "Go on."

"The card has been used today in a place called Halesworth, that's in Suffolk. The card was used twice."

"Suffolk. Saxmundham's in Suffolk, isn't it?" The question was to himself, rather than Miss Parsons.

"I have no idea, sir. Would you like the details?"

"Yes, yes please. Hold on, I'll just grab a pen." Krein rooted through the mess on his desk until a cheap biro appeared, and scribbled the information on a pad, repeating the words quietly for her validation. "The Aulde Antique Shop, oh, Shoppe, twenty pounds, black mock Victorian servant's dress." He paused, his voice now incredulous. "Stop a second. Did you say a mock Victorian dress! What the bloody hell does he want with a dress?"

She was clearly bored. "Sir, I can only tell you what I have here. Shall I continue?"

"I'm sorry, please go on." And again he repeated her for clarification. "Cash withdrawn from the HSBC bank, two hundred pounds."

"That's it."

"Hold on, don't go. The dress, was the purchase chip and pin, or signature?" Krein could hear scrabbling over the line.

"Signature."

"Has anyone checked the signature against her card yet?" Although enthusiastic about the new lead, Krein despaired that the events were happening so far from Oxford. Suffolk might as well be Norway as far as he was concerned.

"We won't get the docket back for a couple of days, but as soon as we do we'll check."

Krein was outraged, impatient. "No, we need to take the slip for forensic testing, I don't want it sent back to you …"

"That's not under my control." Her voice was bland, but the tone final. The phone line went dead.

"Thanks." Krein slammed the receiver down, pushing his aching back against the backrest of his seat. "Raynor." Raynor looked over. "Contact the Suffolk Constabulary, I need an officer to collect this credit card transaction slip before it gets sent in the post." Krein waved the pad in the air. "Make sure they're aware that it's evidence so they don't add to any prints." Raynor collected the notepad and took it back to his desk. "Get a statement from the cashier who dealt with the sale, too, see if they can describe the purchaser."

"No problem."

"Get a copy of the slip emailed to us as well." Krein leant back again, his mind whirring with the latest development. A dress? Why would this man want a dress? He can't be so stupid that he doesn't realise the card transactions are being traced. Why would he risk discovery for a dress?

Police Constable Todd Holden pushed open the glass door and walked into the cluttered antiques shop. Mabel Fairs glanced over and beamed widely in recognition. "Good afternoon, Todd, are you alright?"

"I'm fine, thanks, Mabel. Yourself?" Todd never ceased to be amused with the local vocabulary: he'd only moved to the area a year before. They chatted for a few minutes before Todd explained why he was there.

"Yes, I remember the dress, it was fake you know, and not that good a fake either. But the gentleman seemed most pleased with it. He asked if there was a white pinafore to go with it, but, as you know, we don't usually carry clothing, so I had nothing else to give him."

"Do you remember what he looked like at all?" Todd was editing out the unnecessary details as he scribbled notes on his notepad.

"Oh yes, dear. He was a young lad. Well, dear, I'm seventy-two, so you all seem like babies to me! He was very young."

"How young, my age? Teenager? Forties?"

"Oh dear, maybe early twenties, something that region. He may have been younger, he had a young face. Very nice looking chap, although his hair could do with a decent cut, it was pretty scruffy, but then they all are nowadays, aren't they. Men with ponytails, women in micro skirts. Oh, and the shoes. I blame it on the sixties you know."

"What colour was his hair?"

"Oh, a sort of brown, well, light brown. It was short, spiky, badly cut. If I had a chance, you know, I'd get all these youngsters, scrub them up, put suits on them, and make them look decent for a change!"

"Did you see what he was wearing?"

"Pretty much what they all wear, dear, these youngsters. Those dreadful denim trousers, and they don't even iron them. I liked his jumper though, it was too big for him, but it was Arran, could have been made by my own fair hand. It was too dirty though, I hope he noticed the launderette just round the corner."

PC Holden patiently waited whilst Mabel issued her lengthy replies to a few more questions, and wrote down anything that may be important. He wrote very little. "Did you notice anything else about him, the way he talked, colour of his eyes, anything at all?"

Mabel rubbed her forehead with her hand, deep in thought, and presently she answered. "Not really, he didn't have a local accent, he spoke poshly, then saying that dear, he didn't say much, only to ask about the pinafore. He was just a young man like they all seem to be."

76

"Thank you for your help, Mabel. We may have to question you again, if you don't mind. Oh, by the way, have you got the transaction slip for the credit card he used?"

Mabel's brow furrowed. "Oh dear, you know I'm sure he paid cash, I could have sworn he did. Let me have a look in the till." Todd's heart leapt, he'd specifically been instructed to bring the slip to the station as evidence for a possible murder enquiry. He felt in his pocket for the plastic bag he'd brought to contain the slip.

Mabel rooted through the till, Todd felt nervous at how she was handling the dockets, concerned about adding to the prints. "Oh, here it is. Silly me, he did pay with a card."

Krein fingered through the files on his desk, the documents were all firmly in his memory, but waiting for news from the Halesworth Police Station was exasperating. His computer pinged, he sat up immediately and opened the new email. "Bingo!" Krein hastily downloaded the attachments, and printed them.

"First, the credit card slip." Krein mused to himself, rummaging through the files on his desk for the photocopy of Annabel Keeley's signature. He compared the two. They were similar, but the original was firmer, more confident.

Krein lay the prints down and scanned through the informal statement given to PC Holden by Mabel Fairs at The Aulde Antiques Shoppe. The description of the man who used the card was vague, but had enough detail to convince him that this was the same person who used the card in London, albeit with darker, shorter hair. He would get Raynor to contact Suffolk again, send them another copy of the existing photofit, and ask them to immediately start searching for the man.

Darkness had fallen and Paul was placing the tools he needed for his next duty in the holdall, a knife, matches, paraffin, and a candle lamp he had discreetly stolen from the antiques shop earlier. He'd been annoyed that the old woman hadn't had a pinafore, so he'd snatched the small item whilst she wasn't looking. He'd paid cash for the paraffin, some glue, and a candle

77

from a hardware store, and the matches from a newsagent's across the Thoroughfare.

Paul slipped the old trench coat onto Katie's now limp body, he wanted to keep her warm against the chilly evening air, ensure she remained comfortable on her final journey in his company. He fussed over her hair, it had to be immaculate. Katie and the original Rose Harsent were dissimilar in looks, Rose had had a much harsher face, a dated photo in the book he'd used for research had shown, but that was unimportant. They were both twenty-two when they died.

Paul began to pace, something was unsettling him, he was unsure what. Then he remembered. Rose had been six months pregnant when she had been murdered, and Katie clearly wasn't. He needed her to look as if she was expecting if the body was going to look perfect for the police, and for God. Pregnancy was a factor so important, it couldn't be overlooked.

Paul glanced around, agitated, until he spotted the solution. He snatched a handful of hay, forcing it inside the dress, and another, another, until the abdomen of the garment swelled, bursting at the seams. Standing back to consider the alteration in its entirety, Paul was satisfied that when they discovered the new Rose, the scene would be authentic. The police would be thrilled to find her delicate body, her face exquisite, the following morning.

Paul hoisted Katie to stand, he slid his arm under hers, and reached across her back, tucking his hand into her armpit, supporting her slack body. From that position it would appear to passers-by that she was walking. He held the candle lamp, tucking it into her coat. He struggled to drag her through the rotting barn entrance, but once through, Paul straightened the chignon and the dress, and propped her up again. He guided her along the track, the stream tickling merrily to the right, and passed an array of pastel coloured cottages, their quaintness enhanced by the moonlight.

Crossing the footbridge, they continued along the pavement. "Katie, as you know, you are my new Rose." Paul was so enamoured with Katie, it seemed important he explain what he was doing. "I'm going to show you where Rose is buried."

Although Katie was petite, her weight was burdensome, and Paul stopped frequently to heave her body back into position. He took her left into a small lane, struggling against the slight upward gradient. Providence House was to the right, on the corner. "She lived there, she was a maid, her room was at the top. Do you see Rose, can you see? Can you put yourself in her place? I would take you in and do the duty exactly where Rose Harsent died, but the book said it had all changed in there. The layout is different. That won't do, we'll have to make do with outside, if you don't mind, Rose?"

The road swung to the right, a backdrop of a striking church to the left. Paul stopped, he turned Katie to face the graveyard. "That's where she is, they put her in there. I would like them to put you in there with her, but they probably won't. It would be so nice if they did." Footsteps approached, and an elderly man passed the couple. He acknowledged them with a 'Good day', but Paul made no reply.

Paul turned Katie back, shrugging her upright again, and continued her final journey. A middle-aged couple were now approaching, Paul chatted quietly to Katie to appear as if they were a normal couple. As the couple neared, Katie's body sagged, Paul scrabbled to retain his grip on her, desperate not to attract attention. But it was too late.

"Bit too much to drink, was it?" The man grinned amicably at Paul.

He had no choice but to answer, he couldn't raise any suspicion, not now. Not so close to this perfect duty. "It's her birthday today, she celebrated just a little too much!" He continued to walk, hoping his abruptness was enough to end the exchange.

"Ahh, I'm sure she had a good time, maybe she'll remember some of it in the morning." To Paul's relief the couple walked on, oblivious to the woman's comment on the foul stench of the young lovers to her husband.

Paul steered Katie's body to the right, into a tiny lane that lead back to the main road. They were heading towards the gardens of Providence House. On reaching the pre-planned area, he glanced around to make sure they were alone, but, to Paul's irritation, three inebriated teenagers were heading towards them. He swung Katie in front of himself, appearing to the boys that they were kissing. The youths walked past, oblivious to Paul and his corpse. Although the street was lit, there were enough shadows for Paul to hide with Katie. He dragged her into a bush at the end of the garden and, tucked away from undesired eyes, Paul took the knife from his pocket, holding it to Katie's neck.

He gazed at her, serene, peaceful, and his heart swelled with pride and anticipation. Her face was so beautiful, her closed eyes adding to her vulnerability, he steeled himself to slash her neck, but her loveliness prevented him. It was no good, he couldn't do it. Not facing her. If this recreation was going to be authentic, the cut would have to be deep, from ear to ear. Rose Harsent had bled a lot when her killer had savaged her, but this new Rose wouldn't. There was no heartbeat to pump any out. Still, the grisliness of mutilating this girl that he loved, he couldn't watch the act, however much he was looking forward to it.

Paul flipped Katie around, the smell of her hair wafting under his nose. He clenched at her abdomen, holding her body close to him, and returned the knife to her throat, the blade skimming her delicate skin. Resolute, he pulled the blade towards himself, and, piercing her neck, it glided across with ease. A shudder of excitement ran through Paul's body, he'd been anticipating this moment for so long, and the small drop of blood which fell on his hand stirred emotions he'd long forgotten. Sexual emotions. They sickened him.

The stream trickled daintily beside the bush he was hiding in, the gentle sound bringing him back to the present, and, as planned, he pushed the body towards it. It settled near, but not in, the water. Paul removed the muddy trench coat to expose the plain gown, took the container of paraffin from the bag and poured the entire contents over the body. He could hear footsteps approaching, so he ducked back into the bush, leaving Katie's form to blend into the darkness of the mud on the bank of the stream. The footsteps heightened, then diminished, and Paul returned to finish the job.

He took the candle and matches from the bag, lit the taper, and placed it into the candle lamp. He carefully held it beside

Katie's body, and soon a mesmerizing flame danced along the dress. Satisfied that she would continue to burn, Paul laid the candle lamp beside Katie, the final detail of Rose's murder recreated. He ran over the wooden footbridge that led to the main road from Providence House, and slowed to a brisk walk, in order to not draw attention.

It took half an hour for Paul to gather his, and some of Katie's, belongings from inside the barn, and he was striding along a twisting lane towards Halesworth. He'd only been walking for minutes when the sound of distant sirens pulsed in his ears. He guessed his destiny Rose had been found, and when the speeding police car shot by him, he dodged into the undergrowth to avoid being seen. He'd have to find somewhere to stay, ready to arrange the next duty.

Sunday 1st June

The ringing brought Krein from a deep sleep, he reached over the bed covers and dragged the receiver to his ear, yawning.

"Krein. It's MacReavie. We've got a body."

Krein pulled himself upright, suddenly wide awake. "What's happened?"

"The body of girl matching Katie Joyce's description has been found in a village called Peasenhall, in Suffolk. It's early days but it seems that her throat was cut and the body was semi-burned. The Halesworth force, who you've already been in contact with, are the headquarters for Suffolk Constabulary's Eastern Area, so they're dealing with the investigation in conjunction with us. Anyway, the Super's been talking to them, they want to issue a press release, and the Super agreed it would be a good idea at this point."

"This early?" Krein's first reaction was that they were being hasty.

MacReavie's voice quietened, his revulsion apparent. "Krein, this one's different. Whoever mutilated that body is clearly sick, I haven't given you the whole picture yet. I will, on our drive over there, the Super wants us to furnish them on the background, the Keeley girl, and what we know of the credit card transactions. Can you pick me up, as soon as possible? I've agreed to be there by nine-ish."

Krein glanced at his clock, it was four in the morning. Through a gap in the drawn curtains he noted the sky was still dusky, the remnants of nighttime serenaded by birdsong. "Give me twenty minutes, Guv." He replaced the receiver with a sigh. That poor girl. They were too late.

Katie's butchered, charred remains lay, draped in a white sheet, on a metal preparation table. The room was cooled, and the light intense. Her body had been discovered nine hours previously, but the attending police surgeon had not been willing to estimate a time of death, there were vast anomalies with the state of the remains and the injuries afflicted. So, having been identified by her mother and Caroline Merris by video link, she was first in line for a post mortem this bright, summer morning. Now a fatality was linked to Annabel Keeley's disappearance, the case had taken priority over everything else.

James Alder, the pathologist who was to perform the post mortem, alongside Ewan Fielding, his junior, entered the room. They were followed shortly by Detective Superintendent Jackie Goodman, of the Halesworth Major Investigation Team, who was, by rank, in charge of the case.

Krein steered his steel grey Audi slowly through the gateposts and into the car park of the Halesworth Police Station, parking it neatly. The journey had been long, and having met rush hour at the tail end, he was grateful to switch the engine off.

"Thank God we're here at last. It's further away than I realised!" MacReavie huffed as he stretched his legs in the foot-well.

Krein, who had been behind the wheel for the entire journey whilst his superior snored blissfully, glanced at him, incredulous. "Wasn't it just, Guv." His sarcasm didn't register.

MacReavie clicked the door open, clambering outside into the warm, fresh air. Krein followed, stretching his stiff body. Together they strode to the main reception desk, rang the bell, and waited for the desk sergeant to allow them into the recently modernised building.

Paul awoke, he was surrounded by grime, layers of dust, and greying cobwebs. He scrabbled to his feet, his eyes adjusting to the brightness of the summer sunshine streaming through the open doorway. Once he'd regained his bearings, he remembered arriving at the derelict cottage in the early hours of the morning, and a smile flickered across his face.

It all came back to him now, the long walk from Peasenhall, ducking into the bushes whenever he heard a vehicle approaching, many of which held emergency teams en-route to the murder scene. His murder scene. He'd felt so important.

He'd headed towards Halesworth by chance, but fate had intervened in the form of a blackened cottage that lay in the corner of a large agricultural field. The windows were firmly boarded up, but the back door gaped open, leading to a small room. It was derelict, it was filthy, but it was private, unused, and it had hidden him securely during the massive police activity of the night before.

Paul dusted his grubby clothes with hands that still had traces of crusted blood dribbled over them. He knew that the people he'd passed on Katie's last journey the previous evening would now come forward as witnesses. He'd been astute enough to disguise himself slightly by using a heavy duty glue on his cheeks to attach clippings of his own hair, but still, his description would now be circulated through the police forces, maybe even to the newspapers. From this moment on he needed to be vigilant, and fastidious, about leaving no trail to avoid being caught before his duties were complete. He also needed to find some replacement clothes: he'd been wearing the same jeans and jumper for weeks, and they'd not been washed since he'd stayed at Katie's flat.

Feeling an irritation on his face, Paul scratched at his cheeks, pain emanating from the welts caused by the harsh glue. He pulled his hand away and noticed the fresh blood on his fingers. He needed to find somewhere to wash, clean his face, wash his foul smelling body. Paul scooped up the holdall and braved the brightness outside. Now he could see his surroundings with clarity, he noticed the dishevelled house lay on a main road, and he wanted to avoid being seen if possible.

A dirt track led away from the road, so, after checking he wasn't being watched, he started along the path.

He hadn't walked for long when a cluster of buildings came into view. It appeared to be a farm. The track was open, and Paul realised he was conspicuous, but there were no bushes or trees to give him cover. If anyone spotted him, he would have to improvise.

Nearing the largest of the buildings, Paul noticed the windows were open, and probable signs that it was currently inhabited. However, a rambling, albeit small, cottage lay to one side, and it looked to be empty. The windows were all closed, the curtains drawn, and the washing line was clear. Paul veered from the track, trotting eagerly towards the building. He grasped a short length of wood from the undergrowth, slamming it powerfully against a ground floor window. The glass shattered easily. Paul ducked behind a bush for a minute in case the noise had been heard, but nobody appeared. He plucked the remaining jagged edges of glass from the frame with his gloved fingers, and clambered through into the warm, stuffy room.

The cottage was dark inside, the curtains holding most of the sunlight out. His eyes adjusted quickly, and he could easily find his way round. His stomach growling with hunger, he opened the fridge and tore at some cooked ham, stuffing it voraciously into his mouth. He washed it down with orange juice from the carton. Startled by his barbaric behaviour, he removed his gloves, and pulled a plate and a glass from the wall cupboard. He filled the glass with milk, sliced cheese onto the plate, and finished his meal with more finesse.

Satiated, Paul slid a pair of rubber gloves onto his hands, he rinsed the dishes, dried them and replaced them in the cupboard. He exchanged the gloves for his own, and sauntered up the creaking, uneven stairs. Pushing the first door ajar, the blue room was littered with discarded toys, so he tried another. Spotting a double bed, Paul entered, he tugged the wardrobes open, and wrenched through the hangers. He removed a pair of combat trousers, a T-shirt, and a hefty navy fleece. The owner was obviously very large, the clothes would smother Paul, but at least they were clean, and would disguise him further. As an afterthought, he grabbed some clean socks and boxer shorts, dropping several pairs of each into his holdall.

Paul pulled the curtain aside slightly to check that nobody was approaching the house, listening carefully to the distant farm machinery. Satisfied he had more time, he found the tiny bathroom and gratefully scrubbed at his sore skin, rubbing at the traces of glue, and the itchy scabs. Blood oozed from the rashes, and he dabbed at them with toilet paper until they calmed. A mirrored wall cupboard housed a tube of Savlon, which he rubbed gently into his skin, before tucking it into his bag for further use. Paul peeled his putrid clothes off, dropping them onto the floor, and filled the basin with steaming water to cleanse himself fully.

Appreciating the freshness, he tugged on the stolen outfit, and sponged the scum from the basin until it sparkled in the dim light. He gathered the discarded, soiled clothes, and stuffed them into the holdall. Trotting down the stairs, his cleanliness giving him a spring in his step, he grabbed a baseball cap from coat hook and settled it firmly on his lightly scented hair.

Now the hard part was about to start. His next duty was to be done in London. He had to travel there, un-challenged, and find lodgings where he could prepare his next duty. He had just over two weeks before the next was due, on the eighteenth of June. Hopefully this was enough time for any fuss to die down.

Detective Superintendent Jackie Goodman entered her office, pale from witnessing the autopsy. She was hardened to them, having attended many as she worked her way up the career ladder, but this one was particularly distressing. Usually she could distance herself from the victim easily, but a death of such violence was rare, and that, coupled with Katie Joyce's youth and beauty, made that task harder. Jackie laid her jacket across the back of her seat and sat down heavily. Taking a few moments to compose herself, she buzzed on the intercom to ask the two detectives from the Thames Valley force through.

An ardent feminist, Jackie held back a sneer when the two men entered. She stood and shook their hands, introducing herself, and gestured to the visitor's seats in her office. Together, they all sat.

"As you know I have just attended the autopsy. I'm afraid it's not a simple death, and James Alder, the pathologist, recommended that the body is retained for now."

Krein and MacReavie were listening intently, they issued a swift glance at each other, knowing this was highly unusual.

"The victim has been identified as Katherine Joyce, as we expected, and that in itself means that Suffolk, Thames Valley, Dorset, and the City of London police forces need to work as a team. Thank God for the Holmes System!" Jackie allowed herself a light smile, but it wasn't returned. She cleared her throat, referring to the notes on her desk. "James believes that Katherine …"

"Katie."

Jackie glared at Krein, she wasn't used to being corrected, especially by a Detective Inspector. "Katherine didn't die from the neck wound, nor from the burns injuries. He believes she died of asphyxiation, caused by being immersed in water."

"She drowned?" Krein was shocked.

"There was a small amount of water in the stomach, and a tiny amount of water in the lungs. Samples of both have been sent for analysis, but so far there are no other indications to believe any other verdict than drowning." Jackie picked up the notes. "Although bruises to the wrists suggest she had been shackled prior to death, there were no signs of a struggle, and due to the small volume of water in the lungs and stomach, she must have died in shallow water. She appears to have had a strong laryngeal reflex, which diverted the water away from the lungs and into the stomach, but as there was no apparent struggle, we cannot say that she was held under water by force. We may have to assume that the cause of death was accidental."

Krein stood up, angry. "For God's sake, her neck was sliced open and her body burned. That's not a bloody accident."

"No, but they were inflicted on a body that had been dead for about four days. It's possible someone was trying to cover up an accident."

"No. No." Krein shook his head. "Burn a body to hide it maybe, but not the throat, that does not make sense. No."

George Walters sat on his comfortable fireside chair facing Jackie Goodman and Detective Sergeant Washington. He, and a couple of other witnesses to the dead girl and her companion, had called the police station that morning on hearing the news, and they were all being interviewed in turn by detectives working for the Major Investigation Team. However, Jackie wanted to see George and his wife personally because they had actually spoken with the man. It was possible they may give the best description yet. She was starting with George, and would see Lucy Walters afterwards. It was important they were interviewed separately.

"Mr Walters, could you give me a description of the couple that you saw last night please, in as much detail as possible."

"Certainly." George Walters was an affable man, he liked to help when possible. "The man was about my height, maybe a bit shorter,"

"Your height is?"

"He was five foot nine or ten. He had a fine, downy beard and short hair, I'm not sure what colour it was, it was dark."

"His hair was dark?" Jackie was scribbling in her notebook.

"No, the sky was. He was quite scruffy, you know, big jumper, tatty jeans, trainers. And he spoke quite well, he had a gentle voice. Not from round here. We come from Sussex ourselves, and I could recognise the southern tones in his voice."

"Thank you, and the girl?"

George laughed, stopping as he remembered she'd been murdered. "She was drunk as a skunk, totally blitzed. She was swaying all over the place, he was having trouble keeping her up. She had her eyes shut the whole time. I did notice that she was wearing weird clothes. She had a long black dress on, and one of those big coats that either women or men wear."

Jackie scribbled the words in capital letters, there wasn't a coat on the body when it was found. "Can you describe the coat better? Colour, style, length?"

"It was longish, and quite pale, had a big belt with a buckle on it, but it was tied a bit, not buckled. I thought she looked a bit of a mess, tell you the truth, but saying that, she was very pretty. Her hair was neat, tied back nicely."

"I understand you had a brief conversation with the couple. Could you tell me what was said?"

"Mmmm, I'll try. Lucy and I had had a bit to drink ourselves, I think it started when the girl stumbled, I said something about her being drunk, jokily. The man said it was her birthday, and she'd drunk too much. I said something else, but I can't remember what it was."

"Did the girl speak at all?" Jackie knew she couldn't have, but she wanted to check Mr Walter's credibility as a witness.

George's face strained in recollection. "I don't think so, if she had it was only a murmur, but I don't recall her saying a word."

Krein was angry, he felt usurped. He understood that the four police forces needed to work together on this investigation, and he was happy with that, but he wanted to be with Jackie Goodman whilst she took statements from the witnesses. After all, he knew the background intimately, he'd been working on this case since the twelfth of May when Annabel had gone missing. He'd worked late into the night, sussing out the killer's psyche, the way he operated. So why had they driven two hundred bloody miles just to sit on a press conference, when he could offer so much more than that. Anyway, that bloody Jackie Goodman was another story. Fine, she had worked her way up to a position of respect, and good for her, but if she was too ignorant to even address Katie by the name everyone used for her, what else would she miss in her questioning? He should be there, with her.

Krein paced up and down the functional room, his mug of coffee going cold on a nearby desk, he could feel the tension in his back and neck from frustration.

MacReavie eventually broke. "For heaven's sake, Krein, will you bloody well sit down!"

Krein stopped mid step, this was the excuse to blow that he needed. "No! It's not on, Guv! We should be with them on these interviews." He was trembling with fury.

MacReavie, in his usual manner, missed the point. "Quite agree, quite agree. A woman interviewing important witnesses, not on, not on at all. But you know how the system works. This is out of our jurisdiction."

Blatant sexual discrimination in this day and age, how did he get away with it, Krein mused to himself. He restarted pacing, hands clenched into fists. "Well, I'm sure she's capable of doing the job, woman or not ..."

"Rubbish, Krein. Detectives and Inspectors should be men, women shouldn't be allowed on the force, unless it's for typing and making cups of tea."

Krein cringed, maybe he could now understand why Jackie Goodman's manner was so direct: she must have needed a tough skin to get to her rank. He felt an unexpected glimmer of respect for her.

"Hello Mrs Walters, thank you for agreeing to make a statement today. I shall be as quick as I can." Jackie sat back down on the sofa alongside DS Washington, as Lucy Walters seated herself in the chair her husband had vacated minutes before.

"The couple you saw last night, can you remember what they looked like?"

Lucy's manner was calm and confident, her words concise. "Yes, clearly. She was elegant looking, she wore a pale trench coat, loosely tied in the middle rather than buckled. It needed ironing, but that's par for the course at the end of a night out. She had a long black dress on, it looked dated, but wearing vintage fashion is all the rage nowadays, isn't it. Her hair was beautifully done, in a neat chignon with a couple of long tendrils falling on either side. To be honest, it looked far too neat for someone who was as drunk as she appeared to be. And strange, but I think she may have been pregnant, she looked it, but most women don't get drunk when they're expecting, do they?"

Ahh, the straw inside her dress, why was Katherine made to look as if she were pregnant? "Lovely, Mrs Walters. I need to clarify that the girl you saw was the victim we have found. I have a photo to show you, would you be able to tell me if it may be the same girl?" Jackie produced the recent photo of Katie Joyce that had been supplied a few weeks previously by the Thames Valley force.

"Goodness me! Isn't she lovely. That is the same girl, without a doubt, but last night her skin was a lot duller."

"How could you tell?" Jackie was impressed with Lucy's observational skills.

"Oh, I know it was dark, but her skin looked unnaturally pale, it just seemed odd. You know when you have a drink, well, it always brings a bit of colour to your cheeks. Well, this girl was drunk to falling down, but she had no colour, she was almost grey, if that were possible."

"Yes, I think I understand you completely." Of course she'd been pale, grey. She was dead, not that Lucy Walters knew that yet, and Katie had been heavily made up. "What about the man?"

"Well, before I describe him, could I just point out one thing that may or may not interest you?"

"Please do."

"It was the smell, there was a really horrid smell, and it was coming from her. It wasn't like stale perfume, but a sort of, I don't know, just an unpleasant, heavy smell. Quite horrid."

Jackie could well imagine, having attended the autopsy, however she kept the morning's revulsion from her face. "Thank you, I'm sure that will be an important point. So, tell me about the man."

"Very handsome, scruffy, but handsome. His hair was dark, not black, not dark brown, but a sort of light chestnut. It was quite greasy, and had been cut badly. He had a wispy beard, a very fine beard, but it wasn't as dark as his hair, it looked blond, but that may have been a trick of the light."

"How can you be so sure of the colour?" Jackie found it easy to respect Lucy, she was a wonderful witness.

"The streetlight was on him, of course! He wore a lovely Arran jumper, which I can imagine cost a fortune, but again, it wasn't well looked after. It was grubby, and it was snagged in several places. He wore jeans and trainers. He was a slim man, about George's height, probably mid twenties."

"Would you be prepared to help us create a photofit of the man?"

"Of course."

"Thank you. Just one thing, though. Could you just tell me if you heard the girl speak at all?"

"Yes, she quite clearly said 'home' at one point, I watched her lips move as she said it. It was quiet, but I'm sure she said 'home'."

Damn you, woman, thought Jackie. A bloody good witness, but a defence attorney would make mincemeat of her statement if that comment was read in court. She was sure the girl Lucy had seen was Katherine, but any defence lawyer would claim it wasn't. She sorely wished she hadn't asked the question now. The interview continued.

Jackie Goodman waved to Mr and Mrs Walters as they pulled away in their car. They had agreed to come to the police station so Lucy could assist in preparing a photofit of the man, and George had agreed that it was a good likeness. Jackie strode back to the station, climbing the stairs towards her office, where she had left MacReavie and Krein to compare the new photofit with the previous one.

"The hair has changed, but it's definitely the same man." MacReavie sat up straight, satisfied, as Jackie entered the room.

"I believe so too. It's lucky we've got this so quickly, it will be a great help at the press release, the newspapers will help to make this a nationwide search."

Krein glanced at his watch. "Twenty minutes, looks like we got it just in time."

The Thoroughfare in Halesworth centre was virtually deserted as the newly disguised Paul strolled into Forbuoys newsagents. He grasped a copy of the local newspaper, folding it to conceal the bold headlines, and paid. Keen to read about his murder, it was bound to be the major story, he wanted to board the train before starting. Paul headed towards the station, the bulging holdall tossed over his shoulder, and the newspaper loosely folded in his hand.

Apart from a woman who was on a bench, engrossed in a book, the station was desolate. Paul scanned the timetable briefly, noting the arrival time of the next train to London, and sat down on another bench. He unfolded the paper and a light smile settled on his lips as he absorbed the article about his duty.

The train arrived within minutes and Paul, along with the woman and a group of breathless teenage girls who had just dashed onto the platform, stood, patiently waiting for it to stop. Paul followed the woman into a carriage, and sat, re-opening the paper to continue the report. The train pulled away.

A few minutes passed and the platform remained silent, until a train approached in the opposite direction and slowed to a stop. A group of excitable reporters and photographers alighted, they were visiting the quiet town for one reason: the press conference. They murmured and chatted, hustling and bustling, enthusiastically keen to head for Halesworth Police Station.

One man pointed to the large building that overlooked the station, its nineteen seventies architecture bland yet functional, and pointed. "That's it, there's the police station." And they marched together, retracing the steps of the man they pursued, unaware that they had just passed him on the train just minutes before.

Having welcomed the vast bunch of reporters to the conference, and briefly explaining the circumstances, Jackie passed the microphone to MacReavie.

"Good afternoon gentlemen." MacReavie cleared his throat dramatically, ignorant that Jackie and the female reporters were bristling at his disrespect. "According to witnesses, the man we are looking for currently has short, chestnut brown hair and a beard." He held up the latest photofit. "A copy of this photofit is available for you to take back with you, and your help in publishing it will be invaluable." He replaced the sketch on the extended table. "We believe he is roughly five foot nine or ten, and every witness so far has described his clothes as a large, probably an Arran jumper, blue denim jeans, and trainers. He is early to mid twenties, slim, and talks with a soft voice in a southern accent, as far as we can tell."

Having not been as involved in the investigation as Krein, MacReavie had little more to add, and his speech was over rapidly. He passed the microphone to Krein, who continued relating the case succinctly, yet thoroughly. He detailed from the very first day, the abduction of Annabel Keeley, finding her car in Dorset. He mentioned the bloodied clothes, but deliberately omitted the discovery of the foetus, that was only relevant to the gore-hungry vultures, therefore unnecessary at this point. However, Krein realised he would have to divulge that nightmare to Gregor Keeley soon, now this had become a public matter.

A brief mention was made of the motorcyclist, Alan Benton, being killed in a hit and run collision with the car, emphasizing it was likely the crash was accidental.

Immediately a reporter stood up, she waved her hand and coughed to attract Krein's attention. Krein nodded at the woman. "My name's Victoria Threlfall, I'm a reporter with the Sun. Do you not find it of interest that Alan Benton's death was likened to Lawrence of Arabia's, and that Katie Joyce's murder is so similar to Rose Harsent's in nineteen-oh-two?"

Krein stared at Victoria, his mouth briefly gaping. The silence in the room was palpable. He fished for words, before asking, "Rose who?" He realised immediately that it was the wrong thing to say.

Victoria was enjoying this, her lifelong studies of murders and their perpetrators finally being of some use. "Rose Harsent, aged twenty two, pregnant, was murdered in Providence House, Peasenhall on the thirty first of May, nineteen oh two. Her neck was slashed from side to side, and the body was drenched in paraffin before being set alight."

Krein visibly paled, Jackie focused on the back wall, her lips taut, and MacReavie's face reddened. Satisfied at the reaction, Victoria continued. "Katie Joyce, aged twenty two, made to look as if she was pregnant, was murdered beside Providence House, Peasenhall on the thirty first of May, two thousand and eight. Her neck was slashed from side to side, then her body was drenched in paraffin and set alight. I rest my case" She sat down smugly, the analogy over, the resulting embarrassment severe.

And suddenly the noise was tremendous, talking, shouting, laughing, groaning, the collective result becoming white. Sternly, Jackie stood, her presence stilled the outburst within seconds. The crowd waited as she scanned the room, her confidence enviable. "Thank you for your help, Victoria, this is certainly an avenue that we are aware must be investigated, we have already linked the two and are doing our research accordingly." Krein gasped inwardly in amazement, aware that the reporters had swallowed the lie. "However, now that you, yourselves, have spotted the possible connection, I must point out that Katie Joyce actually died approximately four days ago, the official cause of death is asphyxiation by drowning."

Gasps resounded throughout the room, and the murmuring restarted. Krein, having now digested what Victoria had said, realised that they were searching for a man far more sinister than he had imagined. A ritual, serial killer who researched his methods, selected his targets, and killed by choice. He stared directly at Victoria, she smirked subtly and winked.

Now that Krein and MacReavie had gone, Jackie sat at her desk with her head in her hands, her mind whirring wildly. She glanced out of the window: it was late, the summer sun was beginning to sink slowly. Grabbing her keys, she jumped up and hastened to the door. She needed to see how her team were doing at the scene of the crime.

The area was still cordoned off, but there wasn't much to see now the body had been removed and the evidence bagged up. Scene of crime officers and forensic specialists from the Scientific Services Unit at Halesworth Police Station milled around, looking for anything that may help to solve the case. Jackie sighed deeply, sifting through the evidence they'd recovered so far in her mind, she knew they still had little to go on.

There was no Low Copy Number DNA on the touch points on Katie's body, leading them to believe the killer had worn gloves. Jackie was preparing to drive back to Halesworth when she spotted a constable rushing towards her. She got out of the car.

He was breathless, and excited too. "Ma'am, we think we've found where Katie was imprisoned. There's a derelict barn down there." He bent over, gasping, rubbing at his side.

A determined expression flooded her face, she strode briskly in the direction he'd pointed, he followed. Crossing the stream, Jackie waded through the undergrowth, the dew soaking into her trousers. Her pace quickened when the constable indicated the entrance. She pushed the rotting wood aside, and clambered into the darkness, grabbing a torch offered by a colleague. Her decision was instantaneous. She climbed back into the fresh evening air, and stood tall. "Cordon it off, we need SOCO's, forensics, the whole damned team, and we need them now. He can't escape now, we've got him."

The rapping on the door awakened Jackie, she sat upright, her neck aching and her face reddened from resting on the desk. She winced as she stretched her numbed arms. "Come."

Detective Inspector Dormer entered with a pile of papers, he laid them carefully before Jackie. "A list of the evidence found in the barn, and the tests we've run so far."

Jackie's tired eyes scanned the top page. "Black trouser suit. Soiled with urine and excrement. Proven by DNA profiling to have been worn by Katherine Joyce. Fibres. Footprints in the mud. Casts have been taken. Fingerprints that match Katherine Joyce's. Blah. Blah blah. Anything in this lot that has given us any leads yet?"

Dormer shook his head. "No, but the details have all been fed into the Holmes System, it's all catalogued."

Jackie nodded slowly. She clicked her PC on. "I'll email DI Krein, let him know we've got more evidence. He'll be interested in these."

Due to retire the next month, Dormer had been in the police force for thirty years, but in all his time he'd never known a colleague so committed to the job. His eyes gazed at her softly. "Come on, Jax, it can wait until tomorrow. Krein won't be there at four in the morning, anyhow."

Krein sat at his desk, a steaming, deathly strong mug of coffee keeping him awake. But his fatigue dissipated when the email from Jackie pinged on his computer. He clicked it open hopefully.

Sunday 8th June

Mary Krein opened the door and carried the tray into the bedroom, the aroma of bacon and eggs wafting into the room. Unusually her parents were both still asleep, so she laid the breakfasts on the bed. "Hey, you two, wake up. Happy anniversary."

Krein groaned, work had been so intense recently he could do with sleeping all day. He tugged a pillow over his head, while Linda propped herself up. She nudged him in the back. "Dave, look what Mary's brought for us."

Mary grinned proudly as Krein shrugged the pillow away, raising his head to see the food. The tempting aroma of bacon drifted under his nose, prompting his tummy to growl hungrily. He hauled himself up, awash with tiredness, but aware of his fatherly duties. "This looks delicious, Mary. Breakfast in bed! What have you been up to?"

Linda gazed at her husband, bemused. "It's our anniversary, Mr Unromantic. She's trying to make it special for us."

Under the covers Krein's toes curled. How was he going to smooth this one over? How could he forget their twenty fifth wedding anniversary? From the day he'd first seen her flowing blonde curls, her impish, cheeky smile, the day he'd first held her hand and kissed her tenderly, Linda had been the love of his life. To the consternation of their families they'd sneaked away to get married, it had been so romantic. And now? He'd not even got a card, let alone a present. He wished he could die there and then, anything but deal with the row that was about to happen. Unless he did some quick thinking.

Krein leaned across the covers and kissed Linda's forehead. "I know, love, I was only joking. Happy anniversary, I've got a surprise planned for you later." That should buy some time. Hastily, he took the knife and fork and unwrapped them from the serviette, and lifted one of the plates closer. "This looks delicious, Mary, thanks love."

Mary was still beaming. She did a little skip and trotted out of the room, pleased that her idea had gone down so well. "Mary."

Krein called after her, she peeped around the door. "Has the paper come yet?"

"I'll just get it."

Krein had eaten most of his breakfast by the time Mary returned with the newspaper. She carelessly dropped it on the covers, and Krein's face paled as he read the bold headline.

"Oh, fuck! Fuck, fuck, fuck, fuck, fuck!" He threw the unfinished meal onto the tray, and snatched the paper up. "Fuck! I'm going to be crucified." Krein dropped the paper and sprang out of bed, tugging his jeans on in the same movement.

Linda's hopes of a romantic anniversary plummeted as she read the words that grieved her husband so dramatically. 'NO BODY YET, BUT FOETUS FOUND'. She sighed. Twenty-five years of this, and it never got any better. She watched her husband race from the room, and presently listened to his car engine fire up.

It was nearly four weeks since Annabel had gone missing. Greg had been to hell and was slowly clawing his way out of the vicious pit he'd fallen into. He'd even been to the barbers to have his hair neatened and beard trimmed the previous day. Gail had been delighted, it had meant he was slowly coming to terms with the terrible tragedy they were part of. Obviously, as a mother, she was deeply upset at Annabel's disappearance, but one of them had had to remain stable for the children, and Greg had completely fallen apart, so that left her to be the strong one.

Until today. The headlines glared at her, and, unable to even faint in shock, she had no choice but to comply with the compulsion to read the article. Tears, hot, furious, tumbled down her cheeks, flowing uncontrollably over their redness. Annabel's baby, reported on so mercilessly. Her grandchild, a mere sensation for Sunday reading.

She'd trusted DI Krein, on the surface he had seemed to keep them fully informed of all the developments in the investigation, but he must have known about this, and this was one snippet she'd have preferred to hear in person. Anger burned as she recalled Krein telling them about the press conference. But when she and Greg had subsequently read the details in the newspapers, seen the photofit of the bearded suspect, read with horror about Katie Joyce's death, they'd been prepared. To find out that Annabel had been savaged so monstrously, and like this. Gail couldn't hold it in, it was uncontrollable. The scream resonated throughout the house.

Greg thundered down the stairs, bursting through the door. "Gail? What's up?" He tried to grasp her shoulder for comfort, but she angrily shoved the paper into his hand before he made contact. She could feel his confusion bubbling into anger.

The doorbell sounded, and Gail automatically rose to answer the door, dabbing at her tearstained face. Unlocking the latch, she was suddenly overwhelmed by flashes and urgent voices. She tried to push the door closed as the cameras sparked and the microphones were thrust in her face, but a foot held it open. The questions rang in her head.

"Are you Annabel's mother?"

"Did you know about the foetus?"

"What are your comments?"

"Are they hiding her body from the public as well?"

Faintness washed over her body, her head reeled, her heart raced. Her breathing quick and shallow, Gail squeezed her hands over her ears, eyes tightly shut, desperate to stop the noise, the horror. As her knees buckled and her body dropped to the floor, Greg rushed forward, kicked the foot holding the door ajar, and slammed it. "Piss off, the lot of you, you fucking vultures." He screamed, scooping his mother-in-law's body in his arms.

Three pairs of young eyes watched the scene from the top of the stairs, terrified, oblivious, and blissfully naïve.

Krein trudged along the corridor towards MacReavie's office, his colleagues averting their eyes, uncomfortable. The headlines, and the ensuing calls from a furious Gregor Keeley, were the talk of the station. Opening the door, Krein was surprised to see Detective Superintendent Walker. The two men glared at him, their anger palpable.

"Sir, Guv." Krein desperately tried to sound more confident than he felt.

MacReavie shook his head slowly, he turned and stared blankly though the window. Walker's cheek was twitching, an uncontrollable tic caused by anger. His outburst was sudden. "What the fuck did you think you were playing at, Krein?" Krein knew better than to answer, he hung his head. Walker stepped close, Krein could feel his breath. "I've had Mr Keeley on the telephone three times this morning, twice in tears, demanding to know why he wasn't told about the foetus."

Weeks of pent-up emotions exploded, Krein found himself shouting. "What the fuck was I supposed to say to him, damn it! By the way, not only has your wife probably been murdered, but your unborn child was found ripped from the womb and thrown into the bushes! Gregor Keeley was already losing it, that information would have taken him over the edge."

"You're a fucking detective, Krein, not a bloody social worker. If you didn't feel able to tell the family the whole truth, you should have informed MacReavie, let him do it."

MacReavie shuddered, pleased Krein hadn't mentioned it, but he wasn't about to tell Walker that.

Krein knew his job wasn't on the line over the foetus, but it may be soon if he didn't control himself. But he couldn't. He jumped in, double-barrelled, his voice resounded through the building. "Let's get this straight, shall we? If you bastards weren't so fucking money conscious all the time, we may even have caught the killer by now. You fart around, not wanting to spend the money testing Annabel's friends' DNA, so we've got roughly fifty samples taken from her car, and we don't know who they belong to. I've been pissing up a fucking tree for the last month, with pretty much no help or expenditure from my seniors, unless it involves the glory of standing in front of a press conference," Krein shot a look at MacReavie, his eyes challenging, "all your bloody distraught words to the press, then you go off for your important game of golf."

MacReavie glared at him, furious. He strode up to Krein, grabbing his collar and thrusting his gritted teeth threateningly close. "You will never, ever talk to me, or my superiors, in this way again. Do you understand?" The hollering was followed by the stench of stale garlic.

Unperturbed, Krein glared back, his frustrated anger overwhelming. He lowered his voice and stated, clearly, slowly, exaggerating each word. "Your breath stinks." Krein turned, and strode purposefully out of the office, leaving the two remaining men to glance uncomfortably at each other, dumbfounded.

Krein drove straight to Caisten, he had to see the family, he needed to explain his reasons for withholding the sickening details. He had built up such a respect and attachment to them, he could only hope they could understand he was trying to protect them.

"Oh you're lovely, you are." Eduardo Delfini gently stroked Paul's cheek. He took his hand and ran his index finger along each of Paul's long fingers, one by one. "Such lovely, elegant fingers, you must be a musician, you must be gifted. Do you play an instrument?"

Paul shook his head and smiled modestly.

"When you come to my house, Pauly?" Delfini was desperate to get this gorgeous young lad into bed. "I want you so, you know I do. I think you tease me for no result."

Paul stood up and smiled again. "I'm no tease, Ed, believe me. I will, but when the time is right. You're special to me, and I want the first time to be special. We've known each other four days, I want to know you at least fourteen."

Delfini shook his head and waved his arms in mock disgust. "Ten days is too long for me to wait for you."

Paul laughed and took the glasses from the table, stacking them high in his crooked arm. "You'll wait." He crossed the smoky room and deposited the empties on the bar. The music was deafening, and the strobe lights that flickered occasionally tired his eyes. Heading away to clear more tables, a strong hand wrenched him back.

Jack Weston was not a homosexual himself, no, he liked babes, buxom blonde babes, preferably with no brain and a healthy interest in sadomasochism. But he was an entrepreneur, he knew a profitable business when he saw one, and buying this gay bar eleven years before had made him an affluent man. He no longer had to buy his girls on the side, they threw themselves at him. Marlene, his second wife, and mother of his two growing sons, wasn't concerned about his extra-curricular activities as long as he kept the big money coming in. He had a couple of sidelines, not strictly straight and narrow, but on the surface he was a respectable business owner.

"You gonna go with that Iti or not?" Jack nodded in Delfini's direction.

"One day." Paul shrugged.

"You better do it quick, and you better give me my cut, or you'll be skkk" Jack ran his finger sharply across his neck.

Paul sneered at Jack, unconcerned, he shrugged again. "I'll shag the ugly slime ball when I'm ready, and not before, so get off my case." He sauntered away from the bar.

Jack watched him go with interest. Most of the rent boys who came to work for him were younger, and they stayed firmly in their place, never a smart word back to him, they wouldn't dare. Usually Jack would have been furious, but there was something about this Paul, he was intriguing. Something told Jack that Paul would be an excellent ally to have, and he didn't want to do anything to disrupt that. Paul had the killer instinct, it was clear in his eyes.

Linda turned the oven off. Inside, the lovingly prepared celebratory feast was overcooked, dry and spoiled. She lifted the champagne from the cooler and replaced it in the fridge, then cleared the candles, tablecloth, flowers and crockery from the table.

She checked her watch for the hundredth time that night. It was eleven o'clock. She sighed, deflated, and poured a large whiskey from the Waterford Crystal decanter they'd received as a late wedding present from her parents. Knocking it back, she poured a larger one, carrying it miserably up the stairs. Sitting, forlorn, on the side of the bed, stroking the fresh covers nonchalantly, Linda realised her silver anniversary had fallen as flat as their wedding had quarter of a century before. She downed the drink, shuddering as it hit the back of her throat, and climbed under the covers. She was lonely, yes, but she'd lost the ability to cry years before.

Tuesday 17th June

"I need a gun and some ammo." Paul stared, unblinking, at his boss.

Jack Weston was rarely ever flustered, but he verged on the edge now, not that his eyes would ever admit that to Paul. "When?"

"Today. I need it before I leave work this evening."

Jack shook his head slowly, buying himself time, and slammed his fist on the desk. He knew he could acquire a gun, that wasn't a problem, but he was curious. This was his territory, and if there were any shootings, he wanted to know about it. However, he knew better than to ask Paul directly. He would have to send out some feelers, and quick. "I'll get you a gun, but it'll cost you."

"I've got five hundred." Paul's demeanour was calm.

Jack waved his hand, dismissive. "I'll need a grand at least."

"I've got five hundred." Something in Paul's icy eyes, in his muted voice, Jack couldn't put his finger on it, but he felt uncomfortable. Unable to hold his stare, he looked away, walking around the desk, and stood in front of Paul. His bravado was false, but he only admitted his fear to himself. He thrust his face at Paul's threateningly, and growled in a menacing tone. "Five hundred. But you owe me." Pulling back, he had the afterthought. "What do you need it for?"

The vacant glare silenced him, Paul turned and walked out.

PC Bray sat beside the graffiti covered desk in the interview room, Mr Jennings and Miss Ball were opposite him. "So," he started, warmly, "you say you want to report a burglary."

Lisa glanced at her boyfriend, her manner awkward, and Bray found her innocence attractive. She was young, twenty-one maybe, and she was unusually pretty, her eyes wholesome, her long hair beaded. "Shall I say?" Her fiancé nodded, whilst hushing the two toddlers that were playing noisily behind them. Lisa returned her focus to Bray. "It'll probably seem silly to you, we never thought about it really. It's just someone smashed our window a couple of weeks ago. I was at work, I work at The

Cunningham Arms on Sundays, and Jay took the kids to his mum's."

Bray could feel the boredom arising. "Go on."

Jay finished concisely. "I think he nicked my trousers." If it wasn't for the screaming children, the room would have been silent.

Lisa shifted, uncomfortable, she glanced at Jay, turned to the kids and shouted. "Shut up or you'll get a wallop."

Incredulous, Bray raised his voice to be heard over the children, suppressing the urge to laugh. "What makes you think your trousers were taken?"

"It's obvious! They aren't in my wardrobe." Jay shook his head, perplexed at the perceived idiocy of the question.

Lisa continued. "I washed them, this is silly, because I put them away, and Jay thought they were in the wash. He shouted at me yesterday because he said I was taking too long to wash them, and I said I already had. He said where were they then, and I said I bloody well didn't know. He said I probably threw them away 'cos I'm mean like that, and I said he probably left them in some tart's bedroom."

Bray needed to calm the situation a little. "When was the window smashed, what date was it?"

"It was a Sunday, I already told you, because I work at The Cunningham Arms on Sundays. I work Monday, Thursday and Friday too, but that's when the kids are at nursery, so Jay doesn't have them, so we know it was a Sunday because he had the kids at his mum's house. It was a Sunday."

Count to ten, slowly, Bray thought to himself. "How many Sundays ago, can you think of the date?" Why was he even persevering with this farce?

Lisa sniggered, embarrassed. "Oh, right, um, what's the date today, er seventeenth, and today is a Tuesday, that would have been, um, one, two, two weeks last Sunday. I'm right, aren't I, Jay?"

"Sounds about right to me, I think." He scratched his head.

Bray checked his notebook. Sunday the first of June. He remembered that day clearly, and alarm bells rang in his head.

"Mr Jennings, Jay, could you please tell me exactly what these trousers were like?"

MacReavie had summoned Krein to his office, who entered holding two steaming mugs. "Guv." The argument nine days previously had not been mentioned since.

"We've had a call from Jackie Goodman in Halesworth. A young couple have reported that their house was broken into on the first of June, just outside Halesworth. Some mens clothes were taken."

"It took them two weeks to report it!" Placing the coffee on the desk, Krein noticed his boss's breath smelt minty.

"The couple had a misunderstanding, apparently. Anyway, the man had thought his window had been broken by kids, so he just boarded it up. Their forensics team have been unable to lift any prints from the frame, unfortunately. They've dusted the furniture and looked for fibres as well, but two and a half weeks is a long time, nothing's been found."

"So we're assuming the killer's been in and changed his clothes?"

"I suppose so. Anyway, I'll give you a copy of the statement that the couple made. You can add it to your case notes."

Krein left the office, this investigation was increasingly frustrating. Katie Joyce's mutilation was so similar to that of Rose Harsent's that it had to be significant. But how?

He sat at his desk, filing the latest statement neatly, and deliberated over the facts they had. The Major Investigation Teams in both Kidlington and Dorset had done some research into past murders, but there appeared to be, from their findings, no precedent for the situation surrounding Annabel's disappearance. Maybe the Rose Harsent: Katie Joyce similarity was a decoy, even a coincidence. Alan Benton's accident was unlikely to have been planned, however similar the situation was to Lawrence of Arabia's death. Krein supposed it was possible that pregnancy was a link, after all, Annabel was pregnant, and Katie was made to appear so. Maybe this weirdo was obsessed with pregnancy?

Krein sipped his coffee, he knew the killer was one step ahead, and possibly, probably, the only way they would gain the distance on him would be if or when he committed another murder. Krein's heart sank at the appalling thought.

"What do you mean you can't find nothing on him?" Jack Weston was furious, and time was running out. It was half past eight and Paul was already working the tables.

"We went through his room, top to bottom, under the floor, everything, boss. If there was anything to be found, we would'a found it." Dunny Thomas looked nervously at Jack, he'd seen his temper too many times, and he knew for sure he didn't want it directed at him.

"What about that bag he brings every evening? Have you been through that?" Jack was pacing, his hand to his forehead.

Dunny glanced at Reno, exchanging a nervous glimpse. "Er, Reno here, said he would do it now."

"So what you bloody waiting for, you should have checked it already." His roar made both the boys jump.

Reno hurried from the room, Jack continued to pace until he returned a short time later, flourishing the holdall. Jack unzipped it, and gasped. "What the fuck?" Dragging out a long length of sturdy rope, he placed it on his desk, and followed it with some pieces of brick and stones in varying sizes, three pairs of boxer shorts, and two pairs of socks. Dunny and Reno's curiosity brought them closer, Jack glared at them and they backed away. A can of diet cola was next. A pair of scissors, a pair of gloves, and a torch were removed and the bag was empty. "Where's that little computer thing I've seen him playing with?"

Reno shook his head. "I think that's just a gameboy."

Jack refilled the bag, remembering the order they'd been in, zipped it, and slung it at Reno. "Put it back and sod off. Dunny, get Paul."

The door slammed behind the boys, Jack breathed a lengthy sigh, his snooping having yielded no results. What was that damned man up to? And why did Paul disturb him so much?

Paul pushed the door wide and strode in, shoulders back, with an air of confidence. He closed the door. Jack frowned at him, and, sighing once more, opened the top drawer of his desk and withdrew a Colt Python .357 Magnum pistol. He placed it on the blotter, then pulled out a box containing fifty bullets, which he laid beside the gun. Paul leant forward to grasp the pistol, Jack grabbed his wrist. "Money first."

Paul's cold glare sent a shiver along Jack's spine as he reached into his trouser pocket, he threw a brown envelope onto the desk. Eyes fixed on Paul's, Jack opened it and flicked through the notes. "I won't count it, I trust you. Take the gun."

Unspeaking, Paul took the gun, lifted his trouser leg, and tucked it into his sock securely. He shook the trousers down, forced the box of bullets into the pocket of his fleece, and left the room.

"Fucking hell! What is that bastard up to?" Jack was unsure if he admired Paul's steely reserve, or if it terrified him. One thing he did know was that he never wanted to make an enemy of him.

Paul sauntered towards Eduardo Delfini's regular table and slid onto a chair beside him. Eduardo couldn't conceal his delight. "It's my gorgeous tease, you still tease me today?" He winked, his hand straying onto Paul's leg.

Paul stared directly into Delfini's soul, the edges of his lips curled into a slight smile. "Tonight's the night, I want you tonight." Delfini gulped, surprised, and he felt his penis throbbing as it hardened. "On my terms, though. We'll meet up after the bar closes at one o'clock, not here, but down the road, by Blackfriars Bridge, this side of the Thames."

Delfini, his breathing shallow and fast, could barely speak, his imagination anticipating the feel of Paul's robust body, of being inside it, coming inside it. His voice was gravelly. "You want Jack Weston not to see. I do as you say, I can't wait."

Paul laid his hand gently on Delfini's leg, Eduardo groaned, his pants straining with his pleasure. "Believe me, I can't wait either!"

Delfini arrived at Blackfriars Bridge just past one in the morning, the warm night air hugging his body whilst the Thames rippled gently beside him. He could barely contain his excitement.

Surveying the river, the gentle undulation twinkling in the light of the many lampposts, he could see the HMS President. Although the roads were still busy with a constant stream of traffic, the sound of the lapping water was soothing.

Glancing at his watch, Delfini scrutinized Temple Avenue, screwing his elderly eyes to see more clearly. He was pleased to see Paul's boyish form striding towards him. He grinned, and once more he felt his manhood stiffening within his pants.

As Paul reached Delfini he dragged him under a tree, and dropped his holdall on the dusty pavement. Eager, Delfini tried to kiss him, but Paul pushed him away. "My terms, remember Eddie, my terms."

"I remember, my lovely tease, I always listen to what you say to me." Delfini pushed his hardened groin into Paul's, disappointed to meet with softness. He gyrated his hips, forcing his stiffness at Paul, desperate to have his rigidity returned.

Paul shoved Delfini back, a sneer of distaste fleeting across his face. "I like it rough, Eduardo, I like rough games."

"Pauly stop, you make me come too soon." Delfini gasped as he fondled his own crotch, a drip of saliva running down his bristly chin.

Paul studied his watch. "It's half past one now, I want us to do it at exactly two o'clock. Do you understand?"

"Oh, yes, Pauly, yes." Delfini's pupils were fully dilated as he groped through his trousers.

"So take your hand off yourself." Paul's eyes were full of contempt. The bulge in Delfini's trousers subsided as Paul continued. "We will stay here and be silent until quarter to two, then I will take you to the bridge. You will do exactly as I say." And grew again.

"I will."

Paul took Delfini's hand and led him to the centre of the well-lit bridge. Several cars passed, but Delfini was too enraptured to notice. Paul was oblivious. He stopped, dropped his bag on the ground, undid the zip, stood up and pushed Delfini roughly against the edge of the bridge with his body. Delfini's penis pulsed against the taller man's leg, Paul smiled. "I want to tie you, will you do that?"

Surprised, Delfini hesitated, but not for long, he was too anxious for the act to continue. "Anything for you, Pauly."

Deftly, Paul pulled the rope from the bag, he slipped the ready prepared noose over Delfini's neck, tightening it. Delfini stiffened, his native Italian skin paling. "I not sure, Pauly, tie my hands, my feet, but not my neck."

In one flowing movement, Paul lifted his leg and removed the unloaded gun, he forced it against Delfini's chest and cocked the hammer. Delfini flinched. "You said you would do exactly as I say. I don't like people who lie to me." The twinkling in Paul's eyes had gone, replaced by a cold, hard stare. Delfini felt his bladder empty.

"Pauly, you do what turns you on, I will enjoy you anyway." He knew he wouldn't, not now.

Paul tucked the gun into his trouser pocket, took the length of rope and tied it securely to the railings at the edge of the bridge, Delfini could feel but not see the movement. Paul checked his watch, the time was eight minutes to two, he needed to get a move on if the duty was going to be on time. He reached back into the bag, took out half a brick, and placed it in Delfini's jacket pocket. A quarter brick was placed into the left trouser pocket, and four large stones in the right.

Delfini's body was tense, he was terrified. In his sixty-two years of life he had never been so scared. But suddenly he felt Paul's hand on his groin, and his terror began to dissipate, everything was going to be fine. Paul tugged at his flies, and Delfini began to stiffen once more. The zip fully opened, Delfini felt Paul's hand grope inside, then a cold, hard feeling replaced the hand. Paul dropped a broken brick in Delfini's pants, and roughly pulled the fly up again. Delfini's panic had returned.

"You're ready." Paul stated indifferently as he zipped his bag and tossed it over his shoulder.

Now trembling, Delfini wondered if this was a joke, perhaps all this was a plot to shame his family, embarrass his employers. "How about I pay you to let me go?"

Paul's answer came without words. He bent down and tucked both arms tightly around Delfini's legs, and, lifting his body with ease, he hurled it over the railings. Paul heard the crunch of Eduardo Delfini's neck snapping, and a faint splash as the dying man's brogues entered the water. Paul leant over to ensure his duty was complete. Eduardo's body, or was it Gian Roberto Calvi's, hanged there beautifully, just as it had done twenty-six years before. Another destiny completed, and Paul was relishing the role God had chosen for him. Very much.

Wednesday 18th June

The time was three fifty five in the morning and the police patrol boat neared Blackfriars Bridge on its routine daily patrol. Along the riverbanks birds chirped the dawn chorus, cheered by the summer warmth as the sun tentatively peeped over the horizon. Two disinterested constables sat at the helm, half-heartedly scanning the familiar surroundings. It appeared to be just another regular day, until they spotted the unusual, albeit not unknown, sight of a body hanging from the railings of the bridge. They radioed for assistance, and soon the road across the bridge was teeming with constables and paramedics, investigating what they believed to be a suicide.

Juan Delfini was woken by the doorbell chiming, he clambered wearily from under the snug covers, swearing when he noticed it wasn't even six in the morning. Maria haughtily tugged the pillow over her head. He dragged a silky black housecoat over his nakedness, and traipsed downstairs towards the front door. Surprised and somewhat apprehensive, he moved aside to let the two uniformed police officers through.

"What's all that noise, Juan baby?" The naturally nosy Maria had heard the voices below.

"It's just the police, honey. I'll deal with it, you go back to sleep." A hint of resignation tinted the words, which crime of his had they discovered this time?

Maria sat upright, relief seeping through her as she realised her husband was about to be arrested again. She lifted her hand to her face and gently probed the scabby swellings and bruises, wincing at the sharp pains. Juan had always been a bad boy, that's what had attracted her to him, but she'd never expected the beatings once they'd married. She was resolved to them now, it was just a part of her life, and the only time she didn't need heavy make up was when he was locked up. Go back to sleep, she thought, not a chance! Maria wanted to wave him goodbye.

She climbed out of bed, expecting to see Juan from the top of the stairs, handcuffed and being lead away. But he wasn't. She strained to eavesdrop on the conversation as she trotted down, and gasped.

She shoved the door open. "Dead?" She questioned. "Who's dead?"

Juan was pale, he was balancing on the edge of the sofa, his shoulders slumped. He raised his eyes to her inquiring face. "My father is dead, honey. I have to identify the body."

Maria flicked her wrist at Juan, dismissive. "Rubbish, that is! That old bugger, he don't just die. They got the wrong man, baby."

"They found him hanging from a bridge, they say it's suicide."

"No way, baby, the old bugger wouldn't do that, they got the wrong man."

Juan, dapper in his charcoal grey Armani suit, the hairs on his exposed chest cushioning a hefty gold medallion, gasped, and turned away from the limp, mottled body. "That's my father." Involuntary tears stung at the back of his chocolate brown eyes, and he swallowed hard to keep them at bay. He would grieve later, in private.

The constable led him away from the chapel of rest. "I know this is difficult for you, sir, but we will need to speak to you about your father. Let me know when would be a good time and we'll come to you."

"You taking me back to my house? I speak to you then, my father was a good man, I tell you all about him." Juan wiped the stray tear from his eye with his jewelled hand, before it could be noticed.

After the horror of Katie Joyce's death, it had occurred to Krein that there may be other deaths around the country that hadn't been attributed to her murderer. He had appealed to MacReavie, and subsequently to Walker, that all recent deaths across the country, regardless of their cause, were now logged onto the Police National Computer. The idea was to investigate each death to establish if there had been a previous death within the last hundred years or so under similar circumstances.

With over half a million people dying each year in Britain, this would be a huge operation, and expensive too, and the idea was met with incredulous opposition. Krein pushed, and pushed, standing his ground, and eventually his nagging bore fruit. Walker managed to persuade his superiors, in conjunction with concerned government officials, to allow them to investigate any deaths deemed as suspicious, see if they bore any comparison to a previous death.

The cost of the operation was justified, amazingly, within a few days, when Eduardo Delfini's supposed suicide was found to be strikingly similar to the death of Gian Roberto Calvi, dubbed 'God's Banker' by the press, in nineteen eighty-two.

Krein read the report he'd printed from the Holmes System avidly. Known as Roberto Calvi, sixty-two at the time of his demise, the president of the Banco Ambrosiano of Milan had been found hanging from scaffolding at Blackfriars Bridge in the early morning of the eighteenth of June, twenty six years before. Although the death was initially considered to be suicide, various anomalies were discovered during the investigation, and his family was insistent that Roberto wouldn't take his own life, so eventually the case had been reviewed. To date no one had been found guilty of killing him.

Delfini and Calvi were both sixty-two, the order of stones and bricks in their pockets were identical, and, when the bodies were discovered, the bottom of the trousers were sodden. They both wore dark suits, both were Italian, and both died at approximately two in the morning on the eighteenth of June.

Krein relayed his suspicions to a stunned MacReavie, who contacted the investigating officers in London. The pending post mortem was brought forward, and a murder investigation launched, linking Delfini's death to Katie's, Alan Benton's, and Annabel's, should they ever discover where her body had been dumped.

Krein had never dealt with a case like this one before. It had him baffled, and he wanted to understand the killer's mind, he felt it would assist with his detection. Jaswinder Kumar, a criminal psychologist with an extraordinarily good reputation, agreed to a meeting to give her views of the murderer, based on the information Krein had.

She knocked and entered his office, he drew a sharp breath, her beauty was outstanding. His speech faltering embarrassingly, he gestured a chair, and spent the next thirty minutes furnishing her with the notes he had. She listened politely, registering his words, taking her own notes, and asking question when she needed to. He finished, the room remained silent as she digested and deliberated the information. Finally she was ready to impart her psychological summary.

Jaswinder's speech was slow, each word stressed carefully to ensure Krein understood. "Obviously this man is planning his crimes meticulously, and the results are unfortunately fatal for his victims. However, I do not think he is evil, per se, I think it is far more likely that he is ill."

"Sick!" Krein spat the word vengefully. She stared at him, the contemptuous look in her eye silencing him.

"There appears to be psychotic and schizophrenic tendencies, I think that the man probably believes he is being 'told' to commit these acts in the form of hallucinations that are very real to him, and that is a symptom that occurs in psychosis, although some believe it is an exclusive condition of schizophrenia. I personally think that the symptoms of the three main forms of psychosis tend to overlap, as do many others. However, saying that, I think there are other psychiatric disorders to contemplate."

Jaswinder took a deep breath, considering her next words carefully. "What do we know about this man? He is by all accounts scruffy, self-neglect is a common sign of several mental illnesses, from depression through to schizophrenia and psychosis. Yet conversely, he seems to be obsessively tidy, orderly. When he broke into that house in," she consulted her notes for the first time, "Halesworth, he cleaned the basin after using it to wash himself."

"How do you know that?" Krein was dumbfounded.

"The statement. The woman mentioned that she'd noticed that day that the basin was very clean, stating that she and her partner weren't the tidiest people." Krein felt ashamed, that

114

hadn't seemed important when he'd studied the statement. Jaswinder continued. "Katie Joyce's flat was impeccably tidy when her mother first went to look for her daughter, and she tells us that Katie was messy by nature. There is also continual attention to detail in the killings, and the reproduction of past murders, even to the stones in the pockets of the latest suspected victim. Think of the candle lamp that was in Katie's hand, her black dress, her neat chignon. The man is obsessive, he researches the murders, selects a suitable victim, I mean age, perhaps looks, general similarities, and then he plans to commit the copycat crime in the same place, at the same time, on the same day."

Irrationally, Krein was annoyed with Jaswinder, she was thorough to the point of tedium. He snapped, foolishly. "Tell me something we don't know, we've already guessed he's mentally depraved, I mean you don't slice through someone's neck if …"

That stare again. Ashamed, he stopped ranting. "You have an unfortunate choice of words, Mr Krein."

And his indignation towards her was back. "Look Miss Kumar, his victims, robbed of their life, their families, robbed of their loved one. They wouldn't mind me being politically incorrect."

Why did he dislike her so much? He glared into her eyes, feeling himself melting into the velvety chocolate, wishing he could loosen her hairpin and watch her silky black hair tumble over her shoulders. Shocked, he realised he fancied her.

Her words broke the uncomfortable silence. "Mr Krein. May I remind you that it was you who asked me to meet with you. You wanted my opinion on the wanted man's psychological profile. It is not my fault that this man is killing, it is not my fault that the victims' families are hurting. If you want my cooperation, then please have some consideration for my professional ability, and some respect for me personally."

Chastised, and humbly sheepish, Krein bowed his head. "I'm really sorry, Miss Kumar, this case has become the most difficult in my entire career."

Jaswinder's face softened into a smile, and his heart leapt. He guiltily glanced at the photo of Linda on his desk. "Yes, probably the most frustrating I should imagine. This man is good, he appears to be a chameleon, he blends into society without so much as a suspicion against him."

"So what next? What will he do next?"

"Another murder, undoubtedly. I think he will be feeling very clever by now, I think his mind will be so numbed that he will be finding the act of killing pleasant, I think it will make him feel powerful, in control. In my opinion, you need to find out when, where, and how past murders in this country were committed, and you need to increase policing in the areas of these cases at the time and date of the previous killing."

"Needle and haystack, then. I don't think the bigwigs would be willing to allow us to finance an operation that extensive."

"Then more people are going to die in tragic circumstances. Your man won't be predictable for you, I'm afraid. I feel that, at this moment, he is probably more interested in recreating the detail, more so than in actually committing the murder. But he will be getting some enjoyment from the act of killing, quite probably sexual, and that will intensify the longer he carries on."

"Let me understand this fully. If he continues to kill ..."

"He will."

"Okay. As he continues to kill, he will stop paying so much attention to the details of the recreation, and will enjoy the actual act of killing more and more."

"You got it." She smiled again, he fixed his eyes on Linda's photograph.

"Where can I find him?" The question was addressed to his wife for fear of his feelings should he focus on Jaswinder.

"He's an obsessive person. You'll probably find him at a library!"

Krein stood up. "Thank you, Miss Kumar, and I'm sorry about before, I'm not normally so rude. Look, would you be willing to write a report based on your conclusions. The Super may be willing to put the idea forward if he has the detailed facts you've given me in front of him."

Pushing open the canteen door, Krein's stomach growled in complaint. He had been so engrossed in the new developments,

116

he'd forgotten to eat, and now his body was taking charge. Piling sandwiches and snacks onto his tray, he paid, and looked around for somewhere to sit. His shoulders slumped when he saw MacReavie waving him over. Krein trudged to the table and sat.

A lecherous grin spread across MacReavie's face. "What's with the Asian tea girl then?"

Krein was disgusted. He was used to his boss's sexism, but racism too. He glared at him, and unwrapped his first sandwich.

"Well, who was she. Quite a stunner, wasn't she?"

"She," Krein emphasized the word, "is a criminal psychologist who is intelligent, articulate, and above all, nice. She doesn't deserve your derision."

"Come on, Krein, you'd love to give her one as much as I would." MacReavie laughed, his thick skin cloaking his arrogance.

"She," he stressed the word again, "has given me a psychological profile of the killer, and when her report lands on my desk, you and I are going to take it to Walker's office, and you are going to make sure that he applies for extra funding on this case. If you refuse I am going to make public your repeated, shameful acts of sexism and racism over the past year I have worked alongside you."

"Piffle!" MacReavie wasn't smiling any more.

"Try me!" Krein's shoulders were squared, his determination undisguised.

MacReavie concentrated on his food, playing with the mashed potato with his fork. He mixed the gravy into the mash, stirring in the peas, pushing the meal from one side to the other. Finally he relented. "Why do we need more funding?"

Bingo, thought Krein. "You know the Crime Museum in New Scotland Yard?" MacReavie seemed puzzled. "Used to be called The Black Museum."

"Ah, yes. Didn't know the name had changed."

"You know they have exhibits and documents relating to murders going back to the late eighteen hundreds. I thought we could set up a team of investigating officers there, specifically to analyse old murders, dates, so forth, and set up a database which all the involved forces can refer to try and pre-empt the killer before he strikes again."

"Come on Krein, get back into the real world. That would cost a fortune."

"And not doing it is going to continue to cost lives. What's more important?" Krein was impressive when he was resolute.

Jack Weston had already heard through the grapevine that Delfini had died, so it was no surprise to see the detectives enter the club. They spied Jack and descended the stairs to the empty bar, where he was standing.

Jack knew that Paul was involved, he'd seen the rope in his bag, but even so, it surprised him that Delfini was hanged, not shot. Jack had no intention of splitting on Paul, firstly the man scared him, and secondly his own dodgy dealings meant he had too much to lose by getting involved. He would just act the shocked club owner, distraught that one of his customers had been found dead.

"Good evening, Mr Weston."

"Boys! How nice to see you." Jack grinned widely. "Can I get you a drink?"

"No, thank you. We need to ask you some questions about one of your regulars, Eduardo Delfini. Are you familiar with him?"

"My dear Eduardo, he's one of my greatest friends, he's been drinking here for years." Jack knew he was overacting, but he couldn't stop himself.

The two policemen looked at each other, stunned. "So you haven't heard that he was found hanging from Blackfriars Bridge this morning?"

Jack's jaw gaped, he staggered slightly, and fell against the barstool behind him. His eyes looked pained, and his voice quietened dramatically. "Eddie! Dead! No, it cannot be, dear Lord." His performance was worthy of an Oscar.

"I'm sorry to shock you Mr Weston, but I need to ask you some questions. Could you tell me if Mr Delfini was here last night, please?"

Jack tried to force a tear, but that was impossible. "Yes, dear Eddie, he came in at nine, as he does, did, every night. Oh, to think I will never see him again! He left soon before we closed at one. He doesn't usually stay that late."

"Did he leave with anyone?"

The face of a man pondering. "No, no, I remember him leaving, he was alone."

"Did he mention that he was to meet up with anyone?"

"Why no, he always went home to bed, or so he told me."

The officer was getting tired of the blatant lies, he sighed, annoyed. "Look, Mr Weston, we know that you employ rent boys. In a case like this facts like that are overlooked in order to obtain the truth. This is a murder enquiry. So let's try again. Were you aware of Mr Delfini making any attachments with anyone."

A face of concern. "Oh no, I think Eddie just came here for the company."

Paul was packing his few belongings into the holdall. He had worked at The Weston Avenue Club for exactly thirteen nights, and although the pay had been meagre, the tips had more than doubled the sum. After the five hundred for the gun, buying some clothes from a charity shop, and his moderate rent, he now had roughly six hundred pounds left. Enough to leave the credit cards behind. That would help to keep everyone off his trail.

Paul had deliberately waited for evening's disguising darkness to leave the room he had rented for two weeks. He knew Jack Weston wouldn't mention him to the police, he was a bad boy, definitely not a stool pigeon, which bought him time. He scanned the room, not wanting to leave anything behind, and he made sure everything was clean, tidy. Satisfied, Paul was about to set off when Jack burst in, followed by Dunny Thomas. Jack grabbed Paul by the throat, throwing him roughly against the wall.

"Leaving were you? I don't think so. You owe me, big time, and I intend to collect."

Paul made no attempt to struggle, he stared deep into Jack's eyes, cold, snakelike. Once more Jack had no choice but to look away, those eyes were evil, he released his grip and stepped back, shaking his head slowly. "Just tell me, Paul. Why Delfini? What did he have on you?"

The glare continued, unblinking, Jack shuddered uncontrollably. No one had ever had this effect on him, he was too hard. The silence continued, the stare maintained. Jack's heart raced, and for the first time he considered whether Paul intended to kill him.

The answer came suddenly, the unwavering stare relentless. "No-one has anything on me. Including you." Paul brushed past him, his footsteps echoed along the corridor, and the flustered Jack tried to regain his bravado for Dunny's benefit.

"I never saw no-one get the better of you, boss. Why did you let him get away?"

Drowning out the dissipating footsteps, Jack was enraged. "He didn't get one over on me, and don't let me hear you say it again. Get it? Me and Paul, we have an understanding, got it?"

Dunny recoiled, chastised, as Jack spied the credit card on the bedside table. He snatched it and waved it before Dunny's eyes. "See, he left me this, it's what he owes me."

Dunny continued placing the items in a carrier bag as the cashier took his payment. Unknown to him she pressed an alarm underneath the counter, alerting the security staff. Dunny glanced at her, nervous: this transaction was taking too long. "What's taking so long?"

The lady, inwardly wary, smiled. "Oh, sometimes when the phones are busy it can take a while for the authorisation code to come through."

Dunny nodded, but jumped as a security guard grabbed his arm from behind. "Could you just come with me, please sir." Dunny shook him off and ran, pushing the queue and their trolleys aside with force. He was a fit man, well built and athletic, but the trained guards were faster, they tackled him to the ground, and the police were called.

"But it wasn't my card." Dunny protested.

"We know that," DI Gordon Spencer growled at the young man, "it belongs to a young mother who we believe may have been murdered."

Dunny's face paled, this was serious. Where was his boss, why wasn't he here to speak for him. What was he supposed to say? He hadn't murdered anyone.

Dunny had no idea that Jack already knew of his arrest, news travels fast on the underground grapevine. But there was no way he was getting involved with this one. Whatever, whoever, Paul Joyce was, scared him, and his interest stopped here. He intended to keep quiet, and deny everything if Dunny blabbed. Dunny was unimportant, he could find a hundred new idiots to replace him.

Thursday 19th June

Detective Inspector Spencer of New Scotland Yard had managed to crack Donald Thomas very easily the night before. He'd been reduced to tears, begging for his mother, it had taken barely any interrogation to get the full story. Jack Weston's involvement was no surprise, he'd been under surveillance for a few months due to his extra-curricular activities. But what Dunny didn't realise, and Jack too, was that they were important witnesses to the movements of a suspected murderer.

When Dunny had tried to pay for his shopping with Annabel's credit card, it automatically alerted the cashier to call the police. So now he was tied into the investigation, and a murmuring had circulated that Paul, as they now knew him, was becoming careless at covering his tracks. Arresting Dunny had caused many detective's hearts to sink across the country, because it meant that Paul had managed to remain a step ahead of them. The credit card company informed Krein, as were their instructions, just before MacReavie heard the news from the Metropolitan Police force.

It was the early hours of the morning, and Krein sat at his desk, his coffee stone cold, and digested every line of Donald Thomas's statement. He hadn't known Paul very well, and hadn't wanted to, he didn't like him. Paul had started working for Jack roughly two weeks before. He had been great at his job, chatting easily to the punters, encouraging them to buy plenty of expensive drinks. Dunny wasn't aware if Paul had sex with the customers, for money or not. He didn't think so, but then how would he know? Paul had definitely flirted with Delfini, but Dunny had never seen them leave together.

When asked if he knew that Delfini was dead, the shock on Dunny's face was genuine, and when told that they suspected Paul of his murder, Dunny paled. Hence, he freely divulged the contents of Paul's bag, tears flowing abundantly, the rope, the bricks. The statement was immediately fed into the Holmes System, alerting all the detective teams involved. The gap between the police and the killer had narrowed.

Jack Weston was brought in, totally against his will, for questioning. It was now three in the morning and Spencer's eyelids were drooping with tiredness, only the excitement and the extra strong coffee kept him alert. But even so, he was increasingly irritated by the cocky man's evasiveness. His patience tried one time too many, he snapped. "I'm not sure if you're aware of the seriousness of the situation you're in, Jack. The man you employed for the past two weeks is suspected of killing at least four people so far, in fact five if you count the baby ripped from the womb."

"What? The foetus found in the bush? That case?" Jack's barriers slipped momentarily, he struggled to mentally replace them.

"Jack, we need to track Paul down before he kills again. Believe me, he doesn't intend to stop this spree with Delfini. Your help could be imperative to catching up with him."

Jack debated how much he could tell them, he didn't like men who hurt women, but every time his conscience decided to play ball, he remembered the gun. Divulging that would send him to Shit Street. "I hardly knew the guy. I paid him a wage, he came in, did work, went away again. That's all. He was a nobody to me."

Spencer let out a deep sigh, he knew he'd nearly cracked Jack, but he'd managed to lose him again. He drank the coffee, grimacing at the bitter thickness. "Can you describe him to me?"

"Reckon so. Five nine-ish, er, shortish dark hair, good looking, but he was older than most of my boys though, maybe mid twenties. Is that enough?"

"Facial hair?" Spencer scribbled on his notebook.

"No, he was always clean shaven. When he first turned up he had a touch of acne, but that didn't last."

"Eyes?"

"Two!"

Spencer realised he hated this man. "Come on, Jack, this is serious. What colour were his eyes?"

"Hell, I've got no idea, light I think. I'm not into guys. I don't check them out, I employ them."

Spencer stood up, he rubbed his eyes with his fists, stifling a yawn, and began to pace the room. "Jack, do you read the papers?"

"I read The Sun, News of the World at the weekend."

"The case we're investigating? Have you read up on that, or do you just buy the paper for the tits?"

Jack bristled, he had a keen interest in current affairs, and that comment was harsh. "I read about it, but it didn't interest me, I don't like reading about sicko's who mutilate women. Anyway, there's always some nutter going around killing somebody, we read it every day."

Spencer had to try to break Jack's defences down again, he changed his tack. "How old are you, Jack?"

Confused at the irrelevance, Jack frowned. "Sixty two. Why?"

Spencer leaned across the desk, close to Jack, resting on his elbows. "Delfini was also sixty two. Do you realise that every victim Paul selects is to recreate a past murder. In this instance he needed a sixty two year old man. Now think to yourself, Jack, what if Paul had selected you instead of Delfini? Does it occur to you that it could have been your body we found hanging from Blackfriars Bridge?"

Jack laughed uncomfortably. "No way, he'd never have been able to get me."

Spencer's tone was grave. "I think you'll find that he would. Paul is a clever, very clever young man." Jack swallowed hard, remembering Paul's cold, unwavering stare, and he knew that Spencer was right.

Jack Weston had done what he never thought he would, he had assisted the police with their enquiries. He hadn't told them about the gun, it was irrelevant. However, a new photofit was produced based on his, and Dunny's, descriptions. It was a good likeness, but the one thing the computer couldn't recreate was Paul's eyes. The emotionless, icy stare, the fearsome chill that haunted Jack every time he slept, and would do for a long time ahead.

The media didn't take much persuading to publish the photofit of the serial killer, the whole nation was engrossed in the investigation. Office staff speculated, factory workers theorized, mothers and fathers worried. Secure that the killer would never affect their own families directly, everyone waited apprehensively for the next murder in order to have a good gossip. Unsurprisingly, newspaper sales were high when the latest details were published.

Krein scrutinised the newest photofit, comparing it to the previous two. He couldn't help but marvel at the way Paul managed to change his identity, effortlessly blending into the background again. When Annabel had disappeared, the suspected abductor, based on an eyewitness, had a full beard and dark blond, bushy hair, and he'd progressed through these three photofits to a clean-shaven dark haired lad. Krein had no doubt he would look different now, he would have changed his identity and become invisible again. The worst part was knowing that Paul would kill again, and the only way they could save the next victim's life would be to pre-empt him.

Due to the urgency of the situation the Police Resources Unit at the Home Office had hastily arranged a substantial grant to take the monetary pressure off the search for the killer, and a room on the first floor of New Scotland Yard, next to the Black Museum, had been allocated as a central incident room, with Deputy Assistant Commissioner Falder-Woodes officially in charge of the investigation. A further room was designated for a team of twelve experienced officers were in the process of being transferred to research past murders within the past hundred years, and the team was to be led by Detective Chief Inspector Barry Harner, an officer for two decades, whose attention to detail was legendary. Almost immediately the new specialist team were dubbed the Black Museum Bunch.

Within hours of his arrival, Harner had dredged up details of murder anniversaries that were due in the next couple of weeks. There were few, but, although the sex of the victim was irrelevant to Paul, for some reason Bella Wright's murder on the fifth of July stood out to Krein. He read through the scanty details, she had been shot, the killer was possibly a man on a green bicycle who had been seen with her, but nobody had ever been convicted for her death.

Krein gasped, he scrabbled through the files, searching for the details of the murders that had been copied so far. And remarkably, in every case the killer had never been convicted. Was that a coincidence? Was it the unique fact that attracted Paul to that case? If he was going to recreate Bella Wright's demise, he would need a gun, and that cocky character, Jack Weston, was the type of small time idiot who would supply him with one. Krein hastily emailed his thoughts to Spencer, requesting he interrogate Weston further on this point. Maybe he was being paranoid, maybe he was seeing a link that wasn't there, but if his over-dramatisation would save a life then it was worth the potential shame.

Friday 20th June

Shaking out the excess water, Paul wrapped the fleece around his head to soak up the rest as he had no towel. The light in the train station toilets was dim, and the air was dense with the smell of faeces and urine. A few men came and went, they took no notice of him. Paul rubbed at his head for a short while, then stuffed the damp fleece into the holdall, leaving his newly dyed, vibrant black hair moist. He glanced at the cracked mirror, pleased to see the latest transformation, and positioned some cheap, dark rimmed, reading glasses on his nose. His appearance was significantly different, and he could relax slightly, the chances of being spotted lessened.

Paul needed to find somewhere to stay, somewhere remote to reduce the chances of anybody recognising him. His likeness was on the front page of every newspaper this morning, so he really needed to be careful now. Grabbing his bag, Paul marched from the loos, and away from Leicester Station.

Elaine casually chucked the newspaper onto the reception desk, she'd have to go through the handover with Sarah before she could read the latest affairs. Sarah was leaving for Spain that afternoon and she was eager to finish work early, buying plenty of time to get to Gatwick. She updated Elaine with a quick summary of all the residents, and hastily left the building, her goodbyes met with have funs.

Having made a welcome mug of sweet tea, Elaine sighed as she settled into the chair. The home was neat and tidy, the patients behaving, and she decided that whilst the day was uneventful, she might as well read for a while. She unfolded the paper, and dropped it on seeing Paul's face staring at her. The hair in the photofit was shorter and darker, but the face was just almost identical. Reading the headline, nausea threatened, and the more she studied the article, the higher the bile rose. She'd always thought it odd that he'd never returned to see Maud, after all, he wouldn't know she was dead, but now she could see that the situation was far more sinister. Elaine rushed to the bathroom,

127

spilling her breakfast into the toilet until the retching finally subsided.

It felt like hours to Elaine, waiting for the police to arrive, but in reality it was only minutes. The telephone call had immediately been logged onto the Holmes System, even though her statement had not been taken, which showed how seriously Sussex Police force were taking the matter. DI MacIntyre and DS Wilson, pleased to be involved in the dramatic nationwide hunt, found Elaine to be a helpful and succinct witness. Having detailed the events of nearly a month before, fully aware that her job may be in jeopardy for her failure to adhere to the rules, she read through the statement, initialled corrections to the anomalies, and signed her name confidently.

After speaking to detectives in the incident room at New Scotland Yard for advice, MacIntyre requested the address of Maud Blessing's daughter, Julia Anton. The body would need to be exhumed for an autopsy as foul play was now suspected.

Within minutes the Black Museum Bunch had discovered a past murder in Eastbourne, on the same date, the victim being the same age as Maud Blessing. There was controlled pandemonium on the first floor of the Metropolitan Police headquarters.

Julia Anton stood by the door, her pinched face severe as always, she stared at MacIntyre after he'd introduced himself, unspeaking. "Mrs Anton, we need to speak to you about some developments that have arisen regarding the death of your mother, Mrs Maud Blessing."

Julia moved back to allow the detectives entry to her modest, semi-detached home. They all sat in the lounge, Julia listening intently as she discovered the possibility that her mother had been poisoned, murdered. She soaked in the details of how the potential killer had been allowed access by the incompetence of a member of staff at the nursing home. Her diligence surprised MacIntyre, but nowhere near as much as the apparent lack of emotion.

"So, Mrs Anton, may we please have your permission to exhume your mother's body?"

"I'm sorry but no. Mother was cremated." Julia stated, simply.

And later, Julia stated just as simply to the manager of The Ridings Nursing Home, "I want her fired."

Elaine, a competent nurse with an excellent track record collected her belongings, resolved tears spilling down her cheeks. For her entire life she'd been intrigued by Alzheimers, her grandfather having died from the illness, and she'd loved the residents individually for their inner beauty. It was possible she would never work in this field again now, and it was all her own stupid, naïve fault. She left the building, hopeless.

Krein sat at his desk with the report he'd printed from the Holmes System in front of him. Maud Blessing, eighty-five years old, had died in Eastbourne on the twenty seventh of May. Foul play had not been suspected at the time, and the body had been released for burial without an autopsy.

Julia Bradnum, aged eighty five, had died in Eastbourne on the twenty seventh of May, nineteen fifty-two. Initially foul play had not been suspected, but her body was later exhumed. The cause of death was never found as the body had decomposed too much, but it wasn't cerebral haemorrhage as stated on the death certificate. Later, her doctor, John Bodkin-Adams, who was the sole beneficiary in her will, was arrested on suspicion of murdering Edith Morrell and Gertrude Hullett, the police having also investigated Bradnum's, and Clara Neil-Miller's deaths

Krein sat up straight and gasped when he read the next line. 'The case went to trial, but John Bodkin-Adams was never convicted for any of the deaths.'

"Fuck!" He would need a stiff whiskey now, this was too much of a coincidence. He needed to speak with Barry Harner to express this theme in the murders Paul had selected to copy.

Hundreds of sightings were reported on the Incident Hotline during the morning, apparently Paul had been seen in Scotland, Wales, London, Portsmouth, Leicestershire, Manchester and East Anglia, to name a few. All in one day. Jurisdiction stated that every report had to be followed up, but the London sightings interested the police the most, as they knew he had been living in, or around, London for the past couple of weeks. Unfortunately, none of the calls led anywhere.

Until twelve thirty in the afternoon. The detective who took the call immediately contacted Leicestershire Constabulary requesting they interview Mrs Brenda Taylor, who had called from DH Edwards Pharmacy.

Brenda was adamant that the man she had served that morning was the same person as the man in the photofit. He had purchased a lady's permanent hair dye, and, although she couldn't recall what colour it had been, the electronic till confirmed that it was a black colouring. She stated he'd remained silent during the cash transaction. He'd been wearing a pair of baggy, pale combat trousers, a black, hooded fleece with a logo on the chest, but she couldn't recall what the logo was. He was young, nice looking, in fact all the things they already knew.

This interview, coupled with a few sightings reported in Leicester city centre, convinced the police that Leicester was probably where Paul was hiding. The Black Museum Bunch had already found a past murder near to Leicester, and the anniversary was just over two weeks away.

Barry Harner replaced the receiver, he took the prints from his desk and strolled next door to Spencer. He waved the papers in front of Spencer's face, and laid them on the desk. "I'm not the only one whose gut feeling is that this case will be next recreation. I've pointed it out to you before."

Spencer scanned the document, reading aloud to drive the words into his memory. "On the fifth July, nineteen nineteen, Bella Wright, aged twenty one, was shot in the head whilst cycling along the Burton-Overy Road in the small village of Stretton, near Leicester. She had been either followed or companioned, the distinction wasn't made, by a young man on a green bicycle for the last couple of hours of her life, he was later found to be a Mr Ronald Light. He was taken to trial, but was not convicted for her murder."

130

Spencer ruffled through a pile of printed emails, he pulled out the one from Krein that had waited for him first thing in the morning. "You mean Krein suspects this one too?"

Harner nodded. "He's pointed out that in the original investigations of all the recreations, including Maud Blessing's, nobody was ever convicted for the killing. I think he's on to something."

"It's a great theory for a bloody country bumpkin. He emailed me last night asking if I'd go and see Jack Weston about the possibility of him selling Paul a gun."

"Come on, mate, don't give him shit. He's been on this case since day one, he's really determined. He's even spoken to a criminal psychologist who says his hunch is feasible." Harner had spoken to Krein on several occasions, he liked the man, and respected his persistence and dedication.

"I'm sorry, it's just when I'm working on a case, I don't like being told my job by outsiders."

"He's not an outsider, mate."

Krein needled Spencer, he couldn't put a finger on why. Maybe it was because the investigation was centralised now, and Krein refused to butt out. He shrugged, concentrating on the page before him. "Well, if Paul intends to recreate this murder, we've got fifteen days. I'll have a word with my Guv'nor, see if we can set up an undercover operation in Leicester. As long as the sightings continue there, I can't see much opposition to the idea."

Harner smiled, Spencer wasn't usually the type to accept someone else's gut feelings, he was an arrogant man, albeit an excellent detective.

Paul settled himself in the wooden chair, a hot mug of tea steaming beside him on the formica covered table. The blended smells of grease, bacon, eggs, sausages and toast wafted heavily throughout the small café, and his hungry stomach growled in anticipation of the fry-up he was awaiting. He'd chosen this seat specifically for the unused socket in the wall, and he plugged the lead of his organiser in to recharge the battery whilst he updated his notes and familiarised himself with his next duty.

The waitress smiled seductively as she brought the heavily laden plate over, Paul was aware that the ladies found him attractive, even more so in his latest disguise, maybe the glasses made him look distinguished. He'd not found a place to stay, and he didn't want to waste too much cash, so while the hot spell held out, he intended to sleep outside. He would find a park, sleep behind the bushes somewhere inconspicuous. No one need know, and if they did, he could just shoot them, God wouldn't mind an extra body.

Tuesday 24th June

That extra body just happened to be a copycat murder, one he hadn't expected to do: but with the heavy onslaught of police activity in Leicester, Paul knew he needed to put the police off his trail, and he'd headed to Essex by train that day after a couple of hours research in the library.

The thrill Paul felt as the latest life-robbed body fell was almost sexual: he smiled as he hastily retraced his steps along the dirt path under the twinkling glow of the moon. He needed to get away quickly, this was a residential area and he'd not realised how loud a gun firing would be. Although it was late at night, any of the locals may be reporting the sound to the police.

Mary Goodey lay in her bed, unable to sleep, regardless of having taken two Temazepam sleeping tablets. She was worried, the noise had been so loud. After checking the time, she rolled over, tugging a pillow over her head. Her and her bloody imagination, she really had to stop being so dramatic, the silly trait had already caused her husband to leave. It was just a car backfiring.

Wednesday 25th June

A temporary incident room had been set up in St John's, the headquarters of the Leicestershire Constabulary, and Operation Bella, as it had been dubbed unofficially, had been launched. Details of Paul's victims and movements, and the murders they copied, were pinned to notice boards to give some background to the newly drafted detectives in the Leicester force, and Krein, much to Spencer's disgust, had insisted that he was a part of the operation, alongside five officers from the Metropolitan force. Krein had brought with him a detailed psychological profile of the murderer, and a brief summary for ease of reading, compiled by Jaswinder Kumar. MacReavie had been offered a place in the investigation, but had refused due to an important golf tournament, not that he admitted that to his superiors.

Once the team of detectives had been briefed on every aspect of the Bella Wright murder, four plain clothed officers were shipped out to the sleepy village of Little Stretton, patrolling discreetly, on the lookout for a man matching Paul's description, however loosely. On the twenty first of June, the whole operation had been compromised by an eager newspaper's report on the investigation being relocated to Leicester, but urgent discussions had encouraged the team to stand firm, hoping the leaked details wouldn't alter the killer's plans.

The Burton-Overy road had been examined thoroughly, the exact spot where Bella Wright had taken her final, dying breath was estimated from police records dating back nearly eighty-eight years. Thirty-six bicycle shops over Leicestershire were given strict instructions to inform the police of all bicycle sales, the name and address of each purchaser needed to be taken to eliminate them from enquiries.

All young women within the Little Stretton area whose age would be twenty one on the anniversary of Bella's death were located, without their knowledge, in order to track their movements on the fated day, and two female constables were moved into the village, both bicycle riders who claimed to be twenty one to as many people as they could, hoping Paul would target them rather than an innocent member of the public. The team was satisfied that the plans were flawless. Now they had to bide their time until Paul walked into their trap.

Evelyn Dupont screamed, shocked rather than frightened, she hastily retraced her steps along the footpath, nearly colliding with a red bicycle, the rider braking sharply. Kevin Hammond leapt off the bike, angry at first, but when he noted her expression he was concerned.

"Body. Girl. Blood." Evelyn gasped, adrenaline causing goose bumps to emerge on her arms. She pointed along the dusty path, the mud cracked from the lengthy hot spell. Kevin lay his bike down and followed her directions. A few feet further, he saw a heap of clothes, soon realising they were covering a mottled body, and bile rose to his throat. Trembling, his fingers managed to press nine nine nine on his mobile phone.

Within an hour the area had been cordoned off and Scenes of Crime Officers in paper suits were waiting for the Forensic Medical Examiner and the Home Office Pathologist to examine the body.

Candice Albrough, heavily pregnant with her unborn son, was unharmed, except for the entry and exit holes of the bullet on either side of her head.

The killing was automatically fed into the Holmes System, and was quickly picked up by the team in New Scotland Yard. As instructed for any suspicious death whilst the search for Paul was on, the Black Museum Bunch were given the details. They'd only researched murders within the previous hundred years, so it took a while to discover that in eighteen ninety four, a woman named Florence Dennis, unmarried, aged twenty three, and eight months pregnant, had been shot once in the head in the same area on the evening of the twenty fourth of June, her body being found the next day. Although the method of killing was unfamiliar to Paul, the similarities of the latest killing to a past murder immediately led to it being attributed to him.

Krein sat on the table in Leicester headquarters, his heart weary, and scanned the details of the latest case. He knew

Prittlewell having holidayed in Southend on Sea three years before. Now a mainly residential area, it had once been a small village, an ancient settlement that had been mentioned in the Doomsday Book, in Essex. The victim was twenty-three, seven months pregnant, and was believed to have died the night before. Krein shook his head again, slamming the paperwork on the table. Pregnancy could be a link, but that didn't make sense, because Eduardo Delfini's murder ruled that theory out.

Krein folded the document in four and tucked it into his pocket. He needed a beer, maybe that would help him think.

Paul was exhausted, he'd walked for miles. In the early hours of the morning he'd settled in a small copse within a rape field for a few hours sleep, but had set off again with the sunrise, making his way back, via north London, to Leicester, using his return ticket.

Walking, and being a passenger, had given him plenty of time to think. Paul had bought a newspaper the previous Saturday, horrified to see the headlines stating that the police investigation was centring on Stretton, exactly where he planned to be next to recreate Bella Wright's murder. He'd needed to throw them off the scent, he'd had to find an additional duty well away from Leicester. He'd hurried directly to Leicester Central Library, researching past murders furiously, and eventually found one in Essex that was due three days ahead. The time scale had been short, but it was necessary. He had to get the police off his trail.

Now that his face was on posters everywhere, Paul had needed to disguise himself further. He quickly realised that if he appeared to be a woman, he was less likely to be recognised, so he'd visited Oxfam for some female clothes, and purchased a black hairpiece, a long pigtail, from Claire's Accessories. Convincingly dressed as a woman, he had taken the coach to London, then another to Southend on Sea.

Night was falling, the sun low in the sky, the array of beautiful summertime colours indistinguishable as dusk settled. Paula, as he now had to remember to call himself, laughed to himself as he remembered his latest victim's face when he'd raised the gun to her head. He'd met Candice on the Sunday before, she'd been to

Church and he'd walked alongside her as she made her way home.

Paula had been amazed how easily it had been to befriend her, and even more amazed to find she was the right age, and almost the right stage of pregnancy, for his recreation. He'd expected his search for a victim to take longer, and was prepared to relax on some of the details just to get the duty done, but Candice was perfect.

On the Tuesday, as they strolled through wasteland on the outskirts of Southend on Sea, Paula had told Candice all about Florence Dennis's murder in Prittleswell a hundred and fourteen years before. She'd been interested, so he offered to take her to the area she'd died in. Expecting resistance due to the recent press reports, he'd been astounded when she'd come freely. Paula had no idea that Candice suffered from mild autism, the resulting lowered intelligence causing her to trust like a naïve child, the inability to read preventing the newspapers' warnings from reaching her. It had never occurred to Candice that the friendly woman would ever try to hurt her.

The shock in her eyes had been fleeting, Paula pulled the trigger instantly. It can't have hurt, it was too quick.

Krein leant against the bar, the dregs of his seventh beer warming before him. He was distraught, two more victims, a young woman and her unborn child. He'd suspected pregnancy to be a link, but Eduardo Delfini's murder didn't fit that theory. And he'd also suspected the failure to commit anyone for the original murders to be a connection, but that could be ruled out now because James Canham Read had been hanged for Florence's murder.

Ordering a large whisky, Krein racked his brains. He had to get into the mind of this killer before any more people lost their lives. As he knocked the warming, mellow shot back, he waved at the barman for another, grimacing slightly with the aftershock. His head was spinning and he knew he'd have a hangover the next morning, but he had to relax somehow or he'd never get to sleep. Startled, he grabbed his beeping mobile.

"It's Macreavie. Where are you?" The sobering effect was instant. Krein lied, saying he was in his hotel room, planning an early night. MacReavie continued. "DAC Falder-Woodes at the Yard has ordered an urgent meeting, tomorrow at two, at the incident room in London. They want us both there, and your psychologist friend, because we've been in this since the start. Can you get there?"

"What good's talking going to do, for fuck's sake!" The alcohol had made it easier for Krein to snap. He could hear his boss bristling.

"I'm having to miss an important golf match for this, and I'm not complaining. Be there!" The line went dead. Krein knocked back his second whisky and waved for another.

Thursday 26th June

Now that Paul had got used to being Paula, he was surprised at how naturally behaving like a woman came to him. Paula glanced in the small mirror she'd bought alongside the cosmetics five days before. Satisfied that her make up was intact under the unflattering glasses, and her blue toned black hair convincing with the hairpiece, she replaced the mirror in the bag. She stood, dusting down her fitted trousers and loose tunic, slipped on the worn trainers, and left the tatty outhouse that had housed her the night before.

With so many miles to travel, Paula needed to hitch a lift. She could head for the A1(M), but if she managed to get onto the M1, it would take her directly to Leicester. She chose the latter, and headed along the road parallel to the M25, heading west, lifting her thumb hopefully each time a car approached on the quiet road.

The third car that passed, a gleaming, black Mercedes, slowed and stopped a short walk ahead of her, and the driver waved his jewelled hand out the window. She half trotted, half ran to meet him. Jackson Brooks observed the striking woman approaching in his rear view mirror, and as she neared the car he watched her over his shoulder, lowering the electric window on the passenger side. Paula leant through and he gestured to come inside. Opening the door, she threw her bag into the foot-well and climbed in. Not saying a word, she fixed her eyes on the road ahead, aware of his eyes contemplating her.

"Well, go on then, lady, where are you heading?" She was taller than he preferred his women usually, but she was a stunner. Long, glossy tresses, lightly curling at the ends, her features strong, yet feminine. She wasn't beautiful, but she was handsome, and he wasn't about to say no if he got the chance. Which he intended to.

Paula shrugged. "The M1 would be best for me, are you going that way?"

"Then it's your lucky day, lady, I'm going to Darlington, so I can take you anywhere along the M1." Checking the mirrors, Jackson pulled back onto the quiet road.

"Where do you live? You sound southern." Jackson smiled at her, but was met with silence. "I live in Potters Bar. It's nice and busy. I like that." They passed a sign indicating Junction 22 of the M25 was approaching. "My name's Jackson, what's yours?"

Paula glared at him. "Shut the fuck up and drive, shithead."

Furious, Jackson span the wheel and the car bumped up the verge. No way was some fucking tart going to talk to him like that. He pushed the automatic lock on his door, trapping Paula in, and lunged at her, intent on raping her before dumping her outside. He'd show her to give him respect. "You fucking bitch!" With one hand groping at the tunic to feel her breasts, the other pawing at her flies to expose her, he felt himself hardening in readiness. He wasn't expecting the sinister click that stopped him instantly. He looked up to see the shiny barrel of a handgun pointing at his head. He removed his hands and struggled back.

"Come on, lady, I was joking, lady. I was kidding, okay. Come on, put the gun down." His mouth had barely closed before his shattered brain splashed over the window, the gore seeping down slowly to meet the seat. Paula tucked the gun back inside the side pocket of her bag and, grimacing, leant across the lifeless body to unlock the doors. She knew she'd had no choice, but shooting someone in an enclosed area was far more gruesome than Candice's duty, and she had difficulty controlling the retching sensation. She opened the door, breathing the air, regardless that it was heavily polluted, with relief.

Having recovered her composure, she opened the boot. Inside lay a travel bag, a briefcase, a toolbox, and some rags. She took the two bags, setting them beside her own in the passenger side foot-well. Aware of her exposure, the M25 overlooking the road, Paula knew she needed to act swiftly. She threw the rags onto the ground, checked both ways to ensure no traffic was approaching, and dragged the body out, hauling it as quickly as she could manage, looking around all the while. With all the strength she could muster, she heaved Jackson's bulky body into the boot, pushing him bit by bit, until finally his feet flopped in. Panting, she slammed the lid down.

Paula glanced around once more, and checked to make sure no cars on the M25 had pulled over. Satisfied that no one had seen her, Paula took the rags and wiped the mess from the windows, leaving a light, pinkish smear. She threw the reddened rags into the undergrowth, and, noticing a car approaching, jumped into the car, grabbing Jackson's mobile to appear as if talking. She couldn't be seen like this, the front of her trousers and tunic were bloodstained.

Starting the engine, and pulling back onto the road after the car had passed, Paula glanced at the travel bag. She hoped Jackson has a spare set of clothes in there, she was going to need to change her appearance yet again, just in case somebody on the M25 had seen her transferring the body to the boot and reported it to the police.

Deputy Assistant Commissioner Falder-Woodes regarded the team of detectives who gazed at him, awaiting his speech. For many of them, this was the first time they had seen the man who headed the investigation they were desperately, and unsuccessfully, working on. "I'm disappointed to say that we still have no idea who we are looking for. We have many good eye-witness descriptions, and as a result we know that he dyes his hair to change his look, we know that he changes his hairstyle, and we know that sometimes he is clean shaven, other times he has a beard."

The audience were captivated by his authoritative stance, his confident manner. "We have managed to lift one print from a credit card docket, but it is not a clear sample. We have DNA from various hair roots that were found in Annabel Keeley's car, but we have been unable to match any with a suspect. We have had the results on the bullet that killed Candice Albrough, it was point 357 Magnum, 180gr lead, fired from a Colt Python. As yet we don't know how the killer got the gun."

Spencer shifted his feet uncomfortably, he'd never got round to revisiting Jack Weston.

"This man could even be one of you for all we know. Somehow we have got to find a way to get one step ahead of him."

Krein waved his hand to attract Falder-Woode's attention. "What about Operation Bella?" Krein stood.

"I'm scrapping it. There's no point wasting our time in Leicester, if he was ever planning to recreate Bella Wright's death, then the leaked reports seem to have put him off."

"But Sir, I think he's more likely to do the recreation if he knows we've backed off. I think we should keep the Operation in place."

Falder-Woodes glared at Krein, as did many of the detectives. "I said it was scrapped. May I continue?" His sarcasm reddened Krein's face as he sat down once more. Falder-Woodes took a stapled pile of papers from the podium. "The Black Museum Bunch have kindly compiled a list of possible forthcoming murder sites, and summarised them here. You may all furnish yourselves with a copy as you leave." He glanced around the room, his shoulders back, his head high. "We need to pre-empt this man, and we need to do it quickly. None of us want any more lives lost. I will hand over now to Miss Jaswinder Kumar, the team's criminal psychologist, she will hopefully give more insight as to where this man is heading next."

Jaswinder crossed the stage to take the podium, she settled her notes down and scanned them for a moment. Looking up, her own confidence radiating across the hall, her distinct and detailed account of the killer was no more than she'd told Krein weeks before. Only this time she implored the officers to take Paul's attention to detail more seriously, once again stating that they should begin policing libraries.

A general sniggering erupted. Jaswinder's expression was severe, she caught the eyes of several detectives who wilted under her gaze. "If you were to take me a little more seriously, you might find you catch your man before another life is taken." Her glare caught Falder-Woodes, now seated at the side of the stage. "I also suggest you keep Operation Bella, even if you scale it down. I have worked with Detective Inspector Krein for a while now, and I respect his hunches."

Jaswinder shifted her feet, regarding her notes once more. "Our man may be suffering from a form of psychosis, but I feel there are possibilities of other mental disturbances. He is an ill man, but this sickness may be physical, such as a brain tumour, which could cause a personality change.

"In most cases of psychosis, the illness and symptoms will appear over a matter of time, and will be detected and dealt with before it reaches this stage. In our man's case the speed could have been caused by two things. One, a tumour, as already discussed, and two, a hugely stressful event that has 'taken him over the edge', if you like."

A detective raised his hand, Jaswinder nodded. "When you say 'stressful event', what type of thing are you talking about?"

"The death of a loved one, sudden unemployment, divorce or marital separation, even post-traumatic-stress-disorder, you know, major life events."

The detective sat down after thanking her. Jaswinder continued her summary, concluding that she could not help them to decide where he was likely to attack again. The only thing they could be confident of for now was that it would happen at a previous murder site, and with a similar victim.

It was Spencer's turn to speak, he smiled at Falder-Woodes. "First of all, some potential good news. I have a suspicion I know where the gun was acquired from, and I will be following that lead once this meeting is finished." He glanced victoriously at Krein. "Now, we have compiled a list of males who have been reported missing in the past year, and two of them loosely match our suspect's description. We have the DNA of both men, however their DNA does not match any we have so far found at the crime scenes." He checked his notes. "The first man is Callum Bates, a twenty two year old factory worker from Dunstable, last seen on May first, and the other is Graham Tyler, a thirty year old unemployed actor from Stepney, last seen May the eleventh. Again, the photographs of these men are with your briefing."

Spencer waved the paperwork that Falder-Woodes had left on the podium. "We have extended the Black Museum Bunch's search by an extra fifty years after Candice Albrough's murder.

Each of these sites must be heavily policed on the anniversary of the murder. And, most importantly, we have to put an embargo on press coverage of our investigations. Our plans must remain top secret to avoid this man continuing to get the upper hand. The only person who will be talking to the press from now until we catch the killer is Deputy Assistant Commissioner Falder-Woodes. Any failure to comply, and any leaks, will result in instant dismissal with no appeal. Thank you all for coming. " Spencer left the stage.

MacReavie checked his watch, and nudged Krein. "Bloody waste of time, this meeting. We're no further on, and I've missed my game of golf with the Chief Super."

Krein rolled his eyes and stood to leave.

Jack Weston sat at the empty bar of the Weston Avenue Club, The Sun spread wide in front of him revealing the story of Candice Albrough's death, and it's similarity to Florence Dennis's. Not usually apparent, Jack's conscience was hounding him. Paul killing an aging Italian queer was one thing, but a young pregnant girl so close to bearing her child, that was too much. That man was one sick puppy, and if he was holding the key to stopping Paul's murder spree, well, he was going to have to come clean, even at the risk of his own dodgy dealings being investigated. For the first time in his life, Jack was going to have to tell the truth.

Coincidentally, Spencer and Detective Sergeant Pulowski came through the doors, they descended the stairs and walked over.

Jack stood up slowly, his Oscar winning days put firmly into the past. He spoke quietly, resigned. "I was just going to call you guys."

"Oh yes?" Spencer was intrigued.

Jack pointed at the newspaper, his eyes focused on Candice's pretty, innocent smile. "This murder, this pregnant lady, well, I can't keep things I know from you any more. There's some things I haven't told you." Jack gestured with his head that they sit at one of the tables. Spencer and Pulowski followed him to the nearest, and they all sat.

"The gun. The Colt Python .357 Magnum. I sold it to him."
Silence. No questions. No surprise. Just silence. Jack continued.
"I sold it to him for half a grand."

"Ammo?"

"Fifty. How long am I going to get for admitting that?"

Spencer leant close lowering his voice. "If you continue to be
frank with us, with this investigation being so high profile, I
doubt my superiors will want to take the matter any further, but
please Jack, no more messing."

Jack visibly relaxed. "No more messing. I know where he was
living. It was a room in a house in Shoe Lane. I often let it out to
my rent, um, my staff if they don't have nowhere to stay."

"It's yours?"

"Yes."

"Will you let us search the premises, we may find something
there that could help with our investigation or with identifying
the man."

"There's another fella staying there now, but I'm sure he
won't stop you if I speak to him first. And don't give him no
hassle, he's a good worker."

"Thank you. Anything else, Jack?"

Jack agonised, he'd never been so co-operative in his life.
"The night Eddie was hanged, well that was the night I sold Paul
the gun. I was suspicious, I don't like upstarts operating on my
territory, so I sent Dunny and Reno to check out his room. They
found nothing, so we looked in the bag he always takes round
with him."

"His bag? You've never mentioned a bag."

"It's a black sports bag, he took it everywhere. Anyway, inside
there was a rope, must be the one he used to hang Eddie, and
some bricks. There was the usual stuff small-bits carry around,
you know, torch, gloves, a knife, and there was some scissors.
That's about it, except for some smalls."

Spencer stood up. "Thank you Jack, you've been very helpful.
I'm not going to take a formal statement, if I did I would have to
use the content to prosecute you for what you've told me. This
way you can remain anonymous. I do, however, need to arrange
for a forensic team to search the room in Shoe Street."

The dial on the dashboard was low, Paula was going to have to stop for petrol, but she needed to get changed first, the blood on her clothes would draw unwanted attention. She left the motorway at Junction 12, turning left towards Toddington, then right towards Milton Bryan. The road was deserted, so she pulled into a lay-by, and stopped the car. Leaning into the foot-well, she hoisted the overnight bag to her lap and checked inside. Relieved to see the jeans and selection of T-shirts, Paula threw them into the back, climbed over the seats and changed her outfit once more. The clothes were excellent quality, and her trainers looked out of place, but there was nothing she could do about that.

Paula clambered back into the driver's seat, she reached inside the bag once more, and pulled out a handkerchief, which she rubbed harshly on her face to remove the make up. She unclipped the hairpiece, placing it in her bag, and ruffled her short hair into a more masculine style.

Glancing in the mirror, Paul could see that Paula was gone. He could call himself Paul again now.

Inquisitive, Paul opened the briefcase, rooting through the paperwork. He stuffed Jackson's driving license in his pocket, regardless that he could never pass himself off as a black man. Nothing else took his interest, and it occurred to him that the body in the boot might have a wallet in the pocket. He climbed out of the car, shoved the briefcase inconspicuously under a bush, and opened the boot, grimacing at the heady metallic smell. He tried a trouser pocket, then pushed the body over and tried another. This time was more fruitful, he tugged out a bulging wallet. Closing the boot with relief, he flipped the wallet open and spied the two credit cards and a large wad of notes. Smiling, he got back into the car and drove back onto the M1. He would stop at the next service station, he had plenty of money again.

Tuesday 1st July

The incident room at Leicester had been disbanded, Krein reluctantly returning to Kidlington. Once more he relentlessly pored over the documents he had, trying to get into the killer's mind, but one thing kept springing up at him. Bella Wright. The more he thought about things, the more certain he was that the Candice Albrough shooting was purely a ruse to get the police off the killer's trail. If Krein's gut feeling was correct, then the ploy had worked. Paul wasn't stupid, he would have realised that the operation in Stretton would stop, giving him an open page to continue with the planned copycat killing. Krein's instinct, his understanding of Paul, it made sense.

Krein knocked on MacReavie's door, entering when beckoned.

"Krein, what is it."

Krein shifted his feet, knowing he was about to be humiliated. "Guv. It's the Operation Bella business. I want to go back to Leicester, I want to restart the surveillance." MacReavie took a bite of his sandwich, his face registering nothing as he chewed slowly. Krein wasn't sure which way the conversation was swaying, he tried his luck again. "I don't care if it's on a smaller scale, even if I have to do this alone. But I'd bet my life that Paul's going to strike there on Saturday."

"So I lose you for another week?"

"No, some twenty one year old girl gains me to save her life, if my hunch is correct. Look, even if I just keep a watch out, and if anyone at all decides to cycle along the Burton Overy Road that evening, well, at least I can make sure they're safe."

As MacReavie took another bite, Krein could see his suggestion was hitting home, he felt hugely more confident than he had five minutes previously. "I wouldn't normally say this, Krein, but you've got a proven track record, and you're a good officer, when you're not mouthing off. I'll have to clear this with Falder-Woodes, but I'll make no objection if he doesn't."

Amazed, Krein felt like hugging the man he had grown to abhor: instead he turned to leave with his dignity intact. "Thank you, Guv."

The previous Sunday one of the tabloids had featured an in depth series of articles about the movements of the murderer, dubbing him the Kopycat Killer. They'd commissioned their own psychologist to comment on his state of mind, a man far less sympathetic and compassionate than Jaswinder, and, as a result, he had solely blamed schizophrenia, convinced that this was the illness Kopycat was suffering from. He emphasised that the Government should bring a law in to protect the public by keeping all 'mad' people safely locked away. The gullible nation had swallowed the information unquestioningly, leading to gossip at best, campaigning against psychiatric hospitals at worst. Britain's masses were in uproar, and the possibility of vigilante teams was real.

It was nearly two months now since Annabel had gone missing, and the Keeley household had no choice but to get back to normal, however difficult that was. Greg had finally gone back to work at Gordon and MacIntyre Chartered Accountants on the Monday, grateful for the firm's patience over the past few weeks. They had raised no objection to the extended, paid leave, and the other employees, whose workload had increased during Greg's absence, were pleased to have him back. If Greg was honest with himself, he was glad to be back too, working gave his shattered life some direction again. Gail had agreed to mind the children until a suitable childminder could be found.

It was eleven thirty in the morning, and she'd just collected Petra from her nursery. She was helping the three year old to take off her shoes when the telephone rang.

Gail held the phone in the crook of her neck, still undoing the buckles on Petra's tiny sandals. "Hello."

"Mum?" Gail nearly dropped the phone. She grabbed it securely, pushing it into her ear, the red shoes forgotten.

"Mum? It's Annabel."

"Annabel?" Gail sank to the floor, her legs weakened, the surprise tingling all over her body. "Annabel. Is that really you?"

"Mum, you can't tell anyone I've called, especially Gregor. I need money. Can you arrange that?"

The voice was harsh, the accent difficult to place, but the inconsistency didn't register with Gail, she couldn't bear for her hopes to be dashed. Her mind also glossed over Annabel calling her husband Gregor. Annabel had always hated the name, only having used it once during the marriage ceremony. All she wanted was her baby back. "How, darling?"

"Into my bank account, it must be cash, and it must go in today. Have you got a pen, I'll give you the details."

Her foolish hope destroying her common sense, Gail snatched the pen that lay beside the telephone. "Yes I have, tell me then."

"Barclays, sort code twenty, one six, four four, account number two two three four, nine six seven six, in the name R G Bates. I need a thousand."

Tears were threatening. "Are you coming home soon, baby?" The line went dead. Gail let the tears flow, Petra's confused face looking on. "That was your Mummy." Gail started to re-buckle the sandals, they had a trip to make to the bank.

Maureen Isley, a bespectacled, hunched woman, was fifty-two years of age, but could easily pass as a decade older. The glistening sun highlighted her deep-set wrinkles as she briskly walked her elderly miniature dachshund, Bibby, along Charles Street, heading towards the Haymarket Shopping Centre in Leicester. It wasn't her usual route, but after losing her beloved husband three weeks before, she'd needed to alter her routines, the painful memories everywhere reminded her of her bereavement.

Soaking in the warmth, the beauties of summer, Maureen was immersed in her daydreams, until Bibby's incessant pulling on the lead snapped her into reality once more. She tugged him back, but he was determined, overruling her, leaping into the mound of black bags, foul rubbish and vegetable peelings littering the alleyway to the side of the pavement.

Curious, Maureen followed his foraging nose, and tentatively opened the bag that had incurred his interest. It contained some clothes, some appeared on early inspection to be stained, but recoverable. They appeared to be well tailored, and Maureen felt it would be a shame to waste them. She resolved to wash the garments before giving them to the charity shop just around the corner of her home, and snatched the bag from the reeking pile of rubbish.

Turning the key in the door, Maureen entered her small terraced home, the comforting fragrance of lavender hitting her nostrils. She sauntered through to the kitchen, removing the lead from Bibby, who gratefully curled in his basket and snoozed off the walk. Emptying the bag onto the work surface, Maureen recoiled at the stench of stale body odour, which curled almost visibly from the material. In a sweeping movement, the items were off the surface, and inside the washing machine. Against her habits, Maureen switched the machine on without even checking the labels. That odorous experience had been most unwelcome.

Rachael Bates impatiently fed her card into the cash machine for the third time that day. Relief washed over her when she saw the balance of eight hundred and forty two pounds, fifty-seven pence displayed on the screen. This was the first time in weeks that her account had shown a credit balance. Rachael couldn't believe the stupid woman had fallen for it, not that she was complaining. She'd give her another two weeks before phoning again. Until that missing woman's body was found, she now had a source of easy money. What a brilliant scam!

Rachael withdrew two hundred pounds and headed straight for the shops. This was worth a celebration! And a visit to New Look was a great place to start.

Allie Brooks let herself through the front door of her state of the art flat, hassled from a particularly stressful day at work. She grabbed the handful of letters that lay at her feet, noting they were mostly bills, and took them to the kitchen, dumping her bags before switching the kettle on. Whilst preparing a welcome mug of coffee, Allie noticed the logo for Butlers Plc, the company her husband worked for, on an envelope. She picked it up, it looked official. Jackson was away on business, he had been since the twenty sixth of June, but he was due back tomorrow. Should she open it? It was addressed to him, but it did look important. Intrigued, she tore it open: he would understand.

'Dated thirtieth of June. Dear Mr Brooks, We are concerned that you have been absent for four days without contacting us with a reason for your absence. We have tried both your mobile and home phone numbers, but to no avail. Would you please contact the undersigned immediately. Yours sincerely, J K Brown, Human Resources Department.'

Puzzled, Allie looked at the clock, it was just past six in the evening, they'd probably have all gone home by now, but she decided to try anyway. Dialling, she was surprised when J K Brown collected the call. Giving her name, she continued. "I opened the letter because as far as I knew he's away on business. For you."

"He should have been, Mrs Brooks. He was supposed to attend a meeting at our branch in Darlington on the twenty seventh, but he never turned up. He was booked into the King's Head Hotel in Darlington, but he never turned up there either."

"I haven't heard from him, he never calls when he's away. He set off last Thursday, he was definitely on his way, I saw him off myself before I went to work." Allie was furious, she just knew that Jackson was having another affair, and couldn't understand why he needed to, she gave him everything he wanted in bed.

"I see. Right. This is strange. Do you think that you should alert the police?"

"Police!" Allie almost laughed the word out, they wouldn't be interested in a guy who couldn't keep his dick to himself.

"It might be an idea."

"You're serious, aren't you?" Allie could feel a sinking feeling drifting down her body, a stark realisation that things may never be the same again if she made that call. The silence prompted her to decide. "I'll phone them now."

Greg had worked late into the evening and was pleased to be home. Although his colleagues had done their utmost to keep on top of his work, there was still a sizeable backlog. It would take a few weeks to catch up. He sat at the table with his father in law, Ted, tempted by the delicious smells wafting from the kitchen.

Gail entered the homely dining room, setting a plate of steaming pasta in front of her husband, and another for Greg. She smiled happily, and returned for her own meal.

"You've got a spring in your step, darling. Are you having an affair or something?" Ted chuckled, pleased to see her eyes sparkling for the first time in weeks.

Gail brought her small portion through, laying it down and hungrily taking a mouthful. Greg and Ted glanced at each other, confused. Gail had been off her food since Annabel had disappeared, finally resorting to Complan in compromise to their worry. She smiled enigmatically, avoiding their eyes. "I've, er, I just had some good news today, that's all."

Greg shook his head slowly, he dropped his fork onto the plate, his own appetite now vanished. The raw sorrow, the intense pain, his voice cracked. "How can any news be good when Annie's still missing?"

That was it. Gail could contain it no longer, she had never been one for secrets or lies, and she couldn't let the poor man suffer any more. She jumped up, her excitement energising her as she danced about the room. "I've got to tell you, I can't keep it a secret any more. I heard from Annabel today." Ted choked on his food, Greg's jaw dropped, they both gaped at Gail, stunned. "She called me this morning, eleven thirty two exactly. But she told me not to tell anyone, so keep it quiet, boys. But she's okay, she sounded fine."

It took a while, but Greg finally pieced some words together. "Where was she?"

"She didn't say." Still excitable, Gail sat down.

"This doesn't make any sense." It was Greg's turn to circle the room, agitated. "What did she say?"

"She needed some money, so I paid a thousand into her bank account this afternoon. I'd pay her anything as long as she comes home soon."

"For God's sake. Annabel would never ask for money, she's too proud. Have you got the details of the bank account you paid the money into?" Ted was as rattled as Greg.

152

"Yes, somewhere, just a mo." Gail sprung through the door, returning moments later with her handbag. "Here we are." She passed a slip of paper to her husband.

"R G Bates. That's not Annabel!" Her idiocy amazed him.

Gail chuckled nervously, the sparkle leaving her eyes, the grey pallor returning. "Of course not, she's obviously using another name for some reason." Her face fell as she uttered the words, the foolishness of her actions, of her desperate hope, registering clearly for the first time.

"You stupid bloody woman. I'm going to call the police." Ted clenched the scrap in his hand as he marched into the hall to use the telephone.

Greg, totally understanding Gail's desire for the caller to be genuine, leant over and held her tightly as she sobbed uncontrollably. "I just wanted it to be true."

Rachael Bates paced the cold, stark police cell, the church bells heralding midnight on the civil side of the bars. Why had the stupid, rich cow talked! She could have had some real fun for once in her life. All these wealthy people, swanning around like they own the place, her with her three kids trying desperately to make ends meet. Why should they have all the money and leave her in poverty on the benefits queue. Bloody bitch. When she got out she was going to make the rich bitch pay.

Luckily for Gail Rackham, the courts were going to decide to keep Rachael behind bars for a while, irrespective that her children would be under the care of social services. After all, this was a crime of seriously bad taste.

Saturday 5th July

The morning newspapers heralded the worrying headlines: 'Vigilante Teams Blitz Schiz'

Thelma Pilkington's blood chilled as she read the horrifying headlines. She had been, like most people, following the movements of the Kopycat Killer, as he was now known across the country, but this acceleration of hatred towards mental disorders was unwarranted. Obviously she agreed that if a person was deemed dangerous, they should be confined in a secure hospital, but this blood hunting was vulgar, and served no purpose.

The shop was empty, so she took advantage of the quiet to read the report. The previous night a group of vigilantes, incited by the tabloid reports nearly a week before, had viciously beaten a twenty eight year old man. David Perryman was a schizophrenic who had been released from the Tower Mental Institution into community care two weeks previously. His disorder was controlled by risperidone, an anti-psychotic drug, and he was being introduced back into society having responded well to the treatment.

Unfortunately for him, a group of men in Manchester had taken it into their own hands to 'rid the streets of these 'weirdos', as they labelled schizophrenics, without any clear understanding of the condition. The police vouched to stop such uneducated behaviour, but the 'our view' column of the newspaper appeared to be supporting the vigilantes. Thelma felt it was all so hypocritical, David had done nothing wrong, he was no harm to anybody, having been sectioned after trying to commit suicide. His illness made him punish himself, not others.

Thelma was disheartened by the lack of understanding, her nephew suffered from paranoid schizophrenia, so she had a vast knowledge of the disease. As she read the tail end of the article, the bell on the door chimed as an aging lady entered the shop, clutching a carrier bag. She walked over and passed the bag to Thelma.

Maureen Isley clearly didn't want to just leave the clothes and go, she was intent on a conversation. Thelma listened patiently as she explained how she'd found the clothes, how they were filthy and stained, but after painstakingly working on them, they'd come up as good as new. She elaborated on their superior quality, and how she would have liked to have kept some of them herself, but she was just a small woman, and the clothes were large. Thelma thanked her profusely at every stage of the brief conversation, and smiled with relief when Maureen eventually tired of her self promotion and left.

Thelma opened the bag, the pleasant aroma of washing powder breezed out, and lifting the green tunic, she couldn't disagree that the clothes had been laundered beautifully. But as she removed the carefully folded items one by one, a gnawing started in the pit of her stomach. There was a pair of men's jeans, a pair of men's combats. A pair of lady's emerald green trousers, size fourteen. An Arran jumper, a navy fleece, both men's, a couple of T-shirts, and a muddied woman's trench coat, size ten, olive coloured. Hadn't she read in the papers that the Kopycat Killer had worn clothes like these? And wasn't one of his victims supposed to have been seen wearing a trench coat before she was murdered, that young girl in Suffolk. Without a second thought Thelma called the police.

Krein couldn't decide if he was excited or nervous. He had just arrived at the roadblock that had been organised at the entrance of the Burton-Overy road, near Stretton, that morning. Any person who wanted to use the road was to be stopped and questioned before being allowed through. If Paul was planning to recreate Bella Wright's murder, this would undoubtedly alter his plans, but at least it would save a life. Krein's mobile rang, he answered. "Morning, Guv. Yes, just got here."

He listened intently as MacReavie informed him of the clothes that had been delivered to the charity shop earlier, and how they had possibly belonged to Paul. They were being examined by forensic experts and would hopefully reveal some DNA.

Krein grinned, this was really hopeful, he looked to the sky, silently thanking the God he didn't believe in for finally giving them a lead. As he ended the call, a young girl, early teens, rode up to the roadblock on her pink mountain bike. The two constables manning the barrier consulted her, and let her through. Krein watched her cycle away, the lunchtime sun reflecting from the metal of the bicycle, towards Burton-Overy.

The officers pulled up beside the badly parked, black Mercedes, and an elderly man joined them as they got out from the car. "I'm Jack Phillips, it was me who called the police." He offered his hand to be shaken. "The car's been there for four days now, I've counted each and every day, and to be honest with you, I can't bear walking past it no more, it stinks to high heaven."

PC Adams had already noted the unsavoury smell, and it alarmed him. He radioed the registration number through to the control room, and strolled around the expensive vehicle, inspecting it carefully. Moments later his radio crackled, the car was registered to a Mr Jackson Frederick Brooks, of flat 6, Warmingford Court, Bedford. Disturbingly, his wife had reported him missing four days previously. PC Adams requested a locksmith immediately.

Having overheard, Jack Phillips had to show his importance. "See, told you it was four days, see, I'm obversant me!" Witholding a smile at the dyslexic speech, and nodding politely, PC Adams took a closer look at brownish staining on the rear number plate.

It took half an hour for the locksmith to arrive, but only moments for him to break into the body of the car. A foul stench emanated, a clawing, rotting smell tinged with hot leather. The weak tones of air freshener were drowned pitifully. On the surface, nothing obvious stood out to Adams as being suspicious, but something had to be causing the smell. Jack Phillips, arms crossed and pleased with himself, was watching intently, and had now been joined by a small crowd of children, eager to ease their boredom.

The locksmith, now working with a rag tied across his face in an attempt to block the stench, soon managed to unlock the

156

boot. The lid popped up, and the smell hit them immediately, making everybody recoil. The sight was horrific, and one of the girls in the crowd fainted. A black man, his eyes already rotted away, his body in an advanced state of decomposition clearly accelerated by the heat wave. His head was half blown away, his clothing covered with blood and gore. Instinct took over, and Adams, his diaphragm uncontrollably retching, slammed the boot shut. He composed himself slightly, and radioed for assistance, the horror in his tone more insistent than the words.

Katherine Black had been visiting her grandmother in Houghton on the Hill, and she waved goodbye as she cycled towards the setting sun. Helene Black returned the gesture to her silhouetted granddaughter, and, as she closed the door, she noticed another silhouette move closer to Katherine, also on a bike. Deciding it must be a friend, Helene was pleased Katherine wouldn't be cycling alone, the world was a dangerous place nowadays.

Katherine became aware she wasn't alone, she glanced at the man on the green bicycle, smiling nervously. He grinned back, his eyes full of friendliness rather than threat. She relaxed. "Where are you going?" His voice was childish, his words stilted, it was easy to realise he was retarded. Katherine felt no menace from the man, he wasn't a danger to her.

"I'm going home, I need to get up early tomorrow, I'm going out." She replied brightly, eager not to appear condescending.

"Where home?" He managed after carefully digesting her reply.

"Burton Overy."

A genuine smile. "That make me happy. I go with you."

Katherine laughed, why not, he was harmless.

"Guv?" The day had been uneventful, it wasn't an overly busy road at the weekend, and Krein was sitting on the kerb watching the fiercely orange sun merge into the horizon.

MacReavie's voice was forlorn. "You're not going to like this, but there was no forensic evidence at all on the clothes."

Krein sighed heavily, he stood up and began to pace. "For fuck's sake! How come?"

157

Unknown to Krein, MacReavie was shaking his head. "The old granny who brought the clothes in washed them too well. Not a hair, not a skin cell, no blood, no nothing. She could win a bloody award for being the best bloody washerwoman in history!"

"Fuck!" Was all that Krein could manage before ending the call. He strolled listlessly to the police car, sitting in the passenger side, his feet resting on the gravel. Absent-mindedly, he watched another cyclist ride towards the roadblock, a young woman, and sprang to his senses when he saw a green bicycle roughly a hundred feet behind her, a dark haired man straddling it. It was stationary, the man was watching the girl, and adrenaline flowed through Krein's body as he rushed towards her. "There's a man back there on a green bike. Are you with him?"

Katherine Brown glanced needlessly over her shoulder. "No, but he's been following me for about the last half mile. I don't know him, but he seems okay. I think he just wanted to come along for the company."

Krein and the constables exchanged a brief nod, before he yelled. "After him, now."

One of the officers jumped into the car, the engine firing instantly, and he screeched towards the man. Krein and the other officer were running, determined to catch Paul before he could escape. Fear spread over the man's face, he spun the bike and pedalled frantically, but the Astra overtook and swung in his path, brakes screaming. The man jumped off, the bike crashing to the ground, and ran furiously, but the officer was too fast, he tackled him to the ground with ease.

A gunshot boomed, it's echo resounding through the eerie silence. The moment lasted a lifetime, the quiescence eternal. Until the whimpering. The slight gurgle. The struggled breath.

Almost too terrified to turn his head for fear of the scene that lay behind, Krein's heart nearly burst when he saw Katherine lying, tangled in her bicycle, on the tarmac. Her eyes were wide, the horror apparent, and her straining chest rose and fell awkwardly as her blood spilled ferociously away from her. He sprinted, faster than ever before, retracing his steps to her broken body. Oblivious to the gunman, he threw himself onto the ground and stemmed the hole in her neck with his hand, but the spillage refused to stop. Horrified, he noticed the gaping exit wound on the other side, and just wanted to cry.

Krein felt time stop, he felt his heart cease to beat. Movement happened around him but he was removed from his body, events happening in parallel to his own life. The ambulance pulled up but he couldn't hear the sirens, police cars arrived but he couldn't help the swarming officers to hunt for the gunman. Krein was wretched, that girl couldn't survive injuries as severe, and it was his fault, he'd been in charge of the operation.

Somehow his body moved to the kerb, he sat without feeling and looked without seeing. His private hell burned intensely, searing him, scorching him, singeing him, charring him. As dusk turned to darkness Krein remained seated, oblivious to his mobile chanting angry rings from his boss, unaware of the cordons, the forensic teams, the intrusive spotlights, the baying reporters. And the tears of frustration, of guilt, of inadequacy tumbled noiselessly from his eyes, down his cheeks, into his laughter lines, over his chin, puddling onto the gravel.

Eventually he became aware once more, enough to question how he had got this so wrong. And with no satisfaction it dawned on him. Ronald Light, the man on the green bicycle who had ridden with Bella Wright, he had been found months later, taken for trial, and subsequently acquitted. He had not been Bella's murderer. Her murderer was never found. Just like the others.

Allie Brooks sat, tears cascading freely, as the sensitive policemen gently questioned her. Did her husband have any enemies? "Yes, he was hated by many people. How do you think he paid for an exclusive flat like this" She waved her hand dismissively at her plush surroundings. "He was brilliant at his job, but he was also a gambler, and he made enemies of the people he broke on his way up. We bought this flat, and we've lived a good life, parties, holidays. But he always had to watch his back."

At first it was assumed that Jackson's shooting was a revenge killing, but, when tests run on the bullet proved that it was fired from the same Colt Python that had killed Candice Albrough, it was quickly linked to Paul. Fibres found in the car matched the tunic and trousers handed in to the charity shop. So Paul had killed again, but this time it wasn't a recreation. The horrific realisation was that his psychosis was worsening.

Krein had no memory of returning to his hotel room, the only thought he had, which hit him over and over again, was seeing Katherine's body, sprawled painfully across the road, her life spilling away from her. He couldn't erase it, stop it replaying. Every time he closed his eyes it was there. Every time he opened them, it was there.

The bottle of whisky was nearing the end, he took another slug, no longer wincing at the bite in his throat, and ignored his mobile as it rang for the billionth time. He knew it was MacReavie, and he knew there was going to be hell to pay. For the first time ever Krein was considering retiring from the force.

Sunday 6th July

Krein had gone back to his wife and daughter in Oxford. He wasn't coping any more, he'd been working around the clock for nearly two months, and Katherine Black's shooting was the final straw. Rumours were abound in Kidlington Police Station that the well-respected detective was about to crack. In his absence, Detective Inspector Graham Parker of the Leicestershire Constabulary was handling the investigation, reporting directly to Spencer in London.

Once more, Parker entered the interview room, seating himself opposite Martin Hallissey. He knew that the man was guilty of nothing, it wasn't him who'd shot Katherine. But the fact he'd been riding behind the girl on a green bicycle whilst Paul aimed his gun was more than a coincidence. He'd been placed at the scene for a reason.

Martin's parents had confirmed that he suffered from dyspraxia, but he coped extremely well with his disability, even holding a job at the local garage. However, he had witnessed a dreadful scene, and was having trouble understanding it. At first he just rocked, back and forth, back and forth, and when he'd been ready to talk, the words he used were incomprehensible, almost as if it were his own secret language. They had taken him home the night before, any further questioning was a waste of time, but brought him back in the morning, the hindsight of sleep hopefully spurring him into talking sense. Parker was surprised when Martin began to cry.

"He scared me. He scared me. I had to do it. Wasn't my fault. He scared me."

Parker leant forward, his expression considerate. "Who scared you, Martin, who are you talking about?"

Tears flooded over his cheeks, Martin rocked himself, arms tucked tightly across his abdomen, comfortingly, once more. "He gave me five pounds and said I could keep the bike. I thought he was kind. Then he was horrible, and I wanted to go home. But he told me to follow that girl."

"Who, Martin, who was he?" Parker discreetly checked the recorder was switched on.

In a flash of anger, Martin swept his hands across the desk, knocking the two coffees, and a plastic cup of water flying. The constable at the door jumped forward to stop him, but Parker halted him, force would do more harm than good with this witness. "He's frustrated, leave him." The constable stepped back, the liquids intermingling in a steaming puddle over the floor.

Parker deliberated for a short while, he needed to take the inquiry from a different angle. "Can you remember what he looked like?"

An unexpected smile settled on Martin's lips, amidst the tears. "Yes. I can mister. Black hair and a horrid face."

Little information was gained over the next hour, Martin tried his best, but the description they ended up with was vague. All they knew was that Paul paid the lad to cycle beside Katherine Black. That was it.

A monotone sounded on the monitor, Katherine's heart had stopped. When she had been rushed in the previous day, she'd immediately been fitted with an artificial ventilator, through a tracheostomy in her shattered neck. Doctors had worked quickly to stabilize her, administering painkilling injections, and a drip to keep her hydrated. Once she was settled and comfortable, an X-ray was arranged, and it showed that three of her cervical vertebrae were shattered. She was given less than a ten per cent chance of surviving, and even if she did pull through, she would be totally paralysed.

Responding to the emergency, the crash team half-heartedly attempted to resuscitate Katherine, but it was futile, her injuries were too severe. They had to let her go.

Mr and Mrs Black held her hands as the respirator was turned off, crying for their beautiful lost daughter, praying that she would be happy wherever she was going to.

Linda Krein took the call from MacReavie, writing the message that Katherine Brown had died on a notepad. Her husband wasn't in the bath as she'd lied, he was in the bedroom, but she knew better than to disturb him when he was in a mood like this.

Krein sat on the floor, knees raised, arms wrapped around them, and rocked uncontrollably as the frustrated, angry tears flowed. Two months, victims dropping like flies, and still no closer to catching Paul. If he'd done his research, if he'd paid as much attention to detail as the killer. Bastard. Why had he not done his job properly? As far as he knew Katherine was still alive, and he hoped with all his heart that she would survive the claws of this madman.

Krein jumped up, he grabbed a pillow and pounded it into the wall, anger, exasperation, despairing, futility, the cushion shredding and spilling as he vented his emotions.

But it worked, he'd cried all his tears, his throat was sore and his chest ached. And now he knew he had to pull himself together, the killer was still out there, and he would continue to kill whether Krein fell apart or not.

Krein knew Paul better than anyone else on the case, he understood his mind instinctively, and if anyone was going to undermine that man, it was him. He resolved to be back at work tomorrow.

Linda and Mary sat at the kitchen table, directly underneath the bedroom. Neither could speak, having been witness to the wrenching sobs above. Mugs of soothing tea going cold in their hands, they could physically feel the pain the husband and father was in. Krein didn't talk about his work, but from the newspapers, both knew that he was trying to outwit one of the most terrifying and elusive serial killers ever. They could do nothing for him, this was something he had to work through himself.

By the time Linda relayed the message that Katherine Brown had died that morning, Krein had no tears left to cry, his eyes just acknowledged the sombre news, and that was it. Back to work the next morning, as usual, and no mention of this breakdown would ever be made.

A full examination of the fields and undergrowth surrounding the murder site was made, a special team combing the area on hands and knees, hungry to find evidence. The spent bullet was found, and proven to be fired from the same Colt Python that had killed Candice Albrough and Jackson Brooks, as expected.

No further evidence was found, the killer appeared to be invincible. He would storm into his task, complete it, and disappear, leaving the police standing. After all this time, they still hunted the killer needle in the haystack of England.

Monday 7th July

Krein had recovered from his hiccup the day before, and, now the feelings of frustration and guilt had been relieved, his ability to continue assisting with the investigation was restored. To MacReavie's surprise, Krein breezed into his office first thing in the morning for an update of events.

"I know you're going to have a go at me about taking yesterday off without ..."

"I'm not going to have a go at you." Confusion registered across Krein's lightly tanned face. "Parker in Leicester told me what you were like after Katherine Black was shot. I think you needed a break, you've been working too hard, and you've made the mistake of making this hunt personal." Krein was shocked, he'd never once realised his boss was human, he'd been offered no reason to realise it. MacReavie threw some stapled papers across his desk. "Martin Hallissey, the guy on the bike, this is his statement. Doesn't tell you much. Go and read it. Jaswinder Kumar's meeting me at ten, I'd like you there if you wouldn't mind."

Now Krein was completely bewildered, compassion and manners at the same time. Maybe aliens had replaced MacReavie's personality overnight, or maybe Krein had entered a parallel universe. He took the statement, glanced questioningly at his superior once more, and left the room.

MacReavie had been right, the statement was mostly pointless, apart from, again, showing the killer to be calculating and precise. Krein filed it with his notes, and checked the time. It was nearing ten, he'd get a coffee and bring it into the meeting.

Jaswinder, her work now revolving primarily around the investigation, her excellent track record and reputation catapulting the importance of her theories and advice. She had digested the latest details and was sharing her thoughts. "There is something in particular that interests me." She took a sip of tea, Krein was in awe of her constantly calm manner. "Bella Wright was shot in the head, whilst Katherine Brown was wounded in the neck. Also the two shootings were a few hundred feet from each other." Krein and MacReavie both nodded, but neither spoke. "It seems that Paul may be paying less attention to detail, which …"

"Or it could simply mean that he's a crap shot!" MacReavie had dismissed her idea immediately.

"Or because our presence made it awkward to recreate the killing perfectly." And so had Krein.

Jaswinder nodded, smiling, not disgruntled in the slightest. "Yes, valid points. But in this case I need you to bear with me. You see, what I'm saying is that I've never believed Paul's illness is as cut and dried as schizophrenia, as the press are suggesting. But if he's beginning to show lack of attention to detail, then that backs up my theory that he is suffering from a more general psychosis." Somehow she'd managed to win them both over again, they both considered her, her beauty, her intelligence, and her words, carefully. "Now, there are three generally recognised forms of psychosis. Schizophrenia, bipolar disorder, and organic brain syndrome."

MacReavie laughed. "So he's a healthy vegetable!" The attempt at a joke was wasted, he felt foolish.

"Okay. Organic brain syndrome is a form of psychosis that is brought on by a physical cause, as opposed to a psychiatric cause. It could be brought on by metabolic imbalances, degenerative disease, or injury as in a stroke maybe. Or, as I believe I have mentioned before, a brain tumour. That list is not exhaustive, but you get the idea."

Desperate to appear educated, MacReavie grasped at redressing his credibility. "So something physical has made him go mad." It didn't work.

Jaswinder regarded him pitifully. "It could loosely be put like that! Schizophrenia we have already covered, bipolar disorder we haven't, and I do believe we can rule that out at the moment."

"That's the new term for manic depression, isn't it?" She nodded to Krein. "So why rule it out?"

"I'm not doing so completely, I just don't believe it's the right diagnosis, call it a gut feeling, if you like. Although the condition can, and does, trigger violence, it's counteracted by highs, and this doesn't tally with Paul's behaviour."

"Okay, you know what you're talking about."

"Right, I think we may concentrate on the schizophrenic tendencies as a basis, but we should certainly be aware that there may be a physical cause, and also be aware that the symptoms of various mental disorders seem to, in this case, be overlapping. We cannot label him in any way without being able to complete diagnostic tests on his brain."

Krein's captivation by her beauty ended and frustration took over. "In other words, we catch him, then you can tell us what's wrong." He stood up and began pacing.

Jaswinder ignored his tantrum, unruffled and serene as ever. "The thing that concerns me regarding Paul's next move is that his condition is worsening progressively, that part is scary. Psychosis covers a range of symptoms, including hallucination, delusion, loss of emotion, depression and mania. I can guarantee that Paul has suffered loss of emotion, for example he no longer seems to build up any form of relationship with the victim as he did with Maud Blessing and Katie Joyce. Hallucination, yes, I am sure that he will be 'hearing' instructions from A N Other telling him what he must do. Delusion, well of course! He believes he is a special person who was put on this planet to do these killings.

"Whether an organic cause or a psychiatric cause, Paul is a very ill man who desperately needs medical intervention."

Krein was now standing by the window, gazing at nothing, and his shoulders were tensed with anger. His words were slow, considered. "We can't give him to you to treat, Miss Kumar. He - keeps - fucking - eluding - us."

Her gentle laugh tinkled, agitating him more. "No need to be formal, Dave!"

This bit him hard, he was always referred to by his surname at work. Somehow she'd won the battle, and he glared at her in defeat, before storming back to his chair. "I'm sorry." He didn't mean it.

"I suspect that Paul won't elude you for much longer, he's degenerating fast, and he won't cover his tracks so well. It's common with serial killers who suffer from psychosis. They are smart at first, but eventually they have this desire to let people know how clever they are, how well they plan things, so they leave clues, they contact the police, they play games. I believe Paul is nearly there."

"Okay, okay. So what now? Where is he going next?"

Jaswinder shook her head slowly. "As before, I cannot tell you that. He will still be doing copycat killings, that's his bag, so your team, the Brady Bunch ..."

"The Black Museum Bunch!"

Again the tinkling laughter, she'd been joking and he'd missed it. Krein felt foolish. "Well, they must continue to research previous murders, sites, and victims, and you need to police those areas at the right times. I'd be particularly conscientious over past shootings, the gun makes murdering easy for him."

Krein sighed. "Helpful as ever!" He'd not meant to say this out loud, and realised too late how rude he'd been.

"On the subject of being helpful, I suggest you contact the major hospitals. You see, if there is a physical cause to his psychosis, he may well be getting serious headaches, even black-outs, and this may lead him to needing emergency treatment. It would be a good precaution to ask them to let you know of any male admissions with brain trauma."

Dressed in smart casuals that had once belonged to Jackson Brooks, Paul had cut a handsome figure as he'd boarded the bus in Burton Overy two nights before, and the light trickle of sweat that had dripped from his forehead after running so far went unnoticed. He'd travelled back to London overnight, and now sat on the floor of a disused warehouse in the Docklands. Almost fully undressed, he hugged his knees to his chest and rocked backwards and forwards. Paul was terrified, he was bleeding, and he didn't know why. He'd tripped a few times whilst running through the farmland the night before, but couldn't remember injuring himself. Maybe God was punishing him, maybe the bullet had missed Bella Wright.

Realisation. That was it, he must have missed the girl. He was sure he'd seen her fall from the bike before he'd sprinted away, but maybe he was wrong.

Paul dabbed at the blood with the towel taken from Jackson's bag, it absorbed the flow easily, but he couldn't shake off the pulsing headache. It ground, scraped, grated, scratched, the pain driving him insane. A quiet voice twittered inside his head, he drowned it out, shouting out loud, he hated that voice. "Shut up! Shut up! I will only listen to God. Shut up!"

Mopping once more as the blood oozed, his head exploding with agony, the tears flowed, increasing the pressure on his brain. "Talk to me, God. Please. What do I do? Please." Rocking, back, forth, back, forth, his own hugging arms comforting like a mother to a child. "I'm sorry God, I didn't mean to miss her, I didn't mean to miss her. Please talk to me, forgive me, please make me stop bleeding. Please talk to me." The silence in his head deafened him, he wasn't used to being alone any more.

Krein read the email with interest. Although the investigation had centralised in London once more, he was keeping a close eye on the details. Barry Harner, heading the Black Museum Bunch, had stipulated two more past murders, alerting all interested parties. Krein glanced up as Jaswinder came in, carrying two plastic cups. She laid one before him, and took the other to Raynor's desk. In his absence, she sat, crossing her legs daintily. "Go on." She could tell by Krein's expression that he needed her advice.

He read from the screen. "Case Number One: Ninth July, nineteen forty. Cottage called Crittenden near the village of Matfield, five miles south east of Tonbridge in Kent. One woman found shot lying on the drive of the cottage, name of Charlotte Saunders, aged forty-six. On a subsequent search by the police of the three and a half acres that surrounded the cottage, they found the body of Freda Fisher, aged twenty, in the gateway to an orchard. She was shot in the back. They also found the body of Dorothy Fisher, forty-eight, also shot in the back, at the other end of the orchard. The murderer, Florence Ransom, was convicted."

Krein shifted his position to face Jaswinder. "Three women, I don't think that's Paul's style, do you?"

"No, it's unlikely. For a start he'd have to find three victims, any one of which could overpower him as he went for the others.

And the grounds are bound to have been built on since nineteen forty.

"It can't be ruled out, but my feeling is he won't do that one. Is that it?" Jaswinder sipped her tea, blowing on it gently.

Krein's gaze returned to the screen. "No, there's one more. Case Number Two: Ninth July eighteen sixty-four. On the North London Railway Line. The train left Bow at ten oh one pm. Arrived at Hackney Wick at ten oh five pm. Thomas Briggs, aged sixty nine, was pushed from the train between these two stops, having been hit twice on the head, fracturing his skull. The murderer, Franz Muller, was hanged."

Jaswinder shook her head. "No. That's not Paul. For a start there's no guarantee the victim would die, and secondly there's too much risk of getting caught."

"I agree. Jaswinder, in all this time there's only been one recreation where the original murderer was convicted. Do you think this is a theme worth pursuing, because that alone would rule these two out?"

She thought long and hard before answering. "It may be, but Candice Albrough, Jackson Brooks, and potentially Annabel Keeley, if we ever find her body, don't fit with that theory, so we cannot rely on that. My advice would be to concern yourselves more on the Matfield one, he may just decide to recreate one of the victim's murders instead of all three, so I agree it needs considerable police presence, but I personally don't believe either of these will be of interest to Paul."

Krein nodded his thanks. "I'm going to request a temporary secondment to London. I want to be part of this."

Jaswinder tenderly laid her hand on his, her soft skin sending a thunderbolt through him. "I think you need to be part of this. Regardless of who's in charge, this is your case." He was married, he shouldn't feel like this. But Linda had never understood him in the way Jaswinder did at this moment. Krein withdrew his hand. He was married. Simple as that.

Thursday 10th July

Wednesday the ninth of July came and went. Two dozen officers descended onto the small village of Matfield, worrying the residents, and fuelling the gossips. But their vigilance was unnecessary, nothing out of the ordinary happened: workers left the village in the morning, mothers took their children to play during the day, the elderly residents chatted with each other in the street before they did their shopping. It was as normal as ever.

And neither were any sixty nine year old men thrown from train carriages in London. Nor any men of different ages, or any ladies, children, or dogs. The policing, although necessary, had brought them no closer to catching Kopycat. And the Black Museum Bunch continued researching, hungry to find the next date to cover.

Paul had stayed inside the warehouse in the Docklands, he was scared to move on until the, now occasional, bleeding ceased completely. He couldn't understand anything any more, he was confused, scared, and alone. God had stopped talking to him, the only company he'd had in four days had been the whiney voice that refused to go away. Without God, Paul felt he had no direction, no way forward, and he'd forgotten how to make decisions. He knew he'd messed up somewhere, and this was his punishment, but that didn't make things any easier.

His stomach growled painfully, over and over, he hadn't eaten since he'd arrived, and the only drink he'd had was some lemonade he'd brought with him, the resulting dehydration intensifying his headache.

"God, please speak to me." He begged for the thousandth time.

Nothing. The other voice tried to come through, but Paul clenched his ears tightly, violently shaking his head to drown it out. "Go away. Go away. I don't want you. Go away. I want God."

Finally his pleas were rewarded, God's voice rang in his head, loud, authoritative. "You must kill yourself, Paul. You are too weak to complete your duties. You must kill yourself."

The tired, grateful smile spread across Paul's drawn face. "You'll forgive me for missing the girl if I kill myself?" He knew the answer without a reply. Slowly, Paul took his clothes and pulled them back onto his body, now the bleeding had subsided to the point of barely a drop, they wouldn't stain. He rummaged in the travelling bag that had once belonged to Jackson Brooks, locating six of the remaining bullets, and took the gun from a side compartment.

He opened the barrel preparing to feed it, when God cackled. "Make it more fun, Paul, just put one bullet in." Paul followed instructions and, nerves making him shake involuntarily, cocked the hammer, placing the barrel lightly against the skin of his temple.

His hand trembled, the little, unwanted voice grew insanely until it was shrieking at him. "Don't do it! Don't do it!" Regardless, he pulled the trigger. Silence. Paul clicked the barrel round. "Paul! No! Don't do it!" It got too much, the voice was screaming, screeching, it echoed inside his head until it pounded and throbbed, he quickly cocked the hammer and tugged the trigger. The silence enveloped him once more, and he threw the gun, it skidded across the cement as he clutched his head, tears of frustration flowing. Hugging his knees to his chest, Paul cried like a baby, until the flowing from his dehydrated body ceased.

"You disobeyed me, Paul. I will leave you again."

Now Paul was angry. He was angry at God, angry at the whiney voice, angry at himself. He stood, he grabbed a wooden crate and launched it across the warehouse, it smashed as it landed. He snatched another, and another, he screamed, he shouted, he threw things, he punched things, he kicked, he snarled, he roared. And as he pounded across the floor towards another crate, Paul failed to notice the hook set in the concrete floor. He tripped, landing heavily, his furious head cracking as it hit the ground. And again, silence.

Krein had travelled to London, permission had been granted for his temporary transfer. A meeting had been called by Detective Superintendent Rubenski, and Krein was attending alongside Spencer, Barry Harner, and seven other officers of varying rank. Harner had brought a refreshed list of murder anniversaries, with a summary of the details of each, and the group had discussed each one. Rubenski paced the room, deep in thought, whilst the other officers huffed and sighed, each thinking the same thing. Paul was unlikely to do any of these.

Krein snatched his copy of the list from the large conference table, adding to the collective sighs. "It's not him. Not a single one. Until the Jack the Ripper anniversaries in August." Rubenski stopped his march and stared at Krein, along with nine other pairs of eyes. "That's my opinion, anyway." His manner was not as apologetic as the comment.

Rubenski was striding again, fingers stroking his clean-shaven chin. "My gut is the same as yours, Krein. Can you contact Jaswinder Kumar for her opinion?"

The mention of her name jolted his stomach against his chest, he swallowed hard. "No problem." Rubenski had moved to his desk, and lifted the handset as Krein walked towards him.

Jaswinder listened carefully as Krein summarised each murder anniversary, taking notes, considering each detail. When he had finished he waited, he knew she would deliberate in silence until her opinion was formed and decided. It took minutes, and the officers behind him were restless, regardless of having an elongated coffee come toilet break. Eventually her delicate, yet articulate voice returned a verdict.

"Two things, and they are contradictory." Another pause. "Yes, I agree that, from the list, the only ones that I think Paul will consider bothering with are the Ripper anniversaries. But I don't think he will be able to wait six weeks to recreate another murder. Are you sure Barry Harner's team have found every anniversary before that?"

Krein knew he was attracted to Jaswinder, but she certainly knew how to irritate him too. He bristled. "Of course they can't have, but they've ploughed through books, through the Internet, through police records, they've done their best."

"I know that, I'm sorry. Okay, my suggestion. Police the anniversaries, say, ten extra officers per site. But if you still haven't caught up with Paul by August, then swamp Whitechapel with a hundred extra officers."

No-one in the room spoke after Krein had related her advice.

Natural endorphins helped to kill the pain as Paul's eyes flickered open, but not completely, his head was in agony. His vision blurred, he tried to sit, he needed to see his ankle, the pain he felt was competing with his headache. It was a mess. A large gash across the top of the foot into the ankle, and dried blood surrounded the area. He must have been unconscious for a while.

He tore off his T-shirt and gnawed with his teeth until the material tore easily, making a tourniquet to support the joint whilst soaking any fresh blood. He was desperately thirsty now, his dehydration exacerbated by the blood loss. He tried to stand, but was unable.

Coldness clamoured at his bare arms, he crawled painfully towards his case, his injured head pounding with deep, dull thuds. He put a fresh T-shirt on, followed by one of Jackson's jumpers, and the shivering abated after a minute or two. Paul realised his duties would need to wait until his wounds healed, he dragged himself to sitting, propped against the icy stone wall, and removed his organiser from the case.

Clicking through the database, it dawned on Paul that he had no idea of today's date. He was starving, dehydrated, badly injured, and God appeared to have left him again. Even the whiney voice hadn't piped up for a while. He felt himself bristling with anger again, anger at God. He'd been so good at his duties, and God was punishing him regardless.

Then another emotion appeared: fear. What if God never got in touch again? What would he do? And another emotion: loneliness. What if God wasn't by his side for the rest of his life? He needed God, he needed his instructions. Moreover, he realised he needed to do the duties. They made him feel powerful, strong. He loved the way the bodies fell, their appearance in death, the way they spilled blood.

The pain swamping over in waves tired Paul. He closed the organiser, replaced it in the case, and lay once more. Within seconds sleep was upon him, and he was oblivious to the sirens that howled nearby.

"Detective Krein? My name is Eliza Elliot, I'm the staff nurse in the A and E department of Guys Hospital. I have instructions that we are to contact you if any males matching the description you sent to the hospital are treated."

Krein straightened his back, praying this was the break he'd been waiting for. "Yes, that's right."

"Well, I don't know if this will help you or not, but a young man has just been admitted. He was brought in by ambulance a couple of hours ago, seems someone found him in the Docklands, lying in a coma. We believe from the state of him that he's a vagrant."

"What's wrong with him?" Krein was already pulling his jacket on, trying to catch Rubenski's attention.

"I can't give you that information, patient confidentiality, but I can tell you he has had a brain scan, if that helps."

"Yes, it does. I'm on my way."

It was eight in the evening when Krein arrived at Guys, but the sun was still beating down, the drought now official. The underground had been crazy, especially as Krein wasn't used to ducking and diving like the more experienced commuters. He found Accident and Emergency, and was directed to the intensive care suite. Krein's eagerness was further thwarted when he found the man was currently in surgery.

After detailing his interest in the man, and showing his warrant card, the ward sister agreed to speak with him. She explained that they had no idea who the man was, there was no identification on him at all. The team on A and E had estimated his age to be early twenties. He had been filthy when the ambulance had picked him up, and it was assumed he was homeless. They had no idea how long he had been unconscious, but he was currently having a craniotomy, to remove a meningioma, a tumour of the meninges.

"What does he look like?"

She gave him a scathing look, checking her watch. "I would imagine like the description you sent to our hospital, otherwise A and E wouldn't have called you! You can see for himself, he should be out soon, but go easy on him, he won't be very well for a while. May I get back to my work now?"

Krein drank endless plastic cups of coffee, wasting all his loose change in the vending machine. He paced, he sighed, he was bored, he was excited. And eventually the man was wheeled into intensive care. He wasn't awake, but he wasn't in a critical condition, the operation had been a success. Krein entered the quiet, darkened room, having promised not to disturb the patient. He stood over the bed and studied the man. He was handsome, his eyes closed, his breathing peaceful, and he bore a strong resemblance to the photofits. He was unshaven, and the stubble was dark brown, but his head was bandaged so his hair colour remained a mystery. He didn't look like a murderer, he looked like an innocent boy, fast asleep.

A nurse came in to the room, she plumped the pillows and began her hourly checks on the man. Krein whispered. "His hair, do you know what colour it is?"

She shook her head. "He'll have had his head shaved before the op."

"I take it you won't still have the hairs?"

"No, why?" The man's blood pressure was normal.

"I need a sample of his DNA. Can I swab the inside of his cheek?"

Her expression changed from caring to horrified, she let go of the man's wrist, the pulse count forgotten. "He's just had major surgery! He doesn't need you poking him about."

The tone was equally indignant. "We have reason to believe that this man may be the Kopycat Killer that you'll have read about in your Sunday papers. We need his DNA."

Her eyes widened, shocked, and she glanced down at the bandaged man. "He looks so innocent!" A moment of indecision. She knew it was hospital policy not to allow any such action, and she knew she'd be in severe trouble if she consented. But she'd been following the case intensely, and it terrified her, especially Katie Joyce's mutilation. She glanced around. "Take the swab." Muttered under her breath, she hurried away so she wouldn't witness the act.

Krein removed a plastic container from his pocket, he unscrewed it, and took two swabs from the inside of the man's cheek, placing them in the container, and bar-coding it, before sealing it into a plastic bag. He left the room and located the nurse. "I need to call the incident room to have someone take this to the lab. Can I use your landline seeing as mobiles are banned in here?"

She wasn't doing her routine checks so tenderly any more. "Yes, it's out by reception."

"I also need to speak to the surgeon who performed the operation." She nodded.

A constable had visited the intensive care suite to collect the samples, and Rubenski had authorised a twenty four hour guard on the patient. Krein had spoken to the consultant who had performed the operation. The meningioma had been on his frontal lobe and had been successfully removed. He'd agreed that the pressure of the tumour could have caused a personality disorder, even one as advanced as the murderer's, but he emphasised that most people who have brain tumours don't tend to kill people. If this man was the murderer, it would be highly unusual.

Krein left instructions with the policing guards to contact him, day or night, as soon as the patient awoke, and made his way back to New Scotland Yard on The Broadway to update the notes. He had been allocated a room in a block of flats, owned by the Metropolitan Police for visits such as this, but he wanted to keep working. If he needed to sleep he could nap at his desk.

Paul's eyes fluttered, his head was pounding. He pushed himself up slightly, but the movement exaggerated the pain, so he laid down once more. His surroundings were dark, except for the glowing stream of moonlight that shone eerily through the window. His head pulsed, throbbing with intense waves of pain, he wished for painkillers more than food for his famished belly or water for his raging thirst.

He wished God would come to him, but he felt too ill to beg. He knew he'd failed to commit suicide, and that meant he'd disobeyed God. He was still alive, and God wasn't talking to him. Maybe He never would again. Gratefully, for it was the only time he was comfortable and untroubled, Paul fell back to sleep.

Thursday 17th July

His memory had been badly affected by the tumour, and, on waking, the man had been unable to remember much at all. However, the DNA from the swabs produced a match. The man was Callum Bates, one of the men reported as missing whose description had matched Kopycat's. He was twenty two, had lived in Dunstable with his parents, and was last seen on May the first. His family had registered him missing the next day.

Dishearteningly, the DNA didn't match any found at the crime scenes.

He'd made a satisfactory recovery over the past week, and was released to the police under caution voluntarily in the morning. Krein had attempted to interview him in the hospital a couple of times, but Callum's memory refused to enlighten him, the questions met with an 'I don't know' or an 'I can't remember'. And, frustratingly for Krein, the operation had left him weakened, he tired quickly, so the conversations were stopped abruptly. Occasionally a light would go on in his eyes, but it would soon fizzle away, and again he would state he couldn't remember the past couple of months at all.

The interview room was stuffy, the window painted shut, and the stagnant air was stilled as the heat-wave burned outside. Krein sat opposite Callum, his collar open, top buttons undone. "Can you remember working at the Weston Avenue Club?"

Callum's eyes were gentle, suiting his soft face perfectly. The new hair on his head was that of a baby, it's short silkiness a gentle chestnut. Krein could see he was trying to recall as opposed to conjuring a lie, as his stare was to the right. His voice was as velvety as his hair. "I'm sorry, I don't even remember working, let alone at a club."

"Have you ever used a gun?"

And instantly the light came on, his eyes shone alongside the relieved smile that confirmed he still had some recollection. "Dad had an airgun, we used to shoot at birds in the summer."

"So you have a long term memory?"

179

"I think I must have, Sir. I can't remember things, but when you said gun that memory came from nowhere." His youthful face crinkled into a brief smile, it faded, replaced by concern. "Sir, what am I supposed to have done?"

Krein sighed, Callum wasn't the killer, this felt wrong. He glanced at the constable standing guard at the door. "Did you go to Leicester, or Suffolk, or Essex? Do any of them ring a bell to you?"

And again, desperation to give him an answer. But nothing came forward, and he felt frustrated, he was tired, he was fed up. "I don't think so, I could have done, but if I did it's not there any more. All I remember is sleeping in doorways. I was kicked a few times by drunks, and I remember feeling hungry all the time."

Krein got up, he needed to find Spencer. "I'll be back soon, Callum."

Spencer couldn't explain why, he just hated Krein, he had done before even meeting him. He bristled in his presence, and when Krein pulled a chair up to his desk, his unperformed urge was to slap him. He couldn't restrain the terseness. "What?"

"It's not Callum."

No, not slap him, thump him. "Come on, Krein, he meets every bloody criteria. Right age, right looks, right bloody brain tumour. Not to mention the convenient memory loss."

A deep sigh, Krein wished it was Callum, at least then he could put this whole nightmare behind him. "It's not him."

"Fuck off, isn't it! Get the witnesses, arrange an ID parade. So he's lucky, we've missed his DNA, so get the people who saw the bastard to identify him." The sentence was dismissive, and Krein realised the conversation had finished. Although they were the same rank, there was an unwritten understanding that Krein took orders from Spencer. Now it was his turn to do some ordering, he took his anger out verbally at three detective constables. Chastised, they hastened to arrange the identity parade.

Krein looked at the evening newspaper that had just been thrown on his desk. The headlines glared out, 'Callum the

Kopycat Killer'. His eyes met Spencer's whilst his heart sank. "But we haven't arrested him! Who's leaked that?"

"Probably one of the bitch nurses who wants her fifteen minutes." Spencer's fury was unnerving. "We need to put him in custody now, he'll be mincemeat if we let him go after this."

"Under what grounds? There's no evidence that puts him at any of the crime scenes."

"I don't fucking know! Do him for picking his bloody nose, anything, and get him some legal representation quick. I'll issue a statement to the press, make sure that some of this damage is undone tomorrow morning."

Krein organised a solicitor, and they both had an informal chat with Callum, explaining the situation. Callum was distraught, he was a genuine person, he'd had no idea he'd been suspected of murder. He didn't think he was capable, but with no memory, how was even he to know whether he'd killed or not.

Spencer was convinced Callum was guilty. Krein was not. He refused to arrest him, and the ensuing argument was filled with passion, frustration, and accusations. A furious Rubenski, alerted by the shouting, halted the exchange, ordering both officers home. He arrested Callum himself, the lame trespass being the offence due to being found in the warehouse.

Krein sat at the bar of the unfamiliar pub, his overpriced beer warming too quickly. The paper was spread before him, and he read, and re-read, the libellous articles. Callum's kind face at varying ages was littered through the pages, alongside smiling photos of his supposed victims. Calls to keep mentally ill 'weirdo's' off the streets, community care should be stopped. People with mental disorders should be locked away for good.

His seventh pint sunk, Krein began on the whisky, turning the page with a sickened fear. Kiss and tells. Five girls who had slept with Callum relating their sexual experiences with him. He liked bondage, he was perverse, he liked it kinky. Krein had no idea that the reporters and editors had twisted their words, and that the girls themselves would be as horrified as him at the revelations.

Krein knew that if Callum Bates ever stepped onto the streets again, he would be a hunted animal, emotions around the country were running too high. He hoped for Callum's sake that his gut feeling was wrong, and that Callum really was Kopycat.

And one thing Krein could be certain of was that the newspaper wouldn't be ashamed of destroying this man's life. As far as they would be concerned, they were doing Britain a service by ostracising a guilty man. After all, even if he was innocent, at least the public would 'think' that the killer was off the streets, then everyone could get back to their lives as normal and the fearsome checking behind their backs could stop.

Spencer's hurried press release did nothing to quell the flames. The next day all the newspapers condemned Callum Bates for ever. Innocent or guilty? That was now irrelevant.

Monday 28th July

The identity parade had been held on the previous Saturday in New Scotland Yard. A weekend was the most convenient time for the eye witnesses, and London the most suitable location to travel to. Callum Bates had been certain he couldn't have killed, especially in the depraved manner Kopycat's victims had been, so was content to stand in the line, confident he would soon be vindicated. Although his arrest had expired over a week before, he understood that currently he was safer being under police protection, and his surroundings were more comfortable than the cells. He was under permanent police guard, as much for his safety as for the public's.

The witnesses were driven to London by officers from their local police forces, and no-one had objected. Seven other men, loosely fitting the killer's description, had been picked off the streets to stand in line with Callum, each being paid a token sum for his time.

Krein scanned the results of the parade for the hundredth time.

Witness 1:   Martin Hallissey of Stretton, Leics
               suspect number five
Witness 2:   Brenda Taylor of Leicester
               suspect number five
Witness 3:   Christine Murray of Oxford
               none
Witness 4:   Lucy Walters of Peasenhall, Suffolk
               none
Witness 5:   George Walters of Peasenhall, Suffolk
               suspect number five
Witness 6:   Mabel Fairs of Halesworth, Suffolk
               witness deceased
Witness 7:   Caroline Merris of Clapham, London
               suspect number five
Witness 8:   Felicity Barnham of Clapham, London
               suspect number five

Witness 9:   Elaine Baylis of Eastbourne, Sussex
                none
Witness 10:   Reno Remini of Stepney, London
                none
Witness 11:   Dunny Thomas of Shoreditch, London
                suspect number five
Witness 12:   Jack Weston of Blackfriars, London
                none

Suspect number five was Callum Paul Bates. Once more Rubenski arrested him, this time on suspicion of the murders of Katherine Black, Katie Joyce, and Eduardo Delfini. A psychiatric report was arranged, regardless that his recent operation had cured any disorder he may have had. If the investigators could find anything in his past that could be attributed to an inherent thirst for blood, and shooting birds for fun was an acceptable start, then that strengthened the case against him.

Callum's fingerprints were examined, his writing analysed, his DNA retested, but nothing matched evidence found at the crime scenes. The damning identity parade was the only thing that linked him to the spate of murders. This was enough for the judge, apparently, and he was charged with the murders of Katie Joyce, Katherine Black, and Eduardo Delfini.

Callum stood before Judge Reynolds, listening tearfully to the summary. Reynolds stated that the positive identifications at the identity parades were significant, and Jaswinder Kumar's testimony that Callum could easily have committed the acts whilst suffering from a frontal lobe tumour was notable. The fact he now had no apparent recollection of the attacks was not unusual. It was also more than a coincidence, Reynolds summarised, that Callum had gone missing shortly before the disappearance of the first suspected victim, Annabel Keeley. Callum was remanded into custody, while the case was adjourned until Monday the twenty fifth of August.

The press were ecstatic that the public could safely walk the streets once more. They praised Judge Reynolds for keeping Bates in prison, some even suggesting the death penalty should be re-instated.

Krein, deflated and exhausted, returned to Oxford, back to his wife and daughter. Regardless of the evidence and the Judge's summary, he couldn't shake off the nagging doubt in his mind. He nursed a whisky in his favourite chair, having refused Linda's beautifully presented meal, and mulled over the past few months.

Callum had stressed that he had little short term memory, and his facial expressions, his body language, had supported this. Jaswinder had stated that Callum could have done the killings while the tumour pressurised his brain. Several of the eye witnesses testified that Callum was the man they had seen. Krein sank the drink and poured another. The boldest affirmation that his doubt was justified was that several other witnesses didn't agree Callum was the man they'd seen.

Linda and Mary, the slight to their company having hurt intensely, had finished the meal and the washing up in silence. They brought a chilled bottle of Champagne through, along with three flutes, vainly attempting to welcome the husband and father home once more. They'd kept abreast of the case from the news and the papers, and they knew he'd been intimately involved, but they'd also missed him, and wanted the family back to normal.

Krein knew what they were doing, and he desperately wanted to pretend the past few months hadn't happened, but he couldn't shake the feeling of injustice off. He politely received the glass of bubbly from his grinning daughter, and sipped it slowly. But the chattering television, the insensitive laughter, the irrelevant family life, he could feel the tension rising throughout his shoulders and neck. There was a fine line between leaving the room quietly, or blowing with rage. He chose the former, and his family's Champagne lost its sparkle.

The kitchen was warm from the recent cooking, the aroma of slow cooked meat and creamed vegetables tempted a growl from his gut. He snatched the bottle of cheap brandy Linda used in recipes from the larder and poured a greedy glass, wincing at the harshness as it hit his tongue. More followed, and before long, the alcohol having heightened his concern, he couldn't live with himself one more minute if he didn't offload his worries. He searched through his mobile, Jaswinder had given him her home number for emergencies whilst he was in London. He'd not deleted it.

"Jaswinder, it's Krein."

The second lasted too long, he wandered jealously what he had interrupted. "What?"

"Please don't be mad, I need to talk, I have to, or I'll go mad." He wanted a response, he wanted her kind voice, but he got silence. "Callum Bates. He didn't do it."

"Don't be so silly. Are you drunk?"

The assumption, albeit true, triggered his anger. Jaswinder Kumar could ignite him so easily, sexually and emotionally. He tried to control himself, but it was too late, his mouth was already spurting. "Yes, I've had a fucking drink, is that a fucking crime! Jaswinder, I'm telling you straight, that boy is innocent."

He was grateful to hear the softness return to her voice. "Look, Krein, an investigation that's been incredibly tough for you has come to an end, you've spent so many months living it, breathing it, that you feel unable to let it go. It'll pass, Krein, it'll pass. Have a good drink tonight, have a good cry if you can. Just get it out of your system."

Krein stood up, he was aware he was shouting. "Jaswinder, you're not listening. Who knew the killer the best? Jack Weston, Elaine Baylis, they spent time with him, and neither of them identified him in the parade."

Linda came through, concerned about the noise, the neighbours, while Mary, fed up with her father's behaviour, grabbed a jacket and left the house, intent on staying with a friend. Linda mouthed at her husband. "Shhh, quieten down, it's past eleven." Krein turned away from her, she could feel an argument brewing.

Jaswinder had considered his words carefully, and a flicker of doubt struck her unexpectedly. "Krein, the judge is very experienced, he knows what he's doing." Krein could hear a strange noise in the background, he couldn't place it. Maybe Jaswinder had a cat. "I have to go." The line went dead.

Krein ended his call, and turned to his insulted wife. "Why doesn't anyone listen to me, damn it! They've got the wrong man, can't they just open their bloody eyes and see he's innocent."

The argument was fully brewed. "For crying out loud, David. I've seen the news, I've read the papers. He's obviously the one you were after. Why can't you just stop bringing your work home, let us be a family for once. Mary's already gone off in a huff because of your behaviour, and I'm tempted to! You've got your life out of perspective, you're driving your family away, and all for what? A killer who's already been caught!"

Krein glared at Linda, his eyes blackened with fury. Without removing his stare, he lifted the cheap, bitter brandy, and slugged it down, determined not to show his distaste for her pleasure. His gaze not moving until he was out of the room, he thudded angrily up the stairs.

Linda slept on the sofa that night. For the first time in twenty five years of marriage, she felt unable to sleep in the same bed as her husband.

Friday 22nd August

Callum sat on the uncomfortable bed inside the remand centre cell that had been his home for the last three and a half weeks. As the days had passed he'd been feeling more and more depressed. He was in this place, which he had to admit was better than the little he could remember of the streets of London, for three murders that he had no recollection of at all.

The past month had given him plenty of time to think, and he rooted his memory time and again for a hint of remembrance. He must have been the killer, he was identified by enough witnesses, but he couldn't understand what part of his psyche had been triggered to commit such terrible crimes. Maybe there was a killer instinct at the back of every human's mind? Maybe he had always wanted to kill, but society had restrained him. He wished he could remember more of the past two months, having stormed out after a heated argument with his step-father, a row he could clearly remember, and descended onto the dark and lonely streets of London.

Callum's solicitor had reassured him that the case would be chucked out of court, if it got that far at all. First he'd had diminished responsibility due to the brain tumour, and also the paltry evidence the police had was sketchy. However, that was no consolation to Callum. As far as he was concerned he was a filthy murderer, and the crimes were extremely violent, a trait he hadn't believed existed in him. He deserved to be locked away. And anyway, even if he was set free, public feelings were running so high, he would still be targeted by vigilante groups, he would be a hunted dog. All cried out, the tear pool exhausted, Callum lay on his bed, trying to find a way to forgive himself.

Theresa Francis and her boyfriend of ten months, Joe Allisson, were regulars at the Old Station Inn just outside Burnham, in Berkshire. Theresa lived with her parents in the small village of Eton Wick, but she spent most weekends at Joe's flat on the western outskirts of Slough. It wasn't the nearest pub to either of them, but Joe had been drinking there since he was a teenager, and they had a lot of friends there.

This Friday had been particularly good fun, the crowd had been on top form, and even though Joe and Theresa left the pub well before closing time, they were still laughing. Arm in arm, Theresa tipsy and swaying slightly, they strolled towards Joe's red, much enhanced Golf GTi. He unlocked the driver's door and slipped in, feeding the key into the ignition. He released the lock for Theresa to get in, pushing the door open a little.

Joe could see her standing outside, but she made no move to climb in. "Come on, then." He grunted, fiddling with the stereo. She remained motionless, the door open beside her. Eventually Joe leaned across to see what was holding her up. "Fuck!"

Theresa's eyes were wide, fear emanating. A man behind her held a gun to her head. Slowly, he reached through the open door and unlocked the back. Slamming the front with his foot, he shoved Theresa onto the rug protected rear seat, and, keeping the gun level, threw his bag in, and climbed in beside her.

"Drive." His voice was dull, quiet, yet the threatening tone boomed.

Joe's hands were trembling, he fumbled, trying to start the engine, and soon guided the car to the entrance of the car park. "Right." He followed the instruction without hesitation, the road was clear and dark, except for the receding lights of the Old Station Inn. As if heading towards Theresa's home in Eton Wick along the isolated country lane, as they so often did, the familiar routine was altered with his next direction. "Left." They trundled onto a cornfield at Dorney Reach, not far from the pub. The car bumped over the uneven ground, the suspension creaking, until they were sufficiently far enough from the road for the man to feel comfortable.

"Stop now. We stay here until I tell you to move." Regretfully, Joe killed the engine, his mind whirring with thoughts of escape. "You. Get in the front, next to him." Theresa clambered over the back of the passenger seat, squeezing past the headrest awkwardly, and slipped down. The move was silent, fear controlling the whimpering that threatened. By the gear stick

Joe's fingers rooted until he felt her hand, he grasped it tightly, his love consoling her. The move went unheeded by the gunman.

"Your name is Michael." He stated blandly as he directed the gun at Joe's head. "And yours is Valerie." Theresa could see him from the corner of her eye, the gun was now pointing at her head. She shivered, goose-bumps appearing over her body.

Did he correct him, or would that be a bad move. Joe was unsure. "No, mate, I'm Joe, she's Theresa,"

His rage formed in a guttural growl, the soft voice rising, the words spitting. "Tonight, and for the rest of your life, you will be Michael. Michael Gregston. How old are you?"

The coldness of the voice sent a shudder through him. "Twenty six, mate."

"The girl?"

Theresa shivered again, her bottom lip quivering with threatening tears. Joe answered for her. "Eighteen."

"You're both the wrong ages, but you'll just have to do." And the stillness fell like a heavy blanket.

Finally. "I'm supposed to ask you about your sex life. He did." Theresa and Joe sneaked a glance at each other, neither of them knew what this was leading to, but the conversation ceased, and their tense hands gradually relaxed. Silence floated through the car, apart from the quiet breathing that covered the windows with condensation.

An hour passed, no words were uttered. Aware that the man was constantly aiming the gun at their heads, moving from one to the other, they remained as motionless as possible. Just once Joe noticed the gun lower, he could hear the man was distracted and fiddling with something in the back. He wandered whether he should run, but the destructive range of the gun deterred him.

"God speaks to me. Does he speak to you?" The eerie, lonely lull was shattered by the monotonous tone.

Joe hesitated. Would his answer determine his fate? He opted for the truth. "No, he never has."

"You want to know why?" There was an uncommon kindness now coming through, the man seemed proud. "It's because I'm the chosen one. And you two have been chosen for me through God. Michael Gregston and Valerie Storie, part two."

Valerie Storie? Valerie Storie? Joe racked his brain, he knew that name from somewhere. What was the significance? How did he know the name? The news? Had he heard it on the news? His thought processes were leading somewhere, the vague recollection coming to the fore, bit by bit. And there it was. James Hanratty. The A6 murders. "Oh shit." The comment was under his breath, barely there, but the sentiment was critical. It had all come back to him. Now he knew the direction of their captivation, his fear heightened. He gripped Theresa's hand tightly, and felt a false bravado. Talking was possibly the only way out now. "You aren't Hanratty you know. You do know that, don't you, mate?"

The man laughed. It wasn't evil, it wasn't threatening. More a chuckle, a childlike tinkle. Joe's clenched hand didn't relax. "Of course I'm not Hanratty, they hanged him. But it wasn't him who did it, you know. It was Peter Alphon, he confessed right after they hanged Hanratty, but he was never taken to court for it, or locked away."

Reading about true crime had been a long time hobby of Joe's, resulting in more than a layman's knowledge of the more infamous cases. In two thousand and two, like many people, he followed the news closely when the Hanratty case was re-opened. "No, mate. They got Hanratty on his DNA now, it's been proven it was him, and he was right to be hanged." Theresa glared at Joe, scared he was going to make the situation worse, he mouthed 'it's okay' to her.

He wasn't angry, simply dismissive. "The DNA was contaminated. The evidence wasn't kept separate in nineteen sixty one. It was Alphon. And today, I'm Alphon."

It was as if a light had switched on inside Joe's head. A gripping fear rose through his body as he realised Theresa and he were in far graver danger than he had believed. Callum Bates may be in remand for the Kopycat killings, but he was an innocent man. The man sitting behind them, intermittently shifting a gun between their heads, a gun that had killed at least three people, was the most feared man in Britain currently. Joe had run out of words. Another hour passed.

The silence had lulled Theresa into a false sense of security, her eyes had closed and the alcohol had eased her into a dream. "It's been long enough." Her eyes sprang open, the forgotten fear returned. "Go towards London. Get on the M4."

Joe started the engine, reversing slowly along the track his tyres had trodden through the cornfield, and retraced his way towards the Old Station Inn. The pub was asleep now, the windows dark, the car park empty. Theresa glanced left dismally as they passed their place of joy, and soon the car reached a junction with the A4, the spine of Slough.

Joe was on auto-pilot, the route familiar as he took it every day to work in Hounslow, yet the lack of traffic was unusual as he followed the roads to the motorway. Most of the Friday night congestion had dissipated, the hoards of City workers having scattered to their homes for the weekend. Boy racers shot by at high speed, their manhood enhanced by the acceleration, their street-cred elevated by the thudding beats that rattled their cars. Joe would normally have been racing alongside them, his car fitted with spoilers and body kits and lights and treble bass speakers, but tonight he drove considerately, ignoring the flashing and horns which would normally have fired the competition. The extensive, dirty, industrial Slough passed unremarkably to the left, Cippenham merging into Chalvey, into Upton, into Langley, into Colnbrook.

"Get on the M25, head north, clockwise."

Joe, not totally resigned to his fate, but losing hope by the minute, couldn't resist exhibiting the flaws in Kopycat's plans. "There was no M25 in nineteen sixty one."

"Shut up!" Paul issued a wicked chuckle. "I'm finking!"

Joe bristled at the comment, Hanratty was reported to have repeated the phrase many times during the abduction and shooting of the original A6 victims.

Again, the motorway wasn't too busy, the time was half past twelve, the bulk of the traffic being overnight lorry drivers. The car sailed along raising no suspicions to the plight of the young prisoners held at gunpoint.

The M25 was an arduous and boring road, the darkened scenery often blocked by raised verges. Occasionally a valley filled with twinkling lights would catch the eye, but the journey seemed eternal. Nobody spoke, until. "You want the M1. It's junction twenty one."

The further they headed north from London, the more of 'England's green and pleasant lands', as promised by Blake's words set to Parry's composition, came into view, albeit dulled by the night-time hue. Kopycat directed them through the quiet, brightly lit roads in Luton, and they exited on to the A6, following it for a few miles. In the rear view mirror Joe could see Kopycat looking around, checking the signposts. He almost smiled when he spotted the one he'd read about. "Good, there's Clophill. There's a turning just after to a place called Deadman's Hill, it's a picnic area, that'll show on the sign. Go in there and stop. Turn the engine off." Joe followed the instructions, pulling the car to a standstill and turning the key.

The engine died, closely followed by the driver. With chilling calmness, Paul held the gun to Joe's head and shot twice, killing him instantly. Theresa's screams were hysterical, her hands scrabbling hopelessly for the catch to open the door. Joe's warm blood trickled down her face, soaking into her clothes, she couldn't take her eyes from her boyfriend, the man she loved, the man whose brain lined the inside of the car.

"Shut up! Shut up!" The noise was hurting his head, she was maddening. He flipped the gun round and struck the side of her head with the handle, her blood spilling instantly to blend with Joe's. The door clicked open and she scrabbled onto the gravel, desperate to preserve her own life now she had accepted Joe's was over. Paul followed, easily overpowering her, he thrust his hand over her mouth to quell the screams, but she fought wildly, her tiny body kicking and lashing and biting and twisting furiously.

"Shut up, you bitch! Shut up! Shut up! I don't understand it. I'm not going to rape you. I'm not supposed to kill you. But I will if you don't shut up."

Paul had Theresa in a stronghold, she couldn't get away, but her struggling was aggravating him, and her piercing screams pounded at his head. He shoved her onto the ground, covering her with his body to hold her in place, and steadied the gun against her head. Her eyes were wild with fear, and the screaming stopped. "Fuck you!" He shouted as he pulled the trigger. The tenseness in her body relaxed, a trickle of blood ran from her gaping mouth, rolling into her dark bob, colouring it as it and seeped through to the gravel. Paul sighed, relieved. He released his grip, and tended his ankle. The injury ached if he exerted himself too much, it had healed well, but not fully.

Paul checked Theresa's pulse, and satisfied she was dead, he limped around the car to drag Joe's body out. It slumped onto the gravel easily. Paul snatched the rug from the back seat and cleaned the gore from the wheel and seat, throwing it over Joe's form when he was done. Briefly surveying the scene for the final time, he jumped in the car, fired the engine, and grimaced with the agony from his ankle when he pushed the accelerator down. The car screeched away.

Amongst the trees the golden retriever tugged eagerly at the lead, she could smell the metallic blood and wanted to investigate, but her owner was rooted to the spot, her hand firmly clasped across her mouth to silence her own screams. Rosemary Green's heart thudded a speedy rhythm against her ribs, she wanted to run, but her stunned muscles refused to move.

Suddenly they relented, and she was running, faster than ever before, racing, no idea where, her legs leaping and carrying her far from the horror she'd just witnessed. Her mind was aware that she must contact the police, but her energy, the adrenalin, it carried her further, she was speeding along the road, across the road, heading for safety.

The crime scene had been cordoned off, the trees at the aptly named Deadman's Hill having witnessed murder for the second time. The bodies of Theresa Francis and Joseph Allisson were photographed from every angle, and the area, extensively lit by floodlights, combed for evidence. Having established that Joe had been dragged into the position he lay in, extensive checks were done in the armpits, but no fibres or DNA traces were revealed, the killer had probably been wearing gloves. As the sun rose over the horizon, flooding the sky with oranges and yellows, warmth and light, the bodies were removed to the mortuary, their departure heralded by cheerful, warbling birdsong.

The original A6 murder case was well-known, especially having been re-opened so recently for DNA testing to prove Hanratty's guilt. That, and the controversy over Hanratty's possible innocence, made it easy for the new murders to be tentatively linked into the Kopycat Killer's spate.

Krein was informed in the early hours of the morning. He put the phone down, he hadn't said a word to MacReavie in acknowledgement, he hadn't needed to. Having stressed time and time again to whoever would listen that Callum Bates was not the Kopycat Killer, and being told he was endlessly that he was obsessive, losing the plot, wasting time, being dramatic. Ruining his marriage. He stared across the bed, Linda was sleeping on the far side, her knees hanging over the edge in her attempt to be as far from his body as was physically possible in a double bed. His sigh was long, deep. She was going to take this news badly.

Slowly, Krein climbed from the sheets, the never-ending warmth of the summer's heat-wave swamping his body, promising another tediously hot day, even though the sun was only just rising. He pushed the window open further, the rich smell of lavender wafting through, and pulled on a pair of loose slacks and a T-shirt. He'd go to the station, update himself with all the details.

Rosemary Green, now the initial shock had subsided, proved to be a good eye witness to the murders. She had seen the whole event, and gave an excellent, detailed, and confident description of the man with the gun. Detective Superintendent Claudia Horseferry sat on the chintz reclining chair, a cup of tea beside her, the busyness of the room making her slightly claustrophobic. The interview was being recorded by an officer, and Sergeant Paduch was questioning. Claudia had insisted on attending, the case being so huge: not only was she intrigued by the killer, she needed to hear the woman's emotions, and the camcorder didn't pick up the atmosphere. Paduch made his start. "So, can you describe the gunman?"

Rosemary sipped her tea. "He was fairly tall, not six foot, but not much less. Slim, he wore a white shirt and dark jumper, but the clothes were tatty, torn. He had shaggy dark hair that needed a good cut, but he was clean shaven. Walked with a heavy limp. He killed the man first, that was what made me turn and look, it was, the shot, was very noisy, loud. She tried to get out of the car to run, she was screaming, screaming, Lord, that sound will stay with me for the rest of my life, God bless her. He got hold of her, but then said he wouldn't kill her."

Horseferry, leading the initial investigation whilst the incident room in London was set up once more, stopped her. "He spoke? What was his voice like? And can you remember exactly what he said?" She sneaked a glance at Paduch, aware she'd stepped out of line.

Rosemary considered carefully, her cup poised beside her lips, the steam clouding her glasses. She finally answered. "He was softly spoken, had a gentle voice, even though he was angry at the girl. I think he said, well, he told her to shut up a few times, she was screaming madly, as I said. Then he said he wasn't going to rape her, and that he wasn't supposed to kill her. He shouted that he would kill her if she didn't shut up, then said, well, you know, rude word, um …"

Paduch smiled at the naivety. "What letter did it begin with?"

"F" Rosemary swung her head from side to side, her pinched mouth disapproving.

"I'll fill in the blanks." His manner wasn't as gentle as the smile.

"I'll never forget the look in her eyes just as he pulled the trigger." Recalling the event was so painful for Rosemary, she knew the nightmares would haunt her for a long time. "She was so, so scared."

Krein received the initial statement by email at eight thirty in the morning. He pored over the details, scouring for something new, something to give him a lead, the next place to be. His head thrown into his palms, elbows on the desk, the statement six inches below his face, the words read over and over, etching onto his memory.

There was nothing. Nothing to show him where to go next. Krein thumped the desk, he needed a strong dose of caffeine.

Saturday 23rd August

Krein had phoned Spencer, whose irritation at speaking to his enemy once more was evident, to request that he visit Rosemary Green. "No problem." Was the terse answer, it would keep Krein away from London for a short while longer.

Krein needed MacReavie to authorise his absence again, and he was waiting for his superior impatiently. He wasn't tired, although he'd been awake for hours, but he was agitated at his boss's late arrival. Finally, shortly after ten, MacReavie strolled in. Krein followed the older man into his office.

MacReavie threw his packed lunch onto the desk and sat heavily. "Back to square one then, Krein."

Krein nodded, his mood low. "If you had listened to me they wouldn't be dead." MacReavie avoided the challenging glare, he said nothing. "I'm going over to Bedford in a minute, I'm going to see the latest eye witness personally. The statement that the Bedford force took, it's comprehensive, seems she saw it all, but I want to make sure nothing's been missed." MacReavie's eyes were focusing on the desk, his mind distant. "Guv?"

MacReavie snapped back to attention. "Er, yes Krein, whatever you need to do, yes, carry on. Er, can you fill me in with the latest details."

He'd thought it many times before, and now he did again. He hated his boss. Two more victims, and Krein could guarantee MacReavie was re-living his golf moves. He threw a pile of papers onto the desk. "Here. A copy of the statement from Rosemary Green that was taken soon after the shootings, and the initial enquiries and forensics by Bedfordshire Police are in your in-tray. Oh, and the rough details of the original Hanratty case. I'd already been given them by the Black Museum Bunch before Callum Bates was arrested."

A little flustered, MacReavie fingered the paperwork in his tray. "Ah, um, yes, so they are. Right-ho, Krein. I'll look them through when I have some spare time. Anything else?"

Anger flashed in Krein's eyes. This case should be a priority, in fact MacReavie should be accompanying him to Bedford, not sitting on his arse plotting golf. "Yes, when you have some spare time to concentrate on your job instead of your hobby, could you find out what's happening with Callum Bates now?" Krein knew he should rise above his temper, but he found it so hard.

MacReavie glared at Krein, his nostrils flaring with each breath. "I should throw the book at you!" Krein turned, he knew he'd won, and stormed out.

Neither men knew that whilst they were arguing, Callum Bates's body was being removed from his cell in the remand centre. Unable to live with being a violent murderer, unable to cope with the repercussions, the guilt, unable to comprehend how such a dark side existed within his mind, he'd gathered the courage to hang himself with his bed-sheets. Indirectly, Krein, and the Kopycat Killer, had another victim.

Rosemary Green was far more composed than she had been when Horseferry had met her, if that were possible. She was an orderly woman at all times, she didn't waste money, food, or words. She led Krein into the bright, fussy room, the open patio door inviting the gentle, welcome breeze.
A silver tray lay on the table, underneath a matching teapot with a gentle flow of steam from the spout disbanding in the air. Rosemary poured tea into two waiting porcelain cups, which sat atop porcelain saucers, and added milk and sugar without asking. The spoon tinkled merrily as she stirred the sweetness through.

Krein received his drink gratefully, it had been a long journey and the air-conditioning in his car was broken. "Thank you for agreeing to see me, Mrs Green, I'll try not to keep you long. I have read the statement you gave to Detective Superintendent Horseferry this morning, and it seems fairly comprehensive. One thing, just for my own mind, but could I just ask what were you doing walking your dog at two in the morning?"

A flicker of pain in her eyes, brief, and quickly concealed by her strength of character. She swallowed, adjusting the glasses on her powdered nose. "My son died two months ago, he had a heart attack. He was only forty two. It was very sudden, and I've not really been able to sleep since. My doctor has offered me sleeping tablets, but I'm reluctant, I don't want to become

199

addicted and sleeping tablets are well-known for that. So, when I wake early, or can't sleep at all, I take Lady for a walk. I find the silence, the stillness, therapeutic. The occasional owl hooting, the rustling leaves from night creatures. It's a chance to think, to reflect, with no disturbances."

Krein was taken aback at her clarity, her honesty. "I'm sorry to hear that, Mrs Green. But I understand." He didn't: no-one could contemplate the pain of losing a child, however old, and a sweeping thought of his beloved Mary crossed his mind. He changed the subject with pleasure. "I have the description of the gunman that you gave to DSI Horseferry, I take it you are aware of the so-called Kopycat Killer?"

"Yes, isn't everybody?"

"If I could show you the last photofit that we have of him, could you please say if it bears a resemblance to the man you saw last night." Krein was already taking the picture from his briefcase without waiting for an answer. He knew that showing her the picture could weaken the case if and when it reached the courts, but he needed clarification that he was after the same man. Rosemary looked at it and shivered.

"There is definitely a good resemblance, yes. Except the man last night had longer hair, it was quite shaggy."

"This was prepared a while ago." Krein nodded in agreement.

"I would say that it is probably the same man, they are very similar."

Krein's mobile rang, he apologised and took the call, standing. It was MacReavie. "Three things, Krein. First, the bullets that killed the couple last night were both from a Colt Python, and the markings on the bullets show it was the same gun that was used on Katherine Brown, Jackson Brooks, and Candice Albrough."

Krein began to pace, silently, and slowly, nodding to acknowledge the expected news.

"Right, then, the next thing is they have a clear footprint, set in mud, in the surrounding undergrowth. Probably near to where the victim's car had been parked. Forensics have taken a cast of it, and they should be able to tell what sort of shoes the man was wearing, size, walking oddities even. See if it matches the one at Peasenhall."

"Excellent. Except it still doesn't tell us who he is, or where he is. What's the third thing?" Krein hoped this would be better news, and the sarcasm showed in his voice, albeit missed by the insensitive MacReavie.

"Well, the other thing, Krein, is not very good." Unusually, his voice faltered. "I'm afraid Callum Bates was found hanging in his cell this morning."

Krein grasped for the seat, he fell into it, astounded, hurt, angry. "Hanging!"

"With his sheet. He left a short note saying he couldn't live with the guilt, that sort of thing."

"Oh, Jesus shit!" Remembering Rosemary, he mouthed an apology at her indignant face. "Oh, Guv. Just one day more and he would have been out." Guilt swept heavily over Krein's body, his hands and feet tingling with shock and shame. His words disappeared, he ended the call. Glancing at Rosemary, his weak voice was pained. "Mrs Green, could I just take five minutes, I've had a bit of a, um ..."

"Of course." She gestured to the open patio door that led from the room to the blooming array of beautiful colours, tenderly, carefully raised by talented green fingers.

Krein meekly strolled onto the paved patio, breathing in the summer, the hanging baskets and patio pots revealing hundreds of flowers, drooping, displaying, smiling. The lawn was cut short, it's perfect expanse uninhabited by weeds or moss, and not a ridge or slope to be seen. Krein stepped onto its soft sponginess. He surveyed the beauty whilst his mind purveyed the facts. Another victim, another death related to the bastard he was desperate to catch. The strong midday sun bored into his back, the aromatic honeysuckle nearby oozed its sweetness, and he breathed deeply, the fragrance flowing through his throat and into his lungs. He exhaled, and raised his eyes to the sky, as if in a secret prayer. There was no God, of that he was certain. But evil did exist. It existed in Paul. Jaswinder could fuck her theories, Paul wasn't ill, he was evil. An evil psychopath.

201

Although the interview hadn't raised much more information than he'd already seen in Horseferry's account, he was pleased to have visited Rosemary. Seeing the emotion, the horror in her eyes, it filled in some gaps without words. He could now 'feel' the carnage that had taken place, rather than just read about it. It had become personal.

He found his way to the Bedford Police Station in Woburn Road, and was shown to Claudia Horseferry's office. He was amazed at how striking she was: not pretty, her features were too harsh, but the air of countenance about her coupled with the feeling of authority was intense. She would stand out in a crowd. Her limbs were long and bony, he shook her firm hand. A constable followed Krein in with two coffees, he laid them on the desk and threw some sachets beside them before creeping back out, closing the door.

Krein found Claudia an affable woman, her smile was easy, and he respected her instantly. They discussed the murders in detail, their mutual hunger for detail paving the way to a friendship. Claudia filled Krein with the latest evolvements, occurrences happening after he'd left Kidlington. The registration number that Rosemary Green had somehow managed to memorize within her panic had revealed that the car belonged to Joseph Allisson, the male victim. No sightings had been registered yet, but then why would there be any? Unless the car was being driven erratically, the public didn't yet know the full details of the latest Kopycat developments, only some basic newsflashes. A search for the Golf GTi was logged as high priority to all police forces, and all Krein and Claudia could do was to hope it was spotted soon to help them finally put that first step ahead of the killer.

Satisfied that Claudia would be handling her part of the investigation professionally and thoroughly, Krein returned to Kidlington Police Station, arriving at nine in the evening. Tiredness had overtaken the adrenalin that had kept him going all day, and he needed a strong coffee to perk him up. He had no intention of going home. He settled at his desk, laying his briefcase before him, to unpack the latest notes, when a memo in his in-tray caught his eye. He read it in disbelief.

It was from MacReavie. DAC Falder-Woodes wanted to arrange for the Kopycat Killer case to appear on the next episode of the BBC's Crimewatch. Because of MacReavie's involvement in the case from day one, he was to be the appearing officer, and would therefore need Krein to prepare a statement from his notes. MacReavie would be travelling to London on Monday to meet the Crimewatch team, so he would need the details by Sunday evening at the latest.

Krein threw the memo on the desk, not sure whether he was more incredulous or furious. They were after a dangerous, psychotic serial killer, and all MacReavie was interested in was his fifteen minutes of fame. This was ridiculous. He scribbled 'Fuck Off' across the memo and dropped it off on MacReavie's desk, before going to the pub. Fuck the case, he needed a drink.

Paul had patiently waited for the late summer darkness to fall. Having travelled south after his last duty, he needed to be near London for his next duties, he'd arrived back in Slough before sunrise. He had driven off the road and hidden the car at the edge of a field on the outskirts of Datchet, camouflaging it efficiently with well-stocked branches. It was a busy area, and the endless traffic thundered through all day, and well into the night, but any red that was left uncovered had not been noticed. Not venturing from the car all day, he didn't want to leave it empty before disposing of it, Paul had eaten nothing, but food didn't seem important anymore: he just ate as and when he could.

Finally the skies turned from grey, to charcoal, to a blackened navy blue. The odd cloud floated across, and the stars twinkled like diamonds on a sumptuous velvet cloth. The traffic dwindled until only one or two cars passed every now and then, and Paul decided the time was right. He dragged the foliage from the car, and fired the engine into life. The petrol tank indicator was in the red, he hoped it wouldn't run out before the car was finished with. Paul drove slowly across the bumpy field, mounting the edge carefully. It was fairly steep so he had to accelerate hard, but finally he was back on the road, and the journey to the Thames was short. He found a quiet spot, there was no-one around, so he took his chance.

He drove off the road, and across the grass to the bank of the rippling, lapping river. Once more, he glanced around, and stopped the engine, checking the gear-stick was in neutral. Paul opened the door, threw his bag on the grass, and climbed out after. Moving to the back of the car, he pushed, his hands sweaty in the thick gloves, pushing as hard as possible, all his strength focused on one task. The car inched forward, every step shooting pain through his ankle, and slowly the momentum increased, the car rolling into the calm water. A last heave, and the back wheels had jumped over the bank, air bubbles rising and bursting, popping as the car sank lower, until soon peace was restored, the silence gratifying. Paul smiled, walking away with his bag. He needed to find another hiding place.

Arnold Freeman, who had watched the events with interest, shook his head in dismay. "Bloody joy-riders! He bemoaned to himself as he lightly clasped his fishing rod, not expecting to catch anything. Surprisingly, he felt a tug on the line, a fish had taken the bait, and in the heavily polluted River Thames. A rarity! The car was forgotten, the man was forgotten, and Arnold grinned, enjoying his night fishing more than he had for a long time.

Linda Krein had kissed her excited daughter goodbye at seven that evening. Mary, with a group of friends, was taking the train to London, they were visiting a nightclub in Whitehall for the first time. Linda had never been an overprotective mother, but was naturally concerned about her attractive daughter's welfare and safety. Linda had the benefit of maturity and experience, and at eighteen, she knew Mary was still a mere baby. Her baby. But Mary was still at the tiresomely ongoing stage of believing she knew everything.

It had been a lonely evening, only the television for company, and Linda hadn't heard from her husband since he'd left in the early hours of the morning. She'd seen the news, several times in fact, and was dismayed that David must be back on the Kopycat Killer case. She felt hopeless.

Their marriage had all but fallen apart before, she had felt like a widowed single mother, and now it was all starting again.

Although the cracks in the marriage were still there, they'd managed to paper over them in the past few weeks. The relationship remained celibate, but the conversation had lost the bitterness. Linda clicked the television off, she wasn't watching it, it was just a noise in the background to comfort her. She took a whisky as she contemplated weeks of boring, solitary, isolated, unloved nights ahead of her, shaking the thought from her head with the sharp, acid taste. She sighed. In all these years she'd never resented his work. What was different? Why now. She glanced at the cards on the mantelpiece. 'Happy 45th Mum!" There was the answer. She was aging, and she had no life. She took another whisky, downing it swiftly.

Five hours later, at half past three in the morning, Linda, uncomfortable and cramped, was awoken by the front door creaking open. She realised she'd fallen asleep on the sofa, and from the headache, she assumed she'd had a few too many. A glance at the open whisky bottle confirmed that. Linda stood up, stretching, as Mary, bubbling with excitement, but shattered too, rolled into the room.

Her expression turned indignant. "Mum! What are you still doing up?" Mary could feel anger rising, she was too old for this.

Yawning, Linda eyed her daughter's scant clothing with dismay. Mary hadn't left the house dressed in so little. "I fell asleep on the sofa. What time is it?"

"Don't you think I'm just a bit old for you to be spying on me?" Haughty and defensive, Mary hadn't wanted her mother to see the clubbing clothes she'd sneaked out of the house in a bag. She flounced out of the room, contemptuous, and stomped up the stairs childishly, hoping her heavy feet would deter her mother from waiting up again.

Linda was too sleepy for a confrontation. She yawned again, switched out the light and followed her daughter's footsteps up the stairs, then to her room. Oddly, she was surprised to see David, sprawled across the centre of the bed, snoring routinely in his slumber. She crawled in next to him, turning her back, and fell instantly to sleep.

Sunday 24th August

Arnold Freeman, a fifty four year old man, desperately didn't want to be married any longer. His wife was a miserably boring old harridan, she'd let herself go almost as soon as the ink had dried on the marriage certificate, thirty five years before. He envied the youngsters nowadays, if they were unhappy with their partner, they just nipped to the nearest solicitor and got a divorce. He was of the old school, he knew he couldn't do that. The only pleasures life gave him now were going to work to push paper around his desk, and going fishing.

Every summer weekend, rain or shine, Arnold would cherish the slow, tranquil hours from late Saturday night, to early Sunday morning, listening to the lapping of the gentle waves as they tickled the surface of the water and caressed the muddy shores. He would use the blissfully lonely time to appreciate the nature filled silence. He rarely caught a fish, and even if he did, he'd throw it back. Catching the fish wasn't the point. It was the peacefulness, the serenity, the solitude he craved. No persistent nagging burgeoning his ears, no selfish, materialistic sons waiting for their inheritance, and no grandchildren screaming 'I want'.

The warm air breathed a sigh through his olive green anorak, prompting him to check the time.

Disappointed that his pleasure was due to end for another week, Arnold began to pack his equipment away, but stopped abruptly when he heard a sickening crunch from nearby. He stood and inspected the river. Further along a Bayliner Trophy boat bobbed gently on the water, it didn't appear to be moving forward. Arnold, hands on hips, watched with interest, intrigued. The driver was peering into the hold. "She won't move, something's holding us back?"

"There's creaking from the hull." An annoyed voice shouted, the owner following his words up the steps to the deck. "I think we've hit something."

And at that moment Arnold remembered the car and the joy-rider. Uncharitably, he chuckled, folding his arms, ready to watch the scene unfold. This was the funniest thing he'd seen in a long time.

The first rays of sun were warming the sky, silhouetting the trees and the scenery, and an ancient Orkney Longliner chugged along the Thames. The skipper, an ex-Navy officer, could make out an obstruction ahead of him, he squinted his myopic eyes, assessing the large, grey form.

"Good Lord!" He objected indignantly. "I don't believe it. Does nobody give a damn about the river code nowadays!" Hugh Atkins steered his boat to the left to avoid the stationary vessel and, as he passed by, he yelled. "You can't just land there, you idiots. Don't you know the laws of the river? Moor the boat. Do it now, before you cause an accident." Then to himself in a stage whisper. "Bloody fools."

Mr Atkins didn't expect to be answered, he was used to rudeness nowadays. "It's wedged there, we've hit something. Can you get some help?" A sarcastic tone set in. "Before we cause an accident."

"My apologies, Sir, I will endeavour to find help immediately." Hugh Atkins purposefully steered his craft forward, he was now on a mission.

People across the nation were waking up to their Sunday newspapers, and were disgusted to read that the poor lad, Callum Bates, a victim of injustice, had committed suicide in his cell. It was an outrage, the police should be held accountable. They easily forgot that just a week before, angry vigilantes across the country would have happily strung Callum up themselves. Before they had the proof that he wasn't Kopycat, that was.

The gruesome details of the latest murders were digested and commented on from county to county. In newsagents, buses, queues, café's, pubs, the gossip consisted of little else. Where would he strike next? Was the gun his preferred modus operandi now? What precautions should they take against becoming a victim?

Krein had ignored his usual newspaper, avoiding the headlines. He knew that they would say exactly what he felt himself. Why was Callum wrongly charged, and how was he allowed to kill himself. He knew the phone line in New Scotland

Yard would be buzzing madly with complaints instead of witnesses or sightings. MacReavie had already called him, giving him instructions to head back to London now the incident room had been reinstated. He'd also mentioned that Falder-Woodes was arranging another press conference, so he would be following Krein there later to assist, carefully stressing that he would be missing another important game of golf. Krein knew that MacReavie would have insisted he be part of the press release team, using the old cookie of being part of the investigation from the start, and that the golf comment was purely false martyrdom.

Callum Bates got the easy option, Krein huffed to himself, knowing the thought was wicked, but no longer caring. He'd had enough of this serial killer, and he was more determined to stop him now than ever before.

The rope was attached to the tow bar of the police Range Rover, and the driver steadily tugged the boat free from whatever had trapped it. Fully released, the damaged vessel was towed across the river to the bank. The two sailors threw the mooring ropes to the waiting policemen, who secured the boat to some posts on the shore, and disembarked, grateful to be back on dry land.

The ascending morning sun beat down, it's heat already breaking the workers into a sweat, regardless of the early hour. The officers, sleeves rolled up, and wondering how long the tedious hot spell was going to last, peered into the murky waters, curious of the object that had trapped such a cumbersome boat. The water was dirty, but every now and then, a vague patch of red, dulled by the muddy ripples, was apparent. On the shore four experienced divers were climbing into their wetsuits. One by one they slipped into the depths, following instructions to identify the mysterious object. The waiting officers didn't speak, they watched the still water, waiting for the divers' return. It took less than five minutes, a head popped up and he issued an agreeable thumb, gliding neatly to the river bank, and clambering safely out, closely followed by the other three.

Now in the knowledge that the obstruction was an empty car, an officer summoned for a recovery vehicle with a crane over her radio. It took half an hour, the sun burning hotter all the while, to arrive. The crane hoisted the car out effortlessly, it's operator taking care not to damage it further, and swung the dripping vehicle to the grassy bank. The officer radioed the registration number to the control room.

Within seconds an excited voice crackled back. "It belongs to Joseph Allisson. He's the latest victim of the Kopycat Killer. Bring the vehicle in immediately for forensic testing. Do your utmost not to disturb any evidence."

Krein arrived at the Yard and was immediately told of the discovery. Excitedly he called Slough Police Station, asking if they could help by appealing for witnesses locally. They agreed to contact Star FM, the local radio station, who were honoured to co-operate.

Although regular bulletins were broadcast, as appeared to be the norm with the Kopycat killings, very few sightings were reported, and none of them definite, just possibilities. Krein was astonished that Kopycat had managed to drive from Clophill to Datchet in a stolen vehicle, without any witnesses to note. And he was more incredulous that Kopycat had managed to push the car into the water, probably on his own, and still not be noticed. Was this man invisible?

Due to the colossal interest in the renewed case, a conference room had been hastily arranged at the Thistle Victoria Hotel to hold the press release. The full capacity of the room was two hundred, and it was estimated that this would easily be filled by reporters, and television station camera crews, for the world's media. If anything, the organisers had under-estimated, the room was packed solid.

As Falder-Woodes, closely followed by MacReavie, harbouring a grave expression, walked towards the stage at the head of the room, cameras flashed, newsreel rolled, and the racket was deafening as journalists and reporters shouted questions above each other.

It was four in the afternoon, and the atmosphere in the conference room was muggy, worsened by the intense heat outside, which hindered even the most efficient air-conditioning system. This was the hottest day of the year so far, and the lingering pockets of body odour nauseated Krein as he hugged his back to the wall, near to the stage. He'd wanted to speak to his boss about the ridiculous Crimewatch idea, but he just hadn't had a chance, everything was happening at once. He bristled noiselessly, repelled by MacReavie's performance for the cameras.

The assembled speakers sat beside the table, the stage raising them above the crowd, but Falder-Woodes remained standing, hushing the audience with his authoritative air. It took a while, but when Falder-Woodes finally spoke, the room was soundless.

"Ladies and gentlemen. Thank you for coming at such short notice. You are all no doubt aware that the investigation and search for the so called Kopycat Killer has now been re-opened, after the bodies of a young couple were found near Bedford in the early hours of yesterday morning."

The room erupted again, questions, shouting, angry exchanges. Falder-Woodes raised his voice and leant close to the microphone, his voice was confident, commanding. "We have found the car that was driven from the scene of the crime this morning, and we are currently running forensic tests for any clues that the killer may have left."

Krein stood straight, he turned from the stage and walked slowly from the room, a gesture noticed by MacReavie, which irked him in the manner only Krein could. He would have it out with him later, before going back to the hotel he'd booked as a little expenses paid treat.

Having favoured eating in front of the television to a formal meal in the dining room, Linda and Mary Krein ate the roasted chicken in silence. The food was overcooked, Linda had held off serving it, hopefully expecting her husband home. Eventually she'd had to accept that he was not coming. Again.

The six o'clock news came on the television, neither women were interested until Linda noticed MacReavie's face on the stage. "That's Henry MacReavie. He's your father's boss." She set her meal aside, and scrutinised the screen, listening to Falder-

Woodes speaking, his concern at the latest murders, concern about Callum Bates committing suicide, concern about the nation's worries. Mary continued with her food, disinterested.

Once the news clip had finished, she turned to her mother, a sardonic smile in place. "Shame Dad wasn't up there. I've almost forgotten what he looks like!"

The comment horrified Linda, she tried to laugh it off as a joke, but she knew it wasn't. Although her husband had only been gone for less than two nights, she knew that the short absence was the beginning of a long one. Her mind drifted to the lonely weeks before Callum Bates had been arrested. David had worked away from home, eaten away from home, slept away from home, and, for all she knew, had a sex life away from home.

The despairing thought that her marriage wasn't going to survive this investigation returned. She took her food-laden plate through to the kitchen, her appetite gone.

Arnold Freeman was also watching the six o'clock news, slumped in his easy chair, beer in his hand, with his feet up on the footstool. Some footage about the Kopycat Killer came on, a case he enjoyed following alongside everyone else. A clip came up showing the latest victim's car being lifted from the river, and his stomach clenched as he recalled the joy-rider the previous night. He sat up straight, leaning closer to the television set, turning up the volume with the remote control.

"Turn that bloody racket down, Arnold." His wife's tedious voice screeched from the kitchen.

"Shut up, woman, and shut those bloody brats up, too." Arnold strained to listen to the news. As soon as the report had finished, he snatched a pen and scribbled the incident room phone number on the back of his hand. He reached for the phone and dialled.

Arnold chose to visit Slough Police Station to give his statement, at least he'd be able to speak without his wife and grandchildren hollering and screaming around him. He parked, and introduced himself to the desk sergeant, who, expecting him, immediately showed him to a room.

Enjoying the unplanned peace and quiet, Arnold gave his full statement, laboriously taking his time. Although it had been dark when the events took place, he was able to give the stature of the man, and a rough description. It appeared to concur with previous descriptions of the killer, and the limp that he mentioned certainly coincided with Rosemary Green's account.

The forensics team, overjoyed at first with both the importance of the case and the overtime, had been less pleased to report that no clear evidence of the suspect could be lifted from the car. Traces of Joe Allisson's blood and tissue, the bits that hadn't been sucked away by underwater creatures, were found inside the car. Tiny traces of blood on the outside of the car were proven to have come from Theresa Francis. But the lack of fingerprints on the steering wheel and boot of the car indicated the suspect had probably been wearing gloves, and no DNA taken matched any from the previous crime scenes.

Arnold confirmed that the man had been wearing gloves, he'd queried that on the night as it had been so warm, the man must have been sweltering. Signing the lengthy statement, furnished with irrelevant detail, Arnold was pleased to have helped. He was more pleased to have escaped his nagging wife for a couple of hours.

"You had no reason to be there, Guv, and you know it." Krein's voice was gaining volume, the conversation was taking a turn for the worse.

"I had every reason to be there, I've been part of this investigation ..."

"Since day one, yes, so you keep saying. So give me the names and ages of the victims so far!"

MacReavie's mouth opened and shut glibly, he turned to the window and focused on nothing. "How dare you talk to me like that, Krein, I should ..."

"Have me suspended, so you keep saying. Fuck off, can you! I know more about this case, and more about the killer, than anyone else in this country. You know that, Spencer knows that, Falder-Woodes ..."

MacReavie was facing Krein again. He laughed. "Jealousy. That's what this is. I was getting the glory that you want for yourself."

"You pathetic twerp! You belong on Big Brother!" Krein sneered. "Falder-Woodes stood on that stage, he said everything, and he said nothing. He made excuses for the cock-ups, and he didn't shoulder any blame. There was no reason for that façade, it wasn't beneficial to the investigations ..."

"What about the bloke who came forward after seeing the news?"

"He would have come forward anyway after seeing the headlines tomorrow. This was all just a waste of money and time, both better spent on finding the killer instead of making sure your gentle, caring, and well-rehearsed smile was caught on camera!" Krein was spitting the words now, he was furious.

And so was MacReavie. "That's it, Krein, you've gone a step too far now."

Neither men had any idea that a group of officers were crowded around the door, listening to the raging argument. Spencer was impressed at his enemy's feistiness, he'd not realised how dedicated Krein was, perhaps he needed to review his opinion of the man. The door opened, the officers scattering as MacReavie stomped away, seething.

After dumping the car Paul had limped along the bank of the Thames for a while, the pain in his ankle worsening gradually the further he travelled. Finally he came upon an irregular row of boat houses. A couple lay at the bottom of the gardens to some spectacular, sumptuous houses, the others just small buildings built on what appeared to be public ground. One after the other, he tried the doors until one, in disrepair, cracked open. He climbed inside and shone the torch around. The clammy room was mostly empty, a few bags of junk lay to the edges, and it was filthy, the air heavy with stale, yet moist, dust and vapour. The water in the narrow bay lapped at the cement floor, and, dropping his bag, Paul moved the junk bags between his belongings and the inlet. It was obvious this room was barely used.

Suddenly curious about his new home, Paul shone the torch around once more. In a dark corner lay a gas can, he shook it, hearing the fluid, confirming it was petrol by sniffing. He took one of the bags of junk, revealing some tatty, musty clothes. He spread a few items across the floor, and lay down, transforming them to a mattress. He slept through sunrise to sundown, and on through the night, his tiredness from the previous night's duty extreme. Paul was oblivious to the frantic police activity less than a mile north east, his quiet snoring blending into the sounds of the river.

Monday 25th August

A rumbling stomach was the first sensation Paul felt when he awoke, he was starving, and it dawned on him that he hadn't eaten for a couple of days. He needed to go out to get some food, but he realised that his latest duty would have renewed the interest in him. He would have to disguise himself again, but how, and where would he get the clothes from? Paul rocked gently, confused, but then he remembered his old friend.

"God, are you there?" God didn't talk to him very often any more, he didn't need to, but Paul found that if he asked for him nicely, sometimes He would reply. He was not disappointed this time. He asked what he should do, and God came back, clear and confident, telling him to look through the bags of clothes again, he would find a new identity in them. Paul chuckled his gentle, tinkling laugh. So obvious, why hadn't he thought of that himself?

He moved from the makeshift mattress and held up the clothes, assessing each item individually. They were all women's clothes, and most were quite large. Paul was a slight man, the clothes would hang off him, but really, he had no choice, and he didn't want to anger God by going against his suggestion. Paul peeled off his filthy, odorous clothes, his nose wrinkling. Naked, he stepped towards the inlet from the river, leaning over and washing in the stagnant water, rubbing away the weeks of grime and sweat. Fresher, and grateful for it, Paul stepped into a long, pale pink, flowery skirt, chosen for its elasticated waist. He shrugged a baggy white blouse over his shoulders, deciding against a cardigan because of the heat. The bag contained no shoes, so Paul washed his socks and replaced them on his feet, having wrung them in his hands to remove the excess water, and put his rancid trainers back on.

Now Paul was transformed into Paula once more, vanity made her grateful that the skirt was long enough to cover her hairy legs.

Paula delved into her bag, somewhere inside she was sure she still had the cosmetics she'd purchased the last time she'd changed her identity to a female. After brushing and dabbing for a few minutes in the light from a crack in the door, checking the progress in the compact mirror, Paula was satisfied that her face was suitably made up, and she brushed her shaggy hair into place, fitting the hairpiece skilfully.

Stepping through the door, Paula felt attractive and confident, but modest enough to not draw attention to herself. Her belongings safely stored in the shelter, Paula walked towards civilisation to buy enough food and drink to sustain herself for a few days. Luckily, money was still no object, Jackson Brooks had been a very flash man.

Krein was busy at his temporary desk in the incident room at the Yard. He'd not heard anything more after the argument with MacReavie, and deep inside he knew he'd gone too far, although he wouldn't admit it unless pressed. It was early, he'd barely slept, having had too many beers followed by whiskies just to sleep in the first place. At the first crack of dawn he'd come back to the station, he was more use there than tossing and turning in bed.

So when the door opened and MacReavie stepped in, a three-piece, beautifully tailored navy suit replacing his usual grey, Krein did a double take. MacReavie shot him a hateful glare, and Krein knew that if he wanted to stay on the case he would have to back down. Wincing at the overdone aftershave, Krein waved. "Guv, I need to speak to you. I'm sorry about yesterday."

The room was barely populated this early, but every eye in the room was fixed on Krein now. Including MacReavies', he was shocked. "I, um, don't worry, Krein. I know this case is getting to you. Just don't do it again." Mentally MacReavie kicked himself, he could have drawn it out, had some enjoyment. Too late, he sighed.

Krein nodded at the outfit. "Why the posh suit?"

MacReavie was stunned. "Krein! What planet have you been on! We're going to the television studio today, for the Crimewatch appeal." The incredulous look was replaced with a dazzling smile, which wasn't returned.

In fact, Krein could feel anger bubbling again, he tried desperately to control himself. He spoke through gritted teeth, checking every word. "I don't understand why you're wasting precious time in a television studio when everyone should be concentrating on finding Kopycat."

Aware that their conversation was currently public material, MacReavie pulled a chair up to Krein's desk. He didn't want another argument, because if Krein carried on undermining him he would have no choice but to discipline him, and that wouldn't be beneficial to the investigation: Krein was devoted to the case. "Look, I know you think I have an ulterior motive here, but I don't. Crimewatch will really publicise the whole damned thing, get the nation chatting about the case, we'll turn out hundreds of new witnesses."

Krein sighed deeply, he realised his boss was placating him. "Every person in Britain is chatting about Kopycat already, the case is permanently on the TV and in the papers. Appearing on Crimewatch will just be glorifying it and wasting valuable time."

"The public needs my reassurance that we're doing our best."

Krein snapped. "Fifteen minutes, Guv, fifteen minutes! That's what this is all about, and you know that. Do you not realise that each and every one of those people who calls in as a result of the programme is going to need police time to go and take their statements, verify them, rule them out, and those policemen should be on the streets, at previous murder sites, or getting into Kopycat's mind, making damned sure that he can't get another victim."

MacReavie stood up and banged his fist on the desk, his face reddening. Although irate, his voice was quiet, calm. "Just you make sure that you," and now he shouted, "never, never talk to me like this again." And quiet again. "This is your last warning Krein. Once more I'll forget this because of the strain you're under, but only once. Now smarten yourself up, you look a mess, and I need your knowledge to get the facts across to the Crimewatch team."

Broadcasting House was a short tube journey away, Macreavie led the way through the grand glass and chrome doors. They were meeting Falder-Woodes there. They reported to the receptionist, and presently a young, casually dressed woman led them to her superior's empty office. She returned soon carrying a tray laden with a pot of tea, a pot of coffee, and some biscuits. MacReavie tucked in hungrily, Krein watched London living through the window, seething still for his time being wasted. Moments later Falder-Woodes was brought in, he and MacReavie exchanged pleasantries.

Shortly, in a dramatic entrance of waves and flourishes, a self-important woman strolled in, confidently thrusting her red tipped hand forward for the men to shake. Her voice was as assured as her manner, deep and colourful. "Hi, I'm Maria Ivanov, I'm the Crimewatch contents editor. You'll spend most of the day with me. Sit."

The three officers of the law obeyed like dogs. MacReavie was in awe of the stunning woman, his eyes were on stalks as he searched for something interesting to say. "I have to admit, Miss Ivanhoe …"

"Please call me Maria." She bristled on hearing her name mispronounced, the anger flashing black in her overly green eyes.

"Okay, Maria. I have to admit that I've never done a Crimewatch before. I think you'll have to lead the way."

Dismissive. "Yes, I always do. First we need to decide what reconstructions you want. Have you thought about that?"

MacReavie was enjoying the attention, he'd instantly taken the stage from the other two men. "We don't have a lot to go on, there have been very few good witnesses since the start of Kopycat's killing career. The best one, I think, would be the latest. We can't be sure of the route they took to reach Deathly Mill …"

"Deadman's Hill." Krein got a word in.

MacReavie admonished him with his stare. "But we do have an eye witness to the murder."

Maria clapped gleefully. "So we will recreate the murder scene, sensational, the public will love that. We'll make a point of filming the bodies, that'll attract Joe Public's attention."

"No!" Krein's objection was sudden and unplanned. "No. That won't do. We already know that there was only one witness to that murder, a reconstruction of that would hardly jog anybody's memory. Just remember, we're not doing this for the public's pleasure, we're doing it to find the killer and to stop anyone else becoming a victim."

Maria regarded Krein blankly, nobody questioned her judgement. "So, Mr, er," she made a point of reading his visitor's badge, "Kreeeeen. In your obviously vast experience of my world. what would you suggest, then?" Her sarcasm was weary.

Krein was unfazed, she didn't intimidate, just mildly sickened him. "Katie Joyce. There must be many people who haven't realised they saw Kopycat on his journey north with Katie, or maybe they're even too scared to say anything." Again, an unexpected burst, but more unexpected was the sudden realisation that this Crimewatch idea might actually be a good one.

"No, Krein, I disagree. Kopycat's appearance has changed greatly since then." MacReavie shook his head, Maria smiled at her ally.

"So reconstruct him dumping Joe Allisson's Golf GTi then, as well as Katie's abduction."

"Reconstructions cost money, Krein." The comment was redundant, the BBC would be funding any reconstructions, but Krein missed that jewel.

He was seething, he'd never been so continuously angry in his entire life. His words were marked, forced from the back of his throat for emphasis. "This man is costing lives, Guv, and that is far more important than bloody money."

Maria and Falder-Woodes looked on, incredulous, until Maria stepped in diplomatically. "Boys, boys, let's compromise, shall we. Two reco's, yeah, both of the murders, right, and lots of photos of victims, and photofits of Kopycat. As much cam action on the sites as poss, y'know, it's the visual effects that nudge the viewers' memories. If they know from pre-program adverts that they're going to get a good show, they all tune in and watch. That's what the vultures like."

All three men managed to decipher the compromise, and they had to concede that Maria knew what she was doing, so, frayed tempers calmed, they got back to the discussion, which progressed well. The preliminary date of Saturday the fourteenth of September was chosen to air the show. MacReavie was hoping it would be sooner, but that was the first available slot.

Paula had returned to the boathouse, her hunger satiated. She'd not walked far before she came across a petrol station, and she'd filled a basket with a variety of sandwiches, crisps, chocolate, milk, not that it would last long in the heat, bread, and a couple of large bottles of Pepsi Max. Her ankle ached even though the journey was short, but it didn't overly worry her, it was healing well for an untreated, relatively serious injury.

Opening her bag, Paula emptied all the clothes out, she replaced them with two new outfits, assembled from the bags of discarded women's clothing. Satisfied that her hunger wasn't returning, she felt for the coolest spot in the room, and put the carrier bags of food there, hoping to keep it fresh for a few days until her departure for the next journey.

Paula unzipped the side compartment of her bag and took the personal organiser out. The batteries had gone flat a few days before, and this was the first time she'd had the opportunity to replace them. She slid the battery hatch open and put the fresh ones in. The gadget sprang to life, and Paula smiled widely. Finally she could research her plans for the next duties.

The next one was further ahead than she had remembered, six days away on the thirty first of August, but this didn't faze her, the extra time would give her ankle a little longer to heal. She thought back to the last duty, and her grin returned. She had enjoyed it so much, that wonderful moment when she was completely in control of another person's life, it was her choice to extinguish or save. She found the gore tedious, but the act of killing was tremendous. The power. And the knowledge that she was making God happy.

Six days was a long time, but she wanted to get this one perfect, and that would need plenty of preparation, the site where the next duty was planned was busy, and risking capture was not an option. Swigging absent-mindedly from the bottle of Pepsi, Paula drank the details of her next duty, soaking them up until they were printed on her brain. She would stay in her temporary home until the day of the duty, the re-enactment of Polly

Nichols's mutilation, she couldn't risk being spotted now, because the duties she had coming up were by far the best yet. Paula couldn't wait.

The four ten year old boys sat in a circle, beside the weeping willow that fed from the Thames, munching on crisps and chocolate, barely speaking. An idea came, Billy piped up. "Maybe she's a witch."

The others laughed, and, still chuckling, Craig croaked. "Don't be silly. Witches wear black dresses, idiot. I reckon she's one of those mad people that Dad's always talking about."

They continued to suppose differing theories, each one getting more extreme, of who, or what, the odd lady that had disappeared into the boat shed was. It wasn't long until they all got bored and headed for home, and their waiting dinners. But they mutually decided that they would keep guard of the boathouse every day, and next time they saw her go out, they would investigate what she was up to.

Each boy had exciting dreams that night.

Thursday 28th August

Krein put the phone down, he'd not realised until he'd heard her gentle, intelligent voice again how much he missed Jaswinder. The guilt intensified when he realised he hadn't even unpacked Linda's photo from his briefcase. Jaswinder had phoned to discuss the report the Black Museum Bunch had sent her, convinced that Kopycat would concentrate on recreating the Jack the Ripper murders next. Krein needed to discuss this with Spencer, and was surprised to note the man smiling when he approached with his notes.

Spencer had developed a new respect for Krein having overheard his argument with MacReavie, who Spencer regarded as a pompous idiot. Krein dragged a seat over, placing his notes squarely on the desk. "Jack the Ripper?"

"Yes."

Neither man spoke, each individually contemplating how they could possibly cover the enormity of Whitehall without alarming the public. Krein crossed his legs, leaning back in the seat, and Spencer mirrored the action. Spencer raised his fingers to his lips and gently stroked as he considered privately, Krein mirrored the action subconsciously. With no exchange of words, both men realised the distaste for each other was gone, and that they now had the potential of working together very efficiently. They locked eyes, nodded, and Krein headed back to his desk. He knew that Spencer was a tremendous officer, and that with them both on the same side, Kopycat couldn't win. He felt reassured.

Two days they had spent there. Waiting, pondering, hoping, discussing, and the woman had not left the boathouse once. The boys were bored, this business was wasting their summer holiday. Billy was the first to break. "Maybe she's not in there anymore, she might have gone in the night."

Craig sucked at his fingers, thinking the suggestion through. "We could always look closer." The lads were horrified, each replying with an incredulous stare. Craig persevered, not wanting to lose face. "Just look through the holes in the wood, you know, we won't go in."

"What if she catches us?" Billy was aware he needed the toilet, he didn't need any sudden scares.

"We run." The answer justified the madness. They shrugged at each other, and, one by one, they crept, each carefully placed footstep stroking the muddy grass without making a sound. Closer and closer, and soon Craig was next to the side wall, his hand resting on the peeling bluebell paint, his heart thundering in his chest. Eyes skimming over the wooden cladding, he located a thin gap, the rotting wood having worn away. Checking that his friends were close by, Craig tentatively glanced through. Disappointed, he shook his head, mouthing. "Can't see her, it's dark."

Billy shoved him out of the way, he peered through himself. Leaning to the right, he could just about make out some movement by the door, and adrenalin surged through him. "Shit! She's coming."

"Fuck!" The others whispered in unison as they hurried behind the nearest tree. The door groaned open and the woman sneaked out, her shifty eyes darting around. She appeared to be unaware of the boys, and they relaxed in their hiding place. She smoothed down her skirt, the hem skimming the top of her filthy trainers, closed the door behind her, and limped away from the building.

As soon as she rounded the corner, Billy sprang out. "Here's our chance. Come on you lot, let's be quick." He darted over and pushed on the door, it creaked open easily, revealing the darkness, the stale odour wafting from within. The other three boys still cowered by the tree, but when they watched Billy enter the boathouse, curiosity replaced the fear, and they sprinted forward to join him.

Mooching around the shed, they sorted through the clothes, fingered the food, snooping, prying, desperate to find something that would prove she was a witch, or a murderer, or a burglar, anything to satisfy their childish, adventurous dreams. Craig didn't notice the case in the centre of the floor and tripped over it. "Fuck and bloody hell!" He exclaimed, loving the freedom of swearing.

Clambering up, he examined the bag. "Comrades. I've got something." They jumped over, excited with anticipation. Dramatically, Craig unzipped the case, his chubby fingers rooting through her belongings. He tossed the scruffy, musty clothes to one side, and at the bottom of the bag his hand met with something metallic, he grasped it, grinning, and brought it out.

"What's that?" The boys were mystified by the thin, rectangular, metal box.

Craig played about, pressing and clicking, he pushed a button on the side and the box opened, doubling it's size. "Whoah! Cool!" Craig was giggling, he'd never seen one of these. "It's a little computer, I think." Without warning the door opened, the woman, carrying a plastic bag full of twigs, came in, closing the door behind herself. She was oblivious to the boys, until Craig screamed "Fuck!", and she jumped, dropping the bag.

The boys ran for the door, shoving the shocked woman aside, and piled through, running along the bank, as fast as possible, as far away as possible. And whilst they were escaping, Craig became aware that he still had the organiser clenched in his hand. He knew it was thieving, but he never wanted to see her again.

Recovering from her surprise, Paula darted out of the boathouse after them, furious that they'd been spying on her, but they were well ahead already, their agile, young legs sprinting at top speed into the distance. She waved her fist in anger, but chasing was out of the question, her injured ankle wouldn't endure that. Paula stomped back inside, spitting with fury, and glanced around, seeing what the boys had been up to. Almost immediately she noticed the case lying open on the floor, the stack of clothes piled to one side.

"No." Paula gasped, falling to her knees, she began rooting through the bag. "My duties. My duties. They've taken my duties."

Deflated, Paula sat heavily, she dragged her knees to her chest, her body rocking backwards and forwards, unable to understand anything, confusion obliterating everything. She begged for God's help, over and over, but he wouldn't speak to her, he must be angry with her. But she couldn't comprehend what she had done wrong.

The tears flowed, soaking through her skirt, dripping down her legs, the pressure pounding her head. She had never felt so lonely. Begging. Pleading. Appealing. Imploring.

Then he was there, loud and clear, and the relief flooded over her, washing away the grief. 'You will remember your duties, you can remember, they are in your memory. Just remember what you can, and if the details are wrong, it doesn't matter. As long as you keep choosing people to die, you will still be my chosen one.'

Her body relaxed, and the tears restarted. Grateful tears, grateful to God for still being there, and relieved tears, relieved that she was still special.

Craig stuffed the organiser under his pillow, redundantly checking that nobody was watching. "Dinner's ready." His mother's broken English shrilled up the stairs. Trotting out of the room, Craig resolved to find out how the computer worked later, see if there were any games on it.

Saturday 30th August

Krein pored over the detailed notes for the hundredth time. The first section had the facts of the original murder of Mary Ann Nichols, known as Polly, in eighteen eighty eight. The second section held the extensive details of the operation arranged for the next night. Policing the Whitechapel area of London to ensure that Kopycat could not recreate the murder of Jack the Ripper's first acknowledged victim. He knew the plans by heart, but still read and re-read. Tomorrow he and the expansive team were going to catch the wanted man, and the anticipation was eating away at him.

The phone on his desk trilled, he clasped the receiver, still scanning the notes. "Krein, it's MacReavie. Just to let you know that I'll be travelling to London tomorrow for the stakeout."

Krein's teeth ground at the dramatic term, how did his boss always manage to stir his anger so easily. He bit his tongue, remaining polite. "Any idea what sort of time you'll be here?"

The pause convinced Krein that MacReavie was checking his diary. His assumption was correct. "It's Sunday tomorrow." Slow, deliberate, buying time. "I've got a golf match at ten in the morning, should take a couple of hours, then we're having a family lunch. Expect me there at about six, okay."

"Guv." Krein hated MacReavie, he hated MacReavie, thinking it over and over stopped him rising to the bait.

"Remind me how to get there, will you?"

He hated MacReavie, and his teeth gritted further, his words abrupt. "Get on the Circle line at Paddington, get off at Victoria. Take a cab, they'll know where it is." He put the phone down, knowing he would blow if he didn't. "Bastard."

Mary Krein was in her bedroom with two of her best friends, Nat and Tara. It had taken most of the day for them to preen and pamper themselves into perfect condition, and they were increasingly excited about the evening ahead. Starting with a shower each, they'd moisturised, perfumed, face-packed, nail-painted, hair-straightened, make-up brushed, and finally they all sat in their underwear, ready to leave once they dressed, listening to dance music, and chattering animatedly.

Just after five, Linda had brought a plate of sandwiches up, ensuring they wouldn't be drinking on an empty stomach, and she gave them a mini lecture about the dangers of drink spiking. Mary had been mortally embarrassed, surely her mother knew that people went to McDonalds before going to a club nowadays, and everybody knew about Rohypnol and the others, that's why everyone drank from bottles. Mary had told her mother to leave them alone and stop spying on them, and the dejected Linda had obeyed sadly.

Linda sat in the kitchen, she turned on Radio 4 for company, and sat with her head in her hands. When she heard the girls trotting down the stairs, she didn't see them out, afraid of being reprimanded again. She waited for the door to close and moved to the lounge, pouring herself a brandy, and knocking it back to follow it with another.

The warmth burning her throat, she took stock of her life. She'd not seen or heard from David since the Kopycat Killer had struck again, hearsay told her he was working in London, that might or might not be true. Mary had morphed into a completely different human being, or was it monster, in the past couple of months, one who detested every breath her mother took. Linda was fed up with being taken for granted. It was time she thought about herself for the first time in eighteen years. She needed a hobby, something that was hers, hers alone.

Linda picked up the local paper for ideas, and she was soon absorbed in an article about Jack the Ripper. It mentioned that his first victim died a hundred and twenty years ago on Sunday, in Whitechapel. The journalist had questioned if this was where the Kopycat Killer intended to strike next? Linda stared at the paper, her eyes wide, no longer seeing. Wasn't the club Mary was heading for in Whitechapel? Linda's blood ran cold.

Paula was subdued all day. She was patiently waiting for evening to come before making a move from her temporary home. After her organiser had been stolen, she had bought a pad and a pen from the garage, and had sketched down all the details she could remember for the next, and subsequent, duties. She'd need to be able to move quickly, and with her ankle already a problem, she had decided not to take the suitcase.

Like most things when she was lonely, Paula had run the decision by God, who'd agreed wholeheartedly, and advised her to dispose of any evidence from her stay at the boathouse. Preparing to leave, she put a sheathed knife, wrapped in some of Jackson Brooks's underwear, into a carrier bag, adding the remaining bags of crisps, and placed the bag by the door. She threw the gun into the river.

Dusk was falling, the sky red for tomorrow's delight, and Paula toiled swiftly, collecting all the clothes, the bag, wrappers, everything she could find, and piling them where she'd been sleeping. The final pieces, Jackson's identity papers, were scattered on top, before Paula took the petrol can in her gloved hand, drizzling the fluid throughout the shed.

Moving to the door and grasping the carrier bag, Paula lit a match and threw it, the flame caught the petrol immediately. She watched the growing, yellow flickering, mesmerised for a few seconds, ensuring the fire took hold, and, satisfied, she closed the door behind her. She didn't notice Jackson's driving licence by the door, away from the burning heap.

Paula walked briskly, her limp heavy, towards Windsor. She would take the train to Slough, and change on to Paddington. She was excited, the real fun was about to begin.

Mina Lockington entered her son's untidy bedroom to settle him before she turned his light out. Guilty, he hastily put his hands behind his back, and she was suspicious. "What was that?" Craig shook his head, his eyes wide and innocent, butter wouldn't melt. "Craig. I'm not falling for that face. What are you hiding?" Although she'd lived in England for most of her life, her accent remained heavy with Indian overtones, learned from her parents. Craig still shook his head, his innocent face appealing.

Mina gave up being reasonable, ten year old boys were a pain in the backside. She shoved her hands behind him and snatched the organiser. "What the hell is this thing?"

228

Craig had no choice but to speak up, he'd been busted. "We found it a couple of days ago. By the river."

"What is it?" She repeated.

"A mini computer thingy." He reached up and took the organiser from her, pushing the button to expose the screen and keyboard. An impressed expression crossed her face, instantly replaced with anger as she remembered she was chastising her son.

"You say you found it by the river. Did you steal it?"

Although he shook his head vigorously, Craig's face reddened, betraying his lie. "Where did you steal it from?" Met with an irritating silence, she raised her hand as if to smack him, and the confession tumbled out.

"It was this weird tramp woman. She was all dirty and horrid. We were watching her for some days, then when she went out …"

"Went out where?" Mina was confused.

"She was staying in a boathouse, down by the river, an old blue one. She was living there I think. She went out and we decided to have a look inside, to see what she was up to. We thought she might be a witch." Craig paused, a wailing fire engine passed outside the window. Once the peace was regained, he continued as if never stopping. "She was really scary, mama, she came back in and she was horrid and smelly, we just ran and ran and ran. It wasn't until we were miles away that I realised I still had it in my hand. But I wasn't going to go back, she scared me, and I don't ever want to see her again."

Mina sighed, content that her son was telling the truth. "I'll have to take it to the police station tomorrow, explain what happened." Her soft voice became stern again to act as a warning to her excitable son. "But they may decide to tick you off, boy, you aren't to steal, it's a bad thing to do." She took the organiser, leant over and lightly kissed Craig's forehead, before leaving the room, switching off the light.

Linda rushed through the door, not closing it before picking up the phone and dialling her husband's mobile phone number. She had missed her daughter's train by minutes, regardless of having driven like a madwoman to catch her in time. "David, it's Linda. Where are you?" She was gasping, breathless.

Concern. "Linda? I'm in London. Why?"

"It's Mary, she's gone there with Tara and Nat, train, it's Jack the Ripper, I read ..."

"Whoah, slow down! Slow down! You're not making sense."

Linda knew she was rambling, she breathed deeply to control herself. "Jack the Ripper, David. It's in the Oxford Times. His first victim was murdered on the thirty first of August."

Krein was losing interest now. "I know."

"For God's sake, David, don't you get it! Mary, Tara and Nat have gone to Whitechapel tonight, they've gone clubbing, I just missed them at the train station, I tried to stop them. What if the Kopycat Killer recreates the murder? What if he gets one of the girls? What if he gets our Mary?" The frustration and fear were bringing tears to Linda's eyes.

Krein's voice was reassuring, he hated to hear his wife so distraught. "Think about what you've just said, Linda. The anniversary of Polly Nichols's death is the thirty first of August. It's the thirtieth tonight."

Linda felt like a bumbling idiot, she apologised, saying her goodbyes hastily to get off the phone. She poured another brandy, ashamed for having nothing better to do than worry unnecessarily. Sitting with the oversized shot, she resolved once more to find a hobby. If she had something else to think about, this sort of blunder wouldn't happen again.

The firemen struggled to extinguish the ferocious blaze, with the ongoing heat-wave the surrounding trees and undergrowth could easily catch alight. They needed to contain the fire as soon as possible. Even though the fire was still blazing, the crew already suspected that this was arson. It wasn't impossible for a wooden structure to ignite from a discarded match or cigarette, but in this case it seemed unlikely. They guessed it was kids messing around, taking a game one step too far.

Adelaide Smith worked at the popular Wallingford Bar in Brick Lane, Whitechapel. She was even more popular than the bar, though, with the male clients. She was naturally busty, and wore clothes that accentuated her assets further. Her hair was dyed blonde, long and wavy, and people would turn to stare wherever she walked, she had presence. Up close, beneath the overdone make up, Adelaide wasn't anything special, but she made the most of what she had, and as a result was a woman of many men's dreams.

This Saturday night hadn't been busy, which had given Adelaide a superb opportunity to flirt with a younger man she'd fancied for a while. In company she was outspoken, maybe even brash after a few too many drinks, and Roger Andrews equalled her in these stakes. However, on their own, chatting to one another over the bar, the conversation had been pleasant and satisfying for both parties. Roger was impressed with the older woman, he determined he would try to take her back to his flat. He could do with a good shag.

Unfortunately for Roger, Adelaide, regardless of her public persona, was not a woman for one night stands. Ignorant to this, and with the manager having rung the bell for last orders, Roger decided it was time to make his move. He asked Adelaide back to his place for a coffee, with a sly wink. Chuckling, she refused, as affably as possible, she told him she had an appointment with the doctor early the next morning, and she wanted to go to bed as soon as she got home. Roger, not used to rejection, he was a handsome and persuasive man, he cajoled her, laughing, and when the bottom lip routine didn't work, he pleaded, but her rejection remained firm.

Surprisingly quickly Adelaide went from giggling cheerfully, to being worryingly unnerved. Roger's demeanour was suddenly repugnant. He claimed Adelaide had led him on, she had teased him, and if she wasn't prepared to put it out, she shouldn't make out she was. Adelaide distanced herself from him, she had a discreet word with her manager and friend, Ivan Stulski, who promised her that either he, or his son, would walk her home. Adelaide was an excellent worker, business always boomed when it was her shift, and he didn't want anything happening to her.

A group of young men lurched drunkenly to the bar and, checking her watch, Adelaide served them. She could feel Roger's eyes burning her from the other end of the bar, but she remained composed, ignoring him. Twelve midnight passed, and gradually the revellers moved on to the local clubs, or back to their homes. Ivan and Adelaide systematically cleared tables, wiped surfaces, emptied ashtrays, washed glasses, and all the while Roger sat on his barstool, sipping his pint slowly, his eyes boring into Adelaide's back. Eventually his bitter was finished, he left the bar, shooting Adelaide a final glare.

She breathed a long sigh of relief. "Thank God for that!"

Ivan laid his burly, fight scarred hand on her dainty shoulder. "Stay back half an hour or so, give him time to get bored and go home. I'll walk you back then. Look, let's share a bottle of wine while we wait, okay?"

Adelaide nodded, grateful that her boss was so considerate, and grateful such a hunk of a man would be chaperoning her to her home. The pleasantly fruity Hungarian Merlot, exclusive back of a lorry stock, lasted an hour, and they both enjoyed catching up with each other properly. Ivan and Adelaide had been friends for many years, in their twenties they had consummated the relationship, passionately tumbling in and out of bed as they discovered each other, but after the initial lust had worn off, they had decided they preferred just being mates. Both loved each other, but friendship was as far as it went, and would ever go again. Adelaide had remained mainly single for the last seven years, since she had started working in the Wallingford Bar. She had two daughters, now teenagers, who had lived with their father since the bitter divorce. She was content with this arrangement, she preferred partying to mothering.

Checking her watch, Adelaide stood up, tugging her leather mini skirt over her heavy thighs. She shrugged the tight leather jacket over her shoulders, covering the skimpy vest top. "I'd best get going, I'm dead tired tonight." Ivan nodded, smiling kindly, he grabbed his keys and they went through the door, Ivan locking up once they'd stepped into the unusually chilly night.

The breeze was up, Adelaide trotted ahead, her skinny heels clicking against the pavement, and she hugged the jacket tightly over her ample bosom, whilst Ivan finished securing the bar. He strode his massive, manly steps, and caught up with her in moments. Walking in silence along Old Montague Street, deep in their own thoughts as they travelled Vallance Road, and soon they had reached Whitechapel Road. Adelaide's steps quickened, her arm reached for her boss. Relaxed by the wine she had forgotten Roger and his intimidation, but now the memory chilled her.

"Ivan, I can feel someone's eyes boring into my back." Adelaide, scared, didn't look behind her, but Ivan did.

"I can't see anyone." He took her hand, clenching reassuringly, her fingers like a child's compared to his. "Don't worry, I'm with you. You'll be home safely in no time." And she squeezed him back.

They had been dancing most of the night, they'd come to chill out completely and that's exactly what they were doing. Every hour or so they'd head for the bar, order a refreshing drink to stave away the dehydration. Mary, Nat and Tara, brows glistening with unladylike sweat, shook their booties, lost in their own worlds, lost in the booming beat, lost in the rhythm.

Mary, oblivious to how seductive her hip swinging could be, was pleasantly surprised when an attractive man sidled up and fell into step with her. He caught her glance, and they danced flirtatiously, eyes locked together, the rest of the room forgotten. No words were exchanged, they were unnecessary, their hips and their eyes held the conversation.

After the minutes that felt like hours had passed, Roger Andrews took Mary's hand and led her away from the dance floor, dragging her in the direction of the bar. "I'll get you a drink." His smile beamed, eyes flashing as he undressed her with them, and he fingered the plastic package of GHB in his pocket.

"Thanks, I'll have a Diet Coke please." Roger ordered the drinks, he nodded when the barman offered a glass, but Mary stopped the man. "I'll have mine in the bottle, please."

Fuming, Roger removed his hand from his pocket, bringing a ten pound note with it. He'd have to find some way of getting the drug into her drink. Adelaide had already refused him, and there was no way he intended to go home alone tonight. They took their drinks to a table, Mary's hand shielding the top of the bottle at all times, to his dismay. He broke the ice. "My name's Roger, what's yours?"

The conversation continued, and Roger was surprised at how intelligent Mary was, he wasn't used to clever girls, and he was amazed at how sexy it was. Brief thoughts every now and then made him pleased he'd not managed to administer the drug yet, she was excellent company. But then his penis would stir, and he'd reassuringly feel the plastic pouch.

Tara and Nat had been chatting for a while, neither were getting good vibes about their friend's choice of companion. Eventually, Tara felt the need to intervene. She strolled to the table and, grabbing Mary's arm, yelled "Toilets. Now."

Confused, Mary followed her friend. Walking past the lengthy queue of scantily clad women, they moved to the mirrors, and Tara opened her clutch bag, rooting around for a lipstick. "What the hell do you think you're doing, Mary?"

"What? We were only messing around." Haughty, Mary combed her deliciously long, glistening hair with her fingers.

Tara surprised herself with her unsubstantiated anger, and in turn stunned Mary. "Don't be such an idiot. You were leading him on. You'll get yourself into trouble playing games like that. The Oxford Clubs are bad enough, but this is London remember. You've got to be careful."

The unusual outburst was enough to bring Mary to her senses, she checked her make up, agreeing to lose the guy and stick with her mates for the rest of the night. And no more flirting.

Concerned that another prick teasing bitch was going to get away with humiliating him that evening, Roger closely watched the door to the ladies for Mary, and finally she exited with her friend. Mustering his most dashing smile, his white teeth glittering in the dancing lights, he beamed at Mary as he strolled towards her, grasping the spiked drink to present her. But she blanked him, not even a shrug or a nod, no acknowledgement at all.

He was furious, raging inside his head. Muttering under his breath, the venom more dangerous than the drug he'd prescribed. "Bitch. Bloody bitch. All fucking women are bloody bitches."

And he caught the eye of a timid, petite redhead leaning against the wall. His winning smile replaced the scowl, and he took the Diet Coke as a gift.

Krein walked into the room, it was just past two in the morning, and he'd just packed up work at the Yard. He'd been mulling over the plans for the next evening, and the time had swum by alarmingly quickly. His mind whirred, he knew sleep wasn't on the agenda unless he helped it along somehow. He was dog tired, he'd barely slept in the last week, but nowadays his mind never seemed to let work go. The only answer he knew was stupor, and the whisky bottle beside the bed could provide that. He brought a glass over, pouring an extra large measure. One slug was all it took, and, grimacing with the after-burn, Krein poured another. And another. And another. Still dressed in his casual, comfortable clothes, his shoes in place, his mind went blank, and he was on top of the covers, a drunken snore emitting from his throat. His sleep was peaceful, beautiful, undisturbed, and complete to the next morning.

Ivan and Adelaide reached the front door of Adelaide's small, rented house in Durward Street. She turned the key in the lock and pushed the door open, stepping through. In afterthought, she turned back and gave Ivan a fleeting, grateful hug.

"Thanks ever so much, Ivan, it was really good of you. I'll see you tomorrow."

"No problem, mate, I'll see ya." He turned, his bear like stature ambling towards the streetlight at the end of the short path, and Adelaide watched briefly, before closing the door. Stepping into the kitchenette, she picked up the kettle, but set it back when the doorbell jangled. "What's he forgotten?" Adelaide chuckled as returned to the hall to let Ivan in.

She opened the door, and before her mind could register anything hands grasped her neck, squeezing, squeezing. She heard the door click shut. The pressure made Adelaide's eyes bulge, she thought they might pop from the sockets, her chest ached with the lack of breath. She tried to recognise her attacker, but her eyes were blurred, the tall figure was blurred. Was it a woman?

Adelaide thrust her hands at her attacker, fingers lashing out, scratching, flailing, but the pressure in her head was unbearable. Her chest craved air, it felt caved in, her energy was sapping but her kicking continued. Her body was losing the fight, but the hands squeezed harder, she felt a pop in the front of her neck, and a part of her realised the struggle was futile. Her eyes stopped seeing, the world had turned black. Her hearing was white noise, the world had become monotone.

Paula was thankful to feel the body slump in her hands, but the vixen had put up a vicious struggle, so she continued to squeeze for a count of sixty. When Jack the Ripper had strangled Polly Nichols, he'd ensured she was dead before he'd mutilated the body, that way there was less blood.

Finally Paula relaxed her grip, and Adelaide's lifeless form slumped to the floor, the open eyed look of horror still glaring on her face. Paula checked for a pulse. Nothing. Her hand hovered over Adelaide's mouth. There was no warm breath.

Paula smiled, she was enjoying this, it was going to plan and so much easier than she had expected. She'd suspected the streets would be full of policemen, so maybe she wasn't as interesting as she had thought she was. Or maybe God had spoken to them, and told them how important it was that she did her duties.

Paula cracked the front door slightly, checking there were no passers by, she leaned out and collected her carrier bag from it's hiding place on the porch. Closing the door, she bolted top and bottom, and fed the chain across. After checking the back door and windows were secure, Paula knelt by the mottling body, noticing for the first time how much older the woman was underneath the heavy make up. She scanned her slowly, digesting every detail of her face. Reaching out a finger to touch her still warm skin, Paula's words were tender. "God will be pleased again, you look about the right age, if I remember rightly."

And her mood changed, anger burgeoning as she recalled. "Those bastard children! Stealing my duties. If I ever find them I will cut them up into little pieces, one by one." The outburst was over, the warmth was back as her concentration returned to Adelaide, and her horrified, wide eyed face. "God asked me to do this because I'm special. Your name is Polly now, it will be forever, and you are at peace. You were selected for this special privilege, you are so lucky. You will feel no pain now as I finish my duty."

Removing her gloves, Paula dragged the carrier bag towards the body, she rooted through the underwear and pulled out the knife, removing it from the sheath. She lay it on the floor, cupping her head in her hands as she delved through her memory to remember exactly how Jack the Ripper had mutilated Polly. Throat first, she was sure. She took the knife and pushed heavily against the delicate skin, the sharp edge penetrating swiftly. She forced it deeper until she felt the blade scraping the spine, and her pleasure was mounting.

The next part was the abdomen, she withdrew the knife and plunged it through the leather skirt, her movements becoming frenzied as her gratification heightened. She tugged, and plunged, ripped, wrenched, sliced, slashed, the body yielding, falling apart.

The ferocious attack finished as quickly as it had begun. Paula stood slowly, the blood on her hands mixing with the sweat that oozed, she wiped her brow, mopping the exertion with her sleeve. Regarding the body, she saw there was little blood loss, as with her predecessor's first victim. Adelaide's platinum hair tumbled haphazardly over the lino, blood escaping from the neck wound matting into the roots, and her innards spilled from the multiple stabbings and shredding wounds.

Calm, Paula stepped to the kitchenette, her trainers marching the blood, she rinsed her hands, then the knife, replacing it in the sheath. She'd need it again soon. Paula tugged the gloves back on, she opened the fridge and tucked into a welcome feast.

Mary stepped through the door at half past three, the hall light had been left on for her benefit. Linda was still awake, but after last night's debacle she'd taken her worried waiting to bed, lest Mary's newly vicious tongue should lash out again. The relief flooded through her, maybe she would be able to sleep now, and the welcome sound of her daughter moving around the house comforted her. She curled into a ball on her side, her ears willing to listen long enough for Mary to settle into bed. The fridge door opened. The fridge door shut. The fridge door opened, some rustling, some slicing, the fridge door shut. Footsteps up the stairs, quiet and cautious. Lights off, door closed. Linda drifted off.

The gnawing hunger subsided quickly, Paula passed the body and mounted the stairs. Inside Adelaide's bedroom, she felt comfortable, it was clean, it was tidy, the order relaxed her. She flicked through Adelaide's clothes, she could do with a clean outfit, but her latest duty was a petite woman, and her clothes were tiny. The only thing of use that Paula retrieved was a small, red backpack.

In the bathroom, Paula began running a cool bath, the atmosphere too humid to even cope with a tepid wash. She added bubble bath, the froth appearing across the surface of the water almost instantaneously. Whilst waiting for the bath to fill, Paula stripped off and washed the clothes, concentrating on the blood spatters, wringing them harshly, and hanging them up to dry. She stepped into the refreshing water, feeling the grime, the filth, the spilled blood melting from her body. Her first bath in weeks. It was bliss.

Clean, freshened, revitalized, and relaxed, Paula climbed into Adelaide's comfortable bed, she dragged the covers over her naked body, relishing the warmth and comfort of a real mattress and down pillow. Lights off, Paula felt an embracing sleep descending, she sighed and enjoyed.

Sunday 31st August

Adelaide's body lay, tortured, broken, mutilated, on the cold linoleum floor of her hall. The crusted, blackened crimson spillage that surrounded, although minimal, was sickening. Silence echoed within her house, although outside life continued as normal, and children played delightedly, their voices chirruping happiness and laughter, oblivious to the horror lying behind the small green door they ran past frequently.

Beside the lacerated body, Paula sat with her head in her hands, as she had done since waking at six. She had enjoyed the duty immensely, there had been a slight sexual stirring, but the greatest pleasure had arisen from the power she'd had. She'd felt in control. Although God had been the one to instruct her on the killing, it was she who had done the research, found the victim, carried out the act. Taking in the pulverised body, she knew she had recreated Jack the Ripper's work perfectly.

But somewhere inside her head was an odd sensation, a remorse, and this confused her. Last night she'd relished her task, but this morning she felt saddened as she looked at the result. The cheery voices chiming from the street enhanced her melancholy, they stirred a lost memory. She knew she needed to move on, find a quiet place to stay, remote and undisturbed, somewhere to talk to God in privacy. She needed his reassurance that she was the chosen one more than ever if she was to have the strength to complete the next duty. She pulled the handwritten notes from her pocket, checking. September the eighth was the next one.

Paula stepped into the kitchenette, she prepared a sandwich with gloved hands, carefully cleaning up after herself. Emptying some food into a carrier bag, she placed it inside the new red bag, took a final look at her handiwork, and left the house, closing the door quietly, and walking towards the Whitechapel tube station.

Several children noticed the tall lady, her dark hair scraped into a ponytail, her oversized clothes, scruffy trainers, a pair of black gloves, but they quickly returned to their games, unaware of the carnage the woman had left behind her.

Mina and Craig remained at home while Craig's father, Ronald Lockington, took the organiser to Windsor Police Station on Alma Road. He had severely reprimanded his remorseful son that morning, he wasn't to steal, he wasn't to pry, and he must remember that his father is a company director who isn't willing to have his son tarnish his excellent reputation.

Abruptly, Ronald explained the situation to the desk sergeant, apologising for his son's behaviour, and promising to keep a tighter leash on him from now on. The desk sergeant appeared disinterested in the details at first, but something twigged in his mind. "Where did you say your son took this from?"

"Some old boathouse, not far from Boveney Lock." Ronald, impatient, checked his watch.

"Did he describe it at all, colour, anything at all?"

Ronald checked the door, anxious to get home. "I don't know, blue, I think, wooden. Tatty, run down."

The desk sergeant stood. "I won't be a moment, Sir." He left the room, much to the irritated Ronald's disgust. Returning promptly to the front desk, the desk sergeant took a pen. "Sir, we need to send a constable to interview your son, do you have any objections?"

Surprise flickered over Ronald's face, but he understood quickly, and his smile betrayed his advancing years. "To tick him off, make sure he won't do it again. By all means, be my guest."

Within half an hour PC Adams and PC Granaski sat before Craig and his parents in the decadent lounge of the impressive three story town house. Adams began, his voice and expression gentle to comfort the boy. "I need you to be honest, Craig. Were you and your friends playing with matches or lighters?"

Craig's face was pale, he glanced at his parents, hoping they would believe the truth. "No, honestly, we didn't, never, we wouldn't."

"Do you know that the boathouse you took the organiser from has burned down?"

The fright on his face was genuine. "No, we didn't do it. The old woman was weird, she scared us, she probably did it."

"Craig, I need you to describe this woman, I need you to tell me everything about her."

Craig gave a surprisingly adult account of Paula, her comings and goings, and the oddness of the situation was enough for Granaski, who took notes, and Adams, to believe she may have started the fire to cover her tracks. This was definitely suspicious. They related the details and their hunches to Detective Inspector Burns, copying the statement for him to study.

Burns was interested, arson was usually a destructive hobby or compulsion, but he took his subordinates' suspicions seriously. He attached the Oregon Osaris Personal Organiser to his PC, and noted there was a single file saved, named 'Duties'. He began to read, one page was enough to realise it may be important, and he printed the comprehensive details. Stapling the papers together, Burns returned to his desk and digested them, soaking the details in. Adams walked in, Burns nodded.

"Anything interesting on the organiser, Guv?"

His speech was drawn out, he was a man who liked to take his time, clear things in his mind before acting. "I need to contact the Met, can you find their number for me?"

Adams was back within minutes, brandishing the number. Burns dialled the switchboard, and soon he was directed to the incident room. Krein answered the phone. They exchanged names, and Burns soon got to the point of the call. "I think we have a personal organiser here that may be something to do with the Kopycat Killer."

Krein wasn't expecting this, words failed him for a while. Eventually he managed. "What makes you think that?"

Burns was grave. "The content of the single saved file has comprehensive details of past murders. Several are ones that Kopycat has recreated." Silence again, Burns could not hear the excitement flushing through Krein. "I could forward the file, if you like?"

Krein nodded vigorously. "Yes, yes please, I'll give you my email address. And bag the organiser immediately, have it couriered here. We need to run it through forensics."

Burns followed instructions, adding to the email the statement that Craig had given, and Burns's plans to investigate the remains of the boathouse. He sent constables to the three remaining boys to take statements, and arranged for two forensic experts to accompany him to Boveney to scour the site for evidence. The area was already cordoned off, arson having already been suspected, but the investigation had not been a priority. It was now.

He'd been there literally moments when he spotted the pale pink, charred paper, the plastic folder that contained it partly melted. Using tweezers, he dropped the document into a plastic bag, sealing it to avoid further contamination. Inspecting the writing through the clear pocket, it was apparent that the form was a driving licence. The print was almost totally illegible, but further examination in a controlled environment may reveal more than was currently evident.

The fire had been ferocious, the intensity assisted by the heat-wave, but initial observations showed that it had probably been fuelled with petrol, the molten green plastic container near where the door had been suggested so.

Before sending the licence to the forensic department, Burns noted what he could from the details. Later he discussed them with his colleague. "Come on Sarah, get your thinking cap on. Let's work this out." They scrutinised the notes.

'MR J - - K - - - / - REDER - - - / - - - OKS
FLAT -
WAR - - N - - - - - / COUR -
BEDF - - D
B - - - - -

BRO - -   90 - - - 3   - F 9 - -'

Sarah's initial thoughts came quickly. "Well, it's definitely Bedford, and the first five letters of a driver number are the first five letters of the surname, so the surname must be Brooks."

"Nice one. Right, copy it down, I want you to contact the DVLA, see if their computer can do a search with the details we have, and contact the Bedford station, see if they can help."

Krein printed the emailed attachment, reading the pages avidly. The recreated murders on past dates corresponded with the murders Kopycat had completed, and the next one was dated thirty first of August, the Jack the Ripper mutilation of Polly Nichols. Their suppositions had been right, Kopycat planned to be in Whitechapel tonight, and their vast operation was going to catch him. Krein forwarded the email to a colleague, requesting she send it to every member of the investigation team, and he basked in his new complacency.

Spencer drew a chair to Krein's desk, he listened intently, gradually smiling as he heard about the find in Windsor. He then produced a folder, and discussed the details of tonight's operation with Krein. The exercise would be concentrating on Brick Street, Whitechapel Road, and Durward Street, as that was the route Jack the Ripper had supposedly taken a hundred and twenty years before.

Obviously the area was totally different now. Whitechapel Road was now a main thoroughfare with heavy traffic travelling day and night. Durward Street, which had been Buck's Row in Jack the Ripper's day, was reasonably busy too. Krein considered how Kopycat was planning to kill in the open, without being seen by one of the many passers by. Spencer explained there were many alleyways along the route, and they would ensure that each and every one was policed.

The day was long and slow, Krein yearned for the evening to come, he couldn't wait to finally come face to face with the man he had hunted for so long.

Linda was distraught as she recapped the latest argument with her once wonderful daughter. She poured a large white wine, and turned the oven off, her appetite gone. She had been so proud when Mary had sailed through adolescence with barely a tantrum, she'd had no obvious interest in drugs, although Linda suspected some of her friends weren't so sensible. Mary had a healthy

243

respect for alcohol, and if she drank at all, it would be in moderation. She had a lovely face and a superb figure, and had avoided the trend of bulimia or anorexia. She was uncomplicated, funny, and clever. Quite simply, she had been a joy to raise. Until now.

Although Mary was in touch with her childhood contemporaries, she now favoured Natalie and Tara who she'd met at her first job in a fast food restaurant. Linda had hoped her daughter would hanker for a high profile career, but she was lazy, she was happy to earn enough money to get by and have fun, not understanding how heavily her parents subsidised her lifestyle. Sadly, Linda realised that five months was too long to be 'just a stage'.

Tired from her fitful sleep, Linda had awoken too late, and Mary had already breakfasted by the time she appeared, swollen eyed, downstairs. Initially Mary had excitedly whooped about the fun she'd had the previous night at the fantastic club in Whitechapel, innocently oblivious that she narrowly escaped drug rape. Linda, not anticipating the overdramatic response to come, mentioned the Kopycat Killer, and suggested visiting London on the anniversaries of the Ripper murders was probably not a good idea.

Mary threw a major tantrum, accusing her mother of ruining her fun, her life, stating she didn't want to be tied to Linda's apron strings, and that she must understand that Mary was now an adult, was entitled to go out whenever, and wherever, she wanted.

With the benefit of maturity, Linda remained calm, she reiterated that she was simply concerned, as any mother would be. Mary's selective hearing continued, and after declaring she would rebel if she wanted to, she snatched her jacket and stormed through the front door, slamming it for effect. Linda, lonely, worried, and pouring another drink to drown her fears, had no idea where her child was going.

Paula sat on the bench, her feet were aching, the walk to Victoria Park had been long and her ankle painful, accentuating the limp. She hadn't been unaccompanied, God had chatted away as she travelled, congratulating her on the previous night's duty, justifying its necessity, insisting on the work's importance and how she needed to continue because she was so lucky to have been chosen. Paula had discussed the issues, animatedly, unaware of the consternation in the people surrounding her, and she especially inquired why the duties were so far apart, reasoning that she enjoyed killing so much, she was eager to do it more often.

This had angered her Lord, his voice had boomed, vociferous in her head. She was to stick with the plans. If somebody got in her way, fine, get rid of them, but she was not to question his authority, ever. Paula had thanked God, out loud.

Now comfortable on the bench, she pulled out her notes, re-reading, and instilling the details in her mind once more. Just over a week to go.

Ivan unlocked the doors of the Wallingford Bar, sighing inwardly at the thought of yet another boring Sunday night, with the same boring people, the same boring jokes. At forty three he was jaded with bar work. Eleven years before he had achieved a dream, becoming the manager of, what was then, a run down pub. He'd spruced it up, turned the clientele around, changed the losses into profits. But, now the bar ran smoothly, there weren't any goals left to achieve, and he found each day increasingly tedious.

The work was unchallenging yet hard, the extended hours from the new legislation long, and being the boss came with a distinctive alienation. Ivan now wanted a peaceful life, he wanted a wife, and he wanted to leave the polluted city to enjoy a more rural existence, just take things easy. Maybe next year. He said that every year.

As always, Jim McRae was first in. A downcast, aging man, divorced, grown up kids, small room in a small house, an equally small job. His existence was having a brew or six at his favourite pub every day. He sat on the familiar bar stool he liked to call his own, leaning on the bar, facing the door to watch the punters entering. Without being asked Ivan brought him a pint of Guinness.

Jim gulped half the pint, and breathed out heavily with pleasure, licking the froth from his lips. "You pour a good pint, Ivan. No Adelaide tonight?"

Ivan glanced at the clock on the wall. "She's probably running a bit late. You know what she's like!"

Jim finished his pint, slamming the glass on the bar. Regular as clockwork, he stood up and went to the Gents, Ivan took the glass and refilled it, muttering. "Work was bloody awful today, I bloody hate it."

And Jim returned to his seat, stating. "Work was bloody awful today, I bloody hate it." Not realising that Ivan, his back turned to Jim, was mimicking.

One by one the special team of officers bundled into vans and squad cars for deportation to the designated streets of Whitechapel. The briefing had been intricate, and the officers were enthusiastic. Most Sundays were spent trawling the streets, diffusing bar fights, removing illegally parked cars, mundane duties. So hunting a national killer, the most dangerous man in Britain today, broke the monotonous tedium at every level. Spirits were high.

They were deposited in Brick Lane, each one strolling, vigilant, to their designated patch. PC Gooding sauntered into the Wallingford Bar, clocked Ivan, and went to meet him. Ivan had always found it paid to be friendly with the police, they turned their backs a little more easily. He issued a welcoming smile. "Evening."

"Evening." Gooding removed a photofit of Kopycat from a folder he carried. He passed it to Ivan. "Have you seen this man at all?"

"No." Ivan shook his head, his clientele tended to be older.

Gooding continued. "Would you keep it behind the bar, please Sir, and if the man comes in at all tonight, or even a tall woman resembling him, could you please contact us on that number." Gooding's finger traced the incident line number at the bottom of the page.

"You want me to put it on the wall?"

"No, let your staff see it, put it under the bar, but keep it discreet."

As Gooding left Ivan's thoughts turned to his staff. Adelaide. It was half past eight, usually she would phone if there was a problem. And then he remembered Roger Andrews the night before, and a vivid shudder spiralled down his spine. He took Jim's glass, as if on automatic pilot, and refilled it. Perhaps he should phone her?

Considering the ongoing heat-wave, it was surprisingly cold as the clocks ticked towards midnight. Krein sat with DS Panton in the unmarked police car on Durward Street, wishing he'd brought an overcoat. The pair observed life happening on the busy road, watching for unusual movements, irregular happenings.

The excited momentum of the day had long gone, Krein was overtired, and fed up. The adrenaline that had pulsed through his veins as the operation had begun had drifted away gradually, as nothing untoward happened. Krein sighed, it was going to be a long night. The original murder hadn't happened until roughly three thirty in the morning. Hours to go yet.

Paula was freezing. Although her damp clothes had dried in the heat of the day, a light blouse and flimsy skirt weren't enough to stave off the chilly breeze that rattled through the trees from Crown Gate Lake. Paula shivered as she walked briskly through Victoria Park. She'd spent the past few hours searching for a place to stay, an unlocked shed, boarded up house, anything to keep her from the cold and let her lay her head.

Money was never a problem, she'd replenished her pockets with Adelaide's hard earned cash, but she wanted to avoid bed and breakfast if possible, too much risk of being recognised.

The path met Old Ford Road, and she exited the park, aimlessly walking to keep her blood flowing. A car horn tooted and she jumped, turning to spy the driver; a middle aged, smart suited, bespectacled man. He motioned for her to come over. Lowering the electric window on the passenger side, the driver leant over, and Paula peered in, her face questioning.

The ogling leer on his face answered her simply. "Do you want a lift, love?" His grin, displaying his uneven teeth, was lecherous. To his amazement and delight, Paula opened the door and climbed in. The blood flow increasing to his genitals, Michael Ayrs drove away.

Securing the doors, Ivan left the Wallingford Bar. He was increasingly worried, having tried Adelaide's landline and mobile numerous times throughout the evening. She was a creature of habit, and this wasn't like her. Something was wrong, and his concern was tinged with guilt. He shouldn't have left her last night, should have slept on the sofa, that Roger Andrews was a predator and he was worried Adelaide had been his bait.

His steps were quick in the chilly air as he covered the distance to Adelaide's home. Police officers littered the streets, something was going on, and he guessed it had something to do with the photofit from earlier.

Eventually Ivan reached Durward Street, he stepped up to the green door, his concerns growing as he noted all the lights blazing behind the closed curtains. Adelaide was a penny pincher, and electricity cost money. He knocked, and placed his icy hands in trouser pockets. Waiting. He tried again, but still no reply. Now fearsome, something felt badly wrong, he called through the letterbox. The brightly lit house was silent, so, regrettably, as the scene would not leave him for the rest of his life, Ivan peered through.

Bile surged into his throat, the sight of his former lover's body ripped, shredded, brought the huge man to his knees. An uncontrollable wail surged from his throat, he was howling, baying, out of his macho control.

Krein had watched the colossal man approach the house, he'd noted the desperate knocking, and now he moved instantly towards the horrified figure, springing from the car, and across the street, up the short path. Pushing the hulk aside gently, Krein copied his movements, desperate to see what had broken the man. He saw, and his heart sank.

How could he have missed it? He'd been in Durward Street for over three hours. No one had entered the house. Nobody had left it. Panton, who had closely followed Krein's lead agreed to these facts. Automaton taking over, Krein radioed for assistance, and within an hour the house was broken into, cordoned off, the street alive with flashing blue lights and the buzz of policemen, paramedics, forensic experts. And vultures.

The man staggered across the pavement, not sure where he was, or where he was going. His hand was clasping his stomach, holding his intestines inside. His blood oozed prolifically, pumping from the gaping wound. He was tired, exhausted, but he couldn't stop. He needed a hospital. Now.

Michael Ayrs had been thrown, minutes before, from his own car. Events had happened so suddenly, he couldn't remember much, and his head was getting muzzier by the second. Struggling to recall: there was the attractive woman. Bitch! A flash of metal, then shock. Not pain, just shock. She'd pulled the handbrake. The car skidded full circle. And stopped. She'd pushed him onto the road. Moved onto his seat. Stolen his car. No accident. No cars to help him. Alone. She drove away.

Michael had struggled to his feet. Wobbly steps took him to the pavement. His eyes screwed up as pain overcame the shock. Was this the end? Needed help. Bleeding to death. Headlights shining behind. Muster strength. Got to stop. Stop the car.

It didn't stop. The car tooted angrily as the driver shook his fist through the open window, steering masterfully past the wounded man. Forlorn, Michael saw a ray of hope. A sign. Red sign. White H. Hospital nearby.

As Michael staggered through the doors of the All Saints Hospital in Lambeth his weary body finally gave up. He slumped to his knees, his body falling forward. A nurse shouted for assistance as she rushed towards him. She felt his pulse, it was speeding, signifying major blood loss. She moved his knee, forcing him into the recovery position, but his intestines spilled over the corridor, his grasp released. A hardened nurse, her stomach lurched. Assistance arrived, they needed to get the man into surgery immediately, and within seconds he was attached to a drip, generously donated blood products being pumped into his body, as his own gushed out.

It was doubtful he would survive the night.

Monday 1st September

The crucial members of the investigation team were assembled in the incident room, heads down, shoulders drooping, nobody spoke although they all knew what was coming. The heavy footsteps neared the door, and the hearts of the twelve men leapt into their chests. Falder-Woodes, followed by Superintendent Brannigan, entered, and the men stopped slouching, needing to appear credible somehow.

The two superiors took centre stage, their presence daunting, and through gritted teeth, Brannigan spoke concisely. "What went wrong?" His words were quiet, although they may as well have been shouted for the effect they had. The twelve heads dropped again, feet shuffling, nobody could answer, because nobody knew. "Well?" His voice was rising, his fury palpable. He slammed his fist on the desk before him, and now his yelling could be heard across the first floor. "I'm asking a bloody question, damn it! What the bloody hell went wrong?"

Spencer was the bravest man in the room. "The operation was planned to perfection, I have no idea how Kopycat slipped through our surveillance."

And he wished he hadn't been brave, for the venom was now directed at him. "The newshounds are going to make bloody mincemeat of us. This isn't bloody Mickey Mouse we're playing with! Find out what went wrong, and sort it. I want no more killings, do you hear me! Enough of this. Enough of our time and money has been wasted playing bloody games with this madman."

"Sir." Spencer felt like an idiot now.

"I want a full report, on my desk, by five this evening."

The telephone on Krein's desk began to ring, he didn't move to answer until Brannigan and Falder-Woodes turned to leave. "Krein. Yes, he's here." Krein moved the phone from his ear. "It's for you." He passed the receiver to Barry Harner, whose face paled as he listened. He motioned to stop the superiors leaving, Spencer tapped Brannigan and nodded to Harner as he ended the call.

Harner's voice was quiet and resigned. "I know what caused the error. The buck stops with me. Can I talk to you in private, Sir?"

Krein came through the doors, he took a cigarette from the packet, lit it, and inhaled deeply, his head instantly dizzying, his throat tempting a cough. The doors opened once more, and Spencer stepped out, his own cigarette packet in his hand. "I didn't know you smoked, Krein."

"I don't, I nicked these from Panton." Krein took another drag, he'd given up tobacco ten years before, but knew that the nicotine buzz was the only thing that would relax him right now. "Bloody idiots!"

"I haven't heard the full story, have you?"

A mother pushing a buggy wrinkled her nose with a disgusted glare as she walked by, but Krein just returned her rudeness: he didn't care. "You won't believe it, well, I don't. The Black Museum Bunch gave us the wrong date."

"No they didn't, I checked myself on the Net. Polly Nichols was killed on the thirty first of August, eighteen eighty eight."

"At three thirty in the morning."

Comprehension slowly passed over Spencer's face, soon replaced by disgust. "She died on the night of the thirtieth, not the thirty first as we were instructed."

"You've got it. And I would bet my life that the autopsy will show that Adelaide Smith died in the early hours of the thirty first." Krein took a final drag, the tobacco now burned to the filter, he held his breath in for a while, before exhaling slowly. He had no idea whether to light another or just leave smoking at the miniscule blip of one paltry mistake. He threw the butt, extinguishing it with his foot.

"Shit. Harner's going to be on the firing line then."

Decision made. Krein pulled out another cigarette. "Deserves to be too. He's a great bloke, but that stupid error, or assumption, whatever it was, that led to a woman's death. Somebody's got to be accountable, and as he said, the buck stops with him."

"No it doesn't, it stops with Falder-Woodes."

Krein's face was grey, he felt the guilt as keenly as every other member of the team. His smoky sigh was deep and regretful. "It stops with each and every one of us. We all should have spotted the mistake. We're all to blame for Adelaide Smith's death, and you know it."

Linda threw the newspaper on the table, finished her tea, and stood, stretching away her hangover. Stepping across the room, she refilled the kettle as Mary strolled in, a towelling turban coiled around her head, showcasing her delicate features.

"Morning, love. Cup of tea?" Mary nodded, seating herself at the table. She dragged the newspaper over, the headlines bringing a grimace. "The Kopycat Killer's struck again." Linda needlessly quoted the words.

"I can see." Mary's banality halted the 'I told you so' that was about to follow. "That guy, the one who used to be my father until he fell in love with a serial killer ..."

"Mary!" Although she stuck up for Krein, Linda understood the sentiment.

"Was he there?"

She wanted to lie, to make everything rosy, but she couldn't. "I don't know where your father is any more. I haven't spoken to him since Friday, and even then he was distant."

"You want to divorce him, don't you?"

Linda was completely taken aback, she had no idea where that had come from. She shook her head glibly, unable to answer. In fact, she was scared of the answer.

Mary's matter of factness was back, and her hypocrisy took over. "I think you're being selfish. The Kopycat case is horrid, and you should support him more, instead of harping on about yourself all the time."

Horrified, and despairing, Linda placed a mug of tea before her daughter, she took her own and left the room, only just making through the door before the first tear of many tumbled down her cheek.

Paula woke, soon realising she had spent the night in the driver's seat of the stolen Audi. Her neck was stiff and her back ached from sleeping in such an awkward position. Unsure of her location, Paula glanced through the window, the sky was uncommonly grey, tepid raindrops pattering gently on the roof of the car, which was surrounded densely by trees. She had no recollection of where she'd driven to, but was grateful it was private.

She had a vague memory of getting into the car, of the lecherous man, and a smile spread widely as she saw the bloodied knife lying on the passenger seat. Now she remembered what she had done. He had wanted her, had tried it on, so she'd stabbed him and stabbed him, stabbed him and ripped. His face was a picture, and she laughed at the memory of throwing him from the car. Jack the Ripper had described slashing his victims as 'opening them like a ripe peach', and she now knew what he meant. She hadn't enjoyed the girl anywhere near as much as the man. And now she had a car to live in until the next duty. She was sure God wouldn't mind her doing an extra job, he'd understand it was necessary. She hoped he would speak, but he didn't.

Her tummy growled, she opened the red bag and pulled out an apple, stolen from Adelaide's fridge, biting into its freshness, the crunchiness tickling her taste buds. She took the notes out, eager to re-read the details of the next duty.

The atmosphere was overly subdued in the incident room. Every member of the team reeled with guilt, with stupidity, with lack of attention to detail. Krein doubly felt the angst, because it was he, and he alone, who had cocked up on the Katherine Black shooting. He'd promised himself that he would check every fine detail from then on, and he hadn't. If he'd had been a better officer, dotting the 'i's and crossing the 't's, two innocent women would still be alive. His wretchedness caused physical pain.

Everyone involved with the hunt for the Kopycat Killer felt keenly idiotic, the error was so gaping, so simple.

Spencer perused the details of Michael Ayr's stabbing the night before. He'd died during surgery, and was now classed as a murder victim. It was Spencer's choice whether to attribute it to Kopycat, or treat it, like it probably was, a group of youths out for a bit of 'fun' and some extra money. He picked up the phone. "Is that forensics? I want you to do comparisons on the injuries of both Michael Ayrs and Adelaide Smith before the post-mortems, specifically to know if the same weapon was used on both."

Replacing the receiver, Spencer glanced at Krein, who had overheard. They both knew he was being over-cautious, but they both knew why as well.

The heat wave had finally broken, seemingly for good, and the sky was as grey as the mood in Scotland Yard. Rain had pelted constantly throughout the day, hammering on the windows, relentless. Krein didn't want to stop working. He didn't want to eat, he didn't want to sleep, he didn't want a drink, a cigarette, a coffee, anything. He knew from the personal organiser that Kopycat's next planned 'duty' was the eighth of September, and once more a massive operation was in preparation. He needed to ensure that everything was correct, and they would finally end the hunt for the horrific murderer.

Big Ben had just struck six when two separate reports were thrown onto Krein's desk, he glanced at the disappearing sergeant, and took a look at the paperwork. Autopsy reports. Keen, Krein took the first: Adelaide Smith, at London Hospital. She was forty-three, a hundred and fifty eight centimetres tall, a hundred and thirty four pounds in weight. All internal organs intact, except for her uterus, which was absent.

Krein re-read the last sentence, a sickening gnawing at his stomach, he knew that Jack the Ripper removed the wombs of a couple of his victims. But reading further, Krein was relieved to see that Adelaide had had a hysterectomy four years before.

Adelaide's last meal had been taken approximately at nine in the evening, it wasn't a full meal, a couple of handfuls of peanuts, a bag of crisps. She had approximately eighty milligrams of alcohol per litre of blood in her system at the time of death, so she had been too tipsy to drive legally, but not drunk.

Adelaide had been strangled, the cause of death was asphyxiation. It had been done with bare hands, that was apparent from the bruising on the parts of her neck that were still intact. She was dead before her neck was cut, and before her body was stabbed. There were three deep cuts to the neck, one of them so deep it scratched the cervical vertebrae. There were twelve stab wounds in her abdomen, the knife had been thrust from directly in front, with a right hand, which they could tell by the angle of the stab wound. Before removing the knife, the killer had dragged it down, leaving gaping wounds. One wound, the largest at just over thirteen centimetres long, had been forced open and her bowels had been pulled through and left on top of her skin.

The attack had not been overly frenzied, which was odd for the severity of the injuries. It appeared that the killer had been taking his time to pay attention to detail, in recreating Polly Nichol's wounds a hundred and twenty years before. Definitely the work of Kopycat, Krein thought to himself.

He put the report down, and took Michael Ayr's results. Michael had been stabbed eight times, once through the heart, and that was the injury which had killed him. His spleen, liver, and left kidney were slashed. The knife had been thrust at him from his left hand side, probably with a left hand. Seven stab marks were clean cuts, in the eighth the knife was dragged down before being retracted. This had caused his torn intestines to fall from his body.

Michael's killer was believed to be left handed, Adelaide's right handed. But from the casts taken, they appeared to be perpetrated by a similar weapon. The summary, as yet, was inconclusive.

The phone rang, Krein answered automatically, his mind distant. "DI Krein? There's a man in reception wants to see you about the woman who was killed last night. His name is Ivan Stulski."

Krein knew the name, he remembered the man. He sighed and trotted towards reception, taking the huge man into an interview room. Ivan's tired face was worn, the worries of the world etched deeply.

Seated, Ivan hung his head, his demeanour was nervous, agitated, and he fingered a newspaper in his hand. Eventually he threw it onto the table. "The papers say this was the work of the

256

Kopycat Killer. I know who it was who killed her, but I don't think he's the Kopycat."

Krein was astonished, he hadn't expected that. "Give me a minute, Mr Stulski." Krein located an inactive colleague, and a spare tape, which he fed into the recorder, clicking it on. "I am Detective Inspector Krein, also present are Constable Hopkins and Mr Ivan Stulski. The date is Monday the first of September, two thousand and eight, the time is," he glanced at his watch, "eighteen twenty seven. Mr Stulski, could you please tell me why you believe you know who killed Adelaide Smith."

"It was Roger Andrews, I'm sure about that. He often comes into my bar ..."

"Your bar?"

"I am the landlord of the Wallingford Arms in Brick Lane. Roger Andrews is a rough bloke, he thinks he's God with the ladies. Well, the night before last ..."

"What date, exactly?"

"Um, it was Saturday night, would be the thirtieth of August. Adelaide was doing her Saturday shift, and Roger wouldn't leave her alone. He kept pestering her, asking her to stay the night with him. Well, Addy isn't, er, wasn't that sort of woman, she was decent, and she said no, but he got angry, saying she'd led him on, she was a prick teaser, that sort of thing. Addy was used to problem customers, it was part of her job, but he was so abusive she got scared and asked me if I would walk her home. Of course I agreed.

"Anyway, after closing time, Roger was the last to leave, he kept glaring at Addy, in fact I was just about to ask him to go when he upped and left. We decided to wait a while before I took her home, so we shared a bottle of wine. We ended up leaving at about one in the morning.

"I walked her home and she said something odd. She said she could feel someone staring at her. I looked behind, but I couldn't see anyone, but maybe we were followed, I don't know. Anyway, she got back safely, I said goodbye, and she went in."

"Did you see her shut the door?"

"No, but I heard it as I was walking away."

"So you think that this Roger Andrews followed you both, then somehow got in and killed her?"

"I'm sure he did. As I said, he's a rough guy. Let's put it this way, I wouldn't trust him with any woman, and he didn't like to be turned down. He's got a big ego."

"Do you know where he lives?"

"Sorry, I don't."

"Thank you, Mr Stulski."

Sarah had contacted the DVLA, and the Welsh lady had been extremely helpful, her comely warmth comforting. The driving licence had been deciphered easily, it belonged to a Mr Jackson Frederick Brooks, Flat 6, Warmingford Court, in Bedford. Sarah typed the details into the Police National Computer, and it was immediately tagged to the Kopycat Killer investigation, as expected.

Krein was obviously interested, this was enough to prove the killer had been in residence of a boathouse for the previous week, and he asked for the evidence to be couriered to him. But Krein still realised that the most important part of his job now was not hankering after the killer's past, it was pre-empting the future, and ensuring another life wasn't lost before they halted the twisted man.

Two constables had brought Roger Andrews in just after ten in the evening, after he had returned to his room in Buxton Street. He was drunk, he was abusive, and had refused to come initially. The officers had foolishly, so Krein thought, arrested him on suspicion of murder, which put a timely pressure onto the interview. In normal circumstances, Krein would have left him to sober up before interviewing him, but his need for answers, for explanations, was ripe, and only Andrews would be able to ease his mind enough to sleep tonight.

Andrews sat in the seat that Ivan Stulski had occupied earlier that day, his scorned mouth uttering venomous, irrelevant spewings. Krein turned the tape recorder on, he introduced the persons present.

"Mr Andrews. We have been approached by a witness who states that you were bothering a lady by the name of Adelaide Smith at the Wallingford Bar on Saturday night, the thirtieth of August."

"Bothering her! Fuck off! She's a tart and she was flirting all the way. She's just a prick teaser, you know, make you think you're gonna get it, then cry off. It's bitches like her who get raped, that's what I should have done, stupid tart."

Krein marvelled at how Andrews was incriminating himself. "Are you aware that Adelaide Smith was brutally murdered on Saturday night?" A flicker of his own guilt passed quickly, and the enjoyment returned.

Andrews was openly shocked, his mouth dropped wide, his eyes startled, and Krein had to admit this guy was an excellent actor. Or innocent. Eventually the strangled words came. "You think it was me?"

"Did you murder Adelaide Smith?"

"No. No way. I didn't touch her." And at this point Andrews realised the only way he could prove his innocence would be to admit raping the redhead he'd picked up at the nightclub. The dilemma was terrific, murder or rape. Or maybe both? Roger Andrews had never felt so small.

"You were seen shouting abuse at her in the Wallingford Bar. We have witnesses to prove it."

Andrews was shaking his head, violently, suddenly innocent and childlike. "No. I mean, I did, she wouldn't come home with me, I fancied her, I wanted a shag. But I left when the pub closed, I went to the Vortex Club. Loads of people saw me."

"Any names, addresses?"

Andrews was flustered, he felt trapped. He just wanted to scream, tell them all to go away, leave him alone. His confusion remembered Mary. "There was a girl, Mary I think. Mary Crane, Creen, something like that. I was dancing with her. I've seen her there before."

Krein managed to veil the discomfort of hearing his own daughter's name from the mouth of a potential killer, but he realised it was probably an odd coincidence. He continued to bluff. "You'd better try and remember a bit more about the mysterious Mary, let's just say if she doesn't turn up to back you up, you'll be going down for a long time." Krein knew he had little on Andrews, but fear often produced the truth. "You can stay in the cells tonight, see if you can think a bit clearer tomorrow."

As Krein left the room, he knew Roger Andrews wasn't 'also known as' the Kopycat Killer, and he doubted he was guilty of Adelaide's horrendous mutilation. But the use of his daughter's name, however coincidental, made him uncomfortable. The shout behind him was unexpected. "I can prove I didn't kill Adelaide."

Krein turned back, popping his head back into the room. Andrews had sagged, his head was hung, his shoulders drooping, his stamina and fight long gone. "I was too busy drug raping a red-headed tart." Krein thanked the God he didn't believe in that his daughter's hair was black.

Saturday 6th September

Krein had only returned to his temporary room three times in a week, simply to have a shower and catch up on his sleep. Most nights he spent sleeping restlessly at his desk, having fallen into a fitful slumber over his paperwork. Spencer was concerned, Krein was too deeply involved, but he also knew that Krein's commitment, dedication, and obsession would help them to finally seek out the man they hunted.

A massive operation was being planned for the next night, an enhanced recreation of the previous week's manoeuvre. The Black Museum Bunch had ensured that the details of Annie Chapman's murder by Jack the Ripper were watertight, Barry Harner's ears were still ringing from the disciplining he'd been given. The investigation team who worked from the incident room consisted of twenty-four police officers, and twelve assistants. An extra hundred officers were being shipped in to support the exercise the next evening. The heavy, and visible, policing would hopefully prevent a killing, acting as a deterrent. Nobody, except Kopycat, wanted any more deaths. The Home Office couldn't object to the expense, the public outrage being so great.

The decision to plant eleven plain clothed female officers to act as decoys was controversial, but Falder-Woodes had stood firm, better they with their knowledge and defence skills than an innocent passer-by. They would be wired and tracked.

Roger Andrews's alibi had checked out, the traumatised girl hadn't reported her rape to the police, but was willing to press charges following his admission. However, he'd retracted his statement, claiming he was coerced into confessing to a crime he hadn't committed. He was absolved of the Kopycat murders completely by proving he was in Greece on holiday at the time Katie Joyce was killed, but the police now had to prove the rape, and unfortunately the girl had cleaned herself thoroughly before the police had tracked her down.

Fibres picked from the linoleum in Adelaide's hallway had been analysed, and these matched some found in the remains of the boathouse.

Krein scanned every forensic report he received, feeling increasingly frustrated. They had a forensic trail proving where the man had been from the start, but he remained one step ahead at all times. Krein had been convinced they would catch Kopycat the week before, and when the operation was shown to have been a pathetic sham, he'd been floored. Because of the tremendous disappointment, he was loath to raise his hopes about the coming exercise. He also realised that they had to catch the killer, because he, personally, couldn't take the strain any longer, he could feel himself going under.

Linda was gazing through the window of the quaint teashop, her eyes scanning, subconsciously, the dresses in the Laura Ashley display opposite. Bored and unwanted, unneeded, she'd come into Oxford centre to wilfully waste some cash, but none of the shops along the Cornmarket had tempted her, and she realised she was just trying to fill a void with her credit card.

Absent-mindedly, she stirred her cooling drink, her thoughts lost in the state of her marriage. She had already recognized it was over, but she needed to work out what came next. Did she move out? Did he? Did he even still live there? How would Mary take the news? How would David? A deep voice sounded, Linda jumped, suddenly embarrassed when she saw the handsome stranger beside her.

"I'm sorry, I didn't mean to startle you." With horror, Linda realised her face was reddening. "Would you mind if I sat with you, all the other tables are full."

Suddenly bashful, she nodded without smiling, and turned to the window, extremely aware of his presence, resenting it. He laid his tray down, and sat. "My name is Gordon Watts." She was aggravated. She wasn't in the mood to talk, her mind was elsewhere. But she was also polite, and would hate to be rude. She introduced herself, and the niceties turned into a pleasant conversation, which, in turn, developed into an interesting debate. She was amazed when she next checked her watch, two hours and endless cups of tea had elapsed. And she'd enjoyed herself. And he'd relished her company. Someone on the planet found her intriguing. Her thoughts probing into her past, she couldn't remember the last time she had felt so alive, had talked so animatedly, had captured somebody's attention so fully.

When Gordon invited her for a meal that evening, Linda knew that his choice of restaurant, The Bear Hotel in Woodstock, was wonderful, romantic, expensive, and that his company would suit the setting. Hesitating only for a second, she agreed to go.

The girls had been excitedly shopping for new clothes to wear that evening on their trip to London, and now they were making their way back to the bus stop. They were passing the Laura Ashley store when Nat tugged at Mary's sleeve. She pointed at the teashop across the road. "Isn't that your mum in there?"

Squinting, Mary was horrified to see her mother chatting animatedly to an unknown man, and when she noticed his hand laying over hers, she felt sick. Mary grabbed Nat and Tara's arms, directing them towards the bus stop. "Nope. That's not mum, just looks a bit like her."

At his desk, his new home, in the incident room on the first floor, inside New Scotland Yard, Krein pored over the report on Annie Chapman's death, over the plans for the next night's manoeuvre. Obsessed with a killer. Obsessed with his work. Obsessed with himself. Oblivious that he was about to lose his wife to another man. Would he even notice? And would he even care? Redundant questions. There was only one person on his mind.

It was the fifth day that the Audi had been Paula's hideout. She took frequent walks to stretch her legs, but the rest of the time was spent either sleeping, or preoccupied with remembering the fine details of the Ripper murders. The time was nearing, there was one night to go, and it was essential she got all the details correct, otherwise God might leave her. Her eyes tired with concentration, Paula glanced through the window. The car was parked in a secluded copse amongst the tree filled Burnham Beeches, which lay to the west of Slough. The roads that twisted through the woodland were narrow, and only busy during the morning and evening commuting. Paula had driven away from the roads, along a pinched track, it had been a perfect place to hide from the world. Occasionally people passed nearby, lovers, dog walkers, adventurous children, but Paula had not been disturbed as yet.

The trees surrounding acted like guards, tall and strong, sturdy and mature, their branches dancing in the light breeze as birds flitted over them, hunting for dinner, or just playing. Scenes of nature no longer gave Paula pleasure. Only one thing did. Killing. It was all she wanted to discuss with God, and He felt the same, refusing to change the subject. Sometimes Paula felt a rage, that silly little voice kept piping up, unexpectedly, and she wished it had a form, because then she would be able to kill it, extinguish the pathetic drivelling.

Paula was unaware that her hideout had actually been discovered. Two hours before Mrs Cross had reported the car to the police. She walked her Labrador through the beautiful woodland every day, and had become increasingly concerned about the vehicle, with a single inhabitant, that had been concealed amongst the trees for several days. Uninterested, the police had agreed to send a squad car to the site, laughing behind her back, labelling her a nosy busybody. Regardless, the two young constables were nearing the spot she had directed them to.

Paula, still gazing through the window, jumped when the bright light flashed nearby. She sat straight, peering in the direction, and realised it had been the sun reflecting from the mirror of a police car. It was heading towards her, she was about to be found. Wasting no time, Paula slipped on her battered trainers, leaving the laces undone, there was no time to waste. She grabbed the red bag and scrabbled out of the car, running, speeding, racing away, not giving in to the shooting pains that emanated from her injured ankle. The undergrowth tried to trip her, she stumbled time and again, but she couldn't let the police catch her, tomorrow's duty was too important.

The squad car pulled up behind the Audi, the two policemen stepping out to investigate the abandoned vehicle. One radioed the registration number through to the control room, and soon they discovered that the car belonged to a Michael Ayrs, of Islington, London.

Less than a minute later the radio crackled again, the flustered, excitable desk sergeant stated that Michael Ayrs had been fatally stabbed last week in London, it was suspected that the perpetrator was the infamous Kopycat Killer. He was sending Scene of Crime Officers immediately, and the two constables weren't to touch anything until assistance arrived. The team in London were notified immediately.

Mrs Cross was surprised to see the officers when she opened the door. She'd expected them to check out the car, but without further involvement from herself. She scanned the neighbours quickly to ensure her visitors had been noticed, and let the gentlemen in. Seating the men comfortably she, despite their refusals, produced a tray full of tea and biscuits. She fed a couple to the dog before sitting herself neatly beside her television-addicted husband.

Asked to describe the occupant of the car, Mrs Cross couldn't really help, she'd not been close enough to see the woman properly. She'd had her hair in a ponytail, she was wearing a filthy white blouse. She'd never left the car any of the times she'd been walking nearby, so Mrs Cross couldn't describe any other clothing.

When shown the photofit of Kopycat, Mrs Cross suddenly understood the importance of her find. It hadn't occurred to her that the driver may be a man. Her blood chilled when she realised how close she'd been to the violent filth. But her self-importance and forthcoming gossip more than made up for that. She couldn't wipe the smile from her face.

The car was removed in its entirety from the scene and delivered to the forensics laboratory. Pools of dried blood were proven to have come from Michael Ayrs: they now suspected that he had been killed for his car.

It was getting late, the evening chill was setting in. Again, they knew where Kopycat had been, but they had to find where he was going. As soon as the link to the murderer had been established, all hands at the local police stations had been addressed, and the search for the man, whose locality was now known to be close, became intense. The woodlands of Burnham Beeches were combed on foot, and patrol cars chugged through the streets, searching, probing. It appeared, as darkness began to deepen, that once more, Kopycat was invisible.

When Krein had returned to his desk with a plastic cup of coffee, and found a spray can of deodorant on his desk, he immediately, shamefully, realised he hadn't had a shower for thee days, and sheepishly left the office to freshen up.

The shower had been remarkable, it had perked him up and made him feel nearly human once more. He collected his things together and stepped back out into the light rain. The room was just under half a mile from the Yard, and the journey was pleasant, invigorating.

He was completely unaware that his daughter, flanked by her new best friends, and also freshly showered, was at Oxford Railway Station, waiting for the train to London. Their trips to the Vortex Club were becoming a weekly occurrence, and Mary, Nat and Tara were excitedly chattering about the forthcoming evening to come.

Opening the double doors to the Yard, Krein bumped into Spencer, who updated him on the new developments. At first they appeared to be major leads, but, after digesting facts further, Krein was dismayed to realise that they were still just as far from catching the man as they had been before they'd updated his trail. The DNA would only pin him down in a court of law. The operation the next night was paramount, and the enormity of that worried Krein.

Linda smoothed her dress, checking her reflection in the mirror by the front door. She'd not had the chance to dress up for ages, and was surprised at how well she turned out with a bit of effort. She took her handbag and keys, and strolled nervously to the car.

Starting the engine, Linda pulled away, her mind whirring. She knew she should feel some guilt, but the anger at the way she was treated surfaced in its place. Mary's behaviour had transposed from a genuinely nice young lady, to a vicious mouthed, unruly, nasty brat. Linda realised this was probably a backlash of feeling abandoned by her father, but what about her? She'd been abandoned too, but there was no one for her to direct her resentment at.

She thought of the man she was about to meet up with. He treated her like a precious jewel, he made her feel youthful, attractive, he made her laugh, and he wanted to make her feel special. In comparison, David hadn't phoned since he'd been back in London. The only contact she'd had was the one time she'd called him, and even then he'd easily belittled her.

There had been cracks in the marriage for years, both parties ignoring them, patching them up, scraping on Polyfilla. In retrospect Linda realised that it had died for her on their twenty fifth anniversary. He'd forgotten. He'd worked. She wasn't special enough for him to break with routine. Maybe he was having an affair himself, she didn't even see him often enough to spot the signs. No, Linda didn't feel remorseful in the slightest. She was looking forward to seeing Gordon. If no one else wanted her, why shouldn't she?

Mary stepped into the Vortex Club, the doorman acknowledging her with recognition, followed by her friends. Surprise registered as a policeman stepped towards her, asking her name. Two officers were asking every girl who entered the club. When she replied, he tagged the other officer. "Wilky, I've got her. Can you give us five minutes of your time, please, Mary?" She glanced at her worried friends, nervous, and nodded.

She followed them to an office no bigger than an under-stairs cupboard, and Wilkinson broke the ice. "Well, Mary. I'm glad you got here early. It would have been a real bore to have to talk to pretty young women all night, waiting for you!" The other policeman chuckled.

Mary had no idea what was happening, and her thoughts turned to her embarrassing mother. "Oh God, it's Mum, isn't it?

She's panicking about that bloody killer again, isn't she? How embarrassing can she be!"

Wilkinson shook his head. "I need to ask a few questions about a man who states he was with you for some time last week. Can I clarify you were here on Saturday the thirtieth?"

"We were here, yes." Mary wanted her Dad. She missed him, and she was scared.

"Did you spend some time with a man named Roger Andrews?"

Mary's face paled, had he done something wrong and implicated her because she'd spurned him? "Yes I did. A lot of the evening, actually."

"Do you know the time you parted company?"

"No, I've no idea. Look, am I supposed to have done something wrong? Has he? What's this all about?" Mary was beginning to feel miffed, she was missing out on important partying time.

"A young girl is pressing charges, she's accused him of drug rape."

Mary swallowed hard. She clearly remembered Roger pushing drinks on her, requesting glasses, not bottles. He'd offered her a bottle of what she'd assumed was just Coke when she'd snubbed him. At that moment Mary knew she'd tell these men every detail she could possibly recall. And she remembered every word of warning her mother had issued. And she realised that she loved her Mum, she missed her, and she wished she were here right now.

Gordon gently took Linda's hand in his own, they'd had a tremendous meal, the food delicious, the conversation better, and now he was escorting her to her car. He was a colossal man, inches taller than her estranged husband, and his hand felt protective and loving. The sparks were there, and when they were in each other's company the electric crackled, the room may as well be empty for all the regard they took of their surroundings. Obviously it was early days, but Linda could sense that Gordon would be a special part of her life.

They reached the car, basking in the warmth of their affections, he stooped, and the kiss they shared was sensual, delicious, tempting. He tasted perfect, and she greedily wanted more, but he was a gentleman, he pulled away, leaving her hungry. Starving.

Arrangements were made for a date the next Wednesday, and she climbed into her car, regretfully. Linda wanted to stay, to enjoy the intensity for longer. On the drive home she thought about the conversation they'd shared. She'd been totally honest about the situation with David, in fact he'd been impressed about the case her husband was working on. He'd even attempted to defend David's obsession, Gordon had been following the hunt for Kopycat in the newspapers and could understand the pressure David must be experiencing.

That moment had produced the only tinge of guilt Linda had felt all evening. She'd changed the subject swiftly, moving on to Mary, and how her behaviour had double flipped. Gordon had held her hands, radiating sympathy, and she had absorbed it as sexual stirrings. The smile on her reddened lips was rare for Linda, nowadays, as she drove home, mildly ecstatic. She felt no need for a drink, the whisky, brandy, wine, pain reducing therapies, replaced with being wanted, needed, cherished and loved. Linda slept easily.

When Mary arrived home at four in the morning, she found no waiting light to welcome her, no sleepless mother to admonish, and no father's knee to sit on whilst he cuddled her better. She wanted to cry out her fears to her mother, but for the first time ever, she wasn't there for her.

Paula had run, galloping through the trees, along the streets, past the gardens, beside the pond. The pain hadn't halted her, she knew the police would be on her trail. The night descending had been a blessing, giving her the veil of darkness to cover her tracks. She knew she needed to become Paul again, they knew they were after a woman, but finding the new disguise without drawing attention to herself was a problem.

Paula's resentment seethed, her nostrils still flared with rage, even though hours had passed since she'd had to leave the car.

Someone had ratted on her, and if she ever discovered who it was, she'd rip them to pieces with her bare hands. Paula became aware that she was breaking her skin with her fingernails, she loosened her grip, letting the blood flush out, lightly.

She'd been walking for miles, and for the past three hours had been trying doors, unsuccessfully. People were too safety conscious nowadays. Birds had begun their early hunt for the worm, singing merrily as they toiled, and Paula, drained, trudged up yet another back path. The handle creaked, and the door welcomed her in. Surprise was followed by relief, flowing alongside the throbbing in her lower leg.

Paula felt an adoring cat rubbing around her ankles, she kicked it harshly away, and crept towards the stairs. In the cupboard underneath she found a hammer, arming herself with it in one hand, and her knife in the other. The stairs creaked as she tiptoed up, but the sound of sleep remained constant. Into the room that heralded the snoring, she gazed at the form in the bed, knowing that she was about to please her God.

The old man didn't have a chance. Aware in his sleep of a presence, his eyes had sprung open, fear already radiating from his face. In the darkness he could distinguish a tall woman, he struggled up the bed, but she moved hastily. The blow on his head blackened his eyes, he felt no pain, just surprise, and he could feel the warm liquid flowing through his white hair. Everything went blank. He was gone.

Paula opened the antique oak wardrobe with gloved hands, stripping her soiled clothes simultaneously. The brown tweed trousers that she shook from the hanger would be short and tight, but they would transform Paula into Paul once more. She grabbed a thick jumper, the heat wave was long gone, autumn was advancing. A couple of vests, shirts, a cloth cap, some socks, pushing them into the red bag. The new disguise collected, Paula traipsed to the bathroom, snatching a final glance at the dead man. She'd have a good scrub, spruce herself for the duty the next night, and reassume her alter ego, Paul.

Monday 8th September

It had been a long, tedious night. The church bells tolling midnight had welcomed the chilly, damp Monday, and Krein was exhausted, weeks of stilted sleep behind him. The past six and a half hours had been spent in an unmarked car in Hanbury Street, and nothing out of the ordinary, as far as he and Panton could surmise, had happened.

According to the detailed notes from the recently chastised Black Museum Bunch, Annie Chapman, Jack the Ripper's second acknowledged victim, had been murdered between five and five thirty in the morning, so, if Kopycat's attention to detail was still important to him, then they still had hours to wait. If, indeed, he planned to recreate the murder at all. There was no guarantee he would.

Krein sighed deeply and glanced over at Panton, who nonchalantly picked at the skin on his fingers, he sighed again. They'd barely exchanged a word all night. There was no animosity, just nothing to say, talking would reduce concentration, and that was integral. Krein opened the door. It had been too cold to leave a window open in the car, and the atmosphere was stuffy, reeking of male odour, uncomfortably thick. The pollution of London swooped through the car, but it was fresher than the air it chased out. Krein moved to a low wall, sitting, clearing out his lungs deeply with each deep breath.

A movement in the corner of his eye grabbed Krein's attention. He could see an old man limping into the street at the junction. He jumped back to the car, closing the door quietly, praying the man hadn't spotted him. Through the windscreen Krein logged the man's description into his memory. Fairly tall, his hair was pale. Pale? It wasn't white, maybe ginger. He was balding but it wasn't the usual male pattern, and that intrigued Krein. He hadn't grown through the top of his hair, the patches were sporadic, clumps were missing in irregular places. The tweed trousers were short and tight, revealing white socks, and tatty trainers. Strangely, he carried a scarlet backpack. There were

271

too many anomalies about this character, and Krein's interest was heightened.

The man was level with the car now, walking on the opposite side of the street, and Krein, who had sunken into his seat, was watching in the mirror. The man turned the corner into Brick Lane, and Krein radioed for assistance, he wanted the man tailed.

Immediately after putting out the call, a plain clothed constable arose from behind a low garden wall further along the street, and followed the suspect. He spoke quietly into his radio, detailing his movements, on the seldom-used radio wave the team were using to avoid interference and unwanted hackers.

Paul had a strong suspicion he was being shadowed, he could feel eyes boring into his back. He glanced, but no one was apparent. He listened, but only caught white noise. His intuition told him that he needed to escape, even if it meant losing the duty. But he also needed to be discreet, he had no way of knowing how intricate the surveillance was.

On the other side of the road a welcoming light brightened the dank night, a twenty-four hour shop advertised its wares. Without even checking for traffic, Paul crossed, stepping through the glass door and into the fluorescent lighting. His suspicions were confirmed, Paul noticed the black shadow hovering outside. Calm, he checked products on the shelves, acting as a shopper convincingly, while he located an escape route. The door at the end of the shop was his answer. In a split second, his arm swept along the shelf, the neatly stacked cans, packets and sachets tumbling to the floor, and he was through the door.

Kavi Bhagwat jumped from his stool, furious and shouting, as the tailing officer darted through the door, leaping over the cluttering produce, chasing the suspect. Kavi grabbed at his shoulders, unaware he was a policeman, and the officer pushed him aside, desperate to catch the man.

Outside he sprinted, but the old guy was faster, scrambling easily over the wooden fence. The officer reached the fence, but everything was still, no sign of the man. He radioed for assistance, a brief summary of the fast-paced events, and the back alley swarmed instantaneously with bodies that had seemingly sprung from nowhere.

Krein had left Panton, he was running with an agility he thought he'd lost twenty years before, and, yet again, was chastising himself. His gut had been right, he should have stopped the man before, when he'd had the chance. Why hadn't he? He knew, and his heart saddened. Political correctness. If he'd stopped an innocent old man, walking by himself in the dead of night, the backlash would have been tremendous. Gutted, Krein realised he couldn't win.

Searching redundantly through the back streets and alleys, Paul's adrenaline hastened his heart as he crouched between the two wheelie bins, each one spilling rubbish, and breathed as silently as possible, praying they wouldn't bring on the dogs. His ankle throbbed wildly, and he knew how close he'd come to losing this game. Worse, they were still out there, and now they knew the disguise they were looking for, his new identity was blown.

He needed to escape the area, and speedily, there were too many coppers, and he needed to alter his appearance. The commotion was happening so nearby, he silenced his heavy breathing, he could hear shouting, running, radios. Taking a deep breath, he checked his escape route, prayed instantly to his God, and ran.

Moments later he was in Seer Street, and heading for the church that loomed to the left. Into the graveyard, over to the church. The doors were locked, the windows railed, he swore, desperate. Footsteps running, getting closer, voices, shouting, Paul's eyes bounced to the left, to the right. His thoughts pleaded, he needed God, he needed instructions. And God presented himself in the nick of time, in the form of a black hackney cab. Paul darted over the road, the driver pounded the screeching brakes, stopping, waving his fist through the window. Paul leapt in the car, his hunters closing in on him, and demanded the man drive.

Pissed off with advantage taking punters, he'd already had a fare dodger that evening, Ray Simmons wasn't prepared to take any more crap. "Like fuck I will! Get out of my fucking car you fucking weirdo."

The knife glistened in the streetlight, the female fare in the back began screaming beside the hijacker, Ray gulped, swallowing back the forthcoming tantrum. He lifted the clutch pedal and accelerated, dodging the two policemen who scrambled to the car, demanding he stop. The taxi shot into the distance.

Controlling his nerves, his feet shaking against the pedals. "Okay, mate, I'm driving. Where am I driving to?" The woman in the back was whimpering like a wounded dog.

"Shut up, you bitch! Just drive, anywhere, get away from here, and if anyone tails you, lose them." Paul, leaning through the glass hatch, held the knife, the one he had wanted to use on his next duty that night, threateningly, to Ray's bristly neck.

Ray, jolly in his middle age, raised a smile, typical of his kindly nature. Regardless of the knife, he didn't feel intimidated. "Bit like cops and robbers, innit. What you done, mate? Killed somebody." He chuckled, almost enjoying the unusual interlude to the mundane evening now.

He hurtled the car around a corner, forcing another taxi to brake heavily, horn blasting, and they had turned into Whitechapel Road. Paul spotted the road sign and grinned, God was definitely with him tonight. "Keep driving." He demanded, and pulled the knife away from Ray's neck.

Fiona Windpiper whimpered, the noise an irritation, and she squeezed her body into the worn leather seat, seeking its protection. Paul hovered over her, the knife clenched in his hand. Ray concentrated on driving, he hadn't travelled London so quickly for years.

It didn't matter that it was the wrong road, it was near enough under to the circumstances. Paul forced the knife into Fiona's throat, it slit easily, blood shooting from the carotid, leaking from the jugular. A crack as the blood pressure forced her head back, snapping a cervical vertebrae. The noise disturbed Ray, he checked his mirror, and saw her crimsoned body slump. Her fat cheek hit the window, sliding down, mouth agape, throat agape.

Horror. Fright. Terror. He realised what had happened. What did he do? Fright wasn't his bag. Until now.

"What are you fucking doing?" His words were quiet, pinched, tight. Paul's face loomed through the partition, his hands bloodied, his face dripping with the red fluid that appeared black in the darkness. "Jack did it in Hanbury Street, but I did my best. It's still Whitechapel, so she'll do."

Ray could understand now, the man was a psychopath. And he was clued up enough to realise he could be next. He determined he would do exactly what the weirdo told him to, and in the meantime, would pray. Pray.

The radio waves were full, and every officer on duty in London was aware that the Kopycat Killer was there, and trying to escape. His new persona was old news, the registration number of the taxi he'd escaped in was etched into every officer's mind. Every officer wanted the glory of being the hero who caught the madman, but few were brave enough to really want a tussle with the hardened criminal. The City swarmed with flashing lights and inquisitive, watchful eyes.

The cab was spotted recklessly haring along Mile End Road, and several cars took chase, many more blocking the road ahead. Ray detected them in good time, he tugged the steering wheel heavily to the left, the car hurtled on two wheels into Fairfield Road, Tredegar Road, Parnell Road, leaving deep black tyre tracks at each corner. And it was in Parnell Road that Paul found a chance to escape. He struggled against the wind to open the door, Ray searching the mirror, curious to see what his passenger, his kidnapper, was doing.

"Slow down a bit, slow down, I'm trying to get the door open." Paul puffed, exhausted, urgent, he pushed hard on the door. Instantly Ray braked, the police cars behind lighting the sky red as they followed his lead. Paul tumbled from the car, landing awkwardly on his shoulder, and yelled. "Keep driving."

As Ray accelerated away, the wind forced the door to slam shut, and an intense relief flooded through him, meted with thanks to his Creator.

Paul's body rolled and rolled, grit grating his clothes, entering his skin. The momentum finally stopped, the tarmac firmly embedded into his skin, and he struggled up, pain pulsing through his body. In an instant, he'd hurled himself over the bridge, the bracing water slapping his damaged body as he landed in the Hertford Union Canal.

Twenty seconds later, as his pounding head surfaced, he heard the wailing police cars on the bridge in pursuit of the cab, and in pursuit of him. Allowing a deep sigh of relief, he paddled through the freezing water towards the embankment.

It took a couple of adrenaline filled minutes for Ray to realise he could stop driving like a madman. He slowed to a stop, and, without warning, burst into racking tears. That was how the police found him, howling, distraught, into his palms, leaning against the steering wheel.

In between the wrenching sobs, he managed to describe where the killer had jumped out, and hordes of officers were on the trail. Kopycat couldn't have got very far in such a short time.

Two constables remained with Ray as the others left to join the search, they called an ambulance, believing he would need sedation. Taking a thermal blanket from the squad car, they shrugged it over Ray's shoulders, he shivered, desperately trying to quell his sobbing. Finally the words came. "In the back." His large thumb pointed.

"What are you trying to say, sir?" The officers checked each other, and one opened the cab with trepidation. He could see a pile of clothes on the floor, then the metallic stench hit him. "Oh Christ." His stomach was lurching as he tried to remain in control. "Oh Christ." This was the first body of his career.

His more experienced counterpart stepped in, she leant over and checked the woman's wrist, signalling no pulse, even though the body was still warm. The wound was fatal, the chubby neck had been slashed deeply from one side to the other. She radioed for assistance, the area needed to be cordoned off as soon as possible.

Thirty officers surrounded the canal, floodlights illuminating the scene. An officer shouted, he'd found a patch on the bank where the grass and mud showed signs of recent disturbance. The obvious route would be into Victoria Park, and the suspect would be sodden, thus easy to spot. Four officers remained by the canal, radioing assistance, helicopters with heat-seeking equipment and searchlights, whilst the others trudged into the park, vigilant and eager, wishing the heat wave hadn't broken into constant rain, then they would have a wet trail to follow.

The search continued for the rest of the night, but once more Paul had rendered himself invisible. No sightings, no signs, no clues. Due to the rain, the dogs they employed to hopefully follow the scent, lost the trail.

For Krein, this was the end, he could take no more. He packed up his belongings, and remembered how close he had been to the man. Not even ten feet away. He'd blown it. Too scared of repercussions. Idiot. He realised now that he wasn't up to the job. He was just a Detective Inspector from Oxford. He wasn't capable. Perhaps if he'd taken a back seat earlier, another, more experienced officer would have solved this by now. Krein needed to back out now, before his involvement caused more loss of life. Desperate not to cry in public, but his frustrations flooding all the same, Krein thumped the train seat, wishing he could rip it out and throw it through the window.

Linda was harmonising with Katie Melhua's honeyed tones, barely keeping a smile from her face as she kneaded the dough for a loaf of fresh bread, her jaw dropped as Krein walked into the room. "David! I'd almost forgotten you existed."

He stepped forward, pecking her loosely on the cheek, the shallowness of the gesture speaking a thousand words. "I wish I didn't." He sank into the seat, elbows on the table, head in his hands.

And now her guilt came. Linda dusted off her hands. She soaked a tea towel in hot water, unfolded it over the bowl of dough, and set it to rise in the warmth of the boiler cupboard. She washed her hands, still unable to find any words: she'd heard the tragic news on the radio, which she turned off, the soundtrack not suiting the scene. Silence echoed from the walls. "Do you want to talk?"

He shook his head, climbed the stairs, Linda could hear him running a bath. Mary came in, concerned. "How is he?"

Guilty again. Why had she dated Gordon? "I've never seen him like this. Have you heard the news today?"

Mary nodded, and her face paled. "Mum, I got questioned by the police last night." Linda took Mary's hand, she led her to the table, ready to listen to the story.

Linda rapped on the door, she heard the water stop running. "David, I need to speak to you." His sigh irritated her intensely, it summarised her unimportance to him. The lock clicked back and she stepped into the steamy room, seating herself on the toilet lid as he climbed into the bath. His nakedness stirred no emotion in her. "It's Mary. She's just told me that she was questioned by police in London yesterday." Now she had his attention. "About a Roger Andrews." Full attention, and horror. "I take it you recognise the name."

Krein nodded, sitting straight and washing himself hastily. "He was initially brought in on suspicion of being Kopycat, but was quickly ruled out. However, he did admit to drug rape, although he's denying it now. My colleague Spencer's been dealing with it."

"Nice character then. David, I don't like her going to London while the Kopycat Killer's on the loose."

"Then stop her going." David dropped under the water, soaking the hair that was greying rapidly. The rapidity, the cockiness, Linda wondered if she actively disliked her husband. She didn't credit him with a reply. He lathered the shampoo. "Well?"

"She insists that they're careful, that they stick together, and look out for each other."

"They?"

How little he knew, how little he cared. "She goes with her friends, Natalie and Tara."

"Where do they go?" His hair was rinsed, he laid back luxuriously in the bath, the hot water steeping out London's grime.

"I don't know the name of it, some club in Whitechapel."

A sudden jolt. His expression was anger, shoulders instantly tensed as he climbed from the bath, snatching a towel and aggressively rubbing the dampness from his body. "She is not to go again, do you understand?" The terseness came through gritted teeth, and Linda, weak once, but now strong, knew she didn't deserve that.

"I've had enough of your attitude, David, and your half arsed attempt at being the concerned Daddy. You don't want her to go, you stop her." She was on the point of leaving, and he realised he'd gone too far, he suitably changed his approach.

"He's too clever, Linda, he outwits us every step of the way. I couldn't bear to lose Mary, she's my baby."

"Our baby, David, ours. But it's me who's had the sleepless nights waiting for her to come back every weekend. Me. Because you haven't been here. Work's been your baby, David, otherwise you'd have listened when I told you she was going to London in the first place."

He knew she was right. He knew he'd have to be graphic with Mary to make her understand she mustn't return to Whitechapel. Ever, as far as he was concerned. And he knew he'd have to get over himself and get back on the case. Millions of daddy's babies walked the streets, each of them a potential victim of the worst serial killer in Britain's history. He felt a resurgence, he felt his strength return.

He'd deliberated for long enough. Andrew Hope lay the newspaper down, he took the phone and dialled the number that stared at him. "Incident line. Can I help you?"

"Hi, I, er, I, well, I've just read an article in the Evening Standard about that murder last night, that woman in the taxi." Andrew had no idea why he felt so stupid, as if he was wasting police time.

"Yes sir. Do you have some information?" Hope.

"I think I might have seen the bloke that jumped in the canal." Andrew fidgeted with the greying coverlet on the arm of the sofa, aware he had the woman's full attention. "I was on the tube and this weird looking geyser gets on, he was soaking wet."

"What time was that?" She was waving her arm, she wanted Spencer's attention.

"Mmmm, about half one in the morning, something like that." A needless glance at his watch.

"Sir, I'm going to send someone over to take a statement from you, can I please take some details from you?" Spencer was now hovering behind her.

"Sure, no probs."

"Can I have your name and address?" The pen was poised, ready.

Spencer had gone in person to take Andrew's statement at his flat in West Hampstead, having considered, and ruled out, contacting the nearest station to delegate the task to. He had a gut feeling about the sighting that belied rational explanation. His hunch had been right, the statement was detailed, fantastic, the witness spot on, the information encouraging.

He dialled Krein's home number, interrupting a fiery discussion with Mary, who stormed out of the front door as soon as he picked up the phone. Linda mouthed 'I told you so' before taking her bag and leaving the house. Desolate, Krein's hopes failed to rise as he listened Spencer's new lead, his colleague's enthusiasm not travelling. Replacing the receiver, Krein was faced with a choice. He either stay back and save his family, or he commute back to London and brainstorm with the team to clear the streets of an incomprehensible madman. He waited an hour, neither Mary or Linda showed any signs of returning, and the decision became easier. He jumped into the car, heading for the station to return to London. It was ten in the evening by the time he sat at his desk, Andrew Hope's statement was, as requested, waiting for him. Krein was impressed, the detail was tremendous.

He read the words quietly to himself, speaking them helped to imprint them on his memory. "His hair was a mess, it was pale, but not blond, not white, almost a slight orange tinge, but he had brown eyebrows which looked odd. His hair was patchy, not like a bald geyser, but sort of clumps of it were missing." This correlated with the man Krein had watched, he was certain Andrew was describing the hunted man.

He continued. "His scalp was red and sore, looked a bit scabby, bit gruesome. He wore tweed trousers, they didn't reach his trainers, and he walked with a bad limp. Had a young face, but dressed like he was old, and his shirt was ripped at the shoulder. There was a fair bit of blood and dirt on it, like he'd had a fall or something. Quite tall, well, my height, and he was soaking wet, he was shivering."

The voice made him jump, he had no idea he had company. "Keep going, it gets better." Spencer was standing behind him.

"He got off at West Hampstead, my stop, and I walked behind him out of the station, he went the same way as me. I held back because I wanted to see what he was doing, he looked really suspicious. He didn't seem to know his way around. He went along West End Lane for a while, then went down Inglewood Road, the road I live in. I was walking slowly behind him, he knocked on the door of a house, across the road from mine.

I started to cross the road to go to my flat, I wasn't watching him any more, but I heard the door open and the old guy who lives there said 'Yes?' then there was a thud. I looked round but the door slammed. I thought it was odd, but not worth calling the coppers. But I think it might be the geyser you're looking for."

Krein laid the statement down, he was lost for words. He mulled the words in his head, and slowly turned to Spencer, who had pulled up a chair. "Bloody hell!" Spencer nodded, his enthusiasm beaming with his smile. "Have you sent someone round to the house?"

"Of course! An elderly couple live there, the husband's in hospital with a head injury, his wife won't leave his side."

"Don't tell me, hit on the head with a blunt object."

Spencer's smile abated. "The woman swears he just fell and hit his head. It doesn't make sense."

"So she didn't see Kopycat?"

"She's old, Krein. She says she didn't hear the doorbell, just assumed her husband had gone downstairs for a glass of water. But she says she did hear a thud, and that's when she came downstairs. It probably took her a while, she's slow on her feet. Said her husband was on the floor, bleeding from his head."

"This doesn't make sense. If Andrew Hope says the door slammed, then that means Kopycat was in the house. And why hear a thud, but not the doorbell? I don't like this." Spencer shot a knowing look, he was uncomfortable too. Something felt wrong. "Have forensics checked the scene? Has she been through the drawers to see if any clothes are missing, we all know Kopycat will be after another disguise now his last one's been blown."

Spencer shook his head, and, at that moment, Krein wished he'd never returned to his hometown. Something was hugely wrong, and his stupid breakdown had wasted valuable time. He checked his watch, ten fifteen. How could he justify calling out forensics at this time of night, for a case nearly a day old?

The two men, both exhausted, both wide awake, discussed the latest anomalies. They both knew that events hadn't panned out as described by the old lady, and they needed to speak with her. Unfortunately that would have to wait until the morning.

One thing was certain. Kopycat wouldn't have knocked randomly at that door, ready to knock out whoever answered. Somehow he knew that the owners were aged, that he could issue violence without the threat of being overpowered. This was a major breakthrough. Krein was convinced that by discovering more about the elderly couple, they would find the trail back to the killer. His identity, not his movements. The conversation was long. They shared a bottle of Teachers, knowing the next day would be pivotal. Both slept on their paperwork.

Tuesday 9th September

Michael Dennison, his head swathed in bandages, lay, broken, mute, slumbering, life ebbing in and out of the frail body with each struggled breath. His wife, Elizabeth, didn't notice Krein approaching as she kept Michael's hand clasped inside hers, praying her life would transfer and bring his strength back. He'd been such a sturdy man for so many years, tall and athletic, and now he was a weakened shell.

Krein stooped beside her. "Mrs Dennison?"

Her weary, bloodshot eyes gazed up at him, indifferent. "Yes."

"Mrs Dennison, I'm Detective Inspector Krein, from the Major Investigation Team. Do you mind if I ask you some questions?" Krein swore he noted a hesitation. This woman was definitely hiding something. She knew who the killer was. How was he going to appeal to her common sense, extract the sentiment and replace it with sanity?

"They tell me he was hit. I just assumed he'd fallen."

"Do you know the man who did this to your husband?"

The brow furrowed, her eyes shot to the left. She was lying. "I thought he'd fallen. I called an ambulance."

He was about to tell a lie himself. Not big enough to lay his job on the line, and anyway, he'd laid the rest of his life on the line for this case already, he had nothing left to lose. "Mrs Dennison, this morning I obtained a warrant to break into your house, to enable a forensic team to investigate your property. We believe that the man who struck your husband has committed a number of vicious murders over the past three months. If you are protecting that man, it would be easier for everyone involved, including yourself, to just tell the truth."

Elizabeth struggled to her feet, her arthritic hand loosening its grip from Michael's. Krein was amazed how tall she was for a woman her age. She stepped, frail, to the water jug, and poured a small amount into the waiting glass. Sipping. Buying time. "Mr Kipling, I'm not protecting any man. I thought Michael fell. End of story."

She was good. But so was he. "Krein. My name is Krein. Okay, can you tell me exactly what happened last night, please?"

Her eyes met his, the flash of green unsettling, and suddenly he realised she'd just challenged him. She may be old, she may be worn, but this woman was highly intelligent, and she was about to play him like a grand piano. He knew that whatever came from her mouth would be a fairy tale, she was only going to give him the truth she wanted him to hear. She was talking now, but he wasn't listening. He had to arrange the warrant he'd told her he already had, he needed forensic scientists in that house, and he needed every person related, or known to, Elizabeth Dennison to be checked out.

Krein said his goodbyes, he left the hospital, and as soon as he'd left the room Elizabeth began to cry. For her wounded husband, for her family, for her lies. She would sort out the problems, her family's dirty washing was not going to be aired in public. She was grateful when her daughter came in, elegant, sweeping, attractive. "Mum, oh, Mum." Rushing over, hugging, tightly, desperately, so many months of unsaid words melting away. "I came as soon as I heard. How is he?" Gail took her father's hand. He looked older than ever, smaller, weaker, vulnerable.

"He's alive, darling, that's a good place to start. But he is very ill."

Gail pulled a chair up, she kissed her mother's cheek lightly, and sat. "The police say he was attacked. Have you heard any more?"

Elizabeth shook her head. "I just thought he'd fallen."

Moira Delaney drove into the narrow driveway of her father's home as she did every Tuesday afternoon. Sighing, she turned off the engine and, grabbing the groceries, stepped briskly to the front door, sifting through the key ring. Pushing the door wide, she breezed in. Instantly, something felt wrong. The smell was wrong. "Dad?"

She laid the carrier bags on the kitchen side, concerned. "Dad?" Louder. Ewan Davies wasn't in his favourite fireside chair. She tripped up the uneven stairs of the two hundred year old cottage, and the odour became cloying. Knowing she was about to be shocked, Moira pushed his bedroom door wide, screaming before the sight registered properly. Somehow her fingers dialled the police, and her story was haphazard, laced with intermittent wails and howls.

When they arrived, less than ten minutes later, her face was swollen and reddened from the stunned crying, her shoulders juddering, shaking, and a large brandy in her hand. "He's upstairs." Her voice little more than a croak, before swigging back the alcohol, and lighting yet another cigarette in the usually smoke free cottage.

Ewan Davies lay, on his side, the covers up to his waist, on the bed. His white hair was matted with crusty blackened spillage, as were the blue cotton sheets. The blood loss had been tremendous, he'd survived the murderous blow for a long time, his heart pumping blood whilst his determined body fought death. Death had won.

Another murder scene. Another investigation. The house was cordoned off, the specialists brought in.

Jaswinder's voice trickled over the crackling telephone line as if it were molten chocolate, and, strange as it sounded, Krein understood the logic in what she was directing him to do. He replaced the receiver, wishing he could open up personally to Jaswinder, tell her he had strong feelings for her. Every time a thought like that passed in his mind, he'd guiltily admonish himself: he had a wife already. But he couldn't help it.

He called Panton across. "Could you contact the police department who initially dealt with the Davies murder, I need a SOCO to go back to the scene and check his wardrobe."

"What, for woodworm!" Panton scoffed.

"Get a life! The clothes that Kopycat was wearing when we last saw him were the type of things an elderly man would wear. It could be that Davies was killed purely for his wardrobe, according to our criminal psychologist."

Her hair was cut short, coloured believably, and shaped neatly into a bob. Linda stepped from the hairdressing salon feeling younger than her forty-five years: she felt glamorous, attractive. Now that the weight of her marriage was off her shoulders, she had a vibrant spring in her step, and she almost trotted along the Cornmarket towards Marks and Spencers.

After finding David had left when she'd returned from the library on Monday, she'd alleviated herself of any guilt, any doubts were gone. His heart was in the marriage as much as hers: not at all. She'd been to see a solicitor, Mr Graves, in the morning, and he would be preparing a divorce petition within the next week. Linda had no intention of being greedy with her demands, but she did want to keep the house. Graves had informed her that as long as Mary lived at home that shouldn't be a problem.

She fingered the dresses. Her date with Gordon was tomorrow, and she wanted something elegant, sophisticated, flattering, something that would ensure his eyes were fixated on her. Somehow she found herself in the underwear department, scanning the lace, the delicate filigrees, the sexiness, sleeping with Gordon hadn't crossed her mind before, and she was surprised.

Mary was nearby, deciding which to buy of the three G-strings she held. She noticed her mother, her jaw dropped. The idea of her mother dressing sexily was atrocious, she was way too old. She'd believed that her parents had stopped that kind of behaviour years ago. And she remembered that her father was in London. And that her mother was going out the next night, she'd not said where, or who with. And she recalled the man holding her mother's hand in the teashop. And she felt sick. Her mother was having an affair.

Mary dropped the G-strings, she needed air, her breath was stilted, she had to get away. She ran from the shop, standing in the rain, the thick droplets soaking her but not mattering any more. The icy water ran under her collar, down into her clothes, the discomfort meted by her desperation, and soon her tears intermingled with the downpour.

Another previous murder date was approaching, and the area was due to be heavily policed. Krein scanned the details again. Twelfth September nineteen oh seven. Emily Dimmock, known as Phyllis. Throat slashed, in her room, in St Paul's Road, now known as Agar Grove, near Camden Town, in London. Robert Wood was tried. And acquitted. This was definitely Kopycat's style, and stood out from the others in the Black Museum Bunch's latest report.

He wasn't sure if he wanted to speak to Jaswinder for her professional opinion, or just to hear her voice again. He dialled her home number, she wouldn't still be working this late in the evening. "Jaswinder, it's me again, Krein."

The line was silent, he kicked himself, feeling instantly foolish. Some crackling, and she was back, he guessed she'd just clenched the phone between her shoulder and cheek, her breathing stated she was multitasking. "Quickly, yes. How can I help you?"

Krein was amazed, a baby was crying in the background. "It's about Kopycat, I just wanted your opinion on something."

More crackling, and the crying stopped. "Yep, go on."

He didn't mean to, it was none of his business, but the words tumbled out. "I didn't know you had a baby."

Aggressively businesslike, hostile and abrupt. "Why would you? What can I help you with?"

Krein cringed, she was so professional it was excruciating. He wanted to hold her, comfort her, love her. Quickly, he checked himself. "Are you familiar with the Emily Dimmock murder? It's known as …"

"The Camden Town murder. Yes."

Krein was blushing involuntarily, why was she being so curt? He needed to talk his way through this, it was nine in the evening, and there wasn't another person on the entire planet that he'd rather be talking to. It dawned on Krein that he needed Jaswinder. So he was going to sound informative and adult. "That's the next one, isn't it?" He didn't wait for an answer. "He's getting savage. The attempt on Michael Dennison. The attack on Ewan Davies. I think he's lost it. He's past the attention to detail stage, I don't know. Shit Jas, help me out here."

The desperation in his voice was evident, and Jaswinder's tone softened instantly. He had the Jaswinder he loved back. "I'm with you, Krein, I think you're right. From the evidence I have seen with the past two murders, well, I mean the last two recreated murders, I think you're right. He is definitely more savage. He's long past the stage of caring any more, he has a blood lust, he wants to kill, he wants to rip, and I wouldn't be surprised if he didn't even wait until the twelfth. Having killed Ewan Davies and fatally wounded Michael Dennison, neither of them being recreations from what we can gather, I feel it's likely he will just kill now, randomly."

Krein felt his heart sink, his shoulders droop. He'd expected that, but not wanted to hear it. "Jas, help me here, I'm losing a grip. Where will he be now?"

She considered carefully, he loved her more. "It's tempting to say Slough, he's obviously familiar, but, and this is just my gut feeling Krein, so don't be putting an official stamp on it, the last place he killed was in London, and I don't believe he'll be bothered to travel any more. He'll stay there now, satisfying his blood lust, until you guys get him. Off the record."

Krein could hear her tending the baby, "God, Jas, I wish you were here now." Krein couldn't believe his thoughts had been vocalised. The blushing burned, he wanted the ground to swallow him up. But he also wanted to hear her answer.

It was indiscriminate. "Krein, man the streets, bobbies on the beat, cars on the road. Posters. Anything. He's not about to stop now." So professional.

The call ended, Krein clamped his hands to his head, he felt like a moron. Why had he said such idiotic things? Jaswinder had a baby, she was probably married. He must be having a mid-life crisis. The phone rang, he answered absentmindedly, it was Linda. "Mary's left home." Her voice was urgent, distressed.

"Calm down, Linda, slow down, tell me clearly what's going on."

Sobbing. "She's left a note, says she's going to stay with friends. In London, David. She's gone to London." He held back the expletive, Linda was worried enough already. "She says she'll call soon, let us know how it's going."

"No address?"

Wrenching tears. Krein had no idea that Linda was scanning the rest of the letter, where Mary stated she knew about the affair, and she couldn't live at home with a mother who was cheating on her father. "No."

"Linda, don't worry, calm down. Have you tried her mobile?"

"No answer."

Krein checked his watch. "Look, you have a drink, take a sleeping tablet. Anything, just do something to take your mind off this. I'll be working through the night, I'll keep trying her number, I'll find something out by tomorrow, okay."

Paul's figure in the shop doorway was pathetic, a nearby street lamp casting a glow across his rocking frame. Arms clasped about his knees, he swung, backwards, forwards, backwards, forwards, and his mind was in turmoil. He was in pain, having severely grazed his arm and shoulder when he'd leapt from the taxi, and the wounds were now infected from diving into the filthy canal water. The searing, burning agonies that fired through him were unbearable, and he was scared. In contrast to the heat of his agony, he'd not stopped shivering since hitting the freezing water. He was a mess.

The voice he detested crept into his head, his rocking increased, hands pushing against his ears. "Stop it, go away, I only want to speak to God." He kept thinking about the old man he'd taken the train to visit. He'd hit him with a brick. Why? He knew the man from somewhere. The irritating voice chimed in recognition. "Fuck off." Paul answered, unhearing, his rocking intensifying, screwing his eyes tightly, blocking out the sound.

"Are you okay?" Paul jumped, he wasn't expecting company. He glanced up, a young man stood in front of him, bending to his level. Paul ignored him, fixating on the path, continuing to rock. "I can help you, you know." No acknowledgement. "I'm a member of the Salvation Army, I can help you get a bed for the night." John Abbott reached towards Paul, a friendly gesture, he was genuinely concerned about the amount of homeless people on the streets of London.

He wouldn't be concerned any longer. His body flung backwards, landing heavily on the pavement, scooped up and the searing pain ripped through him. Backed into a parked car, searing again, he felt his abdomen fall open, the cold air hitting his intestines. Life pumped away, he could feel it running, his body slumped forward, the tarmac cold and hard.

Paul wiped the knife on John Abbott's clothes, tenderly whitened by his mother, now easily darkened by his blood. He limped away.

Stunned, Mr Murphy had seen the entire events from his bedroom window. Hands trembling, he dialled nine nine nine, requesting an ambulance, police, he'd just seen a stabbing, he couldn't believe it, he'd seen a man die.

Krein pressed 'send' and the fifth text of the evening bleeped on his daughter's mobile. He had no idea if she'd read any of them, she certainly hadn't answered any of the calls he'd made. He was worried. Worried about her, worried about the extent of the psychosis in Kopycat. His eyes were blurring with tiredness. He rubbed them, hard.

Spencer put his phone down, standing and shrugging his jacket on, he caught Krein's eye. "Stabbing just off Brick Lane. Eyewitness's description matches Kopycat. We're on to him, Krein."

"Dead?" Krein was also slipping into his jacket.

"As a dodo."

The phone rang on Krein's desk, did he answer, or did he go with Spencer? "You get that, we don't need two of us at the scene." Spencer was out the door, Krein knew this was sensible. He answered, and was pleased he'd stayed behind. Examination of the bathroom in Ewan Davies's house showed numerous broken hairs in the basin: their structure was brittle, damaged, with traces of sodium hypochlorite. This explained the state of Kopycat's scalp, and the bald patches. He had lightened his hair with common household bleach, the fool.

A complete set of clothing was also found in the room. Pink, flowery skirt, large. White, stained blouse, large. Rank socks, size six to nine. Boxer shorts, men's, soiled, medium. Jaswinder had been right, Davies had been killed for his clothes. Krein could see Kopycat had lost the plot completely now, capture wasn't far ahead, the frustration floated from his shoulders. Then he remembered Mary.

Illogically, she should know better, Linda had hoped that her husband would put his family before work for once, but could see now that her hopes were futile. She had torn through Mary's room, looking for clues, reading her randomly used diary, desperate to find an indication of where her daughter could be. At the bottom of the shoebox in the wardrobe, she'd found a tatty scrapbook, it had some phone numbers scribbled inside. Snatching the cordless receiver, she dialled. "Natalie? It's Linda, Mary's Mum."

Nat was surprised, people over forty didn't stay up late, did they? "Hi, Mrs K. Wassup?"

"Mary's missing, she left a note saying she's gone to London, do you know anything about it? I'm so worried."

"Nope, sorry."

"She's not responding to my texts or calls, and as far as I know she's giving her Dad the silent treatment too. Nat, can you call her, try and get something out of her?"

Linda was placing every hope she had on a girl she couldn't stand. Five minutes later she knew who Mary was staying with, but not where, she had refused to give Nat the address. Linda's fingers trembled, continually pressing the wrong buttons as she texted her husband. 'Mary met a lad called Matt Olsen at the Vortex Club, Whitechapel. She's staying with him. No address. Please locate.' Send.

Mary felt uncomfortable in the studio flat, it stank of cigarette tinged body odour, and the filth was vile, housework didn't appear to be Matt's bag. Clothes were scattered everywhere, discarded shoes and trainers that reeked, newspapers, take away cartons laced with mould and fungi, spilling rubbish bins. It was a tip, and Mary longed for her light, bright room at home. She thought of her parents, and re-read the multiple texts on her phone. But she was more stubborn than sentimental. She couldn't reply.

The thought of her mother cheating on her Dad, every time she thought of it her stomach lurched. She wanted this punishment to bring her mother to her senses. Unwittingly, she was actually hammering the final nail into the coffin that was their marriage.

Wednesday 10th September

The relentlous rain had ceased, and the morning sun was steaming up the puddles, the heat welcome after the recent, prolonged, cold spell. Krein could smell himself, he badly needed a shower, but now that Kopycat was into his final, depraved killing spree, he wanted to be out there, wiping the streets of the maniac. Spencer was an ally, he'd also spent the night at his desk, occasionally drifting into a sleep, labouring through paperwork when awake. Mr Murphy had been a useful witness, there was no doubt in either of the detectives' minds that John Abbott's murderer was Kopycat, and forensic testing was now proving them right.

Falder-Woodes had issued a press statement first thing in the morning, a full description of the hunted man, and his dangerously advanced psychotic state. Usually the police departments would try to repress fear or panic in the public, but the words Falder-Woodes had chosen deliberately encouraged it. He didn't want people walking the streets, potential bait for an unstable and unprecedented psychopath. But cars still lined the network through London as rush hour heightened, commuters still crowded the tubes, throngs still bustled each other on the pavements. However, the atmosphere was dulled, the sun didn't enhance the russets of the floating leaves, it didn't warm hearts or produce beaming smiles. Everybody in the City was aware that Kopycat was one of them, and eyes darted vigilantly, searching for the weird guy with tatty bleached hair. Everybody passed many. London was full of them.

Krein had run Matt Olsen's name through the computer, he wasn't registered at any address, probably avoiding council tax payments, maybe even income tax. Olsen was a Danish surname, it was possible the man his daughter was staying with was an immigrant. She'd still not replied to his texts, but he was somehow calm about the situation, unlike Linda. He knew that Mary was a sensible girl, and she would have absorbed Falder-Woodes's press release. She wouldn't put herself in danger, of that he was certain. No, he couldn't take any risks, not with his baby. He texted Mary. 'Please don't go out today. Kopycat advanced psychosis. Stay indoors. Love you. Phone me if possible.'

Krein's heart skipped, his stomach filled with emotion, a physical shooting pain. Jaswinder was beside him. How did that happen?

"I heard about John Abbott. I can't stand this any more, Krein, we need to work together, intensively, get him before he touches anybody else."

Dancing on air Krein found a spare desk, filled her with coffee, discussed his files, debated her theories, and all the while he wanted to hold her, make her his.

"Do you think I should call him?" Mary re-read the text to her new boyfriend. He laughed.

"Up to you, babe. But I ain't staying indoors, places to go, people to see, and no weirdo's gonna stop my life happening."

Mary cringed inwardly, Matt wasn't the person she remembered from the club. Her memory was of a kind, clever lad, one who adored her. The reality was the opposite. She'd had sex with him the night before, but sorely regretted losing her virginity now. She wanted her Mum, she wanted her Dad. She wanted home. Mary watched as Matt covered his nakedness with designer clothes, wondering how he managed to afford them. From what she could establish, he had no job.

Matt leant towards her, planting a sloppy kiss on her lips, fingering her left nipple. Her stomach lurched, she wiped the slime with the back of her hand, and she was grateful when he left.

"Mr Murphy said he was sitting in the entrance to a shop, rocking back and forth."

"Uh-huh. Probably listening to voices in his head. I doubt he is in touch with reality at all by now." Jaswinder held the statement in front of her. "Says he killed the man with no warning, and once the body had fallen he walked calmly away, not even a glance back to see if he'd been spotted. No emotion at all. This guy's scary, Krein. You should be looking for him, not sitting here flirting with me."

The blush swept over his face, had he really been so obvious? He felt ashamed, unable to think of anything to respond with. Krein's eyes darted around, he needed to make some excuse, to leave, he felt like a fool. And then the electricity shot up his arm, floating through his body. She was grasping his hand, and her warmth was amazing. "When you catch Kopycat, I'll let you take me to dinner." Every Christmas he'd ever had paled into insignificance. She fancied him back.

Jaswinder winked, provocative. "In the meantime, I'm serious about you lot being on the streets. You need to be pulling in anyone who even remotely fits his description. He is so dangerous now, he's indiscriminate, he's killing for fun. He needs medication, he needs restraining, because the public will be dropping like flies as long as he walks the streets. I'm warning you, Krein, this is not an exaggeration."

Paul bit into the hamburger, he was starving, his latest ripping had given him an appetite as well as a new set of clothing, a new identity. He blended into London beautifully, the red and navy Lacoste tracksuit a comfortable fit, the Von Dutch baseball cap covering the painful sores on his velvety scalp. McDonalds was busy, kids fuelling their growth, adults increasing their obesity, bulimics enjoying their binge, and the hustling, the chatter, laughter, the world passed beside Paul without a second glance. He was eating for hunger, and his surroundings were irrelevant. His mind travelled back half an hour, to the look on the man's face when he'd realised he was about to die. A wide smile flourished, involuntary, as Paul chewed.

In an alley, not fifty feet away, a woman screamed uncontrollably, the vision before her was disgusting. Matt Olsen's body lay on the pavement, fallen on empty boxes, surrounded by stinking garbage. Naked, apart from the Calvin Klein pants, the Adidas socks, and the slashed FCUK T shirt, his torso was ripped from the base of the sternum to the top of his pubis. Intestines had been dragged from his body, discarded to the side, glistening in the sunlight. The smell was atrocious.

Police arrived swiftly, Superintendent Brannigan leading the team. Examining the body the blood loss seemed too sparse, and closer inspection showed bruising to the neck and bulging eyes, the final expression of fear imprinted for ever, the swollen tongue protruding through the paled lips. Matt Olsen had been murdered before he was mutilated, probably by strangulation. This would be confirmed by the autopsy.

Brannigan's team bagged the evidence, which lay beside the body. Black male trousers, thirty-six waist, thirty-eight inside leg. Emerald green V neck sweater, forty four inch chest, male. Charcoal long cardigan, male, same size. Blood soaked the wrist areas of both of the woollens.

Krein was informed, alongside the rest of the investigation team, and the air chilled. He glanced at Jaswinder, and felt guilt. "Panton. Have you got the report from the search at the Dennison's house yesterday?"

Panton scrabbled through his paperwork. "Yep."

"What size clothes does Mr Dennison wear?"

Checking. "Trousers, thirty six waist, thirty eight leg. Tops, forty four chest, sixteen neck."

"Bingo. So we know he got clothes from Dennison's house. I still feel there's a link to the old couple somewhere, can you find out the latest on that?"

Spencer strolled up. "We've checked the DNA of the latest victim, it's been matched to a Matthew Hendrick Olsen, aged nineteen ..."

Krein raised his hand, halting. "What did you say his name was?"

"Matthew Hendrick Olsen. Why?"

"Do you have an address for him?"

Spencer checked his notes. "We have his mother's address. A car's just been sent to notify her of the ..."

Urgency thrust through him, he slapped his forehead in frustration. "He's dating my kid, Spence, she's staying with him. I need her out of here. Out of his place, out of Whitechapel, out of London." Pacing, he dialled Mary's number again, the unanswered rings distressing him more than ever.

The untidiness didn't worry Krein, his mind was elsewhere. The distraught woman in front of him seemed so pathetic, he felt murderous, but he checked himself, after all, her son had just been brutally murdered. But his visit was futile, Matt, as he was known, had moved out a month before following an argument, and Mrs Olsen had no idea where his digs were. She'd only seen him once since he'd left, and that visit had ended with a another row.

Krein's baby was somewhere in Whitechapel, and so was the killer. He had to find both. He knew that Mrs Dennison was hiding something, she was the key that would unlock this puzzle, and he was going to have to force an admission out of her, before any more bodies were torn. He paid his respects to the overwrought Mrs Olsen, and directed his driver to Inglewood Road.

The autumn sky was darkening, the red-tinged navy replacing the yellow edged indigo, and Mary watched the changing sky through the window. She was desperately lonely, yet still desperately stubborn, and undecided whether to phone her parents or not. Her mother had texted earlier, said there had been no affair, but agreed she had been tempted, and her honesty confused Mary, she'd not been expecting that.

Matt had not been back all day, and he'd left his mobile behind, so she couldn't contact him. She wasn't sure if she minded or not. She didn't want to have sex with him again, knowing he wouldn't appreciate her spurning him after putting her up, so, for that reason alone she relished his absence. But she was used to company, and she felt desperately isolated.

For the hundredth time she opened the fridge, and for the hundredth time she slammed the door on the rotting food. She was bored. She was hungry. She was lonely.

Krein stepped up the path, it was the first time he'd been to the Dennison house but it was roughly how he'd imagined it to be. Terraced, bay windowed, short front garden with a low wall. The only part he hadn't supposed was the third floor. It was a large house, and probably worth a fortune. He knocked on the door, and tried the handle, surprised to find it was on the latch. Pushing the door open, he called out. "Mrs Dennison? It's Detective Inspector Krein." Tentative, he found the lounge.

Elizabeth sat in the chair, nursing a cup and saucer of tea, she seemed more lively than the previous day. "Mr Kipling." She stated, and her green eyes assured him that she was misnaming him deliberately, affecting a power over him.

He refused to be bullied. "How's your husband?"

A sip of tea. "Much better. He's out of intensive care, awake, and on a ward. He should be home in a few days."

Krein tried not to, but the words were out. "So you have no incentive to grass on the guy who assaulted him."

Cool as a cucumber, eyes challenging as ever. "I don't know the guy who assaulted him. You seem to have a hearing impediment, Mr Kooper. My daughter will see you out."

Krein was unaware they had company, he span around, and faced the elegant, tall, striking woman, aged since he last saw her from worry and stress. The recognition was instant, for both. "Gail Rackham!"

"Inspector Krein!"

The shocked silence boomed, all three parties stunned. Elizabeth Dennison broke first. "You know each other?"

Gail Rackham was shaking Krein's hand now, her eyes now dulled as she recalled the memories his face produced. "Inspector Krein was the investigating officer when Annabel disappeared." And now she queried his presence, he belonged in Oxford, and the realisation dawned, her voice became strangled in her throat. "You think the man who killed Annabel is the same man who hurt my ..." Her voice tailed off.

Krein was searching inside the deeply green eyes. They were tired, they were old, the wrinkles surrounding them drooped, bags holding years of experiences. But they were secretive, and wicked, and they were hiding a murderer. Krein felt stifled, his breathing was laborious. He'd found the key. Now he just needed to unlock the door. "Where, Elizabeth, where?"

Her gaze never left him, she searched his eyes as deeply as he searched hers. Elizabeth Dennison terrified Krein, her evilness burned through him as her words hammered through, each syllable slow and deliberate. "I thought he just fell."

Krein turned abruptly and left.

"Mum, I want to come home." Mary was wracked with sobs, aware how idiotic she'd been, how selfish, how irrational. Now she was trapped in filth, miles from home, and terrified to leave the room after the text her father had sent.

At first Linda had urged her to return, but when Mary explained the warning, Linda changed her mind. "Listen to your Dad, love. He's pivotal with this killer, he knows what's going on."

"Mum, I'm so lonely. Matt hasn't been back all day, I don't know where he is or how to contact him."

"Do you know any of his friends in London?"

Mary thought for a moment, Matt had always visited the Vortex Club in a sizeable crowd. "Yes, a few."

"Phone them, love. See if anyone can come and keep you company until he gets back."

Mary nodded, pointlessly. "I love you Mum. I'm sorry."

The call was ended, and Linda instantly tried her husband's number. And again. And again. No answer.

Krein breezed into the incident room, the urgency emanating from him. Action was needed, and quickly. Spencer regarded him, he could see that Krein was onto something, he was intrigued.

"Have you got anything on the Dennison couple yet?"

The report on Spencer's desk was easily found, he was an intensely organized man. "He was an accountant before ..."

"No, Elizabeth Dennison. I want to know about her." Krein was seated now, and Jaswinder had the foresight to hand him a coffee. He handled the hot paper cup without noticing, or thanking, his mind totally absorbed.

"Aged eighty one. Retired forensic scientist. Acclaimed for her work, two books published on her studies. Four children. Coincidentally ..."

"One is called Gail, married to Ted Rackham. Yes, and it's 'the' Gail Rackham, our first victim's mother. That is why I'm so interested, because we were right, Elizabeth's hiding someone, she knows the killer, and she's protecting him."

"Shit!"

"Tell me about the children. Grandchildren. Great grandchildren. And how can we get DNA from the couple so we can link it to the killer's?"

"You think Annabel was related to her killer."

"I'm certain she was."

Paul was hidden from the road, the ornately decorated porch of the mosque on Brick Lane protecting him from unwanted eyes. He could see the regular police patrols from his vantage point, but they no longer worried him. All he wanted was to rip someone apart again, that was all that mattered. He rocked, backwards, forwards, backwards, forwards, hugging his knees to his chest tightly.

The annoying voice wouldn't leave him alone, it made him angry, in fact it was the reason he wanted to kill, it's persistence enraged him. He kept his words close, not wanting to be discovered. "Go away, bitch, get out of my head. Get out. Get out. I only want God to talk to me." It droned, it nagged, it antagonized, it made him clench his fists, rip at his skin, scratching his eyes, digging his nails into his face. The only way to stop it was to find another duty. That way God would be back, congratulating, complimenting, adoring.

Mary had Matt's mobile, she clicked through the contacts, and eventually, gratefully, spotted a name she recognized inside. Karen Philips was a nice girl, quite a laugh. Mary dialed the number. Three rings. "Hello, is that Karen?"

"Yep. Who are you?" Mary smiled woefully as she remembered the girl's chirpiness.

"Well, I don't know if you'll remember me, I've talked with you at the Vortex Club. My name's Mary Krein."

Her smile showed in her sunny voice. "Yay, I remember you, dude! I didn't know you had my number! Not that I mind you calling!"

Mary felt silly. "I don't, well, I'm at Matt's place," Mary heard the gasp but didn't understand its significance, "and I found your number on his mobile."

The silence was daunting, Mary waited with trepidation, something was wrong. The words were strained. "You haven't heard." Swallowing hard, the imparter of bad news. "Matt's dead." The swallowing met the astounded gasp. "His body was found in Code Street this morning, his Mum phoned me, she's in a right state."

Mary couldn't speak, she had no words, her loneliness imploded in her mind, leaving a vacant cavern. Her chest heaved, her breathing was light. His body. Matt's dead. His body. Found. Matt's dead. The words slapped her around the face, again, again. Slap. Slap. Dead. Dead.

"Mary, where are you?"

Matt's dead. "Matt's place."

Karen was kind, she was a fantastic mate to have at times of crisis. "Don't stay there, honey, not on your own. Look, I'm half a mile from you. Head out of Matt's towards the Vortex, I'm just past, on Brick Lane, flat twelve B, one hundred and two. Come on, babes, I'll look after you."

Sitting at his desk, Krein was frantic. He was searching every member of Elizabeth's family, and all of them appeared to be law-abiding citizens in professional employment. Police were intensively patrolling the streets, and he knew that Kopycat would be too, searching for another victim. His phone beeped, he'd received a text.

'Mary's heading towards Brick Street. David, please, find our daughter.'

The chair was gone, his mind was gone, his senses had left, he had some keys, he was down the stairs, he was in the car. Somehow Spencer was with him. Krein had no idea how he got there, Spencer must have chased after him. The area he drove to was familiar, Krein had surveyed it so often. He parked in a lay-

301

by, engine running, the bright lights of Brick Lane illuminating the busy road.

Spencer finally believed he would get a straight answer. "What do you know, Krein?"

Krein's heart was thudding wildly against his chest, his eyes never leaving the street, searching, scanning, he wanted the man more than ever before. "My daughter's staying in Brick Lane. Elizabeth Dennison is related to Kopycat somehow. Kopycat is here, now, he's prowling for his next victim. That's what I know."

Not stopping his surveillance for a second, Krein left the driver's seat, he walked around the car, opening the passenger door. "I want you to drive, Spence, up and down, up and down, I'll know Kopycat when I see him."

Seats swapped, Spencer manoeuvred the car into the stream of traffic, his vigilant passenger scanning intensely, and, heart sinking, ahead he could see his disobeying daughter, striding speedily. "There's my kid." He screamed, pointing, and Spencer accelerated.

Paul watched the girl pass by the entrance, the mosque porch still housing him, the shadows dark, private. Her head was down, her black hair tumbled down her back, flowing gently in the breeze, she was gorgeous. Paul wanted her, she was the one, he wanted to feel her inside and drag out her entrails.

He was on her from behind, the hands that crackled with Matt Olsen's dried blood sealing her mouth, halting her scream. He dragged her into the shadows of the porch, the extravagant stonework witnessing her plight. She bit at his hands, her own nails scratching, her eyes widening as she felt the cold blade pierce her skin, pain radiating from her left kidney. Reaching behind, self-preservation surfacing, she grabbed for his hair, but it was merely baby-soft stubble. Her nails scratched at his eyes, his face, his mouth and he bit, his teeth sinking into her fingers.

Footsteps were nearing, she felt the blade re-enter, her eyes wide with terror, her blood oozing, weakening her adrenaline filled body. A tussle, the grip was loosened, her body slumped forward, she crawled painfully towards the brightness, her mind in slow motion, not glancing behind to watch the fight between hero and killer. She could hear screaming, unaware it was coming from her.

Krein leapt from the moving car, landing badly and rolling across the ground, he struggled into the porch: he'd seen his daughter snatched, he'd seen the policeman follow. Mary was on the floor, she was screaming, the policeman, fatally stabbed, slumped beside her, and Kopycat was over Mary, the knife looming aggressively. Krein's screams obliterated the world as he launched forward, the knife slicing his forearm as he impacted the attacker, knocking him to the floor, the weapon skidding away.

The enhanced strength borne from his child in danger, Krein flipped the assailant over with ease, and the handcuffs were on. Kopycat bayed, howling, his eyes wide, the noise animal. He struggled, snarling, sneering, the need for blood loss intense, and the wrestling continued until he was led away. Two ambulances appeared in seconds, the heroic policeman who'd given his life to save Mary's was taken in one, Krein and his daughter, who was bleeding prolifically, in the other.

Krein's wound was superficial, and he sat, arm bandaged, beside his daughter's bed in the Royal London Hospital. A ventilator breathed life into her damaged body, the coma making her appear asleep. The hospital had performed emergency surgery on her, and the prognosis was good. She was capable of breathing unaided, but the trauma had weakened her, and the doctors thought it best to reduce any extra strain on her battered body. Krein held vigil, awaiting the police car that would soon be delivering his wife to his side.

He didn't expect to see Jaswinder, and when she came into the room, joining him beside his adult baby, her presence was no longer important. She still had a way of surprising him, all the same. "We've found Annabel."

Shock flitted across his face, his gaze remaining on the prettiness that lay between the white sheets. "Body?"

"Kopycat."

Wednesday 18ᵗʰ September

Krein fingered his mobile phone, undecided, as he strolled slowly from the John Radcliffe Hospital in Oxford. Mary had been transferred there on Friday, her condition having stabilized sufficiently for the journey. He'd just visited her; she was up and about, her wounds healing well. Apart from the desperate worry for his daughter, the past week had been flat.

Spencer had taken over from him after the dreadful night, organizing the reports, making sure Krein could concentrate on those most important to him. Krein had been relieved to return home to Oxford, and although she'd been distant, he'd thought Linda was just distressed about Mary. When he received the divorce petition, he realised he'd lost everything.

Proud, he'd packed a suitcase that day and left the marital home. Linda could keep it all, as far as he was concerned. Material things were irrelevant. He'd seen too much death to ever care about the car he drove, whether his mobile was the latest model, or the store he shopped in was trendy enough.

Krein leant against the low wall; the autumn sun was warm, but chilled by the easterly winds. Jaswinder's number was displayed on his mobile. He needed to talk to her, he needed closure, he needed to understand Kopycat, Annabel Keeley, what drove her to kill so viciously, but he also knew that asking such questions would be irregular, he should wait for the official reports. He pressed dial. So what if his job was compromised, he just didn't care any more.

"Jas, it's me."

He swore he could hear relief in her voice. "David, thank heavens. How are you?"

"I need to see you."

The line crackled, a baby whimpering, soothing, cooing. "I'm at home, you're welcome to come and talk, as long as you don't mind Sam being here."

"Thanks. What's your address?"

The room was efficiently modern, decorated in neutrals, a comfortable quantity of ornaments, none pretentious, dotted around. Sam lay in the filigreed Moses basket; his gurgle had changed to the rhythmic breathing of sleep since his mother had left the room to prepare a drink.

Jaswinder brought the two steaming mugs into the room, Krein smiled, grateful. He'd never seen her so gorgeous, at home she wore her long, glossy black hair down, it tumbled over her dainty shoulders, the ends flicking slightly. Her face was unmade, her beauty natural, chocolate eyes enhanced by swooping black eyelashes. "I need to know what you know, Jas. About Kopycat. About Annabel."

"Have you read the summary? The reports?"

"Yes. I need to hear you tell it. I need you to help me understand." Krein took a packet of cigarettes from his pocket, her disapproving look halted him: he replaced them.

A deep sigh. "Annabel had been depressed for a while. Her body clock was ticking away, and she was desperate for another child. Before conceiving that baby, she'd suffered three miscarriages, all in the first trimester, and her doctor had become concerned about her mental health. He'd asked her to delay trying to conceive, and take medication to stabilise her condition. She had refused."

"Your opinion?" He sipped his coffee, it was welcome.

"She should have followed the doctor's advice. If she was depressed enough for him to make that suggestion, she needed assistance. On the day that Annabel went missing, she'd parked at the Westgate, as always, but as she'd left the car, she'd noticed the blood." Jaswinder opened her briefcase, she pulled out a hefty folder. "Sorry, I need to consult my notes before I continue."

Moments passed, Jaswinder flicked through the pages. "Ah yes, she was seen, her skirt soaked with blood, by Mrs Murray. This is where the assumption that she was injured came in."

"I remember, but Mrs Murray mentioned a man next to her, bearded, if I remember rightly. Where does he come in all of this?"

"An innocent shopper, probably terrified, and that's why he never came forward." Jaswinder glanced at her son, checking his temperature unconsciously, Krein smiled at the tender gesture.

"Annabel had been complacent, having passed the three month mark without miscarrying, and realising that she was losing the child she desperately wanted, that took her over the edge, if you like. She couldn't handle it, she wanted to escape from reality, and she drove, drove, drove, away from everything, pretending it wasn't happening."

"So the foetus was a miscarriage, not ripped from her body as we thought."

"Yes. From talking to Annabel, although she's heavily sedated and has little memory of the past three months, she clearly remembers seeing the headlines suggesting her accident with the motorcyclist in Dorset was a recreation of Lawrence of Arabia's death, and that's when, well, she calls him 'God', it's an auditory hallucination, told her to research past killings, and that became her duty."

They both sighed, it seemed such an odd explanation, but so simple. "If only we'd known." Krein spoke to himself.

Jaswinder laid a delicate hand on his shoulder. "It wouldn't have helped us if we'd known, anyway. It wouldn't have stopped the murdering, we still wouldn't have known where she was. In all my experience, I would never have expected Kopycat to be female. Some of the crimes were so vicious, but, then again, Annabel's a big lady, athletic, and when experiencing a psychotic attack, the sufferer can display amazing strength. It's the emotional side that disturbs me the most, I would never have expected a woman, especially a mother, to have been emotionally capable of the more violent crimes."

"No. Should the doctor have sectioned her when she refused medication?"

"No. No one could have predicted this, Krein. No fingers can be pointed. But lessons can be learned, and I hope they are." They sat in silence, sipping coffee, no more words left, listening to Sam's snuffles as he slept, blissfully unaware of the world. Krein stood, his questions had been answered, he peeked at the baby, smiling warmly, and headed for the door.

"Thanks, Jas, you've been a great help." He turned to leave, his mood still low.

Jaswinder tapped his shoulder, a cheeky smirk on her face. "One more question. What happened to the meal you promised me when this was all over?"

The life was back in his eyes, the hollowness filled, the cavern of despair inflated with hope. A smile crinkled his eyes, and he turned to face the woman he'd expected never to see again once the investigation was over. Their sparkling eyes met, and elation filled the room.

Gail Rackham now understood whom her mother had been protecting.

But she also knew that she would never see her daughter again. Annabel might be ill, but her capabilities were frightening: her family destroyed, their reputations devastated.

Gail would never forgive, could never forgive, Annabel.

And for the first time ever she wished that Annabel had been the first victim, as they had previously come to believe. Gail wished that her daughter, once cherished, now vilified, had been murdered: at least then she would have been able to sleep peacefully at night.

THE END

Biography

Author of Hope's Vengeance, mother of four, and long time writer, Ricki continuously studies the 'mind', the psychology, of people with great interest, and writes to educate and involve.

Lightning Source UK Ltd.
Milton Keynes UK
27 December 2010

164900UK00001B/22/P